Acknowledgments

I would like to thank Susan for pushing me to start writing the story stuck in my head and her honesty when I gave her my first draft.

Sherri, my editor and a wonderful woman, I could not have finished this book without.

A special thanks to my amazing sons who inspire me every day with their brilliance and never ending humor, and to my husband.

I hope you enjoy reading about Kim's journey as she learns what she can endure as a woman, by staying true to her heart.

All of the characters in this story are fictitious and not real. For my fellow wolf lovers, any fights between wolves that occur within this story are fueled by human emotion.

****

I honestly know that, if you take the time to talk to the animals, they will talk to you. You simply need to listen.

Published by: **CreateSpace Independent Publishing**

Cover artwork done by: Image Revision

Editing by: Sherri Angeleri & Bea Allen

Prologue

"Greg!" Andrew Shouts out, "Greg where the hell are you hiding?"

"Andrew I'm right here in the first stall, what's wrong, why are you shouting at me?"

"When were you going to tell Robert and me about Kim?"

Acting naïve Greg replies, "Kim who?"

"The Kim who talks to the animals, the one who could be the woman we have been searching for, you know for only a hundred years or so."

Greg shoves around some straw with his foot looking anywhere but at Andrew. Obviously uncomfortable with the situation he has found himself in. He puts his hands in his jean pockets and looks Andrew straight in the eyes.

"I've known Kim is the one you're looking for… since you and Robert told me that you are both werewolves. I love Kim like family… I've seen how Robert treats women," raising his voice, "I don't want her hurt, in any way!"

"Greg, I won't hurt her."

"But in your legend Robert is the oldest, meaning that she would have to be with him, Right?"

"Well there are ways around it. If I meet her first and she falls for me, she would be mine, not his."

"And just how do you plan on this meeting happening? I don't even know where she is right now."

"Greg, call her cell phone and get her here before the weekend. That will give us a week before Robert gets back for me to sway her in my direction."

Greg laughs, "You sure that's going to work, you're awful sure of yourself."

"Greg have you looked at me lately?" Andrew poses like a professional male model.

"Alright Mr. GQ don't rub it in. I'll go call her now."

CONSUMED

BY

Kellie Zottman

To: CHRISTINE

Kellie Zottman

1

At a bar in Tulsa Oklahoma, I'm dancing with Doug, my date for the night. We are at a bar called Joey's. This place is designed for dancing. It has a large dance floor on one end and an oval bar at the other end. It doesn't look like much from the outside with plain white cinder block, but this place is hopping almost every night of the week. The song that we are dancing to is a newer slow song, which in here is very rare. Mostly they play blues and seventies rock, It's a nice change. Doug is my flavor of the week while I am here in town. I think he is about ready to go to do some other kind of dancing.

Because he asks me, very seductively, "So, Kim you ready to get out of this bar yet?" He has no idea how ready I am. I know exactly where he wants to go… his place. He grabs my ass with one hand, pulling me against his muscular body, placing his other hand on the back of my head. He smirks just before he kisses me with a kiss that could melt an iceberg. I swear if Doug wanted to he could seduce a nun! He is a great bag of tricks. He has looks, charm, and a perfect body. Right from the start he doesn't mince his words either.

"Absolutely, no commitment to any relationship of any kind ever." is his opening line. It worked with me, and from what I can tell from the locals here, he gets a fair amount of tail. He doesn't get jealous, and he doesn't get mad if you don't call. He only expects the same from any girl he sleeps with.

"Where would you like to go Doug?" I tease,

He simply smiles a very naughty smile. It tells me volumes.

"Doug we better get to your place, before Susan comes over here to lecture us about our dirty behavior in public."

"Do you mean, before I do you right here on the dance floor?"

"Yea that too," I laugh.

We quickly exit the bar and jump into his pickup truck. He just barley obeys the speed limit driving to his house. Good thing it's all back roads that we take to get there. I hold on to the handle above the door. I refer to it as the 'oh shit bar' we scarcely make it to his place and in the door, before he has me naked. The man does not waste time getting what he wants.

Doug is by no means a considerate lover when he is drunk it's all about his pleasure, if I get off it's just a bonus. Not that I don't enjoy the process in getting there, maybe I should say "almost" getting there. Normally he's a very passionate lover, which makes up for when he is drunk like tonight.

Afterward we both shower separately, and then I drive us in his truck to Susan's house back in Tulsa. He'll have to drive himself back home. Susan's house is an old country home. She has many rooms there along with many rules. It's where I'm staying at for the time being. I'm here in town helping her out.

As quietly as possible for a drunken tired person, I unlock the back door and tiptoe up Susan's back stairs. I remember to miss every one of the creaky spots on the steps up to my room. I don't want to wake anybody at this late hour.

I open the door scanning the bedroom, for any possible signs of life. But no, I'm alone for the moment. Hopefully they leave me be in the morning. I really would like to sleep in, just this once. My head hits the pillow and I'm out.

But before I know it, the morning is here again. I could swear I just shut my eyes. I am aware that I'm being watched. Patiently they wait for me to move. I feel their eyes burning holes in my skin. Screaming at me to get up, I know what they want from me, I wish just this once they would leave me be. But I know they won't, and my situation is a hopeless one.

They know now, that I'm not fully asleep. They hear my thoughts, and I hear them telling me to get up and open my eyes. It's hard to pretend not to hear them. My head is bursting with their demands.

Slowly I crack open one eye, just enough to see who is the closest to me. I know what is coming, they will attack, I am sure of it. Sure enough the smallest one is first. She sees my eye lid open, damn! She goes directly for my face, her teeth placed firmly on the tip of my nose. Then the largest one quickly lies across my chest. He pins me to the bed, knocking the air right out of me. I instantly become painfully aware, that I need to go to the bathroom urgently!

They are struggling with one another to get their licks in before letting me up. It becomes impossible for me to move. All I can see of the room is glimpses of the white ceiling, nothing more.

There is just too many of them in the room. I could never win against their demands. Now the rest of them are getting their licks in as well. I swiftly become overpowered by all of them. I start to laugh and they know now that they have won.

I don't mind sharing my bed with them. I don't even mind them nuzzling or nipping me. However a face full of wet tongues is just too much even for me. I shoo them all off of my bed as I try to sit up and stretch.

The dogs must have crept in while I was sleeping. It's not the first time I woke up to a bed full of dogs. It would however be a nicer thing to wake up next to a man. If not for Susan's rules, I would have. It is her house so I follow her rules when I'm here.

It's my own fault that I am so tired. Going to the blues bar last night with some friends. We danced so much I really don't feel like getting up just yet. I got in kind of late last night. My alarm clock said it was three when my head hit the pillow.

I did have fun with my Tulsa boy toy last night. Doug sure knows how to make a girl feel good. Yet I dread knowing I'll hear about my sinful ways soon. Susan is not a fan of my lifestyle. She is a good Christian woman, and I don't fault her for that. She would never even think about sex without marriage first. That's why I had to go to Doug's last night to have sex. She would never allow him to sleep with me here.

"Ok guys come on, let's go outside before someone doesn't make it."

Maybe I should stay in the first floor bedroom the next time I stay here. I know we must sound like thunder with all of us running down the stairs.

We somehow all make it to the back door without any puddles. I glance at the clock in the kitchen over the sink as we pass by. It's eight in the morning everyone should be up and not bothered by all the noise we make.

I let the dogs out back and hurry to the bathroom myself that's just off the kitchen. When I'm done I join the dogs outside. I'm greeted there by about twenty more of various mixes. Some of the dogs choose to speak with me telepathically. That's how I could hear them yelling at me earlier. I can communicate with animals, well dogs mostly, though I have spoken with a bear or two. And a lot of squirrels, they are so easy to talk to, but not a whole lot going on in there.

The only animals that I've discovered that I cannot speak with are wolves and alligators. I have no idea why my gift won't work with them. I don't see many alligators but, I do see a lot of wolves. After finding this out, I made it a hobby to stop at every wolf rescue I find in my travels, in the hopes that just one can hear me. However, I find that every wolf in those rescues is a mixed breed. They hear me just fine. The ones in the wild are pure and I get nothing from them at all.

My conversation with the rescue dogs is a simple one. They ask me if I had fun last night. Others ask where is the food, while a few ask to play ball with me.

I have always known that dogs are not complicated thinkers. They are very direct in communicating their needs. And yes they do have emotions just like us but, they can let go of things unlike humans.

Like I've said at the time being I am staying at Susan's place. She runs a dog rescue out of her home in Tulsa, Oklahoma. She is a good person; I do respect her for who she is. Nevertheless, she tends to forget that I don't have a permanent home anywhere.

I don't stay in one place too long. My cell is always ringing with someone needing the use of my gift. I travel all over the United States helping rescue groups. I usually help them with puppy mill dogs, and sometimes other hard to place dogs.

It's my own fault that I live this way. Word did spread fast about my special gift. First with the New Jersey rescue groups then all over. Because of this, I have traveled all over the United States. I once even went up to Alaska. Working with the huskies was a treat for me. They are very vocal as it is, and when they all started howling at once, they gave me chills.

Doing what I do is not always easy, I get very lonely sometimes. Don't get me wrong, I love working with the animals. But I long for human companionship, which lasts longer than just a night or two.

I've also gotten myself in trouble with the law a few times. I have a habit of taking abused animals away from their owners. Needless to say, a lot of small town cops know me by name. That's not always a good thing, trust me, I know.

Anyway, I myself am originally from a little town in New Jersey. I figured out when I was very young, that I could communicate with animals. I thought everyone could hear them in their minds. What did I know, I was young? Once I realized that other people couldn't hear the animals, I chose to hide my gift outside of my immediate family. They of course still thought I was cracked. But they never questioned my gift.

As I reminisce leaning against the outside wall. I can hear footsteps nearing the kitchen, so I call the dogs in for their breakfast. Following in after them, I begin to help Susan prepare the dog's morning meal. I line up the dishes as she pours in the dry food. I wonder how long until she starts to scold me about last night. Hell I might as well get it over with.

I inhale deeply first, "Morning Susan"

"Morning Kim, how's your head this morning?" And so it starts.

"My head is fine. I really don't drink as much as you seem to think I do. I dance a whole lot more than drink."

"Yea I saw you dancing with Doug. I was going to tell you to get a room, but you disappeared before I could get through the crowd of people. Did you have fun?" She says sarcastically, so I reply in the same manner.

"Yes, you know I always have a good time with Doug." Susan gives me a dirty look which I dismiss. It's my life not hers. I'll live it my way.

"Hey Kim the phones for you." calls Mike from the other room. I didn't even hear it ring.

"Thanks Mike." I go to answer the phone leaving Susan to feed the rest of the dogs. She shouldn't judge others. I guess she missed that part in her bible studies.

I lean against the foyer wall, picking at the fake flower arrangement next to me. I can't go and sit anywhere. Susan doesn't believe in cordless phones either.

"Hello this is Kim, who is this?"

"Kim, hi how the hell are you?" A smile takes over my face instantly. I get the warm fuzzes whenever I hear his voice.

"Greg is that you handsome?"

Greg and I have been friends for years. We tried to be more about two years ago. But it didn't work with my traveling all over the place. Yet we have remained friends. He is an animal rescuer too.

"Yes, Kim I need you to get your pretty ass down here as soon as possible. We're going to raid another large puppy mill soon. They have about 200 dogs there.

I'll have to take them all in. The other groups in the area are all full."

"It's about time someone comes down on those awful people." I scoff.

"Your right, we've been getting the go ahead to raid a lot of them breeders down here, so the sooner you get here the better. The faster we can help these guys get into new homes, and hopefully out of mine."

"Ok Greg I'm about done here anyway. I'll pack up and be there by the weekend."

"Thanks Kim, you know it means a lot to me to know, that I can count on you."

"I'll see you then handsome. Oh and could you get my room ready? You know change the sheets and clean towels."

"Do you want breakfast in bed too?" He says mockingly I know what he is getting at. Just by the way he asked with his devilish voice.

"You still have that new girlfriend in town?"

"Yes"

"Then no, I'll get my own breakfast thanks."

I hang up the phone and Susan is right behind me. I sigh with agitation. Great, now she has even more information to pass judgment.

"So, Kim I couldn't help but overhear. Was that Greg from Tennessee?"

I roll my eyes at her. "Yes Susan, he needs me. You'll be ok if I leave tonight won't you?"

"Yea most of the dogs have new homes. The ones I have left all get along, thanks to you."

"You're welcome Susan, and you're good company most of the time." I wink.

"Thanks Kim I think I like you too." She laughs as she gives me a hug.

"I'll miss you too."

"Ok girl you take care of yourself and stay out of trouble if you can. I'll keep you in my prayers."

"I don't get into trouble it finds me." We both laugh and hug each other again.

"Susan you give me a call if you need me." She smiles at me then returns back to the kitchen. I know she will call again she always does.

I go upstairs to pack up my things. I'll say good bye to everyone later. It doesn't take me long to pack. I have mostly clothes and a couple of pictures. After I put my stuff into my van, I make my rounds saying good bye to everyone. The two legged and four legged. I finally get to go back up stairs and take a nap when it's late afternoon. I'll leave out tonight, I prefer night driving. I'll miss all of the rush hour traffic that way.

When I'm ready to go I'll send a quick text to Doug tell him thanks for the fun, and that I'll call him next time that I'm in town. I'll make my trip in my 71 purple Chevy van. It has a twin bed and mini fridge, along with the shag carpeting. I simply love my van it's my home on wheels. Greg has offered to buy me a new motor home, more than once and I decline his offer every time.

I just can't let my van go. I get attached to things and people. Once I love something I never stop. Though, it would be hard to tell that I have deep feelings, I hide a lot. Even if the person wrongs me, I still have love for them.

I start out on route 40 around ten in the evening. I'll take this route most of the way into Tennessee. Then I'll make a left on RT 71. But that won't be for a long time. So I get comfy in my seat. I turn on a country station and sing along.

I packed in my mini fridge a hoagie that Susan picked up for me. I also have a few snacks to nibble on should I get hungry before morning. I remembered to fill my thermos with coffee. Hopefully it will help me stay alert while I drive through the night?

I smile to myself thinking about Greg. He lives in Black Falls a small country town near Gatlinburg Tennessee. It's really beautiful there, surrounded by the Smoky Mountains.

Greg was born and raised in the same house that he still lives in. The house itself is hundreds of years old. It is a huge southern mansion. When His parents passed a few years back they left the house to him and his sister Nancy. His sister is a good friend of mine too. I don't have many female friends. I tend to get along better with men.

Unfortunately, she won't be at Greg's when I get there this time. She had texted me earlier in the week. So I know that she had to go to Washington State on family business. If it wasn't for modern technology, I would have no friends. Funny though, I thought that they were the last ones left in their family tree.

Nancy and I try to keep in touch on a regular basis. We at least text each other when we can. We both have very busy schedules. I travel all over the place helping rescues and Nancy works for People for the ethical treatment of animals. I'm of course a member too, but Nancy does a lot of undercover work for them. That is something that I could never do. The way that big industry treats animals is horrific. The screams from the animals, surely would destroy me.

Greg and Nancy are good people; their parents taught them to love all living creatures no matter what form they come in. At times this led to a few interesting skunk stories for Greg. His parents also taught him how to invest the family fortune. This made it easy for him to pursue his passion for the welfare of animals. The same passion the three of us share, one might say.

Greg also sends me money without me asking for it. It's the same one thousand dollars every month. I know it comes from him, though he denies it. The money shows up in my bank account. There's no way for me to track where it comes from. The account is a numbered one, location unknown. I've tried to trace it many times over the years. I know he does this because he loves me and wants me to continue my work with the animals. I am also well aware that otherwise my lifestyle would not be a possibility.

So, whenever Greg calls for a favor. I always drop what I'm doing, and head straight to his farm in Tennessee. I'll be able to catch up with Doris as well. She is my other mother. Her actual role is Greg's house keeper. But Doris treats everyone as if they are her children. I think it's because she never had any of her own.

I know that I have a weak spot for Greg. He knows it too. But Greg is the kind of person that God drops in your life because you need them. With the grace of God and Greg's help, I get to do what I love!

It will be nice to stay in one place for a while. Lately, all I seem to be doing is spending a week or two in one place or the other. Then, I am off running to help someone else out.

My mind tends to wander a lot when I'm driving alone. I jump from one thought to another randomly. I'm almost always alone driving. Sometimes I do pick up a stray dog along the way. And once in a great while, I give a lift to a rescue worker. I have met some rather fascinating men along the way. Some bring a smile to my face others, not so much.

Doug from Tulsa is one of the ones I smile about. He enjoys living alone. He has a little old farm house that he shares with Jake, his dog. He's a confirmed bachelor and I can respect that. I wish other people would be more opened minded. Whenever I'm in town he always makes time for me. We go out to dinner and usually dancing. I love dancing. I would like to learn ballroom dancing someday. What I do now, is not exactly proper dancing.

Some of the people I help do look down on my personal life style. They can't understand that I'm always moving around. I don't have a permanent home address anywhere. So, how could I have a real long term relationship?

Even Greg and I couldn't make it work. We have a lot of love for one another. But it's an impossible situation. What kind of man would want a woman like me? A woman that can talk to animals isn't a turn on by any means. Animals do critique, trust me.

As I travel towards Tennessee the weather changes from snow to sleet. After I've crossed the state line, I start to see more snow patches alongside the road. The closer I get to the mountains, the more snow I see. I usually love driving through the mountains. They have a calming effect on me, most of the time. But this time, I have a funny feeling in my gut that I just can't shake.

I start to think about the dogs at Greg's, that I'm traveling to help him with. They are all rescues, from puppy mills. Places that Greg and others like him have been trying to shut down for a long time. I'll ask him what kind they are when I stop to stretch.

Since puppy mill adult dogs are mostly used for breeding, they're kept in cages or pens. Most of the time these cages are kept in deplorable conditions, the animals will have a very poor opinion of humans at first. And who could blame them for mistrusting us. The types of people that run these places think of the dogs as profit or expense, nothing more. They forget that dogs have emotions and souls, or they simply just don't care.

I'll have to show the dogs that people can be good. With my gift, the transformation for them will be much easier and take less time. It won't be so stressful. They'll know without a doubt, that I am being honest with them.

After driving a few hours I begin to feel stiff. I really need to get out and stretch my legs. I check my watch it's almost six in the morning. So, I stop at the first rest area I come across. It's still dark, but Greg should be up about now, so I give him a call.

"Hey Greg, its Kim, I just got inside of the Tennessee border a while back. I stopped at the first rest stop to stretch my legs. I wanted to ask what breed of dog we'll be working with this time."

"Chihuahua and German Shepherds," He replies casually then snaps. "You shouldn't stop at those places they're not safe and you're alone."

This struck me funny, Greg sounds upset; I'm always alone. I guess that he is under a lot of stress right now. I look around to see if anyone else is at the rest stop. I spot a woman on the far side.

I roll my eyes, "Greg remember I'm always alone why would this time be so different? Besides I'm not completely alone. There is a nicely dressed woman who stopped to stretch her legs as well. Though, I don't see another car around."

"Kim, isn't it still night time, how close is she, and does she have black hair?"

"Not very close, I can't make out her face. And yes she has black hair. How did you guess?"

"Kim, quickly get back in to your van and don't stop anywhere isolated, not while it's still dark!"

Slightly confused I answer him, "Yea, Greg ok can I stop for gas?"

"Yes, just be careful I worry about your safety that's all."

"Alright Greg I'm getting back in my van now. I'll see you soon."

"OK, bye"

"Bye"

Strange he never worried about me driving in the past. He must have a lot on his plate. But, I wonder how did he know the woman's hair was black? He did say that all of the other rescues were full. The dogs must be giving him a run for his money. He must have his fair share of dogs too. I'll go with that, or, maybe he's finally lost it.

With my experience and knowledge of Chihuahuas, they'll be the hardest to train because they are simply so hard headed. The German Shepherds will be easiest, they want to please and crave attention. Also, they have a high intellect, which makes for an easier time working with them. I know this is going to take a lot of work, but it's always worth the outcome in the end.

I can't count the wounds I've gotten over the years. I know the scars eventually fade. But the lives of the animals that I touch, never fades from my memory.

I can remember the very first dog I spoke with, she was a wolf mix, in my neighborhood. The dog was supposed to be shepherd but I knew better. Ginger was part wolf. She taught me to talk with my body; the way a wolf does in the wild. So that if a dog chose to block me from their mind, they would still be able to understand me, just by the way I move when I approached them.

Ginger and I would play for hours wrestling with each other. Anyone watching would worry about my safety and sanity I'm sure. But, I never received even one scratch from her. Funny I should think of Ginger. She has been gone since I was thirteen. Why would she be crossing my mind now?

I better start to pay attention to where I am; I find my way by looking at the next exit sign. I'm more than half way across Tennessee, almost at the route 71 turn off. Altogether it should only take me thirteen hours without stopping to get there.

As I continue to drive through the mountain roads the skies become dark and gray. Then out of nowhere, it starts sleeting. I slow down. As I travel further, it changes to a light snow, still not the best driving conditions for anyone.

Further on down the road, the snow picks up in speed and thickness. I can hardly see where I'm going let alone keep control of the van at this point. I slow down to a crawl due to the tires sliding on the wet road.

I can barely see the road sign for the next exit. I think this is Greg's turn off, I can't see the name very well though. Snow is covering the sign. I wish the sun would break through these clouds.

As I drive further on, I'm hopeful that I made the right turn; my gut tells me that I didn't. And the road is too narrow to turn around. I find myself in a desolate area. There are no more street lights or other cars. I would turn around if I could. The visibility is so poor I can't tell where the sides of the road are for sure anymore.

I haven't seen a house or any building in a very long time. Usually I'm not very easily shaken. But the sky is so dark due to the clouds being so heavy with snow. I feel a bit anxious. Maybe I'm a little more than a bit anxious. It's really dark out here. I'm having a very hard time keeping control of the van. The road is too wet and covered with slush. Suddenly, I hit a patch of ice, causing my van to swerve to the right, and then to the left. I should have replaced those balding tires before I left Tulsa.

"Keep it on the road," I tell myself,

"Oh, shit! No, please go back buddy to the woods not the road! Not the road!"

A large black wolf comes darting out of nowhere right into my path. I try to stop but before I know what is happening, my van tumbles down a cliff, rolling repeatedly over and over towards the bottom. This just can't end well. I brace myself in the seat trying to minimize my injuries.

The trees and bushes seem to be flying by me at lightning speed. That's not good, I start to panic. I don't want to die like this in the middle of nowhere. It feels like my heart is trying to jump from my chest, good thing I have a set of ribs to keep it in. As I hit what I hope is the bottom I black out.

2

What the hell happened? That's my first thought when I open my eyes and look around to see where I landed. I have successfully put myself at the bottom of a very steep hill. I did such a good job, I should be proud at least the van is upright.

I should have known, only I would crash my van trying to miss hitting an animal. I check myself over and everything seems to be good. Some parts of me are just a bit tender here and there. But my ribs, they are really tender on one side.

I run my fingers gently over the spot that hurts the worst and find a thin cut. I lift my shirt to look at it. It's not bleeding now but, it must have bled during the fall, my shirt is blood stained. I wonder where that came from. Why do I taste blood in my mouth? Looking in the mirror I can't see any reason for it. It's kind of sweet tasting, strange. I wonder how long I was out. I dust myself off and look around trying to get my bearings. Well, I guess I truly went over the edge this time didn't I? I look out of the driver's side window. All I can see is the darkness of the forest. I guess I'll just wait here until it clears up.

I don't smell gas or seem to be on fire. I think about climbing up the hill, but it's much too dark to attempt to climb up the hill. I'll wait until the clouds clear up. Knowing me, I'll just get lost in these woods or get eaten by a bear. Poetic justice I think they call it, me always looking out for the animals. I would be the one to get eaten, and become someone's dinner.

I turn my head quickly and catch a flash of something as the moon momentarily peaks through the clouds. Wait, was that the moon? Was I out all day?

What in the hell was that? I know I saw something move out there. I don't hallucinate, yet. Hear things that others can't yes, but no hallucinations.

I know that I saw something. What is it? I strain my eyes to see through the darkness, but the cloud cover is too dense. I can't make it out. As I stare out my window finally the clouds break. I can see clearly. It's the wolf, Oh shit! Maybe I hurt him. Damn, I can't just leave him out there. I swallow hard he sure is a big one. He must be about seven feet long and four feet high at his shoulders. I just have to go check on him. That was a long fall and he might have fallen with me. Otherwise, why would he still be here?

I search in the back of my van, checking to see what I have to work with. I can't hear his thoughts, like I would a dog. I need some bribery. I find a box of dog biscuits a first aid kit and grab a water bottle. That might help, I can only pray.

He's laying about ten feet away from my van. He is slowly licking at the wound on his paw. He stops as I open the van door. He's watching me intently. Very slowly, I start towards him. He looks up at me showing his teeth and snarls. Being afraid of an animal is new to me. I have never experienced this before. I don't like the feeling very much either. I put my head down, looking at the ground, showing him that I am being submissive.

I need to follow his instincts, and use wolf body language. Slowly, I lift my head just enough to see where I'm walking. He tilts his head up and starts to sniff the air. As I slowly approach him he lifts his nose up in the air, and takes deeper breathes, catching my scent in the air. Then he closes his mouth and stares at me. That's strange behavior for a wolf. I stop immediately in my steps. I take a deep breath for bravery. I really don't like this fear thing.

"I won't hurt you. I just want to help you."

I tell him, while I creep to within a yard of him. I watch his body language closely. Making sure that I don't do anything he can confuse as aggression. So far, so good, he's just watching me.

"I've got a biscuit. You want a biscuit? Dogs like them." I say in the way one would talk to a baby. He looks very unsure, but no visible signs of aggression yet.

I toss the biscuit within his reach. He looks at the biscuit, smells it but doesn't touch it. That didn't go as I planned, damn!

"Well boy, looks like your front paw is messed up. Sorry about that, I could take a look at it for you. Will you let me try?" No response, he must be a male.

I inch closer and closer to him. My heart is trying to break out of my chest, it's pounding rapidly. If he were a dog, I could easily talk to him and this would be so very easy. I hope he understands me, because I can't read his thoughts at all, but his body language is encouraging. I'm trying to convince myself.

He lies still, just panting slightly. If only I could get close enough to him to clean the wound. The Clara Barton in me has to try. There's no blood on the ground around him, but his leg is matted with dried blood. The wound could be deep I've got to help him.

I keep talking to him, telling him how handsome he is. As I ease myself closer to his injured paw, I kneel within inches of his head. Swallowing hard, I slowly raise my eyes to his, knowing damn well it's the worst thing to do with a wolf.

We stare at each other for what seems like a very long time. Probably more like twenty seconds. Then he smiles at me letting his tongue hang out from the side, and pants. I look at him a little surprised. I'm not stressing him at all.

"You trust me?" He cocks his head to the left, and then easily puts his head down on his good paw with a sigh.

"That's a very good sign, so you're going to let me fix your paw then? Or you bite me so here we go."

I put the first aid kit and water on the ground in front of him. This way he can check them out. After he is done sniffing them I wet the gauze to clean the dirt from his wound. He stays perfectly still just watching me. I on the other hand am shaking like a leaf. There isn't any open wound, just the dried blood.

"How did your paw heal so quickly?" I question him.

That's just not possible for the wounds to close so fast. Especially with all of the blood matted in his fur. Maybe I was out a lot longer than I thought?

I pick up the trash and stand up to head back to my van. He just lays there not moving. To trust me so easily it's not normal, especially without the telepathy working for me.

Since my adrenaline is starting to go back to normal, I suddenly feel a chill from the wintery night air. It goes right through to my bones, causing me to shiver. I rub my arms to warm them.

"Well it's kind of cold out here would you like to curl up in my van? At least until the sky clears, that way we can both be safe from the bears out here. You know, I could use your body heat to help keep me warm tonight."

He cocks his head and arches his brows then gets himself up and heads to my van. He must understand me. When I turn and look at him he is waiting at the van door, huffing at me impatiently.

"In a hurry are we?" before I open the van door I tell him.

"I have the bed you get the floor. Which is carpeted, yea, I know so seventies. He gets in the back and curls up on the floor and puts his head down to sleep. I take off my coat and shake some snowflakes out of my hair. After I take off my boots, I climb in the back with him.

"So I surmise you must have had some human contact in your life boy? You are at ease with me, a total stranger." I cover myself with the thick down comforter and curl up for a good night sleep. It's real funny that I don't feel any real soreness anywhere. Absentmindedly I run my fingers over the small cut on my side. As far as I fell down, I should hurt more than I do.

I think to check my cell and there is no service. I check my iPod for the time. It says seven, it must be nighttime. I must have lost a lot of hours today. Tomorrow has got to be brighter and better than today.

My iPod has the radio feature and somehow I got a news station out here. The weather woman says that tomorrow will be warmer. I sure hope so.

Sometime in the night I feel the wolf climb into my bed, next to me. He snuggles right up against my back. He is helping to keep me warm. I am sure he knows this. He smells like well, not like roses, I'll tell you that. Nevertheless, he is warm and I am freezing at the moment, so I snuggle into him.

In the morning light, I wake to find that the storm clouds have passed. When I look for the wolf, I see that he has his head buried in the box of biscuits. I also notice that my fridge is opened and the turkey hoagie that I had in there is gone. I scowl looking at the wolf.

"Well, I guess I don't get any breakfast do I? Did you leave me anything?"

The wolf takes his head out of the box. Tilts his head downward, and gives me the puppy dog eyes. I just can't help myself and start laughing.

"Did you practice that look, because you've got it down. Well, now that you're full, I should let you out, you think?" He whimpers in agreement and I let him out of the van.

While he is outside doing his business, I put on my heaviest sweater over my thermal shirt. Then I put on a pair of leggings under my jeans. I slip on my boots, coat and gloves. I get out of the van and see if I can climb up the hill. Or, if by any chance there might be a trail left from hikers. I look around and there's not a trail to be found anywhere.

I do find footprints in the snow. They are partially covered by the new snow fall. They must be from last night, sometime while I was sleeping I guess. I wonder who would have walked by my van and not knocked. I try following the footsteps but they end at the tree line, strange. I figure I shouldn't call out for the one who passed by, something tells me I shouldn't bother.

"Well wolf, at least it's a nice day today no more snow or rain and a little warmer." I grab my cell phone and try for a signal. Damn not even one bar out here. I guess I'm going to have to try to climb this hill, it doesn't look too steep. I look around for a good starting point."Well are you coming with me or going on your own way? I could use the company until I find help, or get a signal."

He looks at me as if he is contemplating it. I check over my camping gear making sure that everything is there. The wolf starts to circle the van and marks it. I shake my head watching him.

"Do you really think that if someone wants to steal it that your urine will stop them?"

I laugh, as I make a mental check list of my gear. Tent, sleeping bag, knife, first aid kit, and three bottles of water are all that I have. It will have to do in case I don't reach civilization before the next nightfall.

As I climb up the hill, he keeps running ahead of me and circling back. Each time he gets back to me, he grunts. He then runs back up the hill, like he's mocking me being so slow or something.

Sarcastically, I ask him, "Am I keeping you from something?"

As I work my way up the hill, my mind wonders. Instead of worrying about my situation as it is. I start to think up a name for the wolf.

"So since we are traveling together, what should I call you?" The wolf raises his eyebrow, as if to say, are you serious?

"Ok, I get the hint. I think that I'll stick with "wolf or hey you, for now until I see more of your character. Then maybe I'll change it to something that better suits you. Sound good?" He trots off up the hill again.

As we, the unlikely pair makes our way to the road, I begin to realize as we reach the top. I probably just finished the easiest part of the journey. At least I know where the hill ends. I check my cell at the top and there's still no service.

The road ahead of us looks as if it will go on forever, winding all through the Smokey Mountains. We walk in silence just listening to the sounds of nature. Occasionally, the wolf runs off into the woods chasing something, but returns with nothing. I secretly hoped that he would bring back something to eat.

I keep thinking to myself, someone should have come and helped me out by now. I'm glad that I have the wolf with me, he makes me feel safer. Not that I'm afraid of animals out here, well, not the four-legged kind anyway.

Some mountain people can be real nice but others can be scary as hell. I sure could use a ride about now. I'm spooking myself with possible horrors. It's not getting any warmer out here. The weather man lied again.

As the day grows longer no one comes to my rescue. Every hour or so I keep trying my cell, but there's still no service. I start to think that maybe I took a wrong turn somewhere. If I was on the right road a car should have passed me by now. Well at least no crazy people have come by.

My stomach has been growling for a while. Each time it does, the wolf looks at me with his big golden eyes as if to say, sorry. He did eat all of the food. I know he was only doing what came naturally to him, but that doesn't help my hunger. The day has turned into dusk, so we stop to make camp.

"We need to set up my tent for the night. Hey, you know if there is any water around here?"

He wags his tale and howls at me. Then he starts into the woods. I start to follow, but holler to him "not too far in." I don't want to get anymore lost than I am already. He howls acknowledging my request.

He leads me to the edge of a stream where there is a small clearing. I start setting up the tent. He disappears into the woods and leaves me all alone in the darkness. It suddenly gets real quiet and eerie.

When he finally returns I already have the tent up and a fire started. The wolf prances around proudly, carrying a small doe in his mouth. He decides to drop it right beside me. Making me jump up and yell! With the sound of the deer's dead body hitting the ground. I fight the urge to toss my cookies.

"Wholly shit!" I squeal, He just stands there mouth draped open, like he is smiling or laughing at me. I try to compose myself, yet my sarcasm shows in my words I'm sure.

"Hey thanks for finding us some food to eat. Normally though I would rather, not see my food it in its natural form. But I'm very grateful for the meal. Do you want yours raw or cooked?"

He just cocks his head, so I cut a large piece of the deer off. Then I search for a stick strong enough to hold the meat over the fire. He drags the remainder of the deer away from me. I figured that it would be a blood fest to watch him eat. But he took his time and ate…almost human like.

After we both finish eating, he walks with me to the stream. We clean ourselves up. He stomps in the water splashing me some. I swear he laughed when I scolded him for it.

"You know this wouldn't be so bad if it wasn't freezing out here." I say sullenly, "I think I'll turn in for the night when we get back to the tent."

He trots on ahead of me. I think he got it that I didn't need to get wet. As I unzip the tent, I turn to ask him if he wants to come in. But before I can say anything he runs by me. He almost knocks me down with his massive size.

"Well I guess you want to sleep with me?" He drops his jaw. Then quickly he snaps his mouth shut. He shakes his head as he lies down. That's odd behavior from a wolf. I settle into my sleeping bag and the wolf slides up behind me to keep me warm. He has no idea how secure this little gesture makes me feel.

Sometime in the night, my sleep is disturbed. I hear faint voices like someone is whispering. At first I think I am dreaming. So I don't pay too much attention to it. Then I realize I'm not dreaming the sounds are coming from outside of the tent.

I start to get scared. I pat around me and find the wolf is not next to me. Great, my protector and personal heater are gone. Now I know why I woke up, my heater left.

I try to listen to the voices. First I hear a man with a deep masculine voice, but who is he talking to?

As I listen to him, I can tell he is mad about something. Then I can hear another voice. And realize they are arguing... about me?

The one is whispering to the one with the deeper voice who is not soft spoken at all. I try to focus on their words; I wish I could hear both sides clearly.

"It's not safe for you to stay with her. You're drawing attention to her," the deep voiced one states.

"Someone has to protect her. They won't harm her at the moment," replies the whisperer.

"True," deep voice pauses, "But what if she's not the one? You can't be that sure you just met her. I really don't like this Nick. You could be sealing the fate of someone innocent."

What does he mean by that?

"I just know it to be true. You must trust me."

"Why, just because she can't hear what you think doesn't mean anything. She can't hear gators either."

"How does he know that? Not too many people know that." I say to myself.

They both stop talking and I try to make sense of it. Where is the wolf? What fate? I've only seen the wolf. No man has been following us that I noticed.

"If she is the one, I should be able to hear her thoughts. I wonder what she dreams about."

I think to myself, *"I'll tell you what she's dreaming about, a hot meal and a warm bed."*

"Wait....Nick she can hear me! This can't be right I can hear her also. She's awake!"

His words are full of fear. Why is he so afraid of me? I can't harm anyone.

"I won't hurt you please don't run."

I'm baffled, what just happened? I hear his feet hit the ground hard and fast leading away from me, then silence. Wait, I wasn't talking, what did he mean he could hear me? And the wolf his name is Nick? I'm guessing I only hear one run away not two.

But wolves don't talk like humans? I peek out of the tent and see only the wolf sitting there staring back at me. He comes back in the tent and curls back up to sleep. He knows that I heard some of what was said. However, I'm sure that I didn't hear everything.

Is there is a man who can hear the thoughts of wolves? He spoke to the wolf, like I would a dog or person. He must have my gift? But I heard two voices… how can that be?

Nick seemed to be sure of what he thought of me. And why was that man saying I could hear him? And how could he know that? He also said that he heard my thoughts.

That's impossible he was speaking plainly. I heard him with my own ears, I think? I can't read the minds of people that would be silly. How did he know I can't communicate with gators? Only Greg and a hand full of rescue people know that. I am very concerned and confused about all of this. But for now, I'll have to tuck it deep down. I need to trust Nick to get me back to Greg safely. Maybe this is all a dream? Yes, that's it, I tell myself.

3

The morning brings the bright sun, and with it, warmer air. It feels nice not to shiver. My first task though is to test something I call out to the wolf.

"Nick!" He jerks his head towards me. I knew it, I squint my eyes at him.

"Your Nick right?" He just stares back at me. I give him a stern look.

"Did you open your mind to me last night so I could hear you?" He gives me the same blank stare.

"Ok, so can you block me? Can I hear other wolves or are you a mix?"

He shrugs his shoulders, and then he takes off into the woods.

"You better come back to me you here!" I yell out to him. But I still wonder who the other voice belonged to. Maybe there were two people out there with Nick? I was sleepy, there might have been two people running away. Maybe there is a man who can talk with wolves. I warm up some of the deer meat for breakfast, and figure that he'll come back. I think that he has deemed himself my personal protector. But, from what is he protecting me? That's what I don't know.

I pack up the gear and make sure the fire is out. Then I tie my jacket around my waist. I don't need it just yet. I slept in my clothes last night, so I don't have much else to do except wait for Nick to return.

I call for Nick and he eventually comes bounding happily out of the woods right to my side.

"It's time go buddy."

We walk back out to the road and pick up on our journey where we left off last night. I notice while we walk along the road that he's scanning the area, like he's looking for something or someone. Maybe he is just as spooked as I am. The woods give no comfort to me now, I want a warm bath and Doris's cooking.

I start to hear the sounds of paws on the forest floor. From the sounds, I think they are wolves. I've learned to tell the difference a long ago. It was a skill taught to me by an Indian friend of Greg's, he thought even with my telepathy, I should know what was approaching me. If a wild animal chose to block me out of its mind.

But the wolves making the sounds are not coming any closer. They seem to be keeping a safe distance between us. Nick doesn't appear to be alarmed by them, so I don't worry about it either. They could be his pack keeping an eye on him.

We walk for the whole morning before we stop. Nick leads us to a spring. It has only a thin layer of ice on it. I fill up my water bottles. The water is cold but it's better than nothing. I put my jacket on, I'm not freezing but I'm not toasty out here either.

I notice the wolves that have been following us, stop to take a drink upstream from us. They are watching me but not coming any closer. At least I know what they look like now. Nick and I eat what is left of the deer meat. Out here in this cold, I had to start a small fire to defrost it, and me. The sun is still shinning but the temperature is going down.

I've been checking my cell for a signal roughly every hour with no luck at all. Finally, late in the afternoon, I get a signal. I thank God and call Greg, he answers uneasily.

"Hello Sunshine where the hell are you? You're late and I've been worried sick! Why haven't you answered your cell?" He shouts not giving me a chance to reply.

"Greg, calm down please. I'm ok I had an accident, I just finally got a signal on the cell." He cuts me off panic filling his questions.

"Are you ok? Are you hurt?"

"No, I'm ok just dirty, tired and hungry. But I'm not all alone thanks to my new friend."

"What friend would that be?" I can hear the worry in his voice.

"Relax Greg it's a wolf. A very large wolf he has made himself my personal protector."

"Ah Kim, is he a solid black wolf or does he have some white?"

"He's solid black, why do you know any wolfs personally?" I snort.

"No," he pauses a moment. Then he continues like I didn't catch the hesitation in his voice.

"I just know that there's a friendly one around the mountains, yours sounds like him. I'm glad you're not all alone out there."

"Are you sure that you don't know him?"

"No, I don't. Do you know where you are so we can come and get you?" Greg says anxiously

"I'm not real sure where I am, it's real desolate here. Not one car has come by in days. I remember turning off of Route 71 on to what I thought was your turn. It must have been the wrong right turn. I've been walking back toward the direction of the turnoff I took."

"I think I know where you might be near. I'll get my friend down there to locate you with the GPS. That will help a great deal in finding you. Do you think you can stay put?"

"Yes, thanks Greg about an hour or so right?"

"If you're where I think you are, less than an hour."

I close the phone putting it in my pocket. I share my good news with Nick. I quickly realize that he doesn't share my enthusiasm.

"What Nick? You knew that I was trying to get to my friend Greg's farm. He needs me there. I told you this while we were walking, don't you remember?" Nick puts his head down and wines a little. I look at him with concern, and scratch his head tenderly.

"Nick don't you worry, if you can be good and not eat any of the animals. Then you can come with me." He wags his tail but still looks sad.

I decide to stop where we are on the road. I might as well. I'm going to have to lead them back to the van. There's no use in walking any further.

"Nick you can go hunt if you need to, I'll be right here waiting for Greg on this rock." Nick runs off into the woods. I sit down on a rather large rock to wait. Some time passes before I hear thoughts in my head that aren't mine. This is nothing new to me. Whatever it is doesn't make any sense though, the thoughts are scattered.

"She can't be the one... Could she...? No she's too pale... He can't be right about this one... could we really finally have found her?"

This really freaks me out because the voice is the same one I heard last night. It can't be a wolf, I can't hear them. Maybe it's a hybrid. It can't be a human, I don't hear humans this way either. What in the hell is going on here? I'm too pale for what? Hey, I like my lily white complexion. Found who?

I look all around me, trying to figure out where the voice is coming from. Then I just sit for a while in silence listening. The voice simply vanishes from my head. I am more than a little uneasy with this. I try to relax on my rock and listen to the birds singing. As the time passes, I realize that I can't get rid of this nagging feeling. Something inside is telling me that I should turn tail and run like hell.

I wait for a very long time alone. Hoping for Nick, or Greg, or somebody, anybody. Even the voice inside of my head, but nope, I'm all alone out here freezing, and hungry, and growing bitchy.

All of a sudden I hear something coming through the bushes toward me. I hope that it's Nick, because I can't hear any thoughts. I turn around looking for him, just in time for him to pounce on me knocking me over to the ground.

I get a mouth full of dirt as he starts nuzzling me. I try to get myself up from the ground to no avail. Nick is much larger than I am. I have no way of winning this battle. I just resign to my loss.

"Nick please let me up," I beg him half giggling. "Nick let me up I think I hear a truck coming."

With a long wet yucky lick on my face, Nick lets me up and he vanishes into the woods. I right myself and clean off the dirt from the attack. Gratefully, I filled my water bottle at the stream earlier. I rinse the dirt from out of my mouth. Yuk, I don't need to look any worse than I already do.

I can hear a couple of trucks coming loudly up the road. I hide myself in the bushes along the road. I figure with my luck lately, it's the safest thing to do.

Then I see that it's Greg's truck coming up the road for me. Yes finally! I step out into the open and call for Nick but he doesn't appear.

Suddenly, I hear a long sorrowful howl from a great distance away. At the same time as Greg climbs out of his truck, he gives me a good hug and a kiss on my cheek.

"What is that about Kim?" Greg looks out into the forest, to where the howling came from, like he might catch a glimpse of the wolf howling.

"Well, I'm guessing that's my new friend. He doesn't want to come to your farm with me. I told him that he was welcome, as long as he didn't eat anyone."

"Did he stay with you the whole time you've been out here? Especially at night I hope he was with you?"

Greg is starting to worry me. He is not acting like his usual carefree self. He seems to be too concerned about my safety.

"Actually, he kind of caused the accident. I was trying to avoid hitting him. I lost control of my van on the slippery roads. He did redeem himself by keeping me warm at night and staying with me the whole time. Someone was out here with us but I never saw them. I heard a man talking one night. I think he was talking to Nick. Do you know of a man around here that can talk to wolves?"

I could tell Greg was scared as shit. He tried desperately to hide it from me. "No, no you're the only animal talker I know of." I notice Greg is fidgeting, and he is scanning the trees surrounding us.

"Kim, please show us where the van is. I want to get you back to the farm before sundown. You can clean up when we get there. You're a mess girl," he looks me up and down with disproval.

With sarcasm I reply, "Thanks Greg, like I didn't know that already."

I ride back to my van with Greg. His friend follows in his tow truck. I show them where the van went over the cliff. They both stand there and stare at me. They shift their eyes back and forth from the van to me.

"Don't ask me, I blacked out at the top and woke up at the bottom. In fact I think it was a whole day later."

"Boy Kim, when you do something you sure go all the way?"

"You should know that I never do anything half assed, it's all or nothing," I remark. I ask the tow truck driver, "Do you think you can get it out of there?"

"Well ma'am I think I can get-r out but I don't know if she'll run."

"Shit! I never even tried to start the damn thing. Not that I could drive it anywhere from down there." The tow truck guy starts talking about my van, over me to Greg, pissing me off.

"Greg, I'll tow it to my garage and check it out for you. I'll give you a call later and let you know what's up."

"Ok thanks." Replies Greg

I give Greg a look that he knows well. He knows that I am getting pissed at being ignored. He ignores me too and turns back to the driver.

"Hey, it's my van remember not..."

"Kim, let's get going" Greg interrupts me before I can finish. He grabs my arm and pulls me to his truck. Once inside, he explains why he let the guy go on ignoring me.

"If we play it right, we won't get charged for the tow or repairs if the guy thinks it's my van."

"Oh in that case, I'll keep my female ego out of it."

"Good girl."

"You're not funny Greg."

"Yes I am, so anything new I should know about in your life?" He hands me a heavy lunch bag.

"Doris sent this for you. She thought you might be hungry or something, I don't know why she would think that."

"Thanks for the food, nothing new with me. I've been doing the same stuff everywhere. Like training rescue dogs and some pampered pouches. I like the pay I get for training the pampered ones. Or, should I say, training the owners of the pampered pets. It always starts the same with the pampered dogs. The dog's first notion usually is. "Thank God they finally called you!" Then I patiently listen to them tell me everything the owners are doing wrong. That's the easy part, listening to the animal. But then, I have to teach the people how to interact with the dog in question. You know the same old thing."

We are quiet for a while as I eat my snack. Doris sent sweet tea, fried chicken with corn muffins and coleslaw, yum. We drive along for a while listening to the radio.

"When you called me, I was in Tulsa."

"Yea and how is Doug these days?" I pretend I didn't hear the Doug part.

"A group of us went to this great blues bar called Joeys. I really loved it there. The best part is the women drink for free on Wednesday nights. Free beer and horny guys, what more could a single girl ask for?"

"Kim you actually left your own little piece of paradise just for me?"

"I only would for you, because you're so special." I laugh.

"Very funny, so Kim, I take it that you haven't found a guy that's to your liking?"

"No not yet, they think it's cute at first that I talk to animals. Then, when they realize that it's not a joke, they all get that I need some space syndrome and disappear. So are you still dating that girl Donna from town?"

"Yes why?"

"Well there goes that idea." I say grinning

"I can make exceptions. I'll never tell if you won't?"

"No that won't be necessary, I'm sure that I can find a friend in town. If I feel an over whelming urge coming on, there are always plenty of single men in Gatlinburg." I smirk

"Well, I don't think you will have to go that far to find someone on this trip."

"Greg, what do you mean? Why did you say it like that? Are you keeping something from me? You've been awfully bizarre since you picked me up, are you about to explode from something?" I say with intrigue.

"You'll see soon enough, what I have as a special gift for you at the farm. Now get some sleep, it'll be at least an hour until we get there." He says with a confident expression. I look at him puzzled. But as I start yawning, I decide a nap is a good idea. I lay my head on his lap and I'm out cold.

I'm stirred by Greg's cell ringing. The call must be from the farm. Typical, Greg leaves his cell on speaker. I guess he thought that I was sleeping soundly. He must have forgotten I sleep light and any noise can wake me, providing I wasn't drinking the night before.

"Hello Andrew?"

"Yea, did you get Kim yet?"

"Yea, she's sleeping right now. She saw Nick in the woods. She also heard someone talking to him about you know what."

"Did she figure it out?"

"No, but she heard that someone talking to Nick. Do you think it was him?"

"I hope not. Are you sure it was a man?"

"Yes she said it was a man, why?"

"It could have been Nick's wife, if it were a woman she heard. I know she was out there to help. About how much longer until you get back here?"

"About 30 minutes."

"Greg you better hurry, if you want to beat Robert back here, so I see her first. Do you think she's the one?"

"I think Nick believes she is. He stayed with her the whole time, protecting her. But I don't think he is convinced yet. Most likely I think because she's so light in color. Her Irish ancestry shows prominently. There's no trace that she's part Indian."

"Yea, you told me about that before. Just hurry but be safe see you both soon."

They both hang up. I continue to keep my eyes closed. I wonder what Greg is up to? I know he would never hurt me in any way, but I'm so very confused. How can he know what a wolf thinks? I know there is something different about Nick, but what is it? What about my Indian ancestry? Nick's wife, that's was an odd way to put it. He should have said mate, Nick is a wolf after all.

4

Greg's driving wakes me up from my sleep, especially with the bumps he keeps hitting. I look around, as we drive up toward the farm. The bumpy unpaved driveway is bordered by the thick forest. The road starts out very narrow, then it widens up as we get closer to the main house. I love this place, I go back in time whenever I see it. It's so lovely here.

The house itself is Victorian style. It's white with black shudders, along with a wraparound porch and wide upper balcony, all of which are trimmed with white wooden rails. The porch itself is littered with mix matched chairs and rockers. The steps are lined with water bowls, instead of flower pots, this tickles me. Most people have come to expect better accommodations for the animal's here. In fact, if it weren't for Doris being here, none of us would have clean sheets or hot meals.

Every room in the house has a doggie door installed into it. Well, except the bathrooms and the pantry doors of course. The dogs that live here all the time have free roam of the entire farm.

Adjacent to the main house there are two red barns. We call them the front and back barn. Each barn has three large paddocks that are surrounded by fence posts. There is at least one three walled structure in each for shelter. There's a thirty horse stable, to the right of the barns.

Greg recently had to build a separate storage room, for all of the food needed to run this place. The dogs were getting into the store room that was in the back of the main house. He had the new storage room made out of steel.

Almost everything on this farm is painted white. I have tried to change the colors a lot of times, but Greg won't let me. I think he's color blind. It took two years at least, to talk him into painting the barns red.

"You know Greg, nothing here ever changes. You do know there are more paint colors than just white."

"Yea, I know, but the price was right and the labor was free."

I smile at him. "The house is as beautiful as ever. I've always loved the porch balcony. When I close my eyes, I can almost smell the magnolia trees that bloom in the summer."

I reopen my eyes as we reach the front of the house. I see something just short of a Greek god. He is standing on the front porch looking directly at me. I pat my chest,

"Oh but wait… who... is... that?" I ask trying to breathe steadily, patting my chest with my hand. "Who is that beautiful creature with the long black hair? He makes my mouth water. Is he for me?"

Greg lets out a laugh that actually startled me. I wasn't sure where the sound even came from within him.

"Kim you look like a dog in heat!"

"Greg leave me be." I slap his shoulder playfully

"That's Andrew, he and his brother Robert are giving me a hand while they're in town." I put my hand on my heart pretending that it is racing.

"There are two of them? And why haven't I met them before?"

"They travel a lot, instructing people about the American Indians."

"Is he single?"

"Yes, they both are as a matter of fact. If you can keep from drooling, I will introduce you to him. His brother Robert is away right now, but should be back soon."

We both get out of the truck. I grab my camping gear from the back of the truck. Greg scans the area around the farm nervously. I catch this but ignore it. I'm preoccupied with the handsome creature on the porch.

"Sorry Greg but that is a beautiful man right there."

Greg sighs, "Kim you better stop before you're stuck to your jeans. And hey what am I?"

I look him up and down with a grin on my face. "Well Greg I've seen you naked." I look him up and down again, "well honestly…"

"Kim I think I see drooling. Let me get that for you."

Greg reaches for my face. I nudge him with one of my bags as we finish unloading his truck. I lag behind him as we head to the house.

Andrew is standing at the top of the steps waiting for us. He is wearing only a flannel shirt over a blue t-shirt that fits snuggly against his muscular body and a pair of tight jeans. Oh my! Oh my!

I catch him checking me out as he starts towards us. When our eyes meet we both turn away uncomfortably. That was awkward. I haven't blushed in forever until just now. I must be exhausted, yes that's it.

I whisper to Greg as we walk toward the front porch. "If I start acting like a fool please pull me away?"

"Ok, should I start now? And really like you've never seen a good looking man before?"

"No true, but looking like that without air brushing. No not really."

"You really need to stop looking in those rag magazines. Real men don't look like that. It's all airbrushing and steroids."

"Yeah, Greg when you stop looking at those girly magazines. At least the men don't have implants," I pause, well I hope they don't."

We are laughing by the time we reach the steps. I stop and stand within inches of Andrew. I'm usually very confidant, but he is making me nervous. I swear I can feel his body heat in the air. He should be freezing wearing just a flannel and t-shirt.

I know I look a mess. I wish I could have showered before meeting him for the first time. My stomach is full of the butterflies, the second he looks my direction. I feel like a school girl. This is ridiculous I'm a grown woman.

"Hey Andrew, this is the one and only Kim McConnor, Kim this is Andrew."

Andrew takes my hand in his, catching me off guard. I didn't expect him to touch me. Wow, as our hands connect. I feel an indescribable rush go through my body. Making my heart race; even my pulse increases. The vein in my neck feels like it will burst any second. The blood is rushing through my veins so fast. Every inch of my body comes alive with electricity. I've never felt anything like this before.

I become overwhelmed by the urgency to, damn why am I so turned on? My hormones are raging and yet I feel so much power running through me. Like I could run a mile and not break a sweat. That is if my knees don't give out on me at any minute. My body is completely confused. It doesn't know how or what it should be feeling. I try to speak but I barely get out a, "Hi."

I look at our hands still attached, wishing he would let go. I can't seem to let go myself. I'm feeling this force pulling me towards him. Wow this is sure strange. Did Greg put something in my food?

Andrew is still holding my hand that I am trying desperately to retrieve. He looks directly into my eyes like he can see my soul. I think that he is having the same reaction. Could something be in the air around here? Am I that hungry? Or that tired?

His face looks strained. Maybe he can't let go? Finally, after what felt like forever, he let go of my hand. My senses return to normal almost instantly. I look down at my hand turning it over in wonder. That was the strangest thing ever. It all was over within in a minute or two but felt like forever to me.

Acting as if nothing just happened Andrew starts asking me questions. "So you are the great Kim I hear so much about. It's nice to finally meet the person behind the legend." I collect myself and attempt to speak again.

"Greg what have you told him about me?" I look to Greg more pleading, than anything else. Clueless he doesn't get it.

"Greg talks about you all the time and I mean all the time."

"Well I can't say the same about you. Greg never has mentioned you to me before today." I give Greg a dirty look. How could he not tell me about Andrew before? And for not pulling me away when he could see me suffering. I'll get him later for this.

"How long have you been helping Greg, Andrew?"

"My brother and I help Greg out whenever we're in town. We do travel a lot educating people about our heritage. However, this time we will be here for a long while. Maybe I can see you in action?"

"Huh, What!" that pulled me right from my thoughts of him naked. I put my head down slightly closing my eyes.

"I think she is just exhausted from her ordeal. We'll see you later Andrew." Greg grabs me by the arm, pulling me through the front screen door of the house. In to the foyer we stop just inside the entrance. The wide stair case is to the right of the hall. Directly on my left is a pine wardrobe closet, with an adjoining bench, and four pairs of work boots under it, all of which are caked with mud.

The hall itself has four doors heading off of it. One door is on the right, just before the stairs, two are on the left wall, and one at the far end of the hall. The left wall is otherwise full of family pictures in various sized frames. The pictures date back to the eighteen hundreds.

I turn toward the right leading to the dining room. I try to play it cool with casual conversation. I am so embarrassed.

"Greg, you know this house never changes. I see you still have your mother's crystal chandelier hanging, and her cherry dining room set is still intact. I think she would be happy you left things as they were."

Once I'm sure that we are out of earshot of Andrew. I grab Greg's arm hard and whisper angrily.

"Thanks Greg, you let me make a fool of myself out there. Where was my back up?"

"Yea, I know he looks like a guy from the cover of a romance novel. I was enjoying watching you squirm. You never looked at me like that." I see the hurt on his face and rethink my attitude.

"Yea, Greg I'm sorry again, I thought you were past us?"

"I'm fine except when you're here. And seeing you drool over another guy doesn't help my ego any."

"What about Donna your girlfriend?"

"Yea, you're just so easy to be with, no baggage. And you never care if I smell like dogs. What more could a guy like me ask for?" We both snicker.

"Greg don't you think that my gift is baggage? You know it is to most people. It tends to make trouble. And I travel a lot, and with no permanent address just a van full of my stuff. Most men I've met don't want a woman that can take care of herself. I only have really one need for a man." I say grinning.

"Yea I know Kim, I would be happy to fill that need." As he takes a step towards me, I put my hand up to his chest to stop him from coming any closer.

"Thanks Greg, but I still believe that you are taken. You know that I wouldn't do that to any woman. It's just not right."

"Yea, I know, I'm not asking, but if things should change. You should know there's always an open invitation." He says almost pleading. I place my hand on his shoulder and look straight in his eyes.

"No you are taken! I think that I'll take a shower alone! Then hit the bed I'm beat. Good night Greg I'll see you in the morning." I give him a peck on the cheek before heading to the stairs.

“Good night Kim.” Andrew yells from outside embarrassing the hell out of me. All over again, I can’t believe this night.

“Oh shit! Did you hear every word? Andrew?”

“Yes I did, and things are definitely looking up around here.”

I give Greg one last look of defeat and walk up the wooden steps. Shaking my head, I can feel my face reddening. I close my bedroom door. I look around the room and notice not a thing has changed since I stayed here last. The room is plain white with only a bed, night stand, one dresser and a small round table with a lonely chair next to it.

I try to make sense of what just happened as I shower, what could reasonably cause the instant attraction I felt from Andrew’s hand touching mine? I dress for bed and wonder about Greg’s strange behavior.

I’m grateful that my door locks here, I can safely wear just a long t-shirt to sleep in. I don’t get this luxury in most of the places I stay. Usually I’m forced to share my room with a stranger. I hate wearing pajama pants to bed, but I do when I share a bedroom.

I lay down on the bed, my mind on overload. I know that I’m exhausted. But I know what I felt was like nothing that I’ve ever felt before in my life. The feeling of urgency to have him was much too strong. I mean, I’ve been really horny but that was over the top.

The electricity flowing through every bit of my body, I’ve never felt that. I think that he felt it too. He had a hard time articulating his words. But when he let go of my hand, instantly we were both fine. I replay our meeting over and over in my head. Exhaustion finally takes over and I am out cold.

I'm in a dream I think? I see wolves running and Andrew he's running beside them. I am standing at the edge of an open field watching them. Then out of nowhere, I hear Greg call my name. He seems to be far off in the distance. I wonder where he is.

Then I realize Greg is knocking on the bedroom door trying to wake me up. At least his voice was real. The dream was strange.

"Greg, did you really have to wake me up just now?" I holler.

"Kim its 9:00 in the morning, I have your breakfast with me, do you want it?"

"Yes just let me grab my robe."

"Oh sorry, do you still sleep in the nude?" he says a bit too cheery.

"No Greg, not nude. This is one of the only places that my bedroom door locks, thank God. So I can sleep comfortably. Beside I cover everything important. It's not like I'm sleeping in the nude. Like you think I do."

I unlock the door and slowly open it for Greg. As he enters I catch the look of surprise on his face.

"Kim?"

"What?"

"Why are there no dogs in your room? Usually every one of them not in a secure pen ends up in your room. You're like some kind of a dog magnet."

"I don't know. I'm as puzzled as you are about that. Is the doggie door in the wall working right?" I think about that. Its true when I'm here I always have a room full.

Greg sips on his coffee as I eat my breakfast, not much of one though, just a bagel and coffee. I'll grab something from the kitchen on my way out the door.

"So where do you want me to start today, since I'm up now?"

"Well since the dogs haven't shown any real signs of aggression, most of them are adjusting well. There's really only one animal that worries me. He's the horse we rescued from the same place as our last bunch of rescues. It was a week ago now. There were fifty dogs and Henry. He's not eating right and the vet said that there's nothing wrong with him medically, so it's up to you to fix him."

"Ok Greg let me finish here and then I'll be right out."

He leaves my room and I quickly dress in my jeans a tank top and a flannel. I grab my coat too. It's cold outside here especially this time of year. But Greg keeps the stables nicely heated.

I head down stairs and out to the front porch. Greg and Andrew are waiting for me. Oh, what a beautiful site to see first thing in the morning! I smile instantly I just can't hide it. I take a deep breath and try to clear my mind. It's going to be hard to concentrate with Andrew along. But I'll do my best.

"Let's get started, where is the horse?" I ask Greg, and he points in the direction of the front barn.

"Andrew is going to join us is that ok?"

"Morning Kim" Andrew says smiling, as he gets up from the rocker on the porch.

"Oh, so you want to see how this is done?"

"Of course if you don't mind me tagging along? I hope that's ok, I would really like to see you in action." I smile timidly at Andrew, Greg laughs. I shoot Greg a look to stop.

"I don't mind just stay far enough back so that you don't distract Henry."

Greg states with a hint of laughter, "It's not really Henry that I'm worried about getting distracted by Andrew being around."

"You're not funny Greg!" I snap back at him. Andrew smiles with a charismatic grin.

I can see that I will be getting into a lot of trouble this visit. "Where is Henry?"

"He is in the front paddock. I let him out for you so that the other horses wouldn't cloud your mind with thoughts."

"Thanks Greg, it will be better this way with him alone."

As we walk closer to Henry. I see that he is a magnificent black stallion. When we near the paddock, Greg puts his arm out in front of Andrew to stop him.

"We stop here. Andrew, she needs the space since this is the first time they have met. You are a definite distraction for Kim."

I holler over my shoulder, "I heard that Greg!"

I slowly approach the horse, mentally calling his name. My arms flat against my sides, my head facing the ground. I pretend to be chewing on something. I carefully open the gate and continue to walk with my head slightly down, not looking directly at him. This way he will not confuse my words with my body language. They will be the same.

When I reach him, I slowly raise my hands to his head closing my eyes. It helps me to concentrate better. Slowly, I rub his nose with soft small circles. I include his temples and continue down his face to his neck. I talk to him with reassurances in my voice. I need him to relax so he will trust me. I introduce myself to him, and then ask him to please share with me what is troubling him.

Greg and Andrew watch me in silence for a long time. Then I hear Andrew quietly ask Greg.

"How long does this usually take?"

"It's never the same. It all depends on the animal."

After a while Henry and I start walking together out of the gate. The horse stays right at my side. Occasionally he puts his nose on top of my head as we walk. I whisper, "Greg where are the large dogs that you rescued with him?"

Greg knows not to speak at this moment and points to the barn. If he talks it could break Henry's concentration. He leads us around toward the rear barn. When we get to the door, I tell them that the dog I'm looking for is a German shepherd mix that is very large. Can you find him for me and bring him out? I think he is mixed with Great Pyrenees or Saint Bernard. It's not very clear the dogs face is furry and it is rather large."

"Hey I know which one she's talking about." Andrew spouts out excitedly, he runs into the barn. Greg gives me a look as if to say sorry. Luckily at this point Henry is so in tune with my thoughts, that hearing Andrew's voice didn't startle him into a panic. Andrew comes back dragging a huge hairy mess behind him.

The horse starts to whinny and flare his tail with delight. The dog looks up and he is so excited that his entire body is wiggling with happiness. Andrew drops the leash and the horse and dog start running around each other making happy noises.

"Well, I don't believe it, we knew he was depressed, but I had no idea that it was because of him missing his buddy."

"Wow! It looks as if they haven't seen each other in a long time," Greg exclaims. The two of them are running and jumping all over the place. I have a hard time getting them back to the paddock. They are so excited seeing each other.

As we lean against the fence, watching the two of them play, Andrew turns toward me. I can see the questions on his face before he asks.

"Ok Kim just how did you do that? I would never have figured it out that they were missing each other."

I give Greg a look of concern.

"It's ok," Greg reassures me. "He is cool with it; you didn't freak him out or anything."

"Ok, Andrew really it's quite easy for me most of the time. I have to open my mind and let their thoughts come in. Some words come but mostly I see pictures of what they are trying to say.

Henry kept showing me pictures of him and a dog playing together since they were babies. By the way thanks Andrew for going in there and bringing out the dog. I don't think I could have dealt with all of their voices at once just yet.

Henry was a bit tough to get through to since he really mistrusts people. The people he came from barely fed him and he had no shelter. After they have a few days together, I'll go back in with them and try grooming them both. It will be the first time anyone will have ever brushed either of them. "

We all stand at the fence watching Henry and his friend play. Then Greg sneaks away leaving me and Andrew standing there alone. No my best friend is not setting me up. I'll get him later for this.

Andrew takes a step closer to me leaving only inches between his elbow and mine. Butterflies have moved back into my stomach. I take a deep breath as he moves closer to me. He smells good too, just a little musky. Why am I letting him get to me? I'm too strong for this. It's not like me to be so attracted to a man. Not this fast I just met him. What the hell is wrong with me?

I look him over again. Damn I might just have to sample the menu. There is something about him besides the electric jolt last night. I think Greg is setting us up. He knows how long I have dreamed of finding a man who can accept me for me. Maybe this could be a good thing.

"Kim are you gonna stay here long?"

"I'll be here as long as Greg needs me. Then I'll move on to some other rescue group that needs my services. How about you, how long are you here for?"

"I'll be here for a long stay this time. I don't have any lectures scheduled until a month from now. I'm surprised that we haven't run into each other before. I've been here many times over the years."

"Funny I was thinking the same thing. Maybe Greg didn't want us to meet before. You know he and I tried dating long distance, but we found out that we are better off just friends."

He gives me a strange look before he asks me. "Is that what you two were talking about last night? How long ago was that?"

"Oh it's been years now, nothing to worry about."

"You mean if we were to possibly … Greg wouldn't mind?"
"No, I don't think that will be a problem if we should possibly?"

Oops did he just proposition me? I'm thinking sex, but I don't think that's what he is thinking, or is it? I need to change the subject and step away from him a bit. He is much too close. I can feel the heat coming off of his body again. I bend down taking a step away. I fix my imaginary untied shoe lace. When I stand upright again I'm standing a full foot away from him.

"Greg said that you have a brother that's coming here. When is he due back?"

"Robert should be back any day now."

I think I now know why Greg was in a hurry for me to get here. So I would meet Andrew first, before meeting Robert. My dear friend is up to something. I'll let this play out for a while first before I confront him.

"Andrew I better get going I have a lot of dogs to work with. I'll see you around later."

I walk away quickly leaving him standing there. Why am I letting this stranger get to me so easily? The adrenaline thing must have been caused by my utter exhaustion.

5

I kill the rest of the morning by wandering around the farm. I stop to talk with some of the animals to see how they're doing. Then I go in the house, straight to the kitchen to see Doris.

We have lunch together and catch up on our lives. Doris is like my other mother. In fact she is everyone's other mother. I'm really not sure how old she is though. Oddly, she never seems to age.

Afterwards I meet with some of the newer rescue dogs in the barn. Greg is in there. He helps me with the large dog's first. Things are going smoothly with most of them. There is one rather large Rottweiler that I try to communicate with, but all I get from him is defensive images and his name William. He is not happy here at all! I try to get through to him for over an hour then I throw in the towel. I meet up with Greg by the barn doors.

"Greg, I think it's going to take a long time getting through, he has me blocked out completely. I'll try to work with him at a later time I'm getting worn out."

I leave Greg to deal with the dogs and go to sit on the porch. Talking with the dogs usually tires me out after doing it a while. Besides I think I'm still recouping from my tumble down the mountain. I rub the back of my neck, its sore, and I'm tired. It sure has turned into a very long day. I rest for about an hour. Then I take a walk to clear my head some.

I notice that some of the helpers are watching me. It really starts to freak me out the way they are staring. They've never done this to me before. I spot Andrew watching me too. I smile back to him, but wonder what the hell is going on around here? I feel like the unsuspecting sacrifice in a horror movie.

I decide to duck back into the barn and work with the dogs some more. The dogs seem to be the only sane ones here. I take off my jacket and go in to a pen of puppies. Big mistake on my part, I get jumped all at once. I let them play tug-o-war with my fingers and shirt. They have sharp teeth but, we all have fun. I tire them out as well as myself.

I drag myself into the main house for dinner. Andrew joins Greg and me at the kitchen table. The helpers eat at the dining room table. There is not always room there, so I usually eat in the kitchen with Doris. I noticed that there wasn't much talking as we ate. After dinner, I go and grab a blanket off of a chair in the living room, and head out to the porch. I love to sit in the night air here.

When I get there, I see that there are a few other people sitting on the porch. They all gaze at me. There's that creepy feeling again. I decide to sit on the porch next to Greg. He tells me that he has built a bunk house off the back of the house since I was last here. It's for the volunteers that are drifters. Doris won't take to them staying in the house. Some, a while back, stole from Greg. So now they have a separate place to stay.

It makes me happier knowing they won't be sleeping in the house, especially now that some of them keep watching me. I stay on the porch, for a while listening to the multiple conversations around me. But none are really worth listening to tonight, so I get up and head for bed.

Andrew gets up as well and follows me in the house and up the stairs. He walks right behind me not talking.

"Creepy" I can imagine the eerie music playing in my head as I walk to my bedroom door.

When I get to my bedroom he is standing directly beside me. I look up into his big brown eyes, my hand on the door handle ready to turn it. He looks at my face for a long moment. Then he hugs me tight and swiftly turns for his own room. I thought that he was going to kiss me. It felt like he was. Oh well, he's a strange one. What has Greg gotten me into?

The next few days are about work with Greg. Sometimes Andrew helps me with the dogs. He seems to be an alright guy. But all the helpers watch my every move. I think Andrew is attempting to flirt with me at times. He seems to be finding reasons to be where ever I am working during the day.

He's not really that good at flirting though. But he's trying and I'm enjoying the attention. Greg not so much, I think he is a tad jealous. I hope Andrew knows that I don't do relationships. I'm not around long enough in one place. I don't really care to break hearts either. Maybe he's just playing too.

On Friday morning I get a surprise. Andrew's brother Robert shows up. I get to find out first by running right into him in the hall. Literally, we run into each other. I trip over Coco a Chihuahua and fall into his arms, face first, smack into his chest. I inhale his musky scent, yum. He catches me in his arms and holds me a bit too long. We both laugh awkwardly with embarrassment.

"You must be Kim?"

"Yea and you must be Robert?" I am so embarrassed; I know it's showing on my red face. I look down and pretend to be fixing my long sleeves.

"Yea I am. What did they tell you about me anything good?" He says playfully.

"Well they actually didn't say too much about you. They could have at least said that good looks run in your family."

"Well thank you miss. I thought you charmed animals not men?" He says smiling

"Well it depends on the man I suppose." He motions with his hand for me to go first but I shake my head no and let him go first, so I can check out his butt. It looks good in his wranglers, oh country boys…

We walk down the stairs headed to the kitchen for breakfast. As I check out his ass on the steps I get caught looking. Of course, I turn red instantly.

"Do you like what you see?"

I giggle like a girl, "Yes I did very much. You must work out a lot, like Andrew?" He gives me a crooked smile.

"I can take Andrew any day Kim."

"Oh, should I ask him who is stronger?"

"No, I'll let him go on thinking he's the stronger one."

Both Greg and Andrew nearly snap their necks. They move so suddenly when Robert and I enter the kitchen laughing together. Neither of them looks too happy about it either.

"I see you've met Kim?"

"Yes I have," he looks me up and down. I roll my eyes at him.

"Your Chihuahua luckily tripped her right into my arms."

Andrew shot him a nasty look, so fast I almost missed it. Hmmm, I guess this is going to be a competition between brothers. This could be fun. Robert looks at me grinning like he knows what I'm thinking. There's that eerie music again and a chill going up my back.

I look around the room, "Greg, no ghosts in this house right?" He looks at me like I'm crazy, and shakes his head no.

"Just checking, I keep getting chills lately."

"It's my awesomeness getting to you. I have that effect on some women." Robert states confidently. The rest of us crack up laughing.

Once we sit down for breakfast, no one seems to be comfortable at the table. I eat my food quickly. I put my dishes in the sink, grab my coat and go out towards the barns to work.

I find myself with two shadows now. They seem to be taking turns following me around the farm. The helpers are even more intense with their staring as well. That is until I stop walking around noon. I check myself for anything not tucked in or unzipped. Making sure that my little display is seen by quite a few people.

Everything is where it belongs. When they see me doing this some of them stop looking so much. Or they got better at hiding it from me. I'm not used to people watching me. Most people avoid me, afraid that I might be able to read their minds too.

Towards the evening, I run in to Greg. He's on the porch sitting with Andrew and Robert. The three of them are talking about their day. I just sit and listen for a while. They go on and on about how hard they worked. I am bored with the whole conversation. So I get up to go in the house.

Casually, I say as I'm leaving, "Could one of you tell the volunteers, that I am not something to watch. If they have questions for me, to ask me and not stare at me all day like I have two heads or something." I let the screen door slam as I enter the house. Not one of them replies to my statement.

Later, we all meet up at the dinner table. None of them say a thing to me. Robert and Andrew are eating like starved dogs. Greg is shielding his face with his hand as he eats.

I know they know what's going on, but no one has clued me in yet. If I get gawked at again tomorrow then I'll corner the weakest one. Maybe they have a bet going on? It wouldn't be the first time. But usually it's between two friends I've come across not two brothers. It's too damn quiet at this table for my liking. I need to stop over analyzing things.

"Hey Greg didn't you say earlier, that animal control found another puppy mill close by?"

"Yup, they did why?" I see relief on his face that the silence is broken. He hates awkward silence too.

"Well Greg, I was just wondering when they are going to raid them."

"They have to wait for the proper procedures to happen first. You know issue warnings first. Then give them time to clean things up, etc. The animals will have to suffer even longer, as we just sit back and wait for the law to do what it has to do."

"Yea I know they have to do this legally. Otherwise the jerks just get the animals back because of some stupid legal loophole. So let me know when it's time to help. I'll go with you to gather the dogs."

"Sure Kim, I can always use your skills."

Robert chimes in, "Greg will you still need me? I thought that I was going with you on the next rescue?"

"Robert, the more the merrier, I can use all the help I can get."

"Oh good, just making sure. Maybe I can witness Kim using her special talent," he says with sarcasm

"Do you doubt my talent, or are you curious about it Robert?" I ask skeptically.

"No Kim, I really do want to observe you talk with the dogs, honestly," he says defending himself.

"Ok but haven't you been watching me already. Between you, Andrew and the volunteers, I feel like I am supposed to do a special trick or something. I've never had so many eyes on me before when I've stayed here. But if you want a private lesson, I'll be doing it every day, free of charge."

"Oh, maybe I'll be able to find some free time tomorrow afternoon. That's if Greg doesn't find too much for me to do."

"Like I work you any harder than I do myself?" Greg moans defensively.

"Well there are times that I wonder." Robert says with humor.

We finish eating our diners with the men talking about tomorrow's chores. I decide to skip the porch tonight. I'm still somewhat tired. I tell them all good night as I get up from the table. They all reply back for me to have a good night too.

Andrew must have gotten up to follow me. He calls out to me to wait as I round the corner towards the steps.

"Hey, I'll walk up with you Kim, wait up."

"Ok Andrew"

He walks up behind me on the stairs and follows me down the hall to my room. I put my key in and turn toward him to say good night. He is right in front of me again just gazing at me. His brown eyes are going to make me melt I'm sure.

He is so close to my body. I can feel the heat generating off of him. Please don't touch me I'll cave. I look up into his brown eyes wondering what he wants.

He hugs me quickly, then he turns crosses the hall and enters his bedroom. I stand there shaking my head not sure what that was all about. Ok, that makes twice he's done that to me. Well at least I didn't get all turned on from it. Maybe that thrill thing was just a onetime thing. I can only pray.

Once alone, in my room, I toss my clothes on the end of the bed then take a shower. When I come out of the bathroom in my night shirt, I hear knocking at my door. Ok which one of them could that be?

"Who is it?"

"Kim, it's me Greg, can I come in for a minute?"

"Yea I guess so, but you have to behave yourself, ok?"

He giggles, "Yes I promise I'll be good. I just want to talk to you."

I open the door and he comes in to sit in the chair by the bed. I sit legs crossed on the corner of the bed facing him. He looks concerned, but I wait for him to speak his mind. Knowing Greg as well as I do, something is really bothering him. However if he comes out with all of it I will be surprised, he's not very good at expressing his emotions.

He sits there for a few minutes before he begins talking. "Kim I know you very well and I also know Andrew and Robert. So I feel I have to say something to you because of how I feel. I'm not trying to be judgmental or something. I saw the way both of them look at you and I know you like what you see also," I chuckle.

"Kim, just be careful please, if you choose one of them stay with that one. I would prefer it be Andrew. I think that he would treat you better than Robert. Robert has a reputation of being… well not nice to his girlfriends."

"Greg, no one said that anything would happen between me and one of them. Is there a bet going on? Is that why everyone is watching me? You're not trying to marry me off are you?"

"No, no!" he blurts out defensively.

"It's not like I wouldn't like to have a man of my very own, to not to have to sleep alone or with strangers. To belong somewhere to someone would be great. But just because they like what they see doesn't mean anything.

You know better than anyone how hard it is for me to keep a boyfriend. It would be great if one of them accepted me for what I am. But too many men think that they can handle it. They either get freaked out or they feel inferior after a while."

"I think that you will find that these men are very different from any others you have met before. There's things about them that." Greg pauses, "That makes them stand out from the other men."

"Greg you're sounding like you have a secret. What are you not telling me about Andrew and Robert? Are they gay? That would just be a dreadful waste of my fantasies?"

"No they are definitely not gay." He laughs

"Oh thank God for that. Then what are you hiding from me?" He wrings his hands in one another.

I know he is hiding something. I'll have to give him some more time to come clean. I have to be patient with Greg. He is not a person that you can push for information. If I do he'll clam up and not give me anything at all.

"Nothing I just worry about you. They are not boys; they are men so just watch out, ok."

"Ok, I figure that I would wait and see which one makes the first move. And go from there. I don't want to get in the middle of brothers. Greg you know that I enjoy male company. But I can live without them just as easily. If dating one of them is going to cause you so much stress, then I'll stay away from them both. I value our friendship way too much." I rethink that though after my hugs from Andrew.

"But it might be too late. I think Andrew already did make a move when he hugged me earlier."

"Did he touch your skin?" Greg blurts out at me anxiously.

I smirk at him, so that wasn't my imagination when he touched me that first night. I did feel something more than just a rush of desire. I think that I'll keep that to myself for now though. Greg looks very distraught.

"No, my shirt covered where he touched. Is everything ok with you Greg?"

"I'm not, I well, I've known them all of my life and I've loved you most of my adult life. I don't want to see any of you get hurt."

I'm sure I saw him shudder which is not like him. Greg is usually a strong person. I go kneel in front of him, he is so obviously troubled. I put my arms out for him and he simply falls into me. I hold him for a while feeling his tension slowly relax. Then he pulls away fast as someone else knocks on my door.

"Who's there?" I ask,

"Robert!"

I give Greg a questioning look. And he just shrugs his shoulders. I walk to the door and open it for Robert. He scans the room quickly and enters sniffing the air like he smells something. He picks up my clothes I had on earlier and sniffs them. That was a strange thing to do.

"Robert is there something wrong?"

"No I thought I heard… Andrew in here but I see it's only Greg."

"Yea we were just talking about stuff. Did you need something?"

"No, never mind I'll see you tomorrow have a good night." Robert turns and walks out my door leaving it open. He crosses the hall to his room. I close the door and stand against it.

"Greg, what the hell was that?"

"Well I would rather not say at this time. I think that I'll call it a night. I'll see you in the morning Kim." Greg kisses my cheek and leaves my room quickly.

I close the door and wonder, what kind of mystery is really going on here. Greg is not acting like himself. With the feelings, Andrew caused me to feel. Robert entered my room sniffing my clothes. Like he could actually smell his brother's scent, only animals can do that, right? They both have strong musk scents but nice, strong, not over whelming or repulsive.

Speaking of animals where are the inside dogs? Some of them always come up and sleep in my room when I'm here. I think I need a dog in here tonight things are getting strange.

I grab my key and head down stairs to find a dog or two. I always sleep better when I know one is close by. The dogs can hear sounds that I would sleep right through. I look first in the living room where I'm sure that I'll find someone sleeping on the couch. And sure enough I find Lakita she is an old German shepherd mostly tan, with a black muzzle which is now mostly gray. I don't want to wake anyone up so I talk to her telepathically.

"Can you make it up the stairs Lakita?"

"No, I can't anymore, my legs are too weak. Oh, and none of the male dogs will go upstairs either while Robert is here. I don't know why. They just don't go up there when he is here."

"Ok Lakita thanks do you know where Coco is tonight?"

"I think she is in the family room she likes the rocker to sleep in."

"Good night girl, I'll see you in the morning."

I walk away from her wondering why the males are scared of Robert. What could he have done to scare them away? I'll have to investigate that.

I walk into the family room and easily pick up Coco. She is a black Chihuahua. She wearily opens her eyes and then gives me lots of kisses. I carry her up to bed. She first apologizes for tripping me. Then, she asks me a hundred questions about where I've been.

6

It's Saturday, yeah! We're gathered around the dining room table eating lunch. Everyone is deciding what they are going to do tonight. The bulk of us decide to go out to New Heights bar for drinking and dancing, in that order. It's a nice local bar with a small dance floor. Their food is pretty good too. It reminds me of Merlotte's but without the vampires since they don't really exist.

Greg figures that it would be a good way for me to get to know the boys in a non work environment. I think he's full of shit and is up to something. But a night out is always a good thing. I love to dance and getting a chance to be close to one of my personal shadows. Not a thing I want to pass up.

When we finish our work for the day everyone showers and puts on their dancing boots. I wear a fringed white bustier and a pair of black lee jeans that fit me like a glove. I check my view in the mirror and think 'not too bad.' I check my face once more before I grab my jacket then head down stairs to meet up with the others.

I get a ride with Greg, while the brothers take Roberts's truck. Everyone else piles into various other vehicles. It's a little ways to the bar, and Greg and I talk some about the boys until we get there.

"So Greg, we haven't really had any time to think, let alone talk. Give me some history on Andrew and Robert."

"Like what?"

"Well where are they from? How long have you known them? And most importantly, why are two men as handsome as they are still single?"

He gives me a sideways glance. Don't think he wants to answer my questions. I'll give him a few minutes. Then I'll pester him again.

"Times up Greg, are you going to answer me?"

He rolls his eyes at me and shrugs. "I grew up knowing them both. Their parents have a house on a piece of land north of me. They are really good people, honorable people. I have always gotten along better with Andrew then Robert. Andrew is shy like I am with women. Robert I've heard can be ruff to his girlfriends. Be careful with him ok?"

"Yea sure, you going to tell me why I got all hot and bothered when Andrew touched me?"

"Nope, I'm not touching that one."

"Some friend you are Greg."

"Hey look Kim we're here!"

I'll leave him be for now. There are too many people around to ask any more questions right now anyway. Everyone breaks apart into their own little groups. Greg and I sit at the bar to wait for Donna, Greg's girlfriend. I'll be meeting her for the first time tonight.

"Hey guys what'll it be?" The bartender asks.

Greg replies, "We'll have two beers Brian."

"Its Kim right, here you go, do you want a glass?"

"Yea that's my name and no glass Brian, I'm good. I haven't been in here in a long while. I wouldn't expect you to remember my name."

"I probably wouldn't have if Greg wasn't counting down the days until you got here."

Brian walks away to help another customer. Oblivious that he put Greg right into the fire. Greg knows it to; he is squirming in his chair. He is definitely up to no good.

"Greg, you only called me last week. How long have you been planning on me coming?"

He doesn't even look my way he knows my expression is one of suspicion.

"Kim lets go dance."

I ignore his request. When he finally looks at me, I scowl at him and he ignores me at first. Since, I don't move from my stool. I leave him no alternative he has to answer me.

"Greg?"

"I wanted to call you earlier honestly, and then Robert and Andrew showed up. I waited a while longer besides you had your hands full in Tulsa. I didn't want to call you until I really needed you."

He's bullshitting me again. He has no idea how transparent he is. I'm going to have to drag it out of him piece by piece it seems. We sip on our beers watching a game on TV.

"Oh, hey when is Donna getting here?"

"She'll be here soon she is probably running late as always."

"What does she do for a living?"

"She's a lawyer, she owns her own practice."

"Does she specialize in anything?"

"Funny you should ask. She is an animal welfare lawyer. But she is also a divorce lawyer for the wealthy." Insert an awkward pause.

"Kim don't be put off, she does come from money. She can come across brash at times, but she has a really big heart."

"I'll be the judge of that." I see the concern in his face and decide to ease his mind. I know how much he values my input.

"Greg, if you love her, I'll love her too."

A voice comes from behind us. "That's good to hear, hi Kim? I'm Donna nice to finally meet you." We shake hands politely.

"Hi Donna, here take my stool, or should we go and get a table?"

"Let's get a table," Greg suggests

The three of us go and select a table near the dance floor. I soon find out Donna loves to dance. And Greg isn't too bad either, once he's had a few beers in him, liquid courage.

We sit and chat getting to know each other. Donna doesn't seem too bad for a rich lawyer. She uses some terms that I don't know. I have her break them down to normal English for me. Otherwise the conversation is light. When we finish our second beer, Donna and I get up to dance again.

They're playing eighties music tonight. She spent her teen years listening to this stuff. I'm a bit young for it, but I do enjoy dancing to it.

When we finally sit back down I look around the bar and notice that Robert and Andrew are sitting with a group of Native Americans. They all are looking this way and talking about something.

When Donna and I return to the table, I give Greg another chance to spill what he is hiding. “Greg, do you know what that is about over there?” I motion toward the table with my eyes. “They keep looking over here and talking and when I catch them, they look away.”

Greg with a wide grin says, “Oh, don’t mind them, their just jealous.” He gloats, “I’m sitting with the two most beautiful women in the place.”

Donna and I just laugh at him. I think he’s already drunk. I don’t ask him again but, it does bother me. It just looks very suspicious to me. The way they quickly look away when I catch them. I try to ignore it and just enjoy my night.

Greg and I talk about dogs. Donna tries to appear interested in our conversation. But I can tell she really isn’t that interested. Robert walks up to our table smiling deviously. Here we go, I smile, let the games begin I think to myself.

“Kim would you like to dance with me?”

“Robert you know how to dance to this music?”

“Yes, can you?” he grins,

“Yes and I know you saw me dancing with Donna.”

“Yea, I guess I did, so you going to dance with me or not?”

I let him lead me to where he wants to dance at. The floor is almost empty. He chooses a spot closer to his table than mine. We dance to two fast songs in a row. I discover he’s not too bad at dancing either.

Then the music changes to a slow dance. I start to feel nervous inside. I gaze up at him. I am five seven and he has to be at least six four. I know he can see the question on my face. But without a word he takes my hands quickly and puts them on either side of his waist.

That was funny, I just got the same rush of feelings that I did when Andrew held my hand. The rush was too swift to seriously affect my self-control. Thank Goodness. Is this an Indian thing? I've never touched one before, maybe?

As we dance he pulls me in tight to his body leaving no room between us. I feel his warmth through his clothes and how firm his um… abs are. I'm really enjoying this dance even without the desire thing going on. I rest my head against his chest and close my eyes. It feels good with his arms wrapped around me. I almost wish the music would just go on. Luckily the song fades into another slow song. We continue dancing until Andrew taps on Roberts shoulder.

"May I cut in big brother?"

They exchange a serious look and Robert gives into Andrew. We pretty much take the same position, careful not to touch skin. Andrew waits until Robert is far enough away not to hear him. Then softly in my ear whispers,

"Kim, are you enjoying yourself tonight?"

The warmth of his breath sends a tingle all through me. I swallow hard,

"How couldn't I enjoy myself? I'm dancing with one of the two most handsome men in here." He actually blushes, I can't believe it.

"Hey are the guys you're sitting with all from the same tribe?"

"They are all members of my tribe."

"Where are their girlfriends?"

"The guys that have girlfriends are meeting with them later. Girls always take longer to get ready to go anywhere." He says with humor in his words.

"Oh really, is your girlfriend coming in later?"

"No, I don't have one."

"Is Robert's girlfriend coming in later?"

"No he doesn't have one either. So you get two dance partners for the whole night to yourself. Do you think that you can keep up?"

"I'll do my best."

When the song ends he turns to go back to his table, so, I go back to my own table. As soon as I sit down, Donna is full of questions about my dance partners. She wants to know which one I like best, if I plan to date one of them. You know the usual girl questions.

The more I talk with Donna, the more I think she is pretty normal. I can tell she has class but, she can hang out with regular people too. I'll have to tell Greg later that I approve of her. Though it shouldn't matter as much as it does to him what I think of his girlfriend.

"Well Donna they both passed the dancing test and seem like really nice guys." I glance over at their table.

"I can't get into a serious relationship with anyone."

"That's a shame; they sure do fill a pair of jeans don't they?"

"Yes, they sure do, and they are both so strong. You should feel the muscles in their chest."

Greg protests with a delayed reaction and a hurt expression on his face.

"Hey, sitting right here."

"Oh Greg, I think that Donna knows she's a lucky women to have you." We change the conversation to the décor of the bar to pacify poor Greg.

As the night progresses, Donna, Greg and I continue to talk and drink. That is, when I'm not dancing with Andrew or Robert. Then about midnight Greg and Donna leave me there alone.

Around the same time the Indian girlfriends show up. They join some tables together. Robert comes over to me and asks me to join their group. As it turns out, I'm the only blonde at the table and stick out like a sore thumb. At least everyone is polite, as I'm introduced to the group.

We all share in the topics of dogs and horses. Some are talking about taking a fishing trip on a nearby lake. Others are talking about race cars. It's a pretty normal conversation in this place.

My two men take turns dancing with me and some of the other women at our table. (Cousins I'm told) I do notice that they hold the hands of the other women when they dance.

Jasmine who works on the farm is one of them. She is sitting on the other end of the table. I would like to talk with her. She could give me information about what is going on around here. She does tend to rattle on when she drinks. Maybe that is why Robert made everyone move down a couple of chairs when I joined them, so that I couldn't talk with Jasmine.

I think that the guys are scrutinizing what they say to me. They seem to be choosing their words carefully but, on the other hand, I am getting drunk. I could be reading something into where it isn't. Maybe I'm overly suspicious lately?

"Kim it's almost closing time we should get you back to the farm."

"Yea, you're right Robert we should."

"Kim it's almost closing time."

"Robert you don't have to tell me twice. I heard you the first time. How I am getting back to the farm anyway?"

Those within ear shot look uneasily at Robert and me then at each other. Maybe I drank more than I thought? But they clink their beer bottles together and smile broadly. Robert smiles broadly, while Andrew puts his face down, with a look of defeat. That I just couldn't explain.

"What did I say?" Looking at Robert and Andrew questioningly, no one answers me, I must be missing something?

"Ok, who is driving me home?" Suddenly, Andrew blurts out happily,

"Well Robert we could give her a ride but do we really want to? What if she gets sick in your truck on the way to the farm?"

"I'll just hose it out. You know like I did for you last time little brother." He chuckles,

"Hey, she doesn't need to know that."

"Don't worry guys. I won't get sick in the truck. I didn't drink that much."

We say our goodbyes to the people we're sitting with. We all make sure to say good bye to Brian before we leave. He is the bartender and owner of the tavern. It's a smart thing staying on his good side.

The three of us are stumbling across the parking lot toward the truck. I walk slower on purpose. I want to admire the view and Andrew catches me looking at his butt. I roll my eyes. Do they have esp. or something? They both have on blue jeans that hug their butts nicely. Their t-shirts also show most of their muscle through the thin material. I wonder why they don't wear jackets.

"Kim what are you smiling at?" Feeling the effects of the alcohol I reply,

"Two very fine pieces of eye candy." they both laugh.

"Kim, I think you're very drunk. Here, walk between us so we can keep an eye on you." Andrew puts his arm on my shoulder. He pulls me close to him. "Greg would kill us both if we show up without you. You just might wander off in the wrong direction."

"You're just too important to lose now that we found you." Robert says as he slips his arm around my waist. He makes it incredibly difficult to walk between the two of them. But it is fun being the center of attention. Robert takes the wheel and Andrew helps me up into the truck. Putting me smack dab in the middle of them. Their bodies are very warm. Being this close and drunk my female hormones start to purr.

My conscious tells me not to do what I'm thinking. It just couldn't end well. The power they both have over me when we touch skin to skin would probably make me explode. But what a way to go! I'll just sit here quietly smiling like a Cheshire cat.

"Kim, you ok? Is it too warm in here? I could open a window if you want."

"You sure Robert, I'm not sure she is even here. She looks like her mind is far away."

"No believe me my thoughts are right here in this truck." They exchange looks that I can't figure out.

"And what exactly does that mean Kim? Where is your mind?"

"Andrew it's where it shouldn't be at the moment?" I wonder which one of them kisses better? A man's kiss tells a lot about him.

"Do you care to share your thoughts with us?" Andrew asks hopefully. I notice Robert has a smug smile on his face. Wonder what he's thinking.

"Andrew, I don't think that would be a very good idea, considering that I am outnumbered at the moment. Ah, how much longer is it until we get back to the farm?" I yawn,

"It'll be a little while, so here put your head on my shoulder, I'll wake you when we get there. I think you need to rest, and sleep off some of the alcohol."

"Thanks Andrew, I think that you're right." He puts his arm around me and pulls me in close to his chest. It feels very warm and cozy. Like, I belong right where I am at this moment.

"Andrew, are you always so warm?"

"Yes we tend to run hotter than most men do. Am I too hot for you?" he jests

"No not at all," I scoot my butt over closer to Robert and place my head in Andrews lap. It might be the alcohol, but I feel very secure between the both of them. Robert rests his arm on my thigh. I think as I feel Andrew stroke my hair. Good thing we are all clothed it could get real messy in here. And that is the last thought I have.

7

The next thing I know, its morning. I wake in my room still completely clothed except for my boots and socks. Well that's good neither of them took advantage of me last night. I shower and dress in my usual jeans and a t -shirt.

I walk down the stairs to the kitchen. As I turn the corner. I see my three men and Donna at the table, eating breakfast. I walk over to Robert and Andrew sitting next to each other. I give them each a kiss on the tops of their heads. I figure they deserve it. Since they didn't take advantage of me, when either one of them could have. The two of them stop eating to look at each other in wonder. As I take my seat across the table from them. They both look at me skeptically. I smile at first then tell them why I kissed them.

"The kiss was because. You were gentleman last night when you brought me home. I must have fallen asleep in the truck?"

I catch the fear flashing across Greg's face. He quickly glares at the two of them. If I didn't know better, Greg looked as if he was about to kill them both.

Robert ignores Greg's fierce look completely. He simply grins at Greg, "Yea I carried you up the stairs; Andrew fell asleep in the truck too. I woke his ass up and made him walk." Andrew play punches Robert in the arm. I snicker.

"Thank you both I had a very nice time last night."

"We did too," they say at the same time and get right back to eating. I honestly don't know where they put it all.

Doris makes sure all of us eat properly around here. This morning she made us scrambled eggs, banana pancakes and bacon. There wasn't much talking going on. I think all of us were a little worn out from last night. I notice that Greg can't get the smile off of his face. I just can't resist.

"Greg did you have a good time last night?"

He never gets the chance to answer me. Because Robert and Andrew instantly, start to rib Greg about the noises they heard coming from his room. They say he sounded like an injured animal. A pancake flies at Robert landing short. Doris smacks the back of Greg's head and the battle is over. She will not stand for wasting food or horse play at her table. They all clear out soon after that. While I stay behind and help Doris clear the table.

"So Kim, I see that you're getting along well with the wolf brothers?"

"Excuse me Doris?"

"Robert and Andrew, their last name is lobo. Didn't you know their last name?"

"No, I haven't asked, and they didn't offer it I guess. But yes they seem like good guys they are, right Doris?"

"Yes they are, just watch it, they can play rough I hear."

"Thanks Doris, I'll keep that in mind."

I head over to the stables to visit with Henry. I need to do something easy this morning. I enter the stables and think his name. He sticks his head out of his stall and whinnies at me. I walk towards him and open his stall to go in. He is so happy to see me. In his excitement he nudges me a bit too hard with his head, and almost knocks me down.

"Henry I'm happy to see you too. But calm down a little please." He whinnies again.

I start running my fingers all over his back. In small slow circles which calms him right down. I found that he likes this motion the best. I bought a book on t-touch therapeutic massage for animals. Believe me I don't have it perfected by any means. But I haven't had any complaints from the animals I have practiced on. I would love to take the classes on the subject. But with what I make, I can't afford it.

I never do anything deep in the tissue. I use a light to moderate touch. I go by what the animal tells me they like the most. I work on most of his body over the next hour.

I let Henry know that I am going to get his brush and lead. So we can go out into his paddock, after I have finished brushing him. I walk to the end of the stable where all of the supplies are kept. I pick out a good brush and a rope lead.

As I turn around I'm thinking of last night. Not paying attention to where I'm going. And I run right into Jasmine. She is a beautiful Native American with long jet black hair. She wears it in a long single braid down the center of her back. She has large coal eyes that compliment her round face nicely. I have always admired her beauty. Feeling like a fool, "Jasmine I'm so sorry I was lost in thought somewhere. Are you ok, I didn't hurt you did I?"

"I'm alright no damage done. I think I know where your mind was. She smirks, "I saw you dancing last night with my cousins did you have fun?" She says with a hint of annoyance in her voice.

"Yes I did, it was fun. They are both very nice guys. I didn't step on anyone's toes did I? Andrew told me that neither of them have girlfriends."

"No, they are both single. But you have to choose one of them. They don't deserve to be led on." Boy everyone is in on this set up thing I guess.

"Really Jasmine, I wouldn't want either of them to get hurt. I didn't realize dancing with them would be such a serious thing to do. I better straighten this out as soon as possible. Maybe I should leave the farm. Come back when they leave again."

Panic in her voice, "Kim, I shouldn't have said… anything. It's none of my business what you do. Please don't leave, you are needed here. Trust me on this. That's all I really have to say. Forget that I said anything at all. If they knew they would… be very upset with me. Kim, you're working with Henry today?"

I snicker at her she spoke so fast I almost missed some of what she was saying. "Yes that was my plan for the morning. I like you Jasmine you have always been kind to me. I won't say anything that might cause trouble. But we will talk again later girl. When I have more insight as to what is going on around here. I'm not as dumb as I might appear."

I leave her standing there with a confused look lingering on her face. I think over our conversation as I walk back to Henry's stall. Something is definitely going on around here. But for now I will just listen and wait until I have enough information to corner one of them. Maybe it is just a setup, but I don't know how it could work out well. They travel a lot too.

I enter Henry's stall and begin to brush him just the way he likes. I start to mull things over. The foot prints in the snow really have me puzzled still. Why didn't they help me get out of the woods? Maybe it was one of those crazy mountain people.

I quickly become aware that I must have been too deep in thought. Since Henry is swaying back and forth, I must have brushed him to a relaxed state. "Henry Wake up! Don't fall on me boy! Shit, Henry! Please, please, open your eyes!" I'm not yelling but I am using a loud voice. He starts to blink his eyes and wakes up in time not to hurt me.

"Kim what happened? Did I step on your foot or something?"

"No Henry you were falling asleep and staggering. I was afraid that you would fall on me. Apparently I relaxed you enough that you are talking to me now, instead of using pictures."

"The other animals told me about you, that I can trust you. But, wouldn't that have been your fault for brushing me too long?"

"Yes, smart ass."

"I'm not an ass, I'm a horse." He states this so seriously, I start laughing.

"Henry I know that you're a horse I was joking sorry. Now that you're talking to me what is your friend's name?"

"William."

I finish up with him in the stall and place the brush back where I got it from. I take him out to his paddock so that he can run with his friend, William, the Shepherd mix.

I decide to stand outside the fence leaning on the post. I watch them play and chase each other. It really is a beautiful sight to see. The two of them are so happy playing together.

I see Robert approaching me from the stables. Funny, I didn't see him in there. He joins me at the fence to watch Henry play.

"Kim, wouldn't it be great to run carefree like them?" I smile at him nodding in agreement.

"Kim, if you could be any animal in the world what would you be?"

"That's very easy, a wolf why?"

I swear that he looked like I just slapped him. He didn't speak for about a minute after that. I wondered what in the hell was going on in his head. And I swear that if I didn't know better. I saw a white wolf in his mind. But that's silly I can't see inside of human minds.

"Robert, did I say something wrong?"

"No, apparently you have given this some thought. You answered my question so quickly."

"I guess you didn't know that wolves are my favorite animal, I grew up with a wolf mix. We were real close when I was a child. She taught me a lot about the body language of wolves and dogs. She said that I would need to know it. Because some animals will block me out of their minds. This way I could still read them by the way they held themselves. That's how I knew the wolf that caused my accident wouldn't harm me. I learned that watching the body language of animals has also taught me to read some human body language.

"Can you read people's minds also?"

“No, I can’t read human minds. Just the animals talk to me with their minds. I have a conversation with them. You know like, I’m doing with you right now.”

“Only no one moves their mouths right?”

“Well out of habit I tend to use my mouth but the animals don’t. Robert, it’s not like a side show or Mr. Ed.”

He laughs, “I didn’t think it was. I don’t doubt your gift. I’ve been watching you with the animals around here.” Like I haven’t noticed that I have two shadows now.

We both stand for a while in silence. I think I worried him with something that I said. The way he is looking at me is weird. He’s looking down at me like I’m a crazy women or something. The silence between us becomes uncomfortable. I try to think of something to change the subject. I remember my conversation with Jasmine. But first I need to know if my gift scares him. I take a deep breath for courage. I should be use to this by now.

“Hey Robert are you afraid of my talent? If you are, I understand many men are put off by it.”

“No, your gift is not a problem. Not at all, I wish I had it. Working with rescues would be much easier.”

“What a relief, I thought maybe I scared you.” I hope he isn’t lying to me.

“Oh and I was wondering. Is Jasmine your first cousin or a distant cousin? I saw her in the barn earlier.”

“She is my distant cousin on my mom’s side. Why did she say something to you? I saw her watching you dance with Andrew last night.”

"No it was all good on her part. She was being protective of you two. She was worried about my intentions."

"Kim did she say anything that I should know about? She didn't share any family secrets did she?" he grins.

I think about that before answering him. I make a mental note for when I catch Jasmine alone again. Maybe I'll take her out one night. Alcohol always gets her talking. As well as other things but I'm not her type.

"No nothing like that, she just didn't want me to break any hearts. It's understandable you are her family. I told her that I don't usually stay around that long. I really don't expect to have a relationship with either of you. Especially if either of you are looking for a long term one."

There's that awkward silence again. He sure puzzles me. He inches his body closer and I can feel the heat coming off of him, even through my coat. How hot do Indians run? He hasn't even touched me and my pulse is racing. He turns to face me and gently puts his hand on my shoulder. Perplexed I look up at him.

With the utmost confidence in his voice, "Well I think that might change this visit. May the best man win?"

"What?"

With a devious look on his face, he grabs onto my shoulders forcing me to turn to face him. Oh shit he's going to kiss me. My adrenaline starts racing.

He pulls me tightly against him trapping me between him and the fence. He kisses me hard. My insides instantly turn to butter. I feel like a rag doll. I quickly grasp a hold onto the fence to steady myself. He walks away leaving me bewildered. He is shaky as he walks but his getaway is quick. I grab on a little tighter to the fence. Ok, what in the hell am I supposed to do with that?

8

I've been at the farm a few weeks now. Greg is totally enjoying the show of Robert and Andrew vying for my attention. I have to admit, I enjoy being treated like a prize to win. They both open doors for me and stand when I come to the table. I think they have worked out a schedule for the days of the week as well. If I have it right Andrew has Monday and Wednesday. Robert has Tuesday and Thursday. Fridays are rotated and the weekends are open to who finds me first.

Today is Friday and I think it is Andrews Friday. I look out the barn window to see if anyone is approaching yet. And sure enough here comes Andrew. He is smiling like he swallowed the canary.

I go back to putting a flake of hay in each of the horse's stalls. I see him coming closer towards me out of the corner of my eye. Yet he still startles me, when he whispers my name in my ear from behind.

I somehow tangle my foot in a water hose. Someone must have left on the floor. It causes me to lose my balance and slip, right into Andrew's arms, what timing! He helps me stand upright again. I am so embarrassed I just stand there looking at him. Like a stone statue I just stand there, waiting, hoping for a kiss. Robert kissed me weeks ago.

I think I might get my kiss. He is inching closer to me. He keeps his eyes focused on my face, as if he is searching for some hesitation on my part. Oh hell, just kiss me!

He slips one hand around my waist and the other gently on the base of my neck. He pulls me into him and kisses me with all his worth. My head spins and my knees become rubbery. The desire races though my body as he backs me to a stack of hay. Putting us both down on the hay he continues kissing me. I wrap my arms around him securing us together. I'm not letting him get away from me this time.

His hands start to wander and I let them. I couldn't resist him if I tried. Not that I want to anyway. If we don't stop this, we could be doing it right here in the barn. We are not in the most comfortable place for the first time. We really shouldn't do this in here, with all these animals around. It might be too late though, the animals are starting to go wild. Especially the mares that are in season, they are so loud with their whinnying, that we barely hear Greg shouting for us over them.

"Damn it!" Andrew struggles to release me. I'm not helping much by holding onto him firmly. I wish Greg would just go away. But of course he doesn't. I know Greg is standing just out of sight when he yells for me. He first clears his throat very loudly. Then he shouts out to us, "Are you two going to the fall festival later today?"

Andrew and I hurriedly adjust our clothes. He refastens his shirt and I make sure mine is right side out. I try desperately to suppress my laughter, because I am so embarrassed. I shout back to Greg.

"Yea that sounds like fun, I would love to go." He waits to round the corner, before he asks, "Why are all the mares in an uproar."

I simply turn red and try to play off the obvious. He looks to Andrew then back to me. I can see Greg is straining to hold in his amusement. He is struggling to keep from busting into a fit of laughter. We know each other much too well.

"I should have known with all the commotion the mares are making. What the two of you were doing in here."

"Excuse me Greg?" I question, suppressing my laughter.

"Robert told me you were alone in here Kim. I should have known better than believe him. I'll see the two of you later around six?"

"Yea, that should be a good time to head out. "

"Andrew?"

"Yea sounds good to me, See you later Greg." Andrew says with a hint of aggravation in his words. As soon as Greg leaves us alone in the barn, Andrew begins to apologize for being rude to me. I giggle, I just couldn't help myself.

"Andrew it's not like we had sex we only kissed. And it's about time if you ask me. Really I didn't mind at all. You gonna explain the desire thing to me?" He starts to shift his feet, visibly uncomfortable with my question.

"Ok Andrew I won't push it right now, but I won't wait too much longer for one of you to explain it. Do you understand me?"

Shyly he responds barely audible with a "Yes."

Robert, with his perfect timing, walks by just then. He is wearing a shit-eaten grin.

"Morning guys you two going to the festival?"

Robert says his face all smiles. He knows damn right well what he just did. Andrew glares at him with looks to kill. I guess the competition is heating up. And so is my libido.

The two of them go off in different directions. I know I need a cooling off after that. I finish up with feeding the horses, trying to get Andrew off of my mind. But damn, we were so close, so very close.

Around six we all pile into Greg's Suburban. I sit up front with Greg; there is no way I'm sitting between the two brothers.

We arrive at the fall festival and it's just like any other. The vendors are all under long white tents. The rides are all off to one side. The farm equipment is all lined up. They also have a hay ride for families. Later tonight, they will set up a bonfire.

My three escorts know everybody here, so there is a lot of stopping and standing around talking. Donna meets up with us and steals Greg away about an hour after we get there.

Now I have two escorts that seem to be parading me around to some extent. Neither of them is talking to each other it seems. They each only address me when they notice something and point it out. Finally, we sit down at a picnic table where an older American Indian is already seated. I notice that the sun has gone down.

Robert leaves to get us some beers. Andrew introduces me to his father Nick. He nods as I say "Hello" ok, not a man of many words. His face shows me that he has had a hard life. It is well weathered almost like leather. He doesn't speak much, as we all sit there drinking our beers. But when the boys go together to get more beer and some food he turns to me, his face is very serious. Then he looks out to the crowd of people passing by.

"Young one, use caution in choosing your man this will be the most important decision you make. Be certain your heart and mind agree with each other. Both are very strong men with good hearts. Yet me being their father and all, I do know that one leads with his head and the other lets his desires lead him. Both will do right by you that I know for certain. Remember though, that the one you refuse may not accept your decision without difficulty."

He turns to look directly at me,

"Do you understand me?" I stare straight back into his brown eyes,

"Yes, I understand, I am well aware of this."

"Good, the boys are on their way back. I hope they got me a sausage sandwich."

That was disturbing to say the least. I've been piecing this together. I'm guessing that these Indians take relationships very seriously. Not like most people these days. They both do seem comfortable with my gift. I would love to have a real relationship. Maybe one of them will be the one? Nah, this couldn't work out we all travel around a lot. But, I think I'll see where this road leads me, at least for a little while.

The boys sit on either side of me when they return. Oh lord, help me if one of them starts. Robert snickers but before I can ask him what's funny. He abruptly gets up and leaves us. I look in the direction he was looking just before he left. I see a beautiful woman approaching. Maybe it is an ex girlfriend?

"Andrew?" I question, but they both stand instantly as she nears us. She must be important to them. I am the only other woman I have seen Andrew do that for.

"Kim, let me introduce you to my mother Lea."

I am in awe of her beauty. She is simply stunning. Not a bit of makeup and she still glows. I would never have put her with Nick. It's not that he isn't a handsome man, he is. But next to her, no one could compare.

"Kim it is my pleasure to meet you. Nicolas my dear, sorry I am late my love."

She places a kiss on his cheek, and then sits gracefully next to him. Her class is apparently something she was born with. It is something I myself have very little of. I hope she doesn't notice right away.

Lea turns to face me, "The men have told me so much about you my dear. Does your gift work on all animals?"

"No not with wolves or alligators. I am not sure why."

"Interesting, that may change in your future."

"What do you mean, Mrs. Lobo?"

An agreeable smile on her face she coos. "Please call me Lea. You will know soon enough my dear. Nicolas, my love, we should be on our way."

He quickly stands up and extends a hand to her assisting her to stand. Not that she needs help she is much younger than he is. But I see gentlemanly ways run in the family. Once Nick and Lea are gone from our view Andrew looks around nervously.

"Kim, we should go and find Robert before he gets into trouble."

"Ok, this should be fun; he must be drunk by now."

"That's what I am afraid of. He doesn't get along with my mother. He tends to drink more when he sees her"

"You are going to tell me why they don't get along?"

"Nope,"

"I didn't think so; let's find him before he gets into a mess."

About an hour later we spot him stumbling alone. Andrew takes one side and I take the other. We try to keep him upright. Robert pulls away from Andrew leaning fully on me. I'm strong but not that strong.

"Andrew, we need to get him to a bench before I fall on my ass."

Luckily we find one close. I sit next to Robert and Andrew stands in front of us like a prison guard. Robert keeps his arm over my shoulder. Though, it's more like he is hanging on. Nothing romantic about this scene, I'm glad I decided to wear a jacket tonight.

Very slurred, Robert asks me what I think about his parents. The smell of booze was almost unbearable. I turn away, and calm the feeling of nausea.

"I think they are nice people. I also think that your mom is very beautiful and classy."

"She was once, not anymore." he adds.

His statement puzzled me. But I let it go for now I don't want to upset him while he's drunk. Robert being the smart ass he is starts to run his finger down my cheek. He causes a wave of sweet desire to run all through me. Damn him!

Andrew grabs Roberts arm firmly then yanks it away from me.

"Don't do that to her here Robert!"

"Why not little brother, you have not marked your territory as of yet, have you? I can do as I wish. If we don't hurry they will get her too. They will kill her or change her just like…"

He just stopped mid sentence. Ok he is really drunk, thinking someone would kill me. I try to reassure him by talking softly. It works with frightened animals.

"Robert, I am right here safe and sound. No one would dare to harm me with both of you beside me. I'm the safest person in the world right now." I rub his shoulder to help reassure him.

"Andrew, we should get him home. I'll call Greg and see if we can borrow his truck. He should be able to get a ride with Donna." I make the call to Greg, as Andrew tries to talk Robert into letting him help him walk instead of me. Robert tries to stand up on his own and stumbles. Luckily Andrew was right in front of him.

"Greg said that he will meet us at his truck with the keys. I'll help you walk Robert, but if you touch my skin we will both be face down in the mud. So you promise to behave yourself?"

"Yes, I promise."

I don't whole heartedly believe him. But we need to get him out of here quick. Somehow we manage to get him back to the truck and in the back seat safely. By the time we hit the pavement he is snoring away. The ride home is a quiet one. We both hope Robert stays asleep, at least until we get him home.

Andrew and I help Robert up the stairs when we get back to Greg's. It wasn't easy with Robert trying to kiss my neck. But we somehow manage to get him to his bed alone. As soon as Roberts's door is closed, Andrew starts to apologize for Robert's behavior.

"Andrew it's not a problem. I remember when the two of you, put me to bed when I drank too much one night."

"True we did but, you fell asleep before you made a fool of yourself."

"That's true but we all can't be perfect all the time. I'm guessing this is because Robert doesn't get along with your mom?"

"Yes, he hasn't spoken to her in years. I don't really understand why though."

"It's none of my business really. We should call it a night."

I reach for my door handle and turn to face him. He doesn't hesitate this time. He presses me against my door, his body firmly against mine. He kisses me hard with a hunger. My heart starts racing, my adrenaline overflowing with desire. I start to turn the handle on my door as we hear Greg and Donna coming up the stairs. Andrew manages to pull himself away from me and darts to his room leaving me there panting, wanting more. Damn him!

I barely get in my room and slide down the inside of the door. My legs are not working properly at the moment. So, I stay on the floor for a few minutes. I finally muster up the strength to get up. I slide myself into bed and dream the sweetest dreams. Funny, Andrew's face keeps being replaced by Roberts. Ah, I'll go with it. It's only a dream after all.

9

At the breakfast table the next day it's so quiet that I can hear myself chewing my pancakes. Robert has only black coffee in front of him. He is holding his head in his hands. He must have a bad hangover from last night. Andrew is avoiding eye contact with everyone. Greg quietly snickers to himself. I just ignore him the best I can. I hope Robert knows that I'm not mad at him. We all screw up once in a while.

I finally snap at him. I'm tired of his snickering. "Greg just stop it!"

Innocents filling his words, "Stop what?"

"You know what, stop snickering, it's not funny."

"Kim what exactly is not funny? Is it Robert getting so drunk last night? Or was it my catching you and Andrew kissing twice yesterday? The first time was in the barn. But that was a bit more than kissing I think. Then I caught you again in the hall last night?"

I am so mad at him for blurting that out in front of Robert. Who seems to already be in a mood? Where's a rock when you need one?

Robert glares at Andrew. "How dare you!"

Robert then turns his glare at me. I swear if his eyes were lasers. I would be dead where I sat. Robert's expression changes to a wicked smile immediately. I swallow hard in fear.

In an instant, he is standing beside my chair. He scoops me up into his arms and kisses me the same way as Andrew did the night before. There go my knees and heart. It's not like I could resist him or move for that matter. He is holding me so tightly to his body. Not here in the kitchen please is all I can think.

Robert lets go of me and I sink back into the chair. He starts to laugh; Greg joins him as they erupt into hysterics.

Andrew literally dives across the table catching Robert in his mid section. He rams Robert right into the wall behind him. Roberts's body hits the wood panel so hard that the paneling instantly splits down its center. I wince, that must have hurt, but Robert comes right back at Andrew. He lunges at Andrew shoving him into the opposite wall. Then Robert rams Andrew against the table so hard that it is forced right into me. I scream from the immediate intense pain.

They both stop instantly and pull the table away with such force that everything on top of it is flying through the air in all directions. I grab my stomach and double over. I can barely breathe, my lungs feel so heavy. I fall to the ground in a thud screaming as the pain takes over.

Robert grabs the truck keys and Andrew carries me out to Greg's suburban. Robert drives like a mad man all the way to the hospital. Andrew keeps me in his lap. He caresses my hair attempting to calm me the entire ride. They are fighting over something about their mother Lea, and wolf blood? I'm not sure what the fight is about though. I keep going in and out of consciousness.

When I open my eyes again I am in a hospital bed. I can hear the boys discussing my condition. No, they are fighting again.

"Andrew, why in hell would you ask her for help?"

Robert must be extremely angry with Andrew. He is almost yelling at Andrew and the vein in his forehead is protruding. His face is a dark shade of red. I have never seen him mad before, not like this.

"She would have died otherwise Robert. You heard what the doctors said."

"The risk is too high if her heart stops she'll never be the same again."

"Well no shit I'll be dead. Guys, am I going to be ok?"

They each stop their bickering and sit on either side of my bed each holding a hand. I brace myself for the desire rush but it doesn't come. I look at both of them confused. Why isn't it there?

"Kim you are going to be just fine. The doctors said that you bruised some internal organs but that they will heal in time."

"Yea but they said that you will have to stay here a few days. So you can heal properly. "

"Really I feel fine, did they give me pain killers?"

They exchange looks with each other, which tells me they are hiding something. Robert pips up,

"They gave you morphine. They had to operate on you. Its night time Kim, it has been for a while now." I glance out the window. I didn't even notice that it was dark outside. How long have I been out?

"What time is it?"

"Its eight o'clock and we'll be leaving."

They both kiss my forehead before leaving me to my thoughts. Maybe I dreamed them here? Otherwise, I would have felt the desire thing? Could the morphine have blocked it from happing?

The next day when I wake up, I have this eerie feeling that I was not alone last night. I remember seeing a man with ice blue eyes. He must have been a doctor or something. Maybe I had a dream about him. He did resemble a young David Bowie a little.

Over the next three days, I see the same blued eyed doctor every night. He never speaks to me. He checks my vitals and smiles at me then leaves. Maybe he is a nurse? The day nurse has told me that the doctor wants to keep me sedated due to my injuries being so severe. But she says I puzzle them all with how quickly I am healing. I question her about the doctor with ice blue eyes. She claims that no one she knows of on staff has eyes like that. I must have imagined him I guess.

Andrew and Robert both visit me while I'm here but separately. They both bring me flowers each day. Neither of them will stop apologizing to me for hurting me. Even Greg and Donna stopped in and brought flowers. It smells like a funeral home in here. I enjoy the attention but I want out of here. I really want to stay awake long enough to know what is going on. I know Greg and the boys have been here but how many times I couldn't tell you.

The next time I am really coherent is the day of my release from the hospital. Greg is the one who picks me up. He doesn't say much to me on the way home. That is until we pull up in front of the house.

"Kim, I guess you see all the people in the yard?"

"They are kind of hard to miss." I snide, "Why are all the volunteers having a cook out?" I just knew he was up to something.

"Well the boys decided that we all needed a party. So welcome to my first ever down home cook out." I give him a sideways glare.

"Oh and by the way, the boys have also decided…"

"Go on Greg this should be good." He helps me out of the truck and plants me at a wooden table.

"The boys think you should make a choice between them. So the one you approach first is the one that wins."

"Are you serious Greg?"

"I am as serious as a heart attack girl."

"You're not right Greg, you know that?"

He leaves laughing as he walks away. When he comes back he has a plate full of food. More than I could ever eat, along with a couple ice cold beers.

"This is going to be fun to see which one tries to come over first. Enjoy your day Kim."

And he is off lost in the crowd. I'm not so sure that drinking beer while on pain killers is such a good idea. I look around to locate Andrew and Robert. I spot them sitting alone on opposite ends of a picnic table. They take turns looking my way but neither of them moves an inch. This is going to be a very long day. I take a couple sips of my beer.

By around three I need to use the bathroom. My body is stiff and sore from being in bed and now sitting here for so long. I look to the two lumps sulking. I decide better then to ask them. I look around for a female assistant and spot Donna. She helps me get there and then leaves me on the front porch. It's much closer to the bathroom. I can make it on my own from here, maybe.

I don't have to worry about getting a beer. As soon as I empty one Greg or Jasmine brings me another. The boys still haven't come anywhere near me yet. Talk about being stubborn, how do they expect me to choose one of them right now, after they together put me in the hospital?

The day has come and gone and the night is approaching. I am getting tired of sitting here waiting. I am not about to walk towards them to choose either. I'm not sure myself yet who I really want. I would like more than a sample to judge by. I smile at the thought. I think I've had enough to drink for the day. I'm starting to fantasize a little too much about them.

John, Greg's right hand man is walking towards me. So I ask him to help me up the stairs. He looks scared to death with my request. He looks over to the two lumps and then back to me. Then terror fills his face.

"Kim I like you and all, but I'm not getting my ass kicked by them. Not for simply helping you in the house."

"Really John, I guess they have been on edge since the fight?"

"Yes ma'am, for well, just about every minute for the last few days they have been at each other's throats."

"Ok John, not a problem, I can make it to the stairs on my own."

"Sorry ma'am I see what they did to you. I'm too old to heal as fast as you. I'll be laid up for weeks."

"It's ok John they won't hurt Greg. I think he is neutral."

I look around for Greg and I don't see him anywhere. With a lot of effort I get myself up out of the chair. My insides are very tender. I glare at the two of them staring at me from across the yard. I give them the bird as I start walking slowly to the door. Amazingly, both of them are next to me in a shot. They support me to the steps that lead upstairs.

"The three of us won't fit together on the steps one of you will have to let go." I say into the air, they both stand silently not letting go of my arms.

"Which one of you is going to help me up to my room?" Neither answers me. I tug my arms from them both and sit down on the third step in a huff.

"I'm starting to hurt, my pain pills must be wearing off." They exchange worried looks between them. Then, they each take a seat a step down from me on either side of my legs.

"Ok here it goes guys. I'm not stupid, something is going on here. I know it is more than two brothers liking the same girl. The desire thing has got me puzzled, but neither of you seem to want to share that little tidbit with me. The truth of the matter is none of us live here. We all travel around for a living. I really can't see any long term relationship blooming any time soon. And I would really like to know about the adrenaline rush I get from the two of you. Is it an Indian thing?" I wait, but not a word is uttered from either of them.

"Honestly I'm not worth all of this fighting and trouble. You two can have any girl you set your sights on. Why you fight over me is just crazy."

The three of us sit there in silence for a while. When Coco the Chihuahua walks by, she turns her head and looks at the three of us inquisitively. We are all unhappy with our dilemma. She climbs up into my lap.

"Mejia, if I were you I would pick Andrew. He gives me treats"

I laugh out loud. They both eyed me like I was insane. I explain to them what Coco had said. They both laugh, and then Robert tells her, that he will work on bribing her. "Guys for now can one of you back off and let the other help me up the steps? I can't make it on my own."

Andrew gets up and walks past me up the stairs without a single word. Robert shrugged his shoulders and picks me up in his arms. He carries me to my bedroom door. Andrew is there waiting to open it for us. I suppress a smile they are not going to make my time here easy at all.

Robert lays me gently on the bed and Andrew puts a pair of my pajamas beside me. They both silently leave together, closing the door behind them.

10

During the next month things go well, weirdly though if that's a word. Robert and Andrew seem to be taking turns keeping me company. I am trying very hard to resist both of them. Nevertheless they are making that a very difficult task.

At first I told myself that they were both just being helpful. Feeling guilty for putting me in the hospital, I thought maybe after me getting hurt so badly they would move on. You know, they realize, I'm not worth the trouble. But they have stepped it up. They help me out by bringing a dog to me or taking them back to their pens. This normally would seem harmless in itself. But when those two are involved the story can't be harmless.

I started to notice right away but ignored it. Each time one of them brought me a dog. Somehow they would find a way to touch my skin. It would always be by accident of course. But each time our skin touched, I would get that overwhelming feeling, if just for a few seconds. It would cause my knees to go weak and my heart to race. I am trying to not flirt back or say anything that they can misconstrue as flirting either. I calculate every word before I speak.

It's the same with both Robert and Andrew they know they are driving me crazy. I'm sure they know what they are doing to me. I see them tremble sometimes after we touch; their eyes get darker as do mine when the desire takes over. I'm afraid to ask what this is all about, because I'm pretty sure that I'm going to cave very soon, but to which one is the question.

I think things over as I give some of the dogs badly needed baths. Andrew is a gentle soul he is very kindhearted in a shy way almost too shy. Robert on the other hand is strong and a little scary. Robert just seems to know where he belongs in the world. When he talks I get the sense that he knows what path to pursue. But Andrew is still searching for his path. He is not so sure of what life has in store for him.

If I don't give in to these impulses soon, I just might explode. I will have to decide which one of them I want. Maybe I should move on and get out of here before it gets out of control, but, I think it's much too late for that already.

I don't want to get in the middle of the two of them, but neither of them is backing down. Yet neither is advancing. Robert has not kissed me since the last time and that landed me in the hospital.

Andrew still hugs me at night if we are alone in the hallway but nothing more. I never over hear them talking about me. They don't flirt with me when the other one is there which is strange. Greg has not said a word about either of them, since he brought me back from the hospital.

The two of them have been driving me absolutely crazy. They keep revving my engine, but we never get out of park. I am so horny that I need to go into town to buy new batteries. Maybe I can ask Greg to pick me some up when he goes to town for supplies. No, he would ask what they are for and figure it out. That wouldn't help me out any; it would just cause more trouble. Oh, the radio in the back barn uses the right size batteries that'll work! I finish with the dogs and go to sit on the porch, still thinking about my troubles.

Speaking of trouble I would like to find out where all the new dogs are coming from. I keep finding dogs in my room up to three times in a week. Some are alone, others are in pairs, and they just show up in my room in the middle of the night.

They are all so afraid of the other humans on the farm. They only trust me to get near them and care for them. They all appear under nourished. I know they're getting in my room with someone's help but whom? I can't get a location or how they got here. They just block that information from me.

So every time a dog or two shows up my room gets fuller. I have convinced some of them to stay in the back barn with other dogs. But I remember that Lakita said the male dogs won't come up stairs when Roberts is here. Some of them are male. They had to pass by Roberts's room. I guess they don't fear him? Maybe he did something to one of the males at another time when he was here. As I sit on the porch driving myself crazy letting my thoughts wonder aimlessly. I spot Greg walking to his truck.

"Hey Greg, are you going to town?"

"Yea, you want to go for a ride or do you need me to pick something up for you?"

"Yea, we need batteries for the barn radio that's all. Greg, I've been trying to figure out where the dogs are coming from, do you have any idea? Or how are they getting in to my room pass all the other animals in the house?"

"No I don't recognize any of them. But I do find that very strange. I wonder how they get that far without any of the house dogs barking. You know Kim; they might use the back dog door, and then slip up the rear stair case."

"Yea, but who is leading them to me. I don't hear them calling me when I'm sleeping. I would you know, whether I am awake or sleeping because of the way we connect."

"Maybe it's a dog that you've helped out before, Who knows you're here again and is leading strays to you for help? That would explain them being so calm with you. A person couldn't let them into your room. You do lock your bedroom door right?"

"Yea, I double check each night. If Robert or Andrew gets in my room, well let's just say, you would know." I say that with deeply mixed emotions. I can tell that Greg is holding back a laugh. He sees the longing on my face.

"Kim if you really like one of them. Then go ahead, but before you do. I think Robert just started dating one of the volunteers. So you better focus on Andrew."

"Oh really, then why did he tease me so much this morning, if he has someone."

"What do you mean, what did he do?" He tries to talk with seriousness in his words. But the smile spreading across his face tells me he is getting a real kick out of this.

"I'm sure that I didn't misinterpret what he was doing. He said that he was burning up helping me with the dogs. He took off his shirt very slowly. He even flexed his muscles as he did it. He made sure that I got an eye full of him and"… I shake my head trying to get the image of his naked chest out of my mind.

"Greg, it's November and there's snow on the ground!"

Greg starts laughing at me so I lose my temper and storm off. I think that Greg is enjoying me suffering a little too much. Some friend he has been lately. I'll think of something and I'll fix them all.

The next morning I get up extra early, knowing that the guy's would still be in the kitchen. I put on a form fitting workout set. I sneak down to the living room to exercise.

I position myself so that I am right in their view from the kitchen table. As soon as I put on the music and start stretching all conversation stops in the kitchen.

I know this is driving them all nuts. I may be a size ten but I curve in the right places to drive a man wild. I continue to stretch everything for about ten minutes. I figure that should fix them.

I gather up my stuff and turn around to face them. Yes! I can see by their faces that I have achieved my goal. I think that it's time to get the hell out of dodge.

I run back to the stairs grinning from ear to ear. I stop on the first step to listen. I hear Doris laughing at them. She tells them they got what they deserved. That she knows they have been driving me nuts for the past month. Then she tells Greg to wipe the drool from his mouth.

I walk fast to my room and I quickly close my door. Just in case I pushed anyone too far. I shower, dress, and head out to the back barn as quickly as I can. I somehow manage to avoid all three of them. After a while I stop thinking about the men that might be in my life.

I get so consumed by my work, that it's early afternoon before I stop working. I guess they thought better than to come and tease me today after my little show this morning. I think I was a little too extreme, I'm sure to pay for it somehow.

I almost forgot what day it is. Today is Thanksgiving, so everyone else has stopped working early. The volunteers have all gone home by now. Shit, I race back to the house to help Doris.

I find the men inside watching the ball game on the flat screen. The Vikings and the Giants are playing today. I check the score before going to the kitchen to help Doris. She is ready to set the table, so, I do it for her. We have roast turkey and all the trimmings of course.

Doris is always in a good mood today, as I remember from the past years I was lucky enough to spend here. We are her kids in many ways, as she is our mother. She calls to the men to wash up. The translation being today is special. So no dirt, hats or boots allowed at the table. I run up stairs and put on a long skirt and a peasant blouse.

Once every one of us is at the table Doris says the prayer. The men restrain themselves today. They nicely pass the dishes around the table in a respectable manner. Most days they grab at the food like they have never eaten before.

Andrew and Robert are discussing the football game they just watched. I really can't follow along since, I am not up on who plays for what team. I use to watch football frequently when my dad was alive, but not since then. It's just not the same without him.

I talk with Donna and Doris about Christmas coming up, and what plans we have to make. I know that Doris and I will be shopping tonight at midnight. Black Friday is so much fun. Then we will come back home, power nap, and go out again.

Two days a year the boys do the cleaning up after the meal, today and Christmas. So we girls head to the living room after we have pie. Doris being the oldest gets control of the remote. There is something twisted about her. We are watching a Walking Dead marathon. After a short time Donna leaves us. She couldn't take the gore of blood. I know it's fake so I have no issues with the show; I actually like watching it. I find it humorous at times. Doris and I watch a couple of episodes then we head to bed for a nap before our shopping extravaganza.

Doris wakes me up at eleven with a cup of hot coffee. I love this woman, she is the best.

We head first to Target then on to Wal-Mart. I get my TV series for next to nothing. I have a DVD player in my van so I can watch them whenever I want to when I travel. We are out of those stores and on our way back to the farm by two. We unload our goodies then head right to our rooms for our naps. I set my alarm clock for seven.

The alarm rings for me to wake up earlier than usual. Doris and I are going to continue our Christmas shopping today, so I hurry with my shower and then dress in layers. The temperature outside is 32 degrees, but the stores will be toasty. I enter the kitchen as Doris is placing my breakfast on the table. While I eat alone in the kitchen she puts breakfast on the dining room table for the boys. It will be strange not having one of them follow me around all day.

We meet at her minivan. Doris has issues with my driving skills. I sip on my coffee while she drives us to Gatlinburg. The first store that we stop at is a saddle shop. Greg has been hinting to the both of us about wanting a new saddle. He has made it easy for us also by printing us a picture of the one he wants. Doris and I are splitting the cost of it.

The next store we go to is a bait shop. I'm giving Robert and Andrew gift cards for this place. They both love to fish, that is when they are not picking on me. Afterward, we hit a couple of craft type places, mainly for ourselves. Doris knits and I crochet some. We both dabble in making stuff out of wood.

By the third craft shop we are hungry for lunch. We decide to eat at a little luncheonette, ordering soup and turkey clubs. I had planned to do some heart to heart talking with her about the boys during lunch. But Doris seems to know everyone in town. People continue to stop and chat with her all through our meal. When we're done eating and make our way out of the luncheonette, we run into Robert and a girl I haven't seen before. He is polite when he introduces me to Liz, and makes it clear that Liz is only a friend. I raise my eyebrow at him in question.

"Kim, trust me she is only an old friend of mine. I'm helping her with her Christmas shopping."

"Robert why are you defending yourself to me, we are not in a relationship. Who you date is none of my business."

"Kim we are not dating. I wouldn't ever date Robert." Ok that was a bit disturbing, just the way she said it was alarming. Doris grabs my arm.

"Child we need to get going we have a lot more stores to hit before we head back to the farm." I look at her confused by her reaction to this conversation.

"Good-Bye Robert and Liz, enjoy your day shopping."

"It was nice to meet you Kim." I smile back to Liz, as Doris pulls me away from the two of them.

"Doris what was that about?"

"Nothing, Liz is like a little sister to Robert. They grew up together. That is why she said she wouldn't date Robert. She doesn't see him the same way you do."

"Ok Doris just how do I see him?"

She doesn't miss a beat, "Like the handsome sexy single man that he is."

I laugh out loud at her. "What gives you the idea that I think he is sexy?"

Her face serious as can be, "Kim unless you are blind Robert is nothing less then what I just said."

"Ok Doris I can't deny it, he is all that you said, but I like someone else a bit more than him, I think?"

"Child, I know, but don't count Robert out just yet. He still has his hat in the ring by the looks of things."

"Doris you should leave well enough alone. I'm not looking for a permanent relationship." I smile deviously, "but I sure am having fun being the center of their attentions."

"I bet you are child. Just be careful, I don't want to see you get hurt."

"I will be mother."

We continue down the street giggling like school girls. After a couple more hours of shopping we finally head back to her car with our arms loaded down with our bounties. We have killed the whole day shopping together. The sun is starting to set as we get to her van. I have just closed the gate when I see Robert walking toward us.

"Hey can I get a ride back with you two?" He hollers over to me.

Joking with him a say, "I think we might be able to squeeze you in somewhere." Doris snickers at me, and I scan the van for room for Robert. I make a space for him to just fit in behind my seat. We bought a lot of stuff today. Doris tunes the radio to a Christmas channel. Before I think about it all of us are singing along with the radio. The sun has set before we are half way home. I notice that Doris is acting a bit strange. She keeps looking out the windows like we are being followed.

"Doris is everything alright?"

"Yes of course child, what could be wrong?"

"Well then why are you looking around so much, and I don't mean through windshield either." Robert combs my hair with his fingers, over the back of the head rest.

"Kim, are you always so suspicious?"

"No Robert, and don't you dare tease me in this van."

I hear a low growl behind me, "Robert did you just growl at me?"

Doris starts driving faster. Which is not like her, normally, she is a very cautious driver. I turn to look at Robert, because I swear he is growling.

"What's going on that I don't know about here?"

Neither of them answers me as we race towards the farm. I look all around us for a sign that we are in danger. There is nothing but trees all around us, no animals that I can hear either. That's strange even for this time of year.

"Doris what's spooking you? I don't see any cars around or anybody for that matter." Robert places his hand on my shoulder and pats it in a comforting manner. That raises my suspicions even more.

"Nothing to worry about, it's an Indian thing, we sense something is wrong. But we will be back at the farm soon. You'll be safe and sound there."

"Ok," He keeps so many secrets that I don't truly trust what he says, I know something is very wrong with Doris driving the way she is. We pull up to the farm house and a number of volunteers and Andrew are standing around the front yard waiting for us. They all scatter as we get out of the car. All but Andrew and Robert, they stay and help unload the van for us. I feel like I am being rushed into the house. With the way they are hurrying me, they are acting odd, even for them.

"Robert and Andrew please put the bags down in the living room. Kim and I will sort them out in there." Her look told me a lot more than her words ever could. She was frightened by something. That's not like Doris to fear anything. As soon as the boys leave us alone, I question her.

"Doris what the hell is going on with you?"

She busies herself with sorting the bags into two piles, trying to ignore my question, but I'm not giving up that easily.

I snap at her, "Doris!"

"Kim its nothing for you to worry about my child, trust me."

"Trust is something that I have little of these days Doris." She turns to look at me, seeing my expression of anger, she gives up and sits down on the sofa.

"Kim sit," I do as she says, and sit next to her.

"Child, there was something out in the forest tonight. Something dangerous to us all, I could feel its presence so could Robert." She pauses and wrings her hands together.

"Kim there is a very large grizzly in the forest. He usually stays far away from humans. This is not his territory normally, and with him being so close its best not to go outside alone, at least for a few days. The boys will lead him away by baiting him with deer meat. They will lead him closer to his last known den. He should be in hibernation this time of year as you know. He must not have eaten enough in the fall."

"Oh, here I thought we were being followed by someone. The way the two of you were acting. That's a good plan to fatten him back up so that he will hibernate. I should go and help them. Grizzlies are easy to talk with. Do the boys know where his cave is located?" I stand up as to leave and help Robert and Andrew.

"Yes they will lead him back in the right direction. You can sit back down Kim. They will be far away by now; no need in going out there to help. "

"Oh? Why wouldn't they ask for my help, though I'm glad that is all it was? And what do Indians have a magical connection to bears?"

Doris laughs, "No my child I saw it chasing us, didn't you hear it?" I look at her questioning what she said. She had me up until she asked if I heard it. I would have, Grizzlies are loud broadcasters. Now I know she's lying to me. I just grab my bags and head up to my room. Looks like I can't trust anyone here. Doris was my last hope at any truth.

I stay in my room for the rest of the night. Keeping myself busy wrapping my gifts. I'm furious though, I wish I could get an honest answer from someone.

I have William with me, for company. Since he has come a long way compared to his first days here. We have not let anyone else know just how far though. I feel safer with him near me. He likes to hang out in my room with me. He is also a good sensor, he hears someone coming long before I do.

11

For the next couple of weeks everyone is acting strange around me. I have escorts if I'm outside after dark. I have asked why, but all I get are vague answers. Nothing to really base anything on or figure out what everyone is up to. Maybe they have been smoking the peace pipe a little too much.

Before I know it Christmas day is here. I help Doris make a huge breakfast, made up of ham and eggs, waffles, bacon and homemade muffins. After breakfast we all take our coffee with us, and gather in the living room to open our presents.

The boys are happy to get the gift cards from me. They each give me CD's, Robert gives me the new Muse CD and Andrew gives me the newest one from Evanescence. I hug them both for their gifts. Rose and I exchange gift cards for the same store, Kohl's. Greg is so surprised that we gave him the saddle he wanted, that he kisses us both and hugs us in turn.

We all go out to tend to the animals in the barns. I was able to talk a major pet store into donating some pet toys. I have them all in two rather large bags. I feel like Santa. I give every dog in each pen a new ball or chew toy to play with, depending on which one they wanted, and a large dog bone. Then I go over to the back barn where we have about twenty cats waiting to be adopted. I go into their enclosure to pass out the toys.

I don't get time to spend with the cats as much as I would like to. But I do make sure to groom the ones that have long hair. Doris is the one who cares for the cats most of the time. She loves cats. That's probably why the same cats are here as the last time I visited, she has named all of them. I like Salem the best. He is a large, black long haired cat.

My last stop is the stables. Henry is the first horse I see. I have carrots and apples for all of the horses. After I finish playing Santa, my chores begin for the day. I clean out about half of the stalls and Jasmine cleans out the others. We only have ten horses here this Christmas. Most years there are a lot more to care for. We leave their stall doors open so that they can let themselves out, if they want to go out to the paddocks, they are all geldings.

Jasmine and I walk back together to the main house. By now Christmas dinner will be ready. She will join us for dinner this Christmas by choice. Her parents have long ago passed and she has no close relatives except for Andrew and Robert. I wonder why they aren't spending today with their parents. I know they must live close they were at the fall festival.

Greg says the prayer once we are all seated at the table. He thanks God for all he has given us throughout the year, and how grateful he is that he is able to help so many animals. Like Thanksgiving we are properly dressed and use all of our manners today.

I'm not sure how, but I'm seated between Robert and Andrew. It was the only seat left, when I came out of the kitchen carrying the vegetables. I'm not crazy about this at all. I'm trying hard, not to think about the two of them beside me. It's getting hot in here and I know it's not the temperature of the room. It's me and my thoughts.

Robert places his hand on my thigh and I just about choke on my turkey. Andrew pats my back, which doesn't help me at all. I look pleadingly at Jasmine for help, and she kicks Robert under the table, he yelps. I stop choking and Andrew stops patting my back. I catch my breath closing my eyes to recover my composure.

"Thanks, Jasmine."

"You're welcome Kim. Some men have no manners it seems." we both snicker.

Greg unexpectedly clears his throat, "Kim, I forgot to tell you that we got the go ahead for the raid at the Browns property. It's set for tomorrow morning. Do you still want to go and help out?"

"Yea, Greg, I figure that I could be useful there, especially if any of the dogs are loose."

"Good, I was just making sure that you are still coming. Robert you are coming?"

Dreamily he says, "Yes, I wouldn't miss it for the world. I'll get to watch Kim all day long." Cupping his face in his hands he gazes at me. Like a love sick teenager.

I roll my eyes at him and Jasmine picks up a biscuit and throws it at him. Of course he catches it just before it hits his nose. They all laugh and I just shake my head. Doris walks behind Robert and smacks him on the back of his head. She is good at giving a "Jethro."

"Thanks Doris harder next time, ok?"

"No problem Kim, he had it coming."

Andrew not to be left out, "I've had the pleasure of watching her on her first day here. She sure is something to watch." Andrew reaches behind me trying to slap Robert on his shoulder. He barely reaching him before Andrew must grab onto the back of my chair or he would have tipped over backwards. I'm guessing they have been drinking while they watched the football game. By the way they were carrying on I think the Vikings won.

"Robert you should pay extra attention when she bends over to talk to the little dogs. It really is a view to behold."

The two of them erupt into a burst of laughter.

"Brother, I believe I got an eye full. You know when she did her little show for us."

"Kim you know it's not nice to tease." Robert laughs; I feel my Irish temper go directly to boil.

"How dare either of you accuse me of teasing? You two have been teasing me since I got here!"

"Ok, all of you knock it off! Some of us are trying to eat our meal." Greg snaps jokingly. "Kim, you know what you did Thanksgiving morning was a bit much." I refuse to answer Greg.

"I'll be in the kitchen helping Doris!" I take my plate with me to the kitchen.

I hang in the kitchen with Doris until they clear out. Then I go in and clean off the table. After we have done all the dishes and put all the leftovers away, we sit at the small kitchen table and have a piece of pie together. She looks around guardedly and then puts her hand on top of mine.

"Kim, I have to talk to you about something." I look at her with concern, she looks very serious.

"What is it Doris?"

"Well, I'm aware that none of this is really my business, but you know that I have adored you since you first came here. I feel that I should speak my mind to you. What you do with it is up to you. I won't fault you no matter what you decide."

She pauses to take a deep breath, and then she takes my hands into hers. I think she is about to tell me what the hell has been going on around here. I'm not sure that I really want to know just yet. I open my mouth to speak and Doris puts her finger to her lips. "Please hear me out before you speak. I know that you are confused, about what is going on here. You know that you have to choose one of them. They both are great men and either of them will treat you like gold. But with what I know, that I can't share with you yet, they have to be the ones to tell you. I really wish they would hurry up with it all… I think that you should choose Robert."

I sigh I was hoping for more insight, not her personal opinion about the whole thing. I know she doesn't miss much around this place.

"Even though I know you like Andrew more. Robert is the eldest and he should wed first."

I burst into laughter, "What year is this?" She continues on ignoring me. I stop my laughing instantly.

"Before you sleep with one of them, you'll have to have your mind made up. With which one you want to be with forever. You cannot go back and forth with them; they will know believe me. I know that you don't know everything that is going on here. I wish that I could tell you, but it's not my place. Robert must tell you when he is ready to do so."

We just sit there for a long moment looking at each other in silence. I think maybe she's been drinking today. Or, maybe she pays to much attention to things pertaining to me. Also, I am beginning to realize, I must be the only person not in the know. If someone doesn't come clean soon, I might just get the hell out of dodge. This isn't so fun anymore it's starting to get scary.

"Kim, Andrew is convinced that you are the one but Robert I'm not so sure about. Even with the physical proof. Really Kim you're one strong woman holding out this long. I was their mother's best friend and she only had to worry about one man touching her. Their father and back then people didn't have sex before marriage. They just barely made it through the wedding day. We didn't see them for a week after that day." She snickers.

"They were so weak from not eating enough and from plenty of, well you know what. They were exhausted."

I look at her face, not sure what to say or feel. I fight the smile that is trying to surface, instead I let the confusion take over my face.

Doris has never been anything but kind to me. But she is not telling me very much, that I didn't figure out on my own. But what does she mean, "The one?" I know that I like Andrew more than Robert. Robert kind of scares me for some reason, I can't decipher exactly why.

"Doris I want to follow my heart. I don't want to hurt anyone either. I would actually like to know what is going on around here first. I guess you're not telling me any more tonight are you?" She just shakes her head no. Then she looks down to the floor.

"I know that something serious is going on here, with the adrenaline rush that I get if either of them so much as touches me. It's like something supernatural. I know it's not normal the urgency I feel… They do feel it too right? I can't be suffering alone?"

She snickers at me a bit, before she decides to answer my question.

"Yes, I can tell you that much. They are suffering every time they touch you." She smiles,

"Kim, you're in love with Andrew aren't you?"

I wasn't expecting that question. I put my head down in shame. I don't want to admit that I have fallen in love. I've been denying it to myself. I hate being weak in the matters of the heart. Reluctantly I whisper, "Yes I'm afraid so."

Panic filling her voice, she looks around nervously. "Kim you must keep that to yourself for as long as you can. Robert has a temper that you don't ever want to see."

"Oh great, I feel so much better now. Didn't you just tell me to be with Robert?"

"Yea, but that's part of the reason. As long as you are in love with Robert he will protect you from his rage. Except that you love Andrew. There's no telling what Robert will do when he finds out."

The expression of fear on her face is scaring the hell out of me. I feel a chill go right through to my bones.

"Oh now isn't that great! Doris thanks for your concern and telling me what you can. I do appreciate it. I wish that you would tell me more. However, I get it, you have told me what you think is allowable. I think I need to be alone now!"

I slowly get up from my chair and turn towards the kitchen doorway. I see Robert standing just outside of it in the hallway. He looks so hurt. I lower my head, knowing that he must have heard me. I whisper his name delicately and his face instantly turns from hurt to anger.

Slowly through clenched teeth he snarls. "Don't you speak to me, you will regret this."

His words frighten me so much that I stand there and shake in fright. I hear Doris's chair slide hard across the kitchen floor. She comes up behind me placing her hands on my shoulders.

"Robert you just leave her alone. She is in a tough spot as you know. It will work itself out in time." He glares at us both and storms away up the back stairs. I swear his eyes just changed color. Doris twists me quickly around toward her and hugs me tight.

"My child things will be good again, just give it time."

I pull back from her slowly. "Doris I'm not as sure as you are about that. I think that I'll go out to the porch before, I risk going upstairs alone." A horrifying feeling runs through me with the thought of going upstairs. Especially, since he is alone up there.

"Good idea, stay close to Greg or Andrew. Oh and don't tell them what just happened."

"Right now, I don't even want to know why."

I grab a blanket from the couch and walk out to the porch. I look all around just in case. Greg gives me a strange look and I shake my head no quickly. He doesn't ask why, but I know that I'll be questioned later. Greg stands up and stretches a bit too obviously.

"Andrew, you're going to be out here awhile?"

"Yeah, I'll be here a bit why Greg?"

"Because I'm heading in for the night, I just wanted to make sure Kim has company out here."

"Oh, no problem, it will be my pleasure to keep her company."

Without a word, I take the seat next to Andrew away from the door. Robert really spooked me. The rage in his eyes, I swear they started to change color from soft brown to black. My eyes change shades of blue with my mood but not complete colors ever.

"Well did you have fun today?" Andrew said, breaking the uncertainty in my head and startles me. I jumped slightly in the chair. I must be so concerned about Robert, that I tuned Andrew right out.

"Kim, you ok?"

"Yea… I'm fine just thinking. Tomorrow is going to be a busy day rounding up the dogs."

"Sorry, I startled you although it was funny seeing you jump. I wouldn't want you to be scared of me."

I try to think of an excuse for being so jumpy. "No it's just so peaceful out here at night. I guess I was just lost in thought. You don't scare me Andrew. I kind of figured that you must be a good person if Greg lets you stay here and help out." Makes me wonder why Robert is allowed to stay here. Especially if he has such a bad temper, like Doris said he does. I feel at a loss. I have so many things I want to ask, but I am not sure I really want the answers. I am getting scared that I may be in danger.

"You know Andrew, people have come here, and many of them thinking this would be an easy job. With free room and board but ended up either quitting or getting fired for one reason or the other. Cleaning up after animals is no glamour job. Greg told me you have been here many times over the years. But, I still think that it's strange that I haven't met you two before now. I know that I would have remembered meeting you or Robert before. Somehow I think that would stick out in my memory."

He smiles smugly, as he sits silently staring at the stars in the night sky.

"At some point you must have proven yourself to Greg. And that's good enough for me. Besides whom would I have to pick on me if it weren't for you and Robert? I think the two of you love having me around just for comic relief."

"No, not just for that though it is fun. I really do like having you around. You add a special light to this old place. Besides you know, you're much better looking than Greg."

"Why thank you Andrew, careful, I could get the idea that you might just like me?"

"Honestly Kim, what's not to like?" He looks me up and down like I'm prime rib.

"You're joking right Andrew?" I look at him quizzically.

"No Kim, I think you're great. Just look at what you can do with animals. You're not hard on the eyes either. And I've caught you looking at me, I think you like what you see too." He says boldly, a smile crossing his face.

"But I'll have to learn what I can do about scaring you again." he says grinning,

"I may not be able to read your mind Andrew. But I get a sense about people. Though it is a strange feeling, I have to say, it's not a bad one."

"What do you mean strange?"

"Well I can't put my finger on it. But I see a wall when I look at you sometimes. It's like you are trying to block me out. Didn't Greg tell you, I can only get into the minds of animals? People are just too hard for me. I usually don't bond well with people.

Greg and I only get along well because of our mutual dedication to the animals. You know self-sacrifice; we always put the animals first. Still it's funny how I can even get the wall from you. I usually don't see anything at all." He does perplex me quite a bit.

"I won't pry; I probably wouldn't want to know what's in your head anyway." I say with a nervous smile.

"You never can tell what a person is thinking or what dark secrets that they could be hiding. It's a good thing that you can't get into my head, it is best that you stay out of there." He says with a devious grin.

"Still not scared, Andrew, hey by the way, Andrew, can you tell me something about your brother Robert."

"What do you want to know?"

"Well, he doesn't seem to know what to make of me. Do I spook him or something? I know some people avoid me because of what I can do. That I understand, but that's not what he is doing exactly. At times he jokes with me or is super sweet and other times, he can be out right mean to me." I adjust myself to face him. I want to see the reaction on his face.

"Did you know that he let that Rottweiler out and the dog almost got me? Robert knows that dog is a trained attack dog. He also knows that I am having a hard time working with him. Why would he do that to me? I don't think I have done anything to deserve that kind of treatment from him."

At least before tonight I hadn't. I see the hurt and anger in Roberts face from earlier when he overheard me. My embarrassment covers my face and I know it. Andrew kneels in front of me. He has an upsetting look on his face.

He puts my hand in his. Here we go again. The excitement goes through my system the instant he touches my hand. Just like before, I try not to react. I know that this is something more than I can understand. It must be supernatural or an Indian thing.

"I don't think that it's you personally," Andrew tries to console me.

"He can be a real bastard sometimes. He never was really good with women. I'll talk with him about his attitude. I didn't realize that he was treating you this way. Sorry about all of this."

"Andrew, could you let go of my hand please?"

A long silence passes and a lot of restraint on my part. I try to stand up feeling the strain of desire. My heart is beating at full force, my blood is racing, I don't want to jump him right here on the steps. Andrew holds my hand firmly restraining me. I close my eyes. I use everything I have to maintain my self-control. I even dig my free hand into the arm of the chair.

"Please don't go just yet," he pleads shyly. I am struggling very hard not to attack him. If he doesn't let my hand go soon I'll…

It's taking everything I have to even think coherent words. He knows what he is doing to me and himself as well. Why won't he let me go? Finally, he releases my hand but he is still blocking me from standing up from the chair. My composure slowly returns to me. My breathing slows to normal.

"Andrew, I have an early start in the morning remember? I'm going with your brother and Greg to help with the raid at the Browns. It might take all day to collect the dogs there. I'll see you tomorrow night. Save me some dinner will you?"

I try again to leave. I know that I am running on with my words, I try desperately to escape as he strokes my hair. Damn him.

"Andrew… please stop… teasing me." I plead.

"I could go with you guys tomorrow," He whispers close to my ear. I feel the warmth of his breath across my cheek. I must be strong, no giving in.

"No, you know that you have to go and pick up supplies in town. You know we'll need them when we get back with the new dogs."

He steps back an inch or two, allowing me just enough room to stand. He stays right in front of me. He is not going to let me go I fear. Gently, he kisses my cheek than my mouth. I'm on the edge, I want him so badly it hurts, but I don't want to rush this. I try to pull away little by little with a lot of effort.

"Andrew, I shouldn't get involved with you… I won't be around here for much longer… I can't start something where one of us could get hurt." Namely me,

He just gazes at me with a longing in his eyes. He pulls me closer to him and kisses me deeply. Putting his hand on my ass he pulls me tightly into him. I do believe that I'm not the only one turned on. I start to think we are about to do something more than kiss. However he releases me turns and walks unsteadily out into the yard, where he fades into the darkness of the trees.

"What the hell? Why can't we ever get out of park?" I yell out to the darkness, and fall back into the chair my knees are so weak from him. I need a very cold shower. Damn and Greg forgot the batteries. I hear a lone wolf's howl echo in the darkness. He sounds close by.

I somehow manage to walk in to the house and up to my room. I creep as quietly as possible to my room. I don't want Robert to hear me pass his door. I reach my door unlock it and enter in one swift motion. I stand frozen, my back against the inside of the door.

I think that maybe it's too late not to get hurt. I get into the shower, warm water, not cold, knowing I have made my choice. Robert and Andrew both have made a move and now Robert is mad at me. He shouldn't have been listening to a private conversation.

I get into my night shirt and climb into bed. I start thinking about what I know so far. I have been told to choose between Robert and Andrew for whatever this thing is. Greg wants me to be with Andrew. Doris wants me with Robert. They are no help there. Andrew is so sweet and gentle. Where Robert has a mean streak and a temper it seems. Though they all are hiding things from me that I need to know.

Physically, I am attracted to both men. Their bodies are like perfection. The adrenaline rush they both can give me with just a touch is spooky. But my heart seems to be leaning toward one direction… Andrew. I know he is my safer choice.

Suddenly, I hear a loud crash. I jump out of bed and open my door looking up and down the hallway. Robert's door flies open and he fills his doorway glaring at me. I can see the rage in his eyes; they are black!

He starts to take a step toward me when Nick the wolf comes out of nowhere. He is flying down the hall towards me. He halts right in front of me, and sits on top of my bare feet.

Nick bares his teeth at Robert. I suddenly become aware of Andrew and Greg standing in their doorways. Apparently trying to figure out what is going on. I just stand there frozen in place. I'm not sure what will happen next, my heart is racing out of control with fear. I smile nervously.

We all stand there looking at Robert waiting to see what he will do. I see all kinds of thoughts flowing through my head so fast. I can't make them out or where they are coming from. I know that it's not Nick because I can't hear him. But I don't see any other animal in the area. And the thoughts are more complicated then I usually get. Nick is still growling at Robert while I'm pondering.

The look of disgust covers Robert's face. He slowly retreats back into his room. I take a breath of relief. I look at Greg and Andrews's faces seeing their concern. Slowly they look down to my friend. Nick gazes up at me with his tongue hanging out to the side panting. I pat his head and tell him that he is a good boy.

"Guys this is Nick, he was the wolf that kept me company until you came and got me, you know, when I crashed my van. He must have been close by tonight I guess. And since he scares Robert, he'll be staying the night. Good night guys, I'll see you in the morning."

Without any questions or comments they both turned and went back in their rooms. That was very strange. I think as I let Nick into my room and double check the locks just in case.

"Ok Nick I know that you can understand me though I can't do the mind thing with wolves. So you stay in here and protect me from Robert tonight. I'll feed you a big breakfast in the morning. Is that a fair deal?" He licks my cheek and I take that as a yes.

That was too strange; Robert must have broken something in his room. When I was thinking that I might love Andrew. How could he know what I was thinking? It's just not possible for him to hear my thoughts. Is it? No, not in the real world, people can't hear each other's thoughts can they?

Well why not? I hear animal thoughts and they hear mine when they want to share… but they can block me out if they want to… can Robert be doing that? Hearing my thoughts and blocking me out? I'll test him tomorrow if I get a chance.

Shit, I'll have to be with him all day tomorrow without Andrew to protect me. I can't take Nick with me because he might scare the dogs we will be rescuing.

I wonder how strong Greg is really, could he take Robert if need be? I better get some sleep. I'll need all of my strength to watch out for Robert and talk with the dogs.

12

I tossed and turned for a good while. Then Nick climbed on my bed. With him next to me I calmed right down and finally got to sleep. The morning turned out to be a clear one. Greg, Robert and I load up the trailer and truck with as many crates and carriers that we can fit. Not one of us exchanges even a single word. Then the three of us cram into the pick-ups cab. The Suburban would have fit us better, but it can't pull a trailer anymore.

The ride is mostly quiet except for a little small talk between Greg and Robert. I of course am sitting in the middle of the two of them. I feel real uncomfortable next to Robert. I know he must still be angry with me so I scoot closer to Greg.

I start to see images that I don't quite understand. Something is running low to the ground. I know that it's an animal, but, I can't see what kind of animal. I don't see anything running out alongside the truck either. It has to be close with the clarity of thoughts I pick up on.

"Greg, do you see anything running outside?"

"No, why, are you getting something?"

"Yes… I was. Funny it's gone now, just like that." I look at Robert, He glares back at me. I shudder and scoot my butt even closer to Greg.

"Are you ok?" Greg asks

"Yea, I'm fine, just a chill I guess."

The truck is silent again as we ride along. The road leading up to the Brown's is dirt. And it's full of potholes, making it difficult not to bounce into Robert. Each time our hands touch, I feel the same rush I get when Andrew touches me. I think about his kiss from last night. I notice Robert suddenly looks angry. WTF?

"Robert, I'm sorry that I keep bumping your hand, but our driver could slow down a bit. I see that it's making you uncomfortable when we bump into each other."

I figure if he's angry enough he might come clean with why they can do this to me. This is as good a time as any. Maybe his anger will get the best of him. But no he just grabs my hand and runs his fingers up my arm, sending electricity all through me.

"Kim," he coos, "I enjoy the feel of your skin it's so soft and warm."

I know the excitement is showing on my face. He knows what he's doing to me. Making me desire him right here in the truck. He inches his face closer to mine. I know he is feeling it too as I inch my face closer to his. This really isn't all that easy with the bumps.

He says nothing and shows no indication of letting go of my hand. I manage with a great deal of struggling to pull it back from him just before our lips meet. I feel the relief instantly. He pulls himself together just as the house starts to come into view. The next one of them that touches me like that will pay for it I promise myself.

The trees open up to the Brown's home. There are a lot of trailers and shacks spread out on the property. I get out of the truck steaming. Greg grabs my arm to assist me. I pull away from him quickly.

"You ok Kim?"

I glare at him, "I will be just fine when one of you come clean about Andrew and Robert. I know something is going on. But no one is telling me what. For now it will have to wait, let's get the dogs crated."

He gives me a look of concern. But he knows better than to utter a word to me, when I'm pissed.

We previously had decided to split up. So we could crate and tag as many dogs as fast as possible. We are not alone so, I decide not to corner Robert here. Most of the people assisting us with this rescue also volunteer at the farm. I'm sure they already know what's going on.

The task of gathering all of the dogs takes all day. By the time we finish it's almost dusk. I take one last look around, both with my eyes and my mind. I spot a lab cowering behind one of the sheds and I yell to Greg.

"I'll be right back, I found one more."

Robert shouts to Greg, "Go on ahead we'll catch a ride with someone else. Your trailer is full anyway."

Greg with severity in his voice says, "No, I'll wait for Kim."

"Greg don't you trust me?" Robert sneers,

"Well Robert, usually," Greg walks up close to where he thinks only Robert can hear him. Greg hasn't realized that I've walked up behind him the lab in my arms. I listen in, I can tell things are about to get ugly between them. Greg is right in Robert's face.

"I'm not stupid Robert. I won't leave her here alone with you. I know that you don't like what you heard last night about Kim's feelings for Andrew. And I know that you're afraid she might figure out your secret too. I won't let you harm her and neither will your brother."

Robert, not missing a beat shouts back at Greg. "Andrew isn't thinking with his head, and it's going to cost us everything we worked so hard to protect. Remember when you found out what we are? You were so scared you locked us out of the house. Then you told us never to come back to your farm. You even went and bought a gun. You're a pacifist Greg!"

Greg ignores him turns and catches the look of fright on my face. Greg realizing I heard everything lowers his voice to a normal tone.

"Hey Kim, the dog can ride with us up front, there's no more crates. Robert can get a ride with someone else, won't you Robert!"

"Yea, no problem, I'll see you later at the farm"

Robert says smoothly as he storms off. Greg and I exchange looks, and get into the truck with the dog. I wait a while then ask just some of my many questions that are floating around in my head.

"What was that about between you two? Can you tell me their secret?" He pulls off to the side of the road. He stares straight ahead.

"No, I can't."

He looks down at his hands. "And I wish with everything in me that I could, but it's not my secret. I never figured that it would get like this. I thought Robert would leave well enough alone. And I just figured that it would be easier on you, not to have to ride back with Robert in the truck."

"Thanks Greg, but why does he treat me this way? It's like he can't make up his mind. He scares me with the way he looks at me sometimes, like he wishes I were dead or something. And at other times he is as sweet as sugar?"

Greg snaps back at me, "Well how the hell would I know what goes through his head? Who cares anyway? I wouldn't worry about him so much. And you scared of someone, that's not like you!"

"Yea, I know but he just confuses me!" We both shut up ashamed of ourselves for yelling at each other.

"Kim, I don't think that Andrew would let him harm you. If Robert does anything you don't like tell Andrew. You know he likes you, don't you?"

"Really, I thought he just liked getting me all hot and bothered, and then he leaves me hanging. Well he did kiss me a few times now. But I guess that you already knew that huh? He really likes me? I figured that I was just a toy for the both of them. They enjoy teasing me and keeping their secrets."

Greg tries to ignore my sarcasm. And I know it.

"Yes, Kim You really didn't know? The man is crazy for you and the sexual tension between you two is killing me. I'm about to do you myself. He needs to get around to it soon."

"Greg!" I exclaim. I just look at him dumbfounded.

"You can't be serious, your girlfriend Donna remember her? She won't like that."

"Well, I wouldn't tell her." He says with a devilish grin, I slap him on his shoulder. Not hard though just enough to get my point across.

"Please, could you drive faster Greg? So that I can get back to the farm and eat something. I'm starving and I want to clean up. Maybe then I can try to forget what you just said."

"Kim, you're going to have to help us unload, before you can clean up." He jokes.

"Yes, I remember, but you'll be too busy to pester me when we get there. There will be people waiting for us. So you won't be able to tease me with other people around. And if you do, I'll just get Andrew on you. If he likes me like you say, he'll take care of you bothering me." I say back to him jokingly.

When we finally get back, I'm a little short with everyone. I need to know what the hell is going on, especially because I know that I'm involved. And no one is telling me what the hell is really going on. Not even Greg, who is supposed to be my friend.

I hurry with what has to be done before going to bed. I only get a moment with Andrew but Robert is standing too close, leering at me.

"Good night guys." I snap as I start toward the house.

"Hey, wait up" Andrew calls to me. I slow my pace for him and notice that Robert is right beside him. His rage is still on his face causing me to answer Andrew coarsely.

"What Andrew?"

"Hey, I just want to know what it is that upsets you so much. You don't have to be short with me." He says with sadness in his voice.

"Sorry Andrew, it's been a very long day, and I'm bushed. I didn't mean to be short with you."

He takes my hand gently and I shudder with the jolt it sends through me. Inside of me a struggle begins between the desire from Andrews touch and my fear of Roberts rage. I notice that Andrew suddenly stiffens his body when we touch. At the same time, I catch Robert glaring at me. I see loathing in his eyes, and I get a crystal clear picture right then and there he doesn't want Andrew and me together.

The light bulb in my head finally clicks on. That's Robert's problem, he's falling in love with me! But I also grasp that I saw that in his mind. Then I see my own thoughts in his head. I start to panic and fidget.

"Andrew I've got to go. I'm just so very tired, good night." I say hurriedly, as I give him a peck on his cheek. I almost lose my balance in doing so. I turn and walk briskly toward the house. I go in the door, right up to my room, closing my door fast and locking it immediately.

Once I'm in my room, I start to pace, as I worry about what to do now? And why was I able to see inside of Roberts's head and he in mine it's just not right, I never see inside human minds. Something is very wrong here. I never was able to see inside Greg's mind or anyone else for that matter ever. I can't see in Andrews mind either. It must be something special about Robert.

I sit on the edge of my bed worried as hell. What do I do and what is happening here. Should I leave tonight without a word to anyone? I'm frightened, why can he hear my thoughts?

"My intentions are not to hurt you, unless you hurt me first."

"What the fuck? Where did that come from?" I look around my room for anyone but I am alone.

"Robert?"

Oh hell I'm going to get a strong drink. I slowly open my door looking both ways down the hall. I creep down the back stairs to the kitchen. I get the Jack out from the cabinet, and grab a bottle of coke. I'll be in need of this tonight so that I can sleep. I creep back to my room.

When I reach my door, I hear Robert's door open. I turn to look at him.

"Robert, can you hear me?"

"Yes, you chose the wrong one."

"I'm truly sorry, Robert it wasn't on purpose."

"Just the same, you're in love with my brother, and here I stand alone with my broken heart."

We stare at each other across the hall, and then he closes his door, without another word mentally or otherwise. I close and lock my door quickly. I can't believe that I can hear his thoughts. How can this be happening? I plan on having a couple of drinks, to calm myself down before I can sleep. I start with mixed Jack and coke, but that lasted for only two drinks. A couple of straight shots later I was able to fall asleep.

13

The next morning I manage to avoid Robert at breakfast and while working with the dogs in the morning. I skip lunch and hide in my room with William the dog for the afternoon.

By dinnertime, I'm starving, and my luck for the day has run out. Robert is seated at the table next to the only empty chair. I do my best to block my thoughts from him. Now that he has allowed me to know he can hear my thoughts, he is toying with me at the table.

I try hard to just eat my dinner, as Robert boasts that he can hear my thoughts anytime, that he can block me out of his head at will. Communicating to me only what he wants me to hear. He taunts me telling me how he has been listening to my every thought. Since the day I arrived here. I look at him appalled that he would raid my mind like that. My stomach is churning, he has me so upset.

"You know Kim, I especially like the way you think when you're drinking. Want to go to the bar later? I would love to play out some of your fantasies."

He starts replaying every sexual thought I have had since we met. I kick him under the table as hard as I can.

"Stop it Robert! And I mean now!"

I try to block him from my head.

"Kim, are you alright? You look pissed off."

"Sorry Greg, my mind was wondering to an unpleasant memory. Oh a change of subject, Greg, you know the dogs are making great progress from the raid before last. Most of them will be ready to go up for adoption soon. Do you want me to post them on Pet Finder or are you going to do it?"

"So Kim, who is it that kisses better Andrew or me?"

I just couldn't ignore that one. He has me so pissed! Glaring right at him with the meanest look I can muster,

"Andrew is the better kisser. You really should get some practice!"

He left me alone after that, now he is pissed. Maybe I should try harder to ignore him.

"Thanks Kim but I already started taking their pictures and writing the bios. So don't worry about any of it this time. If we keep getting more dogs, I'll need your help to keep me organized. I don't want to post the same dog twice, or with the wrong information."

"Ok, let me know. Well I'm done eating, good night everyone."

I get up abruptly and rush to leave the room. They all look at me with apprehension. I left most of my dinner on the plate. That is not like me at all, and Greg knows it.

Later that night Greg knocks on my door, but I send him away. I don't want to talk to anyone right now. He's just as guilty keeping secrets from me, some friend he is.

I'm sure that Greg and Andrew must know something's going on, but they haven't said too much, not that I have given them a chance to either. I manage to avoid Robert most of the time over the next couple of days, except for meals. At mealtime I practice blocking Robert out. There is no way avoiding him there. I rush thru dinner most nights and head directly to my room afterward.

I think the other volunteers must know that I can hear Robert by now. They knew it at the bar when he slipped up. I remember he said that we need to go, twice but everyone else heard him only say it once. And again in the truck with Greg, Robert must have been testing me with him thinking of running.

I have been avoiding everyone when I can. I'm pissed off at them all, but with my weakness for Andrew, I sometimes let him talk me into joining him on the porch after dinner. He has a way about him. I can't fight the truth. I have love for him in my heart. Still I'm mad that he has not come forward with what is going on here.

If Robert comes out with us, I usually find some way to get away from him fast. Because every time Robert is near me, he makes sure that I hear his every thought. He is a very lewd man.

Even if I try to block him out, it's like he is screaming his thoughts at me. That is when he wants to. I'm afraid to tell anyone what is going on because of the anger in his words. At dinner Friday night, I let my guard down so he can hear my thoughts.

"Robert I want to know what's going on."

"I will not answer any of your questions I don't want to. I think since you want Andrew over me that you don't deserve to know."

"Funny, I don't remember choosing Andrew. He kissed me Robert. I didn't make the first move, he did. Are you mad because he thought of it first?"

"No! That's not it! I kissed you first remember?"

He blocks me out of his head. Damn that didn't go so well did it? I have to control my tongue better in the future. While we are fighting our mental fight, Greg asked Robert something. And he has to speak to me.

"What did he say Kim?"

"I don't know I was listening to you."

"Shit!"

"Robert, didn't you hear me? When did you say you were leaving for that lecture in Georgia?" Greg thankfully asks him again. I notice Andrew has a concerned look on his face, wonder why?

"I'm heading out after dinner. I should have left earlier today but with the load of new dogs that we received. I thought that I would stay and give you guys a hand instead."

I start singing *"Freedom, freedom"* in my head.

"Shut up! I won't be gone that long it's only for a week. I'll be back to torment you each and every day."

"I'm learning how to block you out. Maybe by then I'll have it perfected. And by the way, Greg's talking to you about your trip." I smile to myself.

"Well, you have a good trip Robert. We'll see you when you get back."

"Thanks, Greg."

I just sit there grinning like a Cheshire cat. Then I have a thought. With panic in my voice, "Andrew you don't have to go with him?"

"No not this time." he says looking at Robert as they exchange a quick look. I suddenly feel a great relief that Robert will be away for a while. My smile comes right back.

"Bitch"

"Love you too Robert" he smirks at me, as he gets up from the table.

"Well I'm off on my journey. Don't do anything that I wouldn't approve of while I'm gone little brother." Robert says with malice.

"You either Kim" Robert glares at me over the table. I roll my eyes and look away.

"Ok" Andrew says hesitantly, looking at the both of us.

Greg and Andrew finish up then go to sit in the living room. I stay and help Doris clean up the table after dinner. I don't want to go upstairs alone that might be a very bad idea with Robert getting his gear together. However, Greg and Andrew must think I did go upstairs. I hear every word of their conversation, coming from the living room.

"Hey Greg, is it me or has Kim been getting a little touchy recently?"

"I was going to leave it alone. But I think it's the tension between the two of you. You know it's driving all of us crazy. And if you don't take the next step soon Robert will. He says seriously, and then adds lightheartedly. "I offered to be a stand in. You know just for old time sake. I hate to see a friend suffer like this."

Andrew plays dumb, "What do you mean? You two were a couple?"

"Well not really, it just started one night and well neither of us have a good track record with the opposite sex. So it was more for convenience than anything else."

"Greg, is that why you kept Kim from Robert and me for so long?"

"No! Besides that is very old history. The two of you belong together. I know she likes you and I see that you like her too, so get it over with will you? History can be changed. It doesn't have to be Robert."

"She keeps playing me off. I know she feels the desire just like I do. But Greg, she could get hurt." They say some things too low for me to hear. I strain but not in time to catch whatever they said.

"Well the next time the two of you are alone, do me a favor, don't back down. She can handle you, trust me. It would also relieve some of the anxiety that Robert has been causing her. I think he is losing control. Has he told you yet, can hear her thoughts?"

I knew it! It's some kind of Indian thing.

"No, he isn't sharing too much with me lately. I think that he's angry with me. He thinks that I should just back down and let him have her all to himself. But I'm falling for her; she is something real special, even without the legacy."

Awe, that was sweet, but how dare Greg speak for me. That's what I get for eaves dropping. What legacy is he talking about?

"Oh Andrew, and when you two do it, make sure that you are alone, no animals in the area either."

"Should I ask why that would matter?" Good question Andrew, I think to myself.

"Well with the two of you mixed with her gifts, the animals will know what's happening and not all of the dogs are fixed just yet. We could have a puppy explosion no pun intended… Andrew you didn't tell her, did you? You know, what you can do?"

"NO! Greg! She can't find that out, she would never want me then. Besides, my brother will kill me or her, or both. I'm just not ready to tell her yet. I want to know if she likes me for me, before I tell her what I can turn into."

"Andrew, she is far past liking you, trust me."

That can't be a good thing. What does he mean turn into? I stand frozen, not sure what to think about what I just heard. Then quietly I sneak out the back door, and come around to the front of the house, to enter the door like I've been outside.

"Hey! Guy's what's up for tonight?" I say brightly. Greg quickly rebounds with,

"Nothing Kim, we were just talking shop." He gets up a little too fast, spouting his words out quickly,

"Well goodnight, I'll see you both in the morning; I want to go check on the new rescues in the front barn before I hit the sack. I'll probably be a long time, a very long time."

Greg says, as he nudges Andrew. I catch him and just shake my head. How obvious can he be? Yea, like I couldn't tell they were talking about me, even if I hadn't been listening to them, the guilt showed all over their faces.

Just then Robert comes stomping down the stairs. He blows through the front door without a word to anyone. I listen and watch him start up his truck and drive away. I yell a silent Yippee.

Andrew and I exchange puzzled looks then we both dismiss it.

"Who can guess what Robert is upset about?" I say and Andrew turns to me smiling,

"Nice night tonight Kim, do you want to go for a walk?"

"Maybe," I say preoccupied, "I think that I'm going to check the store room first. We are running low on some things and I want to make a list. You know with all the dogs that have been showing up again." I feel it's safe enough that I can go outside alone, now that Robert is gone.

"Oh well then, I guess that I'll have to walk all alone, all by myself." He says coyly. I grin.

"I think somehow you will be safe Andrew."

I start off in the direction of the storeroom. I hope that he isn't going to wait much longer, though I might just have blown my chances for tonight. I know I'm not all that strong to resist him, my strength is quickly diminishing. Especially now with Robert away, we should be safe. Should he feel that he really wants to be with me? Even though, his brother will be very pissed at the both of us if we do. I can't fight this longing for Andrew. He has no idea how hard this has been resisting him this long. But if Robert reads my mind, he'll know, and then what? I'm scared to death of Robert.

I enter the storeroom and turn on the lights. Consumed in my own thoughts and worries, Andrew startles me when he clears his throat standing behind me. I didn't even hear him following me. I turn around to face him.

"Andrew, where did you come from?"

He pulls me to him, holding me firmly against his chest. I try to struggle, to free myself because of my fear of Robert is screaming at me in my head. But I feel the rush of emotions run through my entire body as he kisses me hard. I try to resist him, but to no avail I give in. I kiss him back just as feverishly.

He backs us to the wall grabbing my wrists up with one hand and holding them above me, securely against the wall. His other hand explores my body, and with a single tug, he pulls my jeans down and rips off my underwear, he unzips his pants, raises me up on the wall. I wrap my arms around his neck, without any hesitation he thrusts right into me.

I moan with the sensational pleasure flowing though my body. Finally, he releases my mouth to nibble on my neck, continuing slowly downward, he kisses lightly on my skin until he reaches my breast. He lingers a while, then slowly pulls himself back.

Looking hungrily at me, he curves his mouth into a crooked smile. He then pushes deeper within me watching my face. He thrusts into me over and over, harder and harder, until I feel like I can't take anymore. Instantaneously our bodies shudder with indescribable pleasure.

As we catch our breath, we hear a long sorrowful howl echoing in the surrounding mountains. Andrew grabs onto me tight, when he hears it as if he is frightened by it, but why would a wolf's howl scare him?

He must know what it means. But I don't get a chance to ask him. The howling starts a chain reaction. All the dogs on the farm start to howl and bark like crazy. Quickly we adjust our clothes and race out of the store room. Damn, I liked those panties too, I think as I stuff them into my pocket.

Laughing, at all the commotion we caused as we rush to the barns, I take the front one where Greg is having a hard time. Especially, since he is laughing hysterically. The dogs gave me away. I really need to learn to close my mind when I'm having sex. We finally calm the dogs down after a long while.

Greg and I walk toward the house. He finally stops having fits of laughter. He asks me if I'll be nicer now that I'm not so stressed. I just smack his arm, always the smart ass. It's not like I can deny it, I can't stop smiling. I do wish we had lasted a bit longer.

Over the next couple of days Andrew and I spend every free moment together that we can. We work together in the same barn. We're careful not to touch each other if anyone is near, but we flirt and tease each other constantly. I think I really have fallen in love with him, and it scares the shit out of me.

I just can't tell him how I feel, not yet anyway. I worry about why I get the feelings, from his touch. It's like nothing that I have ever experienced before in my life. And I'm well aware that it's not the thrill of new love. It's much more intense than humanly possible. His touch sends my heart racing with every nerve alive with the feeling of power. The uncontrollable desire for him is just terrifying. I wonder where these bruises come from though. The ones on my back side are easy to figure out, but the ones on my wrists and arms… they couldn't be from him?

I've asked him about the desire thing, but he just plays it off. With me having over active hormones, I know he is hiding something from me. I see the fear in his eyes sometimes, when we are having sex. He tries to be tender but it never stays that way for long. I can't believe that the bruises are from him. Wouldn't I feel it if he caused them?

I have to find a way to get his secret out of him. I'm still very worried about what is going to happen, on the day Robert gets back especially, since he's due back any day now.

After lunch on the last day before we expect Robert to be on his way back. I decide that I would have one last time alone with Andrew. When Robert comes back, I fear that we won't be able to get any alone time. The fear of Robert reading my mind and finding out that I slept with Andrew is frightening. My whole body shivers with even the thought.

I come across Andrew unloading bales of hay off of a pickup truck. He's stacking it just inside one of the paddocks. I sneak up behind him and with my most seductive voice ask,

"Hey sexy, are you about done yet?"

"Yea, why?" he asks as he catches my facial expression. He can tell that I am up to no good. We don't touch each other in public. Only Greg and maybe Doris know for sure. The volunteers all leave the main house by dinner time, so after dinner we have been sneaking up to one of our rooms, but I just can't wait today. With Robert due back soon, it may be our last chance for a while.

"Let's take a walk just you and me. There are enough volunteers here today. We could escape for a while and not be missed." I say cheerfully, he looks down at me suspiciously,

"What do you have in mind, my little flower?"

"Well maybe you and me and a blanket in the open field on the back forty. No one is supposed to be out there today." I say fighting the grin that's taking over my face.

“Whatever my little flower wants, I think we should let Greg know we’re going for a walk. He worries when he doesn’t know where you are. He’s like your own personal protector. Has he always been like that with you Kim?”

“No, just since I’ve come back this time. He’s always been a great friend to me, but, this visit is very different.”

I help Andrew finish unloading the hay. Then we walk side-by-side careful not to touch, to the front barn to where Greg is. When we enter the barn we hurriedly close the door. A large dog has gotten away from Greg.

We see Greg chasing the big Rottweiler aka William. Greg looks distraught and yells for our help. This is the same dog I had a difficult time with that I have made my friend, though no one knows yet. Quickly, I spout out orders.

“Andrew you go around to the right, I’ll go straight toward him, Greg stay where you are in the middle. Randy stay to the left end, box him in towards me, so that I can get his focus.”

By doing as I ask we box him in quickly. I take a stance that reflects authority. He stares at me, not too happy. The others start slowly advancing towards his sides and rear. Then with weight in my voice I say.

“William sit, stay!”

The dog instantly sits down right where he is without hesitation. The guys all exchange looks of surprise. I ignore them to maintain control of the dog. Though inside, I really want to laugh at their reaction and so does William.

“William, go back to your pen!”

He heads right for his pen and waits there for me to open the gate for him. I let him in telling him I am proud of him, that he's a good boy. He barks in response. I walk away from him past the amazed eyes. I wait until we are outside of the barn, and the doors are closed before I speak.

"Ok explain that Kim." Greg questions.

"Well honestly, he was challenging you Greg, he thinks that you're weak." Greg gives me a sarcastic look. "The next time he challenges you, stand your ground and give him commands confidently. He will obey. He was thinking that he could get out of the barn and find me. I figured out that he doesn't respect us when we speak softly to the other dogs. He needs a strong leader to follow, no wimps as he puts it. So I tried something new and it worked. He wants to stay here as a guard dog and his name is William. You know it means protector."

"What do you mean wimps? I'm not a wimp, and I don't think Randy is one either."

"I'm sorry Greg, I'm just telling you what William thinks. But the reason Andrew and I are here, is to let you know that we're taking the afternoon off, Andrew and I that is," I tell Greg as we start to walk off towards the back forty. Greg just shakes his head at us. I hear Randy tell Greg.

"This will not end well, the two of them." I push his remark out of my head for now.

I wait until we're just about to the clearing and I kiss Andrew passionately. I break away from him; giving him a devilish grin. I run as fast as I can toward the middle of the clearing. He catches me easily and pulls me to the ground on top of him. All the while we laugh playfully.

With one arm around me keeping me close to him. He reaches for my hair, pulling it back carefully trying not to touch my face yet. He gathers it all into a ponytail. And in one smooth motion, I'm under him…

Afterward we lay beside one another watching the clouds float by. I should be freezing out here in the middle of February. If not for Andrews coat and his body heat combined, they make me nice and toasty.

I only chose to come out here because. Greg is getting mad at us for having sex in his house. He claims that we're too loud. I know he hasn't said anything to Andrew about it though, just me. I know Greg is jealous, even though he swears that he isn't.

"Andrew, I've never been so happy." He squeezes me a little tighter. Good thing I'm wrapped in his coat.

"Kim you make me happy too, and it's not just the sex."

"Yea, tell me about the sensations we feel when we touch. That's not normal believe me. It's like an overwhelming pull. I can't resist you even when I'm exhausted." I shove my elbow in his ribs gently.

"I felt it when we first met on the porch." Andrew takes his finger and runs it across my bare hand.

"You mean this feeling," he breathes,

"Yes," I say excitedly, "please explain that."

"I can't, maybe it means that we are meant to be together, simple as that."

Yea right, then why would it work with Robert also? And why can't I hear Andrew's thoughts? "No Andrew, there is a lot more to it than you are telling me. I know there is, I will figure it out. Is it an Indian thing?"

"Can't we just enjoy it and not question. Something's just can't be explained Kim."

Well I guess I'm not going to find out today what this is all about. I guess I should just enjoy things while they last. We lay there for a while surrounded by the tranquil sounds of nature, just watching the clouds drift overhead.

A while later, Andrew glances at his watch, Jumps to his feet and exclaims.

"Kim we are late! Its dinner time and we better hurry back."

We must have fallen asleep. We rush back to the farm. He is faster than me and leaves me in his dust. I walk towards the house from behind the back barn. I stop dead in my tracks. I hear Greg shout out to Robert as I round the corner. My heart has fallen to my feet, by passing my stomach completely. I am literally scared to death!

"Hey, Robert welcome back. Did you have a good trip?"

He must have seen Andrew pass by. He knows that I would not be far behind him. Greg takes a deep breath of encouragement and clears his throat. I know he's scared as well. His voice is shaky.

"You know while you were away, your brother and Kim seem to be spending a lot of time together."

My insides churn Damn you Greg! You just couldn't keep your mouth shut, just this once. Greg gets quiet, waiting for Robert's reaction. I am worried about how he will react. I know he isn't happy with me for liking Andrew already. I hope he doesn't punch Greg.

"Yes, I know what's been going on while I was gone, and I don't like it!" Robert says with obvious anger in his voice. Good he didn't hit him, yet.

"The two of them together could ruin everything for me. How do you think she's going to react when she figures out what we are?" Sarcasm fills Roberts every word.

"Well knowing Kim she might be upset at first." What does he mean? What are they? Andrew said something about changing into something. What the hell are they?

"She's falling hard for your brother. She would rather accept what he is, then live without him. She has already stayed much longer then she was supposed to, Because of him, it can't be Doris's cooking. Robert you know Kim's the one in the legend. You've seen the way they look at each other when they touch. They feel the connection, just the same as you do. I've seen your body tense up when you touch her. Do you hear her thoughts?"

"Greg, I gotta go, I need to take a walk, and clear my head. Before I do something Andrew might regret." Robert bellows at Greg then he storms off.

I begin to hear scattered thoughts from Robert. He is very pissed at Andrew and me. He just hates that Andrew is the one I chose. They even had a wager on which one I would like more. How dare they? I listen more, containing my anger and blocking my thoughts from Robert.

His thoughts are confusing to me. He is thinking that he will never find another woman like me, because the others are dead. The other girls were killed by the dirt sleepers. I am his birth right, I should be his not Andrews. He knows that it's just a matter of time. Andrew will tell me what they are. Andrew is weak like their father.

None of that settled well inside of me. I run to the bathroom in the house. I feel sick in my stomach. I play it over and over in my head what he thought. So many questions what are dirt sleepers? Zombies or vampires no they are horror story creatures? Those things can't really exist can they? What do they change into?

Why do I feel sick? Maybe I ate something that was bad, shit I'm going to throw up again. I race back to the bathroom. I stay in there for a long while. Finally, the nausea clears away completely.

I sneak to the front stables and do some busy work. I need time to think things through. I get so caught up in my troubles that I don't grasp that I was followed, until it's too late. I'm in an empty stall my back to the door. Robert encloses me in his arms. I get the rush thinking its Andrew. I accept his touch until he holds me too tight.

"Hey Andrew, let up a little, that hurts."

"Oh it's going to hurt much more than this." He whispers in my ear.

I cry out panicking, "Robert, let me go, let me go now!"

"Sorry love, if you're good enough for my brother, then you'll have to be good enough for me."

"What do you mean Robert? Let me go right now!" I demand.

"No bitch, it's my turn" I try to scream; he covers my mouth with his hand. My back is to his chest, so I try to kick backwards at him. A mare in from the next stall tries to assist me in getting away from him. She goes for Roberts arms with her teeth. He backs us out of the stall.

"Thanks anyway girl." I think to her,

She protests by whinnying and kicking the walls of the stall. He easily carries me to another empty stall.

"Shut her up Kim!"

I still hear her whinnying loudly, even though he has carried me to the other end of the stables. I tell her not to hurt herself that I will get through this. I also tell the other horses not to make noise.

He holds me tightly against him. Adrenaline is rushing through my body, desire and fear intertwined into one emotion.

Unexpectedly, he throws me face down to the ground. Instantly, he straddles me, pinning my body against the cold hard floor. He pulls my hair hard arching my back.

"If you scream, it will be worse, understand?"

I nod yes in response to his threat. He tugs at me to turn over. I roll over onto my back. I glare back at him, he ignores it.

He places his hand squarely on my chest keeping me pinned against the cold hard floor. Damn, he is stronger than I thought. His eyes grow dark and crazed. Fear overcomes me I close my eyes praying he stops.

He unzips my jeans slowly. I open my eyes looking for some trace of the Robert I thought I knew, but he's not there. He studies the terror overtaking my face and mind. I open my mouth to speak. He leans down within an inch of my face. Very sadistically he utters,

"If you yell and Andrew comes here, I'll say you seduced me, do you understand? Who would he believe his brother, or his lover, a known slut?"

That hurt me deeply and he knew it would. I feel horror running through me, filling my entire body. I start to tremble uncontrollably. I want to cry, but I refuse to show him my tears. I will fight them back as long as I can.

"Why are you doing this to me? I haven't done anything to you." I hiss,

"Yes you did, you slept with my brother first, not me. There's only one woman like you left alive. I guess we will just have to share you. I trust that's all right?"

I try desperately to block out everything around me. His scent is enticing and he is so warm. The desire is overcoming me, which I'm fighting so very hard to resist.

"Kim, you can never tell him. It would crush his little heart, and then you wouldn't have him either. Do you understand?" He taunts me then he forces himself inside me.

I close my eyes and try to picture a peaceful place to go to until he is finished. I think of tall pine trees next to a tranquil lake. It works for a few moments, and then I become painfully aware of what he is doing to me. The cold hard ground is scraping my back as he pounds me harder and harder.

I try fighting him, but I know that I'm also fighting myself. I don't want Robert. But the rush of desire… is… too intense to defeat… It's just useless for me to fight any longer. He's too incredibly strong. I could never over throw him. I just stop fighting and lay still in defeat. I turn my head to the side and lay motionless. I try to focus on a spot on the stable wall, but my eyes are overflowing with tears, I just can't fight back anymore.

He moans, "No, keep on fighting me. I like it that way. It's much better than if you just lie there and take it. It makes it more fun when you fight. Don't you think?"

"You disgust me, how could you do this to me? Why with so much anger and pain?"

He tries to intensify the desire effect by kissing my neck. I am so very sickened with myself for the feelings of yearning for him. His touch makes me weak. I find myself reluctantly meeting his thrusts, hating myself for doing it.

He finally finishes torturing me. I pull my legs up into a ball and roll over to cry. I can't hold back any longer. The emotions are too great, I can't contain them. I yell out to him.

"Please… leave me alone… just go away."

"I will for now," he utters, as he dresses himself.

"But if I want you again, I will take you." He kneels down in front of me and lifts my chin so that I am looking at him, "Oh, and Kim, I will want you again. That was so much fun."

I pull my face away from his grasp.

"I hate you Robert!"

He laughs at me as he opens the stall door. Lingering there, he looks at me helpless on the floor. His arrogance is overflows in his mind.

"Did you know that we get the same rush that you get when we touch you? No, I bet he didn't share that with you? Oh well, just another secret he's keeping from you."

When he finally leaves, I lay there totally disgusted and confused. I cry uncontrollably for a long time. I try to pull myself together. William comes to me and he licks at my face trying to console me. I thank him and ask him to stay with me tonight. But, I make it clear to him that if Robert tries to hurt me again, that he is not to intervene. I don't want him to get hurt, and I don't trust Robert at all anymore with anything.

I dress quickly, and head for the house trying to get Roberts face out of my head. I can't believe what just happened. And he said this would not be the last time. He plans on attacking me again I need to get out of here. I make it to the porch before I collapse. William sits right beside me. He is in full blown guard dog mode. The pain Robert inflicted is over whelming. It hurts so much just to walk. I sit here worrying about all of what's happening to me. What am I going to do? I can't tell Andrew, he would think that I'm lying or worse, believe me. He would attack his brother. Robert does deserve a good ass kicking.

A dog comes running toward me from out of the woods. William stands up ready to attack. I clear my eyes to see what is coming and I see that it's Nick.

"It's ok William he's a friend. Oh Nick, I'm so glad to see you." Nick kisses and nibbles on my face, showing that he is just as happy to see me. I tell William again that Nick is a friend, though he continues to growl at Nick. I hug Nick like he is a life line. And for the moment I bury the thoughts Robert down deep inside.

I try to enjoy the visit from a harmless friend, though it is a little tense between William and Nick, I don't understand why William doesn't trust Nick. Nick can see the stress on my face, so I quickly change my expression. I don't want him to know what happened to me, so I pretend to be happy. As we get reacquainted I see some dogs hiding just inside of the tree line.

"Nick, are they friends of yours?"

Nick makes some noises and they slowly approach the house with caution. I start to hear their fears and try to reassure them that I will only help them. When they are in front of me, they tell me that Nick rescued them. The images are coming so fast it's hard for me to keep up with all of them. I'm too drained to concentrate.

I finally tell them, "Ok enough for now, let's get you guys settled in for the night."

I take the dogs to the barn and put them in a pen and feed them. They will be fine together until the morning.

"Nick, I guess now I know where all of the dogs are coming from. It's sure good to see you again. I have to get to bed now before I drop. Are you staying tonight?"

Nick gently jumps up to my face and licks me then he runs into the woods.

"Bye for now Nick, come back soon please."

I call out to him. I pat William on his head. "Let's go to bed boy, will you stay in my room tonight?"

"Yes,"

When we get into my room, I undress and see the bruises Robert left on me. I look myself over in the mirror. I feel so disgusted that I throw up everything in my body until there is nothing left. I take a shower and scrub everything. As I climb into bed I hear a knock on my door, I hesitate, and worry who is there.

"Kim it's me Andrew, you in there?" I breathe a sigh of relief,

"Yes, I'm coming, just a second."

I grab my robe covering up the bruises, and then open the door for him. He enters knowing something is wrong. He scans the room but doesn't ask. He has learned to read my face and I his.

"Andrew, I'm exhausted. More dogs showed up tonight, can we do this another time?"

"Honestly Kim, I just wanted your company no sex, just company, is that ok?"

"That's fine, but you use your own blankets. If you touch me, it'll be all over. Andrew laughs as he agrees to my request. I'm glad he is next to me, I feel safer. I just might sleep tonight after all. I wonder why he wanted to stay with me. He hasn't spent the whole night with me even though we've been having sex. It's strange that he would, especially tonight after his brother raped me.

14

In the morning, as I go to get out of bed. I'm not quick enough with the robe, and Andrew wakes. Catching me walk to the bathroom seeing some the bruising on me, not that he is innocent, some of them are from him. But the ones that hurt are from Robert.

"What happen to you last night?" I can hear the alarm in his voice.

"Remember the dogs last night? Well they were a bit excited. Also the wolf that brought them was a little too happy to see me. I guess I just didn't notice the bruises last night."

"Oh" He says, I know he doesn't completely believe me, but I couldn't think of another excuse. I couldn't tell him the truth.

"Next weekend, when you leave for your trip, can I go with you?" I ask Andrew when I return from the bathroom and lay down next to him.

"You'll be bored while I do the lectures. There's nothing to see or do at the collage that would interest you."

"That's ok I would like to hear your speech. Aren't your lectures on Indian culture?"

"Yes."

"I bet they're good, I might even learn something about you. And where there's a college, there are bound to be animals that need my help."

"What will Greg do without you helping him out?"

"He'll be just fine. He survived without me before, and he can do it for a short while again. Let's go get some breakfast, I'm starved." I'm terrified to stay here without Andrew. I'm glad he is letting me go with him on his lecture trip. It's only for a few weeks but maybe I can heal from Robert's attacks. Besides Robert would have way too many opportunities to trap me.

As it is, four days have passed now since the first attack. And Robert has found me alone twice and assaulted me. He thinks that he has the right to claim me as his. He muttered something about his birth right, whatever that's supposed to mean?

I've been very cautious to stay where other people are. I don't want to be alone anywhere on the farm. William has been glued to my side. He growls when Robert is in the area to warn me. The only reason Robert got away with the two assaults was when William went outside to relieve himself. I now follow William on his potty breaks.

As I enter the barn with Jasmine. I over hear Greg and Andrew talking about something, so I stay out of sight and listen. Yea, I know it's not right, but, I also know something is going on around here that none of them are telling me about. Jasmine looks at me as I put a finger to my lips. She walks away in the opposite direction.

"Hey Greg, did I tell you Kim is going with me for my lecture trip this time?"

"I think that's a great idea for Kim to get away from here. She's been looking a little worn out lately." I can't believe he just said that, like he doesn't know why I'm suddenly so tried.

"I asked her about that, she said that she'd be ok in a few days. That she was coming down with something.

But I think that it's something more and she's hiding something from me. Greg have you noticed the bruises on her?" Andrew asked.

"Yes she told me they were from the dogs playing with her too rough. Andrew don't you believe her story?"

"No, I wish that I could see in her head. I've been so careful not to hurt her. But the darkest bruises appear when I haven't been with her. We haven't had sex since Robert came back, I'm afraid that it might be Robert hurting her. And even if it is, he'll never admit it. I think while Kim and I are away, I'll go set up some lectures for him. You know, keep him away as much as possible."

"That sounds like a good idea for now. But that won't hold him off forever. Robert has a temper and he has put other women in the hospital before. It's not beneath him to force her to keep quiet. All he would have to do is threaten one of us or an animal."

I swear my heart skipped a beat, when I heard Greg say Robert has put other women in the hospital. What in the hell has he gotten me into? He is supposed to be my friend.

"I also think the change of scenery would help Kim. She spends all of her time either with the dogs or one of us. She needs outside contact. Where are the lectures this time anyway?" Greg asks.

"We head out in the morning to Florida. Thinking ahead I made calls about my long trip coming up through North Carolina. We'll be gone about a month on that trip. We'll meet a lot of my people mostly in North Carolina during our trip.

I hope to have told her by that time, but just in case I don't, I'll have to keep her close by. I've worked out how to keep her out of trouble. But I can't be with her the whole time. I've called some of the people that I know. I asked them to line up animals for her to work with."

"Andrew, couldn't the animals tell her what's going on?"

"No, I thought of that, the animals are from the local towns not the reservation. The town's people would have no idea to warn her, I have made sure of that. There will be enough people in place to keep her from finding out. Just in case, until the time is right."

"Andrew, why are you dragging this out? There's no doubt that Kim is the woman in the legend. She deserves to know before she has your puppy."

"Not funny Greg, not funny at all."

"Yea, really it is Andrew. Let Kim know the truth about you and Robert and get it over with. She's already suspicious that something is going on, I mean the touching thing alone that goes on between you three is creepy enough."

"The three of us, what do you mean Greg?" Andrew asks confused.

"Well if she gets whatever you call it with you, shouldn't she get the same feelings from Robert? She wouldn't be able to resist him either, if he were to touch her, would she?"

"No, I guess not… I hadn't thought of that… He could be forcing her to have sex with him. And knowing him he would threaten her." Andrew says sounding distraught.

"Well Andrew, then you better get her out of here first thing in the morning."

"I plan to."

"Andrew, you should know that it won't take long for her to get pregnant, now that you two are having sex and if he is?"

"You knew we were having sex?" Andrew says jokingly.

"Andrew the whole farm knows that you're having sex. It's not like you're quiet about it. And the sound of my furniture breaking kind of gives it away."

"Oh sorry about that, but I fixed what I broke. Well most of it anyway. Greg, while I finish packing, could you find her and make sure he's nowhere around her? Now I'm worried about her safety."

"Yea, no problem, I think she's up stairs, I'll see if she needs help packing."

I slip out of the barn without them seeing me and rush up in to the house. I run up the back stairs and smack into Robert.

"Shit!"

He forces me into his room. As we hear someone coming up the steps. He quickly covers my mouth with his shirt sleeve. He holds me tightly against the front of him. His back is against the door. I can't move even if I want to. His grip on me is so tight.

"Robert, I am really getting sick of this shit."

"Shut up bitch!"

"I know its Greg coming let me go!"

I hear Greg knock on my bedroom door, he gets no answer. He crosses the hall and knocks on Robert's door.

He has no idea that Robert and I are on the other side of it. I manage to stomp on Robert's foot. He makes a low grunt. Greg must have heard it because he raises his voice.

"Hey Robert, are you in there? Have you seen Kim anywhere?"

"No... No, I was sleeping… I don't know where she is and why would I?" Robert replies as if he is groggy.

"Robert, is she in there with you?"

"No Greg, now go away, I'm tired!"

I try to make more noise so that Greg hears me. Robert quickly wraps my legs in his before I can stomp him again. Greg reluctantly walks away down the stairs. I hope that he heard me and is getting Andrew to help. As soon as Robert knows Greg is gone, he removes his arm from my mouth.

"I'm not done yet; you are going to be away from me for a time with Andrew. I have to get in my share before you leave."

"Why can't you just give up and let Andrew have me?"

He grimaces, "What's the fun in that? Besides you don't hate this, as much as you protest do you? Remember Kim, I can also read your thoughts. Even when we're not near to each other, just like you can mine? I see that you are falling for me, which proves to me that you are weak, just like the rest of them."

"I'm not the only weak one here Robert." I state sarcastically to him

"Never say that again," Robert commands as he pushes me down on the bed. He lies on top of me simply looking at my face. My arms pinned across my chest between us.

He is fighting himself with how he is starting to feel about me. His mind is one big confused mess. He loosens his grip on me, enough that my hands are free. I try to take advantage of his distracted thoughts. By digging my nails into his chest, I break the skin causing him to bleed.

"Oh please hurt me, he pleads, I like it so much better that way," he says as he …

The next morning we are about to leave on our trip. Andrew finds me in the kitchen wearing a long sleeved thick sweater and jeans, not my usual attire. I'm sitting alone at the table, eating my breakfast, lost in worry.

He places his hand gently on my shoulder, but, I still flinch. My whole shoulder is bruised from Robert pinning me to the bed.

"Kim, why is your shoulder so tender?"

"I must have pulled something." I reply absently. He looks me over smiling. I know he is happy to be leaving, so that we can have some time alone.

"I saw your bag in the hall. Are you all packed?" he says excitedly. I'm glad one of us is cheery this morning.

"Yes, we just need to get my duffle bag from the hall."

"We Kim, do you have a frog in your pocket?" I scowl at him I'm in no mood right now.

"Remember that Andrew, because I do get even." I say confidently,

"I'm shaking in my boots" Andrew says as he laughs and makes his body shake all over. I go to hit him and he runs towards the hall. I begin to chase him laughing, but before I can catch up, Robert stops me at the doorway. He steps in front of me, successfully blocking me. I come to an abrupt stop in his chest. I try to conceal my fear from Andrew's watchful eyes.

"Morning Bitch"

"Bastard"

Robert knows that Andrew is watching us so he jokingly says to me,

"What did my brother do now? Do you want me to rough him up for you?"

"No, I can handle Andrew, thanks anyway." I say causally, as I squeeze through the doorway pass him. I walk swiftly away from Robert, right out the door with Andrew.

Andrew whispers, "I think he's up to something Kim, Don't trust him." What an understatement that was.

"Don't worry I don't trust him at all." I whisper back. We leave the house to load the van with our stuff. I'll be grateful to be far away from Robert for any amount of time. I look back at the house and Robert is standing on the top of the front steps, his arms crossed and smiling, watching us drive away. I shake off the evil thoughts he is shouting at me. I am not looking forward to returning to the farm any time soon.

15

We cross the Florida state line heading for Tallahassee. It'll only take us about eight hours to get to Florida University. I hear it's a very nice campus. They have lots of palm trees and a water fountain out in front of the main entrance. Back in 1854 it was a school for boys. I searched the internet for a little history on the university. I wanted to have some insight, into where we're going.

I immediately get lost in thought again worrying. What will happen when we get back in two weeks? I know Robert will make me pay for my absence. I keep rethinking everything over and over in my head. My stomach keeps acting up. I think Andrew is getting mad at me, for having to stop so much. But before I know it, we arrive at the University. We are staying with a history professor, Dr. Glenn. He has invited us to stay at his home. It's convenient because he is in walking distance of the campus. This ends up being a good thing for me because after the first lecture, I'm pretty bored. I decide to walk to the Professors home; it's less than a mile away.

It's late in the afternoon, dusk actually. While I walk I can tell that something is following me from just inside the trees. I know it's a dog because of the thoughts that I get from him. I tell him to please show himself to me, but he chooses not to come out into my view.

I just continue to walk toward the professor's home. The sun has gone down and the street lights switch on. I see a handsome man walking toward me. I wouldn't have even looked at him, if not for the dog's sudden fear at the sight of this man. I try not to show on my face, I have been alerted to the possible danger of this man. I don't change my pace or direction either. I look straight head. When he is near enough to me, he deliberately steps in my path. He looks me up and down like I was chocolate cake.

"Yum," he licks his lips,

"Excuse me sir?"

"Oh sorry, let me introduce myself, I am Jonathan. I am a friend of the professors. May I escort you to his home? You really shouldn't be out at night alone?" He extends his arm for me to take it.

"I'm sorry but I am not afraid of the night. I always have unseen protectors around me Jonathan." And with that, he bursts into hysterical laughter.

"Oh my dear, you have no idea what is protecting you in the night. That is partly why I choose to meet you for myself. I wanted to satisfy my own curiosity. Sadly not my thirst," he runs his fingers across his lips. I look at him bewildered.

"Kimberly, you are a site of beauty. I just do not understand why, he simply has not eliminated…? If he truly wants you for himself, he could have you changed at any time."

"I'm very sorry Jonathan, but I have no idea what you are talking about. I think I'll walk alone to the professor's home. Thank you very much for your offer, I have to get going." I start to walk away from him and a question crosses my mind but before I can stop myself, I ask it,

"Who is it that wants me eliminated?"

"No my dear, on the contrary, he wants you for himself. I on the other hand, would have you killed already. Better yet do it myself. That my dear I would take great pleasure in."

He waves his hand like you would at a fly, "But alas he is in charge. I refuse to tell you his name. You will know soon enough I'm sure of that. The pot is starting to boil."

I call the dog mentally. That has now been joined by four more, to come out and walk with me where they can be seen. They do as I ask and Jonathan laughs again.

"Your wolves do not scare me. We will meet again my dear, till then I bid you adieu."

He bowed before he backed away from me, and crossed the street. He snaps his head quickly to the right, and then is gone from my sight. I can't see what it was that made him flee, but, I am grateful for whatever it was.

The dogs stay real close to me as we walk to the professor's. Once there, the dogs all leave me to return to their own homes. I thank them for getting me there in one piece. I decide that from now on, I will stay inside at night. At least while we are away from the farm. That man Jonathan really creped me out.

When Andrew comes in from his lecture it's time for dinner. I don't bring up my encounter with the creepy Jonathan. We eat our meal with Dr. Glenn and his family. He has a lovely wife and two young sons. The conversation is all about the history of peoples that have come and gone from Florida.

At first I learn a lot about past peoples and how much Andrew knows. He really impresses me with his knowledge. But then they discuss statistics. I get very bored very fast. I go with the kids to their play room and we play with matchbox cars. The boys are eight and ten.

We see who can make their car fly the furthest off a table I let the boys win of course.

I catch Andrew watching us play from the doorway. He gives me a broad smile as he continues on down the hall. I'm not sure what that was for. Shortly afterward Mrs. Glenn comes for the children. I go to join Andrew in our room. He is fast asleep, so I follow suit and fall right to sleep beside him.

The next few days while Andrew is at the college, I play with the boys during the day. They are out on a school break. We fill our days with playing with their soccer ball and playing hide and seek. We also enjoy swimming in the indoor swimming pool they have.

Their mother is very happy to have me visit. She told me to come back anytime I want to, with or without Andrew. I told her that I would see what I could do. She really enjoyed having some time to herself. I guess I would too, if I had two boys to take care of full time.

The next stop is a short one on our way back to the farm. It's a small community college. We are staying in a motel this time. The rooms are small but clean. All white walls and brown carpeting. The bed is covered with a gold quilt. At least they have a well-equipped indoor gym.

Since we will be here for few days, I'll need something to do. I look up the local animal shelter and give them a call to lend a hand. Since they know who I am, they arrange a ride back and forth for me. I fill my day by working with the animals on their training and behaviors. I also teach some of the staff how to read the dog's body language. It will help them understand what the dogs are telling them.

Andrew and I manage to eat dinner together every night. Usually a fast food place or small diner, neither of us are wealthy by any means. On our last night, Andrew tells me that we are invited to a party at one of the teacher's homes, Mr. Fort's. I had brought some nicer clothes with us just in case I needed them. I was glad that I did, Andrew already had dress clothes for the lectures. He looks real nice in a suit.

When we get there, we find that it was more a cocktail party with appetizers and wine. Neither of us cares for wine. I ask the waiter if they have anything else to drink. He tells me that he will get us a couple of beers. We try to mingle with the teachers friends. Andrew and I soon find ourselves bored out of our minds. We decide to take a walk out to the gardens in the rear of the house. Mr. Fort's garden has won awards for its beauty, which he made sure everyone at the party knew many times.

The garden is lit up with tiny white lights woven through the wisteria vines. It really is breath taking, even though nothing is in bloom at this time of year.

Andrew and I sit on a wooden bench and just admire the scenery and silence. We are not out there for long before my stalker appears.

"Hello Andrew, I am a friend of Mr. Fort. How are you this evening?" Andrew stands to shake his hand. Jonathan looks down at his own hand with inquiry when they touch.

"I am fine this evening, have you met Kim yet?" Andrew must detect something is wrong here. I keep fidgeting and shifting my feet. I politely shake Jonathan's hand. Since Andrew is with me I feel protected.

"We have met already, have we not Kimberly?" I feel coolness to his touch.

"Yes, we have, when I was walking alone back from the Florida University to Dr. Glen's. Do you make it a habit to follow young women around?"

"Kim!" Andrew snaps, I maintain my defensive tone and body language.

"Oh how rude of me. I am sorry if I might have slighted you in anyway. You were so polite to me before when we met. So polite in fact that as we spoke four dogs came to protect me from you." I turn to look at Andrew, who is astonished by my actions.

"No Kimberly I believe that it was five wolves."

"Wolves," Andrew asks

"Dogs Andrew, not wolves, I don't believe that Jonathan would be here if they had been actual wolves that night." Jonathan laughs his demeaning laugh again.

"Andrew I am suddenly very tired, Can we go say our goodbyes?"

"Yes Kim, let's go inside. Are you coming, ah your name is?"

"Jonathan, we will see each other at another time Andrew, good evening for now."

"Andrew let's get out of here now, please?"

"Yes Kim, he was disturbing."

We go into the house and search for the host to say goodnight. I ask if he knows Jonathan well. Mr. Fort says that there is no one by the name of Jonathan here tonight.

Andrew gives me a worried look and we leave. We grab some fried chicken on the way back to the motel. I just can't seem to get Jonathan out of my head. He is very disturbing to me.

We pack the stuff we won't need in the morning. I know something is amiss about him, for the dogs to come to my aid out of nowhere. He called them wolves, not dogs, certainly he knows the difference. There was something very weird about him. He seemed old world with the way he spoke, and his hands were colder than a normal mans. If I didn't know better, I'd think I just met a vampire. How silly of a thought, I dismiss the whole thing from my mind.

At first light in the morning we are in route to Greg's. It should only take us a couple of hours to get to the farm from here. Andrew drives like always and I just look out the window. Now I have even more things to worry about when we get back. I now know that there is an unknown stranger that wants me in some capacity for his own. Jonathan would rather me be dead, if possible by his own hands. And then there's Robert who will be waiting to attack me at the first chance he gets.

Andrew and I return to Greg's farm much too fast for my liking. Once we are back, I resume my normal routines. I do whatever I can to avoid being alone with Robert. William and I are like Siamese twins joined at the hip. I begin to sneak up to my room. That is if I'm not already with Greg or Andrew. I also take extra care not to be alone anywhere on the farm, especially at night. Now even the night isn't safe for me, even if Robert is not here.

Still Robert finds ways to attack me. He is getting overconfident about it. He waits until Andrew has just left me alone somewhere, then he drags me to a concealed spot. He even pounces on me when I am cleaning the stables. Reluctantly, each time I tell William to go for his safety.

Robert's favorite is when I'm trying to get to my room. He grabs me just as I reach for my door handle, then he pulls me across the hall into his room. Robert has given me only one safe haven, my bedroom if I make it there. I don't understand why no one hears us. I try to make as much noise as I can. I know someone must hear us. But no one ever comes to save me.

Because of his actions, I find that I am disgusted with myself more and more. I hate that I allow him to abuse me. I feel trapped in the secret. I also hate to admit that aside from my guilt and the bruises, I enjoy the physical thrill that comes with each attack.

But I have been feeling weak lately. I'm not sure if it's just stress or maybe something else. I think that it's time for a phone call to my best friend, Greg's sister Nancy.

She always sets me straight when I get into trouble way over my head. I find a quiet place in the den to make my call. I first surround myself with large dogs including William.

I open my cell hoping she will put things into perspective for me.

"Hello"

"Nancy, its Kim"

"Oh Hi, how's it going, and where are you now?"

"I'm in Tennessee, still at your house. And you are?"

"I'm in Washington State."

"Nancy, I have a slight problem, I hope you can help me with, I need your judgment with this confusion in my head."

"Kim what did you do now? Is my brother causing you stress? Are you pregnant?" I laugh, though that's not the least bit funny.

"Funny Nancy, I hope not. Well I seem to be mixed up in some kind of an Indian thing." She giggles,

"Don't laugh it gets better. I think I met a vampire too, but I'm not sure. I know this sounds crazy." Dead silence on the phone.

"Nancy, are you still there?"

"Kim, what are you drinking?" she says light heartedly.

"Nothing I'm sober, I swear. I've been trying to piece together the strange things going on here. Well you know I can talk with the animals. But get this; I can talk mentally with one of the men here. It's really creepy too. He's not very nice to me. But I can't do anything about him right now. I avoid him as much as possible."

"Kim is it Robert or Andrew?"

"Nancy? It's Robert." How would she know their names?

"Do you know what's going on here girl?"

"Well I know you are supposed to choose one of them as your husband. They have to explain all the rest I can't. They might kill me. That's why Greg sent me away from the farm. He knew I couldn't keep anything from you. In fact, I'm surprised to hear from you. I thought he had blocked you from calling me, because he blocked your numbers from me."

"Wait, you knew that there were men that could make me melt with their touch. That I would be able to talk with one of them mentally, and you never thought to tell me? You tell me right now, what the hell is going on here! Is my life in danger? "

"Well now that you have met them, you need to stay where you are. If a vampire did approach you, you need Andrew and Robert's protection. Otherwise your life off the farm is in danger. Pressure them until they tell you what it is all about. I don't think I know the half of it."

My head is spinning. Even the one person I thought I could rely on is keeping secrets from me.

"Kim, what about the vampire you mentioned?"

"I'm not sure if it was, but the way he talked and acted. And his hands were very cold for a normal man. I know it sounds funny, but strange things are going on here that I can't reason away."

"Kim, which one of them is it that you fell for?"

"You know me well Nancy, I fell for Andrew."

"Then, I'm guessing, Robert is the one that is hurting you?"

"Yes, he is."

"Is there any way that Andrew can take you away from the farm, so that you will be safe from Robert? You didn't tell anyone that Robert is hurting you did you?"

"No, of course I didn't, if I said anything Robert would kill Andrew if they fought. He is much stronger then Andrew. And hell, I can take Greg myself."

"Ok get away from there with Andrew, as soon as possible. But Kim, remember, no going out at night."

"Yes mother, Andrew has a two month lecture tour coming up. I'll go with him and just concentrate on working with the animals on our way. Nancy, do you know… what they change into?"

"Kim, I've got to go. I'll call you on the house phone later. Give my love to Greg. Take care of yourself, Ok?"

"Yes, Nancy I will, love you too girl."

Well that didn't help me any, she was my last hope. She obviously is in on this thing as well. But she didn't think I was crazy about the vampire? Oh Hell, what am I mixed up in?

I tip toe up the stairs and luckily tonight, I make it to my room, avoiding Robert one more time. As soon as I close my door and think that I am safe, I hear a soft knock on my door. I close my eyes and pray for anyone but Robert.

"Kim, do you mind if I come in for a while?" Andrew whispers.

I swing open the door and wrap my arms around him. Hugging Andrew in my doorway, I open my eyes and see Robert standing in his doorway. I shoot him a dirty look and he glares back at me.

"You'll pay for that later bitch."

I of course cringe. Andrew quickly turns in the direction I was looking, and sees Robert glaring. Andrew looks back to me.

"Don't worry about Robert. He's just jealous of our happiness." I think to myself as I raise an eyebrow, that's putting it mildly. If only I could tell him what's really going on. I ask Andrew to stay in my room with me for the night. I make him use his own blankets, I'm not in the mood for sex, and just one touch will drive me crazy. I figure between him and William in my room, I am more than safe from Robert, at least for tonight I am.

In the morning, I wake up to Andrew looking over my body at my newest bruises. I look up at his worried face. I'm afraid to ask but I do.

"What's wrong honey?" I say innocently

"Kim, I don't think all of your bruises could have come from playing with the dogs, and the wolf would have left some teeth marks. None of these bruises appear to be anything like a bite? I'm going to figure out what you're hiding eventually. Why don't you just tell me Kim?"

"Well, we all have our secrets to bear, don't we?" I reply mocking him. If he can't spill his, I won't spill mine.

I get out of bed and take a shower. I dress in the bathroom. Afterwards, I go down stairs to the kitchen. I talk with Doris while I eat my breakfast. I ask her if she ever heard of a man named Jonathan. She appears frightened at the mention of his name. But her answer is quite contradicting.

"No Kim, I never heard of him that I can remember. What was he like?"

I describe what he said and how he had acted. She promises to check around. I don't think that she will have to check far from the way she acted. Being Doris, she must have a good reason for not telling me what she knows.

I try to clear my head of all this crap going on. I go to the back barn where I know Greg is today to work with the dogs, teaching them basic commands like sit and stay. The more they know the better their chances of getting a good home. I work with them until just about night fall.

As I start for the house, I turn on my internal extra alert system. I know there is more than one thing that goes bump in the night. I scan the whole yard to the tree lines. I'm a little scared of what might be around watching me.

Lately Nick has been hanging around the farm at night. But he must be off somewhere else. I see a figure in the tree line just beyond the clearing. It appears to be a man. The figure takes a step away from the trees toward me. I observe another shape step forward and the one closest to me retreats from my view. The other man stays where he is just looking at me. I stand still not knowing who is out there. I stare at the man with white hair for a while and take just one step in his direction.

He puts up his hand as if to stop me. Then he makes a slight bow and backs off into the trees, and out of my view. Ok, enough strange things for one night, I head to the kitchen to eat a snack before I go up to bed.

On my way to my room exhausted, I think how glad I am because Robert was supposed to leave today for a few days. I think I might have a peaceful week ahead. But as I put my key into my bedroom door, Robert presses me against my door.

"Damn it Robert!"

"Yes Kim, I didn't leave yet for my trip. Can you guess what I want?" He runs his finger down my arm sending chills throughout my entire body.

"Robert, I'm exhausted please leave me alone tonight?"

"Nope," he says as he gently kisses my neck.

"This is new Robert, gentleness."

"I can change up if I feel like it Kim."

He starts to lead me toward his room across the hall. Both of us distracted by the rush of desire, we don't even see Andrew coming down the hall. Robert kisses the back of my neck once more then he pushes me into his room.

Robert tries closing his door behind us. But Andrew puts his leg in the way stopping the door from closing. Andrew uses his body to force his way in Robert's bedroom. Robert backs us up against his high boy dresser, with me in front of his body, facing Andrew like a human shield.

"Robert what are you doing?" Andrew can clearly see the fear and shame covering my face. "How could you hurt her like this?"

Robert has his arms crossed against my front, holding me tightly against him. Andrew shouts not really asking, "How could you hurt me like this? You've been forcing her to have sex with you haven't you? Kim, you come to me now!" Andrew tells me through gritted teeth, extending his hand to me. I try to free myself, to no avail. Robert starts shouting,

"I'm not letting her go Andrew she should belong to me not you! I'm the oldest living son, she is my birthright."

"Robert let her go! It's not her fault. She can't die you know that. She's the last one alive. Without her, the next generation won't be born. You've been abusing her. You know you could have killed her!"

"Robert please let me go. You've caused enough pain already." I plead.

Sorrowfully I look to Andrew, "I'm so sorry for what has happened. I just couldn't tell you and I couldn't fight him. I never wanted you to know. I didn't want to come between the two of you. It's funny how things happen, because here I stand in the middle."

I can't look at Andrew anymore my embarrassment is crushing me, I look to the ground. My head hangs down in shame.

"I don't blame you Kim. I've seen the bruises on your body! All over your body!" he says angrily at Robert.

"Kim, I know that you can't resist either of us when we touch. We have a special hold on you. It's magic behind it, thousands of years old. It's so much stronger than any simple human could imagine or resist. You were created for us, well one of us."

I look at him puzzled. "Robert let me go." I say very soft and slowly.

"Robert, I won't run to Andrew if you release me."

He looks into my eyes, to see if I am telling him the truth or not, before releasing me.

"Ok but don't test me." I turn to face Robert.

Keeping my eyes fixed on him. I take just one small step backwards in order to position myself between the two of them.

"What do you mean a special hold? Created for one of you?" I question.

Robert states factual "There is to be only one woman born for each man... I turn to Andrew to catch him shoot a threatening look at Robert. Robert stops what he was saying for a moment, and then continues on.

"Though for each man born there is also a mate. There may be many born in a generation. We are sure that the others are dead, all killed by our enemies. They killed our mother too."

"Robert I have met your mother, remember?

"That thing was not my mother! Only reason you are living is that their king has taken an interest in you. I'm glad he did. It made it much easier to find you. We didn't even know you had been visiting Greg all these years."

"I've so enjoyed myself since we've found you."

"Not funny Robert."

I can see the anger building in Andrew. His temperature is starting to boil. The veins in his head are getting bigger by the second. I blink and see his face which seems like its changing shape. I look at him oddly. I back myself against Robert, in fear of what I think I am seeing.

"Andrew what's wrong with your face?"

"Kim you better go it's about to get real hairy in here."

"Kim get out of here, have Greg lock the door behind you. He's running up the stairs now. Once you are on the other side, don't open the door no matter what you hear in here. If you stay until we are done, and I'm hoping that you don't for now, only open the door if you hear my voice. If you hear Robert's, run as far away from here as you can. Look for Nick he'll protect you with his life." Andrew growls slowly through clenched teeth. It is not a human growl and I know it.

I look at the two of them slowly inching closer to the door. I can't just leave. I hug Andrew and whisper.

"I love you with all of my heart, I'm so sorry." I kiss his hot cheek and flee the room. I slam the door closed behind me.

Bewildered, I lean with my back against the door. One hand still holding on to the handle, the other hand touching my lips covering my mouth. The heat from Andrews's cheek is still lingering. He is burning up. The picture is becoming clear in my mind.

Greg is flying down the hall towards me. He pulls me away from it as he locks the door. I think he knows that I am in shock. We can hear Andrew and Robert fighting in the bedroom.

"Kim? Kim can you hear me?" Greg grabs both of my arms and shakes me trying to wake me from the shock. I hear him but can't quite answer. I slowly look up at him with a blank expression on my face.

"Kim you have to listen to me, get your ass out of here! Get out now! Do you understand me? You need to get a safe distance away from here."

I barely understand what Greg is screaming to me. I can only hear the hostile words drifting from behind the locked door. Andrew shouts at Robert, his voice full of rage.

"How could you hurt her like that over and over again? I've seen what you've done to her. You know that I love her and that she loves me. Why couldn't you just accept that?"

"Because she belongs to me, she should be my lover not yours!" Robert shouts back at Andrew.

"I think there's more to it than that. You also fell in love with her? Didn't you Robert?"

"No! That would be weakness. I'm not weak like you and dad. Hey Andrew, do you want to wager who's puppy she might be carrying?" Robert says teasing knowing that I can still hear them.

Disorientated, I ask the air, "Puppy what does he mean Puppy? Wait! I'm not pregnant!" I shout through the door. "And you do love me Robert!"

Robert answers with arrogance, "Are you sure?"

Greg looks at my face then my stomach. He lightly places his hand on my stomach. I stare back at him with wild eyes.

"Kim, he couldn't be right?" I push his hand away.

"No, I'm on birth control."

Suddenly we hear them crash into something, I'm sure smashing whatever it is into splinters. We can hear them struggle and strike each other. I cringe with each blow I hear. We hear furniture breaking, shattering of glass and the sound of tearing clothes. I become petrified when I hear snarling and growls coming from the bedroom. The sound fills the hall echoing everywhere. The animals all over the farm are all in an uproar, I hear their fears and alarm. They are as scared as I am. But I can't comfort them, being all torn up inside myself. I cover my ears I don't want to hear them.

"This is too much. They do change into wolves don't they?" I murmur to Greg, and then I shout as loud as I can muster. "Greg! How could you? Their werewolves! You set me up with werewolves!"

I break away from Greg and start running towards the stairs. What do they mean Puppy? I can't be pregnant. I can't handle this shit right now. I need to get away from here, from all of this.

I run as fast as I can through the hall to the steps, flying down the stairs and out to the yard. I keep running right into the woods. I don't stop until my legs give out, as I fall to the ground. Letting my emotions consume me, I curl into a ball and cry uncontrollably.

My mind races with questions. Who's going to win and how will I know? Why do I care? What did Robert mean Puppy? Could I have a wolf pup? No, it would be human first right? God I hope so I'm not nursing a puppy. I have to confirm what I think I know.

Werewolves oh shit! They can't be part wolf can they? I know that Indians have a strong connection with Wolves but? No, that's just not possible for them to be things like that. Wait I have been with Andrew during a full moon, he didn't shift into a wolf. They don't exist. Do they? Why not, I think I met a vampire. Werewolves are the least of the two evils right?

I can't believe they all lied to me. Especially Greg, Nancy and Doris how could they? I feel like a sacrificial lamb, just waiting to be slaughtered.

I guess all the sex was just about getting me pregnant. I guess neither of them really could love me. I'm just a vessel for their offspring.

16

I wipe my eyes and take a good look around. I must have cried myself to sleep. Where in the hell am I? The sun has long set and it's black as coal out here. Suddenly I get the feeling that I'm being watched. What in the hell do I have left to lose?

"Who's there? Show yourself, I feel you out there. If I'm not going to be your dinner, please show yourself." I hear nothing at all, just silence, it's much too silent. Not even a cricket is chirping.

"Which means a predator is close by. Maybe it's my imagination. I have been through a lot today. My mind can't be working right. Besides what's the worst that can happen? My life has just been shattered. How much more can I take before snapping?"

I say all of this out loud. I'm hoping that if it's a human watching me, they think that I'm crazy and leave me alone. Still, I hear nothing at all. Whatever is out there will either kill me or not, I can't be worried about it right now. It can't be Nick, he would show himself, and crickets don't stop when wolves are near.

I can't find my way back from here to the farm tonight, not that I want to go back there anyway. So I decide to make a bed and shelter to sleep in for the night. If something is going to eat me, I would much rather be asleep when it happens. I guess I should make a fire to keep warm, just in case God thinks that I can handle anymore after today's events.

"If I'm really lucky, maybe a little forest creature will walk right up to me and drop dead so that I can eat." I wait a second, but nothing happens damn! I sure won't starve by the morning.

I make a decent looking bed out of dry leaves. I build a makeshift roof out of some fallen tree branches. I know that something is still watching me, but it has not advanced. I'm not going to waste energy worrying about it. I clear a three foot area for my little fire. I use a thick tree limb to dig a shallow hole to help contain the fire. I add some rock around the edge to complete my fire pit. Why I have a lead rope in my pocket, I can't remember, but I use it along with a stick to get my fire started.

As I settle in my little nest for the night, I unconsciously start to rub my tummy. What if there is a little one in there? What will I do about it? Keep it of course, and somehow keep Robert away and maybe Andrew too.

The fire I set is going strong keeping some warmth around me. I try to close my eyes and get some sleep, I'm so exhausted. It's not too long after I settle in, I hear footsteps approaching. I stay very still and quiet. I can tell it's a human and I use that term loosely anymore.

"Kimberly, are you there?"

Only one man has ever called me Kimberly, and I don't trust him at all. It could be because he wants me dead.

"Kimberly, I won't hurt you. I just want to know how you are faring. You went through a lot this evening. Your werewolves should have told you what they expected of you. Will werewolves ever learn to be honest and open?"

I listen to the voice and I don't recognize it as Jonathan's. The voice is much more soothing, and there's a slight accent that I cannot make out. European of some sort I think, there seems to be real concern in his voice.

"Kimberly, my name is Victor. I am a friend of yours and Nick's." Yea, at the moment I am rethinking the phrase "friend."

"I plan to stay close to you until Nick gets here, as he is away at this time. We've sent word for him to come as soon as he can. He should be back by morning, at which time I'll have to be going."

This person seems to know all about me, but I don't know him. What could he want from me? I notice that he takes his time speaking, his words are not rushed.

"We do not want you to be alone out here. Jonathan is not a nice, creature for the lack of a better term. He may try to harm you if he knows that you are unprotected. I don't expect you to trust me at this point Kimberly. But I hope in the near future you will learn to trust again. Just answer me, so that I know you are ok for now."

He waits for me to answer him, but I keep silent not sure if I should. He waits a few minutes more before continuing.

"Kimberly, I heard you crying earlier, if you should need comforting. I am capable, should you need it."

Many thoughts dance through my head. Like what if he is here to kill me? Or worse, there could be worse, there is always worse. Something deep inside of me tells me that he is not dangerous, maybe I can trust him? I trusted Andrew and he lied to me. Robert, Greg, Nancy, and even Doris they all betrayed me.

Strangely I feel relaxed with him being so near. My racing heart has slowed. I don't know why though. Maybe it's because, I am not all alone out here?

"I'm fine, just leave me be Victor." I squeak.

"Yes Kimberly, I will do as you wish." I hear him sit down on the ground, just outside of my makeshift shelter.

"Victor, you've been standing right beside me this whole time?"

"Yes I have, I told you that I mean you no harm. I would never harm you, ever; I have come to keep you safe. That is all I am here to do. Please rest you will need your strength. I'm afraid that your nightmare is just beginning."

"Oh thanks Victor, I will sleep so much better now." I say with a hint of sarcasm.

"Sorry Kimberly, I wish I could tell you what is happening here, believe me, I really do. I am not one that believes in keeping secrets, well, not from the one that is involved in the secret.

I know someone who will be able to shed some light for you, her name is Lilly, and she works at the town library. She will be more than happy to tell you what you need to know. Here take my cloak, you must be cold."

He hands me his cloak keeping his face out of view. I purposely touch his hand. Good no creepy desire thing but his hand is cool in temperature. Lovely, a vampire is now protecting me.

"Good night Kimberly, do sleep well."

"Thank you, good night Victor."

When I wake in the morning I hear snoring beside me. I also have a face full of black wolf hair. I give Nick a shove, hoping it is Nick that is next to me. He gives me a backwards look over his shoulder. Yes it's him.

"Well, look who's here, my personal protector. You know you could come around a little more often."

Nick gives me another sideways look and puts his head back down and closes his eyes.

"You think I'm going to let you just go back to sleep. No way Nick, you're getting up I need breakfast, I'm starving. So you have to go hunting for me. I can't do it; I couldn't kill a fly, a wolf maybe but not a fly."

Nick takes his time slowly stretching every limb and yawning. He shakes his body a few times and steps on me as he crosses over me.

"You could loss a few pounds you know." I tell him winded.

He walks beside the fire where there is a large wicker basket. He picks it up in his mouth and carries it to me. He drops it in front of me, and then lays back down closing his eyes.

"Grumpy this morning?" he just huffs at me. "I guess so, must have been a late night for you."

I open it and inside there's biscuits and muffins and some orange juice. There are also clean clothes inside, along with soap and lotion.

I look at Nick, "Victor?"

He nods yes; I toss a muffin to Nick. He catches it easily and swallows it in one gulp.

I finish eating and wonder, "Nick, are you going to stay in wolf form, or shift into human while we walk?" He cocks his head and stares at me dumbfounded.

"Nick, I put two and two together and got werewolf."

Once he recovers himself, he drags over a back pack and puts it in front of me. I check it out and it has a tent and a sleeping bag in it, along with clothes and water. I search in it but there is nothing for Nick to wear.

"I guess wolf it is. I don't want to see you naked. I'll get changed now."

Nick goes off into the woods to give me privacy. Victor strikes again but why? I don't understand why he cares at all about me.

I sit around after changing wallowing in self-pity for a while. Later in the day, we decide to walk to where I don't really know or care for that matter. I let Nick lead the way. I have no idea where I am. I'm not ready to go back and face them just yet.

"You have any ideas for us today?"

Really, like he would answer me. I am sure that he must be a werewolf too. That's why I can't hear his thoughts. Must be why I've never been able to hear a wolf's thoughts. Oh my, that means Ginger, must have been a mix, Yuk.

Nick must be older then Robert. Since Nick protected me against Robert at my bedroom door, Robert didn't even challenge him. He must be their father, Nicholas.)

Nick and I have been in the woods for a couple of days just wandering. He chooses not to shift at all. So for the most part, I talk to myself about my problems with his sons. Just saying some of it out loud makes me feel like I'm crazy.

The notion that werewolves and vampires are real, kind of blows my mind. And now, I am supposed to give birth to one? I could be pregnant right now. How scary is that? I can't believe that I somehow got mixed up in this whole mess.

Well at least my friendly neighborhood vampire is delivering me fresh clothes and bathing supplies. The basket is filled with food to last me the entire day. I imagine Nick must know exactly where he is leading me.

One night, I wake up and Victor is still with us. They must think I am sound asleep in the tent. I love listening to Victor's voice it is so elegant and worldly. I've never heard a person speak the way he does. Since Nick seems to trust him being here, I decide to get a look at him for myself. Not thinking what form Nick would be in, if he is talking to Victor.

I open the tent slowly and cautiously peeking out. At first I can't speak, I can't find my voice. He is breath taking, not my type at all. Too perfect, with his face chiseled like it is. But those ice blue eyes, I do like the eyes. His hair is long, straight and white. His clothes are noticeably tailored to fit him perfectly.

His appearance is so impressive that he could be on the cover of GQ. To make things worse, Nick is lying on his belly naked in human form next to Victor. I really didn't expect Nick to be in human form. But since he is, I now know for sure that he is Andrew and Robert's father.

Victor must be who I saw in the trees at Greg's. He frightened off the other figure. He must have been the one at the hospital checking on me, I remember the eyes I saw. Victor looks my way smiling softly. He catches me with my mouth gaped wide open, just staring at them.

"Nicholas, I do believe that Kimberly is awake." He says quite calmly. Nick quickly runs into the woods and comes back in wolf form.

"Thanks Nick, I like you better as a wolf anyway." Nick lays down huffing.

"Kimberly it's nice to see you awake. Though, you are just as beautiful to behold when you are sleeping." Okay, he's been checking in on me when I'm asleep, creepy? I sit down on a large rock facing them.

"It's nice to finally meet you face to face as well Victor. Thank you for the clothes, tent and the food. I presume that you have been bringing them for me?"

"Yes, Nicholas gets your clothes from your room at Greg's house, and I have them washed before I bring them here for you. Have you enjoyed the food I've sent?"

"Yes very much, but some of the clothes I don't recognize as mine."

"I thought you might like the things I added. Some of your clothes are so old and worn. You deserve better."

Snob, "Sorry I don't have a tailor." I make a motion with my hand at his perfect suit.

"Please explain to me why you are so nice to me. You don't owe me anything." I say a bit too sharply.

"Kimberly, I would," and he pauses as he looks at Nick.

"I am glad to assist you in your time of need. Nicholas is my dear friend. I know he cares deeply for you, therefore, I care for you as well."

"That's so sweet Victor, I do appreciate all that you have done for me. Most people couldn't be bothered this much, to help a stranger out."

"Kimberly, you are not a stranger to me. I am not like any human you have ever met before." I try to digest that. I think he just may have alternative motives.

"Nick, you could have told me that you were a werewolf all along. I've dressed in front of you."

He covers his face with his paws and peaks through at me. I laugh at his antics. Then I remember Andrew and Robert. "It was you that I dressed in front of?"

"Yes, the boys have not shifted at the farm. Nick forbids them from doing so in your presence. Until you knew what they really were, he didn't want them to show you in that manner. We all thought you would run away if they did, alas that is exactly what happened."

"Thanks Victor, and thinking back Nick you always turned your face from me when I dressed. Thank you for being a gentleman. Nick you haven't told Andrew or Robert where I am did you?"

"No, he has not. We thought that you should have some time to think things through without them interfering. Nick has told them to heal and let you do the same."

"Victor, you would be a vampire?"

"Yes, you are correct." He grins.

"I thought so. Do all werewolves and vampires get along with each other?"

"No, not at all, Nick and I have an understanding with each other."

"I've been thinking about what you said to me the first night I was out here. I think that I will do as you suggested, and visit Lilly at the library tomorrow. Will she be honest with me?"

“She shall be honest with you. She is the sister of Nicholas here.” He pats Nicks head. “Tomorrow should prove to be enlightening.”

“Good night gentleman, I’ll turn in now. I hope to see you again and thank you once more for being so nice to me Victor.”

“Sleep well Kimberly, we will meet again I assure you.” I go back in to the tent and I’m pretty sure that I’ve seen Victor somewhere else before. I just can’t remember where.

The next day while Nick and I are walking, we start to feel watched. I notice that Nick is looking a lot to the left into the thick of the woods.

I whisper to him “What do you see or hear?”

Before he even looks up at me, I become aware that something is watching us. We exchange worried looks as we keep walking, trying not to let on that we know they are there. Nick walks with his side against my leg. I think he is trying to comfort me. Yet we both keep gazing sideways in the direction of the muffled sounds. I could tell by the steps its animals not humans. I thought the steps were much too soft for something as large as a human.

I abruptly stop walking. Nick puts himself in front of me in a defensive stance. I close my eyes and concentrate very hard on the point of the source. Nick stands guard with his teeth bared. He circles me defensively from the unseen force. With my eyes closed, I stand very still, trying to hear what is nearby. I can’t pick up a thing, must be wolves.

After a short while, I open my eyes and shout into the woods.

"You can come out and walk with us if you like. We won't hurt you, will we Nick?" Nick looks at me as if to say, speak for yourself woman.

"Nick you behave yourself. You know as well as I do that they are wolves. It's not the boys is it?" He shakes his head no.

Well then, I holler into the forest again. "We would rather you be out here where we can see you. It's just creepy like this." I pause to give them time to come out.

"I know that you don't plan to eat us. I don't know if Nick knows you or not, but we will never know if you keep hiding. So please, show yourselves. Surely you must have something to say to us?"

Suddenly Nick takes off into the woods growling and yipping at whatever is in there. I stand frozen, afraid that Nick will get hurt. I yell for him to come back over and over. All I can hear is a lot of growling and yipping. By the sounds, I don't think they are going to fight but, I'm not completely sure of anything right now.

Minutes pass. I'm starting to get scared. Suddenly Nick is running toward me at full speed. It appears to me that he is being chased by a pack of wolves.

My mouth drops in dismay. I'm not sure what to do. My heart is pounding in my chest. I know if I run they will catch me in no time at all. But Wolves don't eat people, because they are people. I tell myself for reassurance.

The pack approaches me with Nick in the lead. Nick stops in front of me in a protective stance. Then everything is silent. I stand there frozen; In front of me are about nine wolves. Some stand in place, while others are pacing back and forth, mouths gapping, some just lie down.

The alphas approach and sit down in front of me. The male and female alpha wolves look directly into my eyes. As they change into human form, I really wasn't expecting that, they proceed to tell me that they have to have a word with me. To have a seat, Ok, I wasn't expecting that either. I take a seat on the ground in front of them in the dirt.

They both have long jet black flowing hair, which reaches the middle of their backs. Their skin is rust in color. Their faces are weathered, not youthful by any means.

I still can't seem to get it in my head that wolves can transform into humans. It goes against nature. I become overwhelmed by everything swimming in my head. The alphas begin to tell me about their long lives. They still don't tell me my exact role in this whole thing, just that I'm a means to the continuation of their heritage. They guess they have lived in these mountains over two hundred years as wolves.

I discover that they are distant relatives of Nick. They explain that they have chosen to live as wolves. They do not walk with humans any longer. They only wanted to meet the next woman in line to carry on their heritage. Since none of this pack is of the chosen blood line, they are unable to have pups of their own.

The male alpha informs me that he is one of three elders that maintain their laws. They are the only ones who can pass judgment on any of their kind that betray their laws. I think about this. Is he warning me?

They then turn to Nick and ask why he is allowing a vampire near me. I raise my brow pretending not to know.

"What do you mean vampire?"

The female explains, “We know the scent is that of Victor, the king of the vampires. This is not a good thing. Victor is our enemy he has killed all of the other females in many generations. We fear he is now after you, and we can’t understand why Nick has allowed him near.

I turn to Nick, “Change and explain what is going on.” Nick walks deeper into the woods and returns covered with leaves. Thank goodness.

“For your information he won’t harm her. He has known about her since she was a teen. How do you think I found her? It was through following him.”

“Nick, what do you mean he has known about me that long?”

Now I know where I’ve seen him. He used to come to the deli I worked in when I was in high school. And come to think of it, I remember seeing him in the bar I used to go to. He never made me feel uncomfortable though, in fact, he was always a gentleman to me.

“If he knew who I was, why didn’t he just kill me then? Why did he go through all of this trouble? He has been so nice to me, Nick?”

“I believe that he is obsessed with you, and has been for a very long time. I know he will not hurt you like he did the others. He had many opportunities over the years. The most that he ever did to you was, frighten away a boyfriend or two of yours, when he thought they treated you wrongly.”

“Are you kidding me Nick? Is that why I couldn’t keep a boyfriend in high school? Oh isn’t that just great.”

“Woman, I still don’t want Victor anywhere you are. You need to get out of the woods, and go back to Greg’s farm. We can keep you safer there." The alpha Male commands me.

"I need to go to town first. Then I'll call Greg to come and get me. I must meet with someone there, before I can face Robert and Andrew again. Unless you care to explain completely, what it is I am expected to do?"

"Simply put, you are to bare as many sons as possible. You may give birth to daughters but they will not be able to bare children of their own. Only the males that come directly from your blood line can reproduce.

The girls will however shift the same as the boys, when they are of age. Your blood comes from the very first medicine women of long ago. One of them was wed to one of my kind. No one knew that the two joining as one would cause a new race. That is when the first werewolves were born and the legend began.

No one can remember just how long ago that was exactly. We do know it was some time after the great flood. It was a terrifying thing to my people. The first boy shifted into a wolf at the age of thirteen.

The people thought that it was the work of an evil spirit. Later, they learned that he was a protector of their kind. They learned to use this new creature against their enemies. The wolf did not exist before that time.

The alpha male then shares with me the names of some of the wolves in his pack. He is called White Feather and his mate is Clover. White Feather explains that the reddish one is Sendoa and the white one is Loki. I nod to each of them as they are introduced to me. He chooses not to tell me the names of the others. For what reason, I don't know.

It is getting kind of uncomfortable talking with naked people. I feel overdressed. However, our unusual group begins walking together. White Feather informs me of places where dogs are kept in cages and barns, most of them are in the neighboring woods. I know what type of places these are. I ask him to show Nick exactly where they are, that is after I have returned to the farm. They agree to help me with whatever I need to get things right. Though, they really don't get along with dogs.

The more White Feather talks, the more I realize that he is speaking in old English. I had been trying to figure it out the whole time. They must have been out here in the woods a very long time. Nick is keeping the lead of where we are headed. I know that he is leading me to Lilly, at the Gatlinburg town library. She works there as a librarian.

We part with the wolves when we reach their territory line. They wish me well on my journey and tell me to hurry back to the farm. They don't like me being out here in the woods unprotected. They will have the wolf pack in the next territory patrol our campsite tonight.

They won't let the vampire anywhere near me. I'm not too happy about this. I won't have a breakfast or clean clothes in the morning. I won't be able to get answers from him that are burning a hole in my head. Nick and I walk a distance further. It's getting later then we thought, so we set up camp for the night.

"Nick I'm glad that I have you with me, let's get some sleep I'm bushed. Nick can tell by the way I'm talking, I'm not too happy about the wolves keeping Victor away from me. He nuzzles me trying to cheer me up. It works of course, and then he settles next to me. I can hear his stomach rumbling.

"I have some food left in the basket for me. But you go and hunt I'll be fine with all of my new protectors watching over me. You won't have to wait for Victor to show tonight, because he won't be coming. Oh and Nick, don't forget to get breakfast in the morning, since my concierge won't be able to."

He just huffs at me. I know he thinks I'm being petty. I think with my newly gained knowledge, Victor is not the one I need to fear, he has been the only honest one with me up to now.

When I wake up in the morning, Nick has gone already. I stoke the fire, not knowing what he might bring back for breakfast. A little while later Nick comes trotting back with a McDonald's bag in his mouth. I start laughing.

"Ok Nick, how in hell did you score a McDonald's bag?" He drops it in front of me.

"Nick you didn't flash anyone did you?" He shakes his head no, thankfully. When I open it there are pancakes and eggs, still kind of warm.

"Good job Nick, which must mean that we are close to town."

As I eat my breakfast, I think over all of what has happened. What do I have to look forward to in my very near future? I hopefully will find out what the hell is really going on. Maybe Robert will leave me alone. Yea right, I'm just wishfully thinking.

I clean up the campsite, putting the fire out. Nick then leads us to the town. When we near the edge of the woods, we stop. I know Nick can't come with me into town. People around here aren't stupid. To fall for me saying it's a black husky mix. Nick is way too large to pass that off.

I tell Nick that I'll see him later at the Farm. And I promise to call Greg after I talk with Lilly. Nick gives me a lick on the cheek and runs off into the woods.

17

I make sure that no one is looking when I walk out of the woods. When I find the street sign it reads, Airport Road, right where I need to be. I pay attention to how the numbers are running. The numbers are going up so, I'm headed in the right direction.

I just need to make a left on to Cherokee Orchard Road, and then I'll go straight to the library. I keep an eye out because I'm not sure who may be looking for me. Since I am reasonably sure that the whole werewolf community knows about my existence, outsiders may know too. I don't know where Robert and Andrew are either.

I'm sure they both survived their fight. If one of them were dead, Nick wouldn't have helped me. He would have no reason to. You know I can't help but wonder though, how do you kill a werewolf? Is it anything like in the movies?

As I walk up the street to the library, the town's people all greet me as I pass by. This reminds me of why I love this place so much, the people that live here are all so nice. Manners and courtesy's still do exist.

The library is like it would be in any other small town. It's a medium size brick building with white trim. I open the squeaky old white wooden door and go right to the desk, where there is an older American Indian woman with black gray hair pulled back in to a pony tail.

"May I help you miss?" she smiles.

"Yes, could you tell me where the books on Indian legends are kept, specifically, wolf legends?"

The old woman looks me up and down, smiling broadly, and asks.

"Are you Kim?" I take a step back, fear crossing my face. I look around nervously. Maybe the boys are waiting here.

"Oh honey, I won't hurt you Andrew told me that you were coming. Are you looking for information on what is happening?"

She waits for my answer but, I just look at her, not too sure of what I should do.

"My name is Lilly. Just give me a minute or two. I have to get someone to cover the desk. Then we'll go get some lunch. You won't find the information you need in any book, I promise you."

She gives me a look of, you should already know this. I wait for her next to the door. I don't know yet if she is friend or foe. She could be getting Robert. I almost jumped when she snuck up behind me, she laughs at my reaction.

"Ok, let's go, there is a diner right up the street."

"I hope you plan on treating, I haven't got any money on me at the moment."

"Yes dear, it's on me today."

We go up the street, not saying a word to each other. Lilly keeps looking at me funny and smiling. I start to think she might be crazy as a loon. When we get to the diner we are seated right away. We both look around checking for prying ears. Lilly starts to talk first by taking my hand in hers.

"Honey, I know things are hard to understand right now but, if you give me a chance to explain, you'll be ok. Greg said that you are one of the strongest women he has ever known. And when Andrew met and shook your hand, he knew you were the one born for him, well one of them. Robert, he is the oldest so it really should have been him. But as long as the blood line continues that is what matters. There are usually many boys and girls born each generation. We have had some trouble keeping," She takes a long pause as if she is deciding, weather she wants to tell me what is on her mind or not.

"Well, that doesn't really matter. The women like you are all descendants of medicine women from any Indian tribe. That is why the boys have to go out and lecture so they can find, well you." She chuckles, "The men are pure Indian. All of them are born here in the Smoky Mountains.

With each generation it gets harder and harder to find the women, with what the white man has done to our people over the years. If it weren't for Victor, we would still be looking for you. Thankfully, he took a liking to you, otherwise, you would be dead too."

"Lilly are you enlightening me or trying to scare the hell out of me? I'm not afraid of Victor. Though I've been told I should be. Now Jonathan he does scare me."

"You've met Jonathan and are still living?"

"Yes, I think it's because of Victor being the king. But Andrew was with me, he was not alarmed by Jonathan. Also Jonathan said that he is not allowed to kill me?"

"Andrew didn't know what Jonathan looked like. We know of Jonathan but, any wolf that had met him is dead. No one has ever been able to identify him before. Did Victor give you any blood?"

"No nothing like that, just his verbal protection. By way of his command, Victor strictly prohibits my death."

"Oh alright, let me get back on track then, I will tell you about their upbringing first. Nicholas and Lea had only three sons. They raised all of their sons with plenty of love and care. They taught each of the boys the ways of our people and to be one with the earth. They showed them how to treat all living creatures with honor and respect. As they aged and the years went on, Nicholas knew that finding one of you was becoming more and more difficult.

We've known that the vampires were the ones responsible for killing the girls. They have hunted down at least fifty girls that I know of, since I have been around. And many more before my birth, I am sure."

"Lilly, how long have you been around?"

"So far, only three hundred years, as I was saying, Then Lea died earlier than anyone expected. Her death was really mysterious. I think she was poisoned. Nicholas kept a very protective eye on her. He didn't allow anyone to visit her in the end. The casket was closed at the funeral. Nicholas said that she wanted everyone to remember her as young and beautiful. Not to see her that way. It was very peculiar for it to happen that way. We usually burn the bodies in a ritual."

Lilly doesn't know that Lea is still alive? Wait that's why Robert hates her, she is a Vampire, she must be.

"Lilly, you know that Lea is still around, don't you?"

Sternly she looks at me, "Lea, my sister in law, is dead."

"Alrighty then," Wait Lilly is three hundred years old, wow.

"Now, in your culture, we are known as werewolves. But we did not come to be for evil reasons. Our nature is to be kind and caring creatures. The first ones came to be for protection of their Indian brothers. They killed only to protect, never for vengeance."

"Wait, I've only a trace amount of Indian blood in my veins"

"It only takes a little Indian blood for the legend to continue." Lilly says with a smile. She goes into a daze of sorts as she continues to explain, I don't think I could have stopped her if I tried.

"The legend as it goes. There is to be one man for one woman born. For every son born a girl is born somewhere, to be his mate. They will know each other by their gift of being able to talk without words. Also when they touch, their bodies will come alive with a desire that will consume them. They will not be able to resist each other, when they connect."

"Well, you've certainly got that part right. Consumed is a good word to describe the feeling."

"Yes Kim, that seems to have caused a big problem. Andrew figured out that Robert was using it against you."

"Yea, over and over he used it against me. I feel so guilty for hurting Andrew like that. Why can't I hear Andrew's thoughts?"

"Robert is the oldest living brother. That's how it works. You know he loves you also? That's part of the problem."

"What do you mean he loves me? How could he with the way he treats me. Do you want to see the bruises? I'm sure some are still here from the last time?" I argue.

"No my dear, I know he never was the gentlest man. Kim, did you check to see if you are pregnant yet?"

"No, I didn't even think I could be pregnant, I'm on birth control."

"Well, the little suckers can be quite potent. I don't think the pill would stop them."

"Ok, I'll get a test before I go back to the farm."

"Here, I have one in my purse."

"Excuse me?"

"Well, it's not like I didn't know you were going to come looking for me. I came prepared for our little meeting."

I frown, putting my open hand out to Lilly. She places the test in my hand and I head to the bathroom. I close the stall door. I take a deep breath before opening the wrapper. Not sure what I wish for more, positive or negative. I take the test and wait for three minutes in the bathroom. I read it and wrap it in a paper towel. I carry it back to the table where Lilly waits. She looks like she could burst if I don't tell her. I sit down and hand it to her so she can read the results. The look of sadness fills her face as she opens the paper towel.

"Sorry Lilly, I'm not pregnant yet."

"Are you sure, Robert swore you were with child."

"Really, he never said a word about it to me. Robert is such a monster."

"Kim! They're not monsters you know that better than anyone else!" I look around to see if anyone is staring at us, and of course, everyone in here is. I smile awkwardly at the noisy faces.

"Lilly, lower your voice. I didn't mean it like that. I don't care that they are werewolves. That's not a problem for someone like me. I meant that he should have been less abrasive with me, especially since he thought I was carrying a baby." She relaxes and sits back against the booth.

"Oh sorry dear, so you don't have any problem with them being werewolves, really?" She appears honestly surprised by my statement.

"No Lilly, that's not my problem. But when I do give birth, what will come out?"

"Oh the wolf part doesn't happen until they hit puberty."

"Oh great, not only will I have to deal with a hormonal teenage boy, but he can eat me if I piss him off." Lilly starts laughing.

"You will be a wolf as well my dear. It's not an easy time for anyone involved. That's why grandparents stay around to help guide their grandsons through the hard times. You should know more than anyone, you can't talk to your parents about everything."

"Yea, that I know only too well, at least I won't have to tell them about this since they have passed. So will everything be normal about the pregnancy and the birth?"

"Yes Kim, it should all go just like normal. You might be a little more hormonal than the average woman. If you have any concerns, just go to the clinic here in town and ask for Doctor Ricks. He can help you with any questions."

"Ok, when do I change?"

"It will happen after you give birth to your first child. One of us will watch over the baby until after you have shifted for the first time.

"Now that I know what will happen to me. Can I stay with Andrew or, must I go with Robert?"

"You must follow your heart, they both love you. And you now know what the legend says about what is to be. But this won't be easy on any of you three. Things would go smoother if we could find just one more woman."

"Lilly, there are other werewolf men why can't they make puppies?"

"To put it simply, their time has passed and when you and Andrew touched, it started the clock on your fertility. We have estimated that it lasts about twenty years. After that you will not be able to have any more children."

"Have they searched everywhere for other possible women?"

"Yes, they have. If you were to have a half-sister she might be a special one, there's no guarantee."

"I wouldn't know if I have one or not, being as I have never met my birth mother."

As Lilly and I sit there eating our lunch, we hear what sounds like dogs fighting. I shout out to the dismay of the people in the restaurant.

"No! Robert! No!" We both dash out of the diner, and come to an abrupt stop at the site of two wolves fighting in the street.

They are ripping at each other's fur, tearing out pieces of flesh. Their blood is dripping to the ground. I swallow hard wanting to keep my lunch in my stomach. A crowd is starting to form and the men are taking bets on which one will win.

"Damn humans," I hiss to Lilly.

"Kim, stop them before it gets worse or one of them is shot."

"Stop it the both of you! Stop fighting look at yourselves! Acting like spoiled children, you were raised better than that." I am shouting and screaming at Robert and Andrew to stop fighting. The crowd starts cheering them on.

A police officer pulls up and draws his gun as he aims at the wolves. I step in front of him and scream to him, "Wait officer! I can control them just give me a few minutes. I'll get them to leave peacefully with no one getting hurt. Please, give me a minute." I plead to the officer.

He looks at me first in anger. I can tell he doesn't want to lower his gun. Then, slowly, his expression changes to a smile, thankfully, he remembers me.

"Are you from Greg's farm?"

"Yes, I'm Kim, just give us some space and I can handle this."

"Ok people, back up she needs some room, but watch this. I've seen her in action before. She's the one that got my dog to stop attacking my wife. I'm still not sure if that's a good thing though." The officer slips out, and then he shouts to the crowd to move back. As the officer is talking, I plead with Robert and Andrew to stop fighting. I beg them to stop and walk into the woods.

We can work it out somehow. We all can live in peace together.

"Please, Robert I know you hear me, look at all the people staring at you two. You're supposed to be leading examples for your people. Right now all they see are two brothers fighting over some stupid girl. Both of you need to grow up before the others realize what's going on."

"Andrew, you have to stop this. Be the bigger brother and end this, it's just not good for anybody. This fighting over me is senseless." They aren't listening to me at all I give up and fall to my knees and start to cry.

When they hear me, they both stop fighting at once. They walk up to me from different sides and nuzzle me. Both of them try to comfort me and stop me from crying, this must be a sight, everyone has instantly stopped shouting.

I thank them for stopping the fight through my tears. Damn these emotions, I'm not good dealing with this kind of stuff. As I hug the wolves in the middle of the street, we hear gasps of shock come from all sides in the crowd.

"They all think I'm crazy, you two happy now? Look at me a grown woman, hugging to wild, bloody wolves in the middle of the street."

"Well you don't see that every day." We hear from somewhere in the crowd. I start to laugh to myself as I get up from the ground.

"Thank you officer, that is for not shooting my friends. They lose their temper with each other sometimes. I'll make sure that they stay far away from the town in the future. If you want, I can have a talk with your dog. So he'll nip your wife once in a while. I owe you one I suppose."

"No, Miss you've done enough. But I hope you're free for the next year or so though."

"Why, what do you mean by that?" I question,

"Well, everyone in town will know what you just did by night fall. They will be calling you for every animal related problem they have. You're going to be a very busy person."

"I'll have to deal with that later. Now I have to get these two back where they belong so if you'll excuse me officer."

"It's Barren ma'am,"

"Thanks again, Officer Barren, I really do appreciate this."

I turn to the wolves, scowling at them. I am so mad at them right now, I could scream! I point towards the trees.

"Ok you two this way!"

18

The two of them follow me to the woods. I turn to look for Lilly but she's gone. I guess I'll just have to thank her later. I look at my werewolves trotting happily beside me. I still can't believe all of this is real.

"The two of you, as soon as we are out of sight, transform. I have no idea who is who. Then we can talk once both of you are in human form. It just feels very strange talking to both of you in wolf form."

We walk for a short distance in silence back to my last campsite. Robert is keeping me blocked the whole time. Making me wonder what he is hiding. Once we approach the campsite, I scan the area. I place my hands on my hips, glaring at them.

"Ok, go change or however it happens, I'll wait right here." As they disappear into the trees I sit down on a fallen tree branch. Robert decides to share his thoughts finally.

"Kim you know we'll be naked don't you? It's not like we can grow clothes."

"Oh shit! I hadn't thought of that! That can make this harder than I thought to discuss."
"Hey guys, grab a leaf or something to cover with please?" I can hear them both snickering just out of my site, and Robert thinking.

"Yes, things could get harder?"

"Hurry it up, the two of you sound like little kids." I yell to them ignoring Robert.

Speaking mostly to myself, "I guess this is as good a place as any. To discuss what we're going to do, with what your people expect from us. Also, how the three of us can get along and live together in peace."

When I finish my sentence, they both come walking out of the trees towards me, wearing nothing but grins. I know I turn a deep shade of crimson. I close my eyes and shake my head slowly. Choking on my words, "Please cover up or sit down or something."

They sit in front of me one on the right and one on the left. They don't even attempt to cover themselves.

"You two are not playing fair." I try to keep my eyes on their faces and find that I am failing badly.

"You were warned, we don't grow clothes just fur."

"I give up, here." I take off my jacket and flannel shirt and throw the clothes at them.

"Cover up please." I look at both of them trying desperately to stay on topic.

"You know Kim, I could use your t-shirt and you can have this jacket back. I wouldn't want you to get cold," Andrew says grinning.

"No, I'll be just fine, please cover yourself." I wait until they cover their manliness. I'm amazed that they have no bruising or wounds from their fighting.

"All right, I suppose I know enough about the legend, no thanks to either of you." I scowl, "but there being two of you and one of me, we have a special problem. Since both of you are in love with me, that certainly doesn't help the situation any. Andrew looks at Robert questioningly,

"Robert, you do love her?"

"Yes brother, couldn't you tell? Just by the way I talked about her. Or, the way I acted around her. Why do you think I stayed around the farm? I could have gone out on more lectures. It wasn't because I liked the hard work at the farm. You weren't the only one that fell for her, you know."

Robert pauses and twists his hands in his lap. I know he is struggling with his emotions. He believes saying "I love you" is a sign of weakness. I study the stress on his face. I see in his mind just how much he does love me. It humbles me having that inside knowledge. Especially since my heart belongs mostly to Andrew. However, I've come to realize that I do have feelings for Robert too. My time in the woods has opened my eyes.

"You know Andrew, all the stories that dad would tell us, I mean mom was a beautiful woman before she changed. I thought that dad just got lucky, with his soul mate. You've seen the pictures of some of the woman from the past. They weren't easy on the eyes. Then when we met Kim, I fell instantly, just like you did. She's stronger than I thought she would be. Especially because she is half Irish, I thought she would be more timid. I'm glad she doesn't scare easily either. Which is a good thing for us, any sane woman would have been long gone months ago." We all laugh an awkward laugh.

"Yea, I know what you mean Robert, but we both can't have her. And I mean we can't share her physically. That's just not right, is it?"

I missed some of what Andrew said. My mind is drifting I'm distracted by their nakedness. Add in the warm fuzzy feelings, that Robert caused by his admitting his love. He really isn't all that bad, I guess. I glance toward him then to Andrew. Their muscular chests, that long black hair, I would love to…get on tract Kim, stop wandering I tell myself.

Robert hears what I am thinking and lets out a laugh startling me from my thoughts.

"Kim, I could quench your hunger if you want me to?" Smiling deviously, not waiting for my reply. He starts talking to Andrew like I'm not even there.

"Well brother, I think we could work something out, we could take turns you know. On who would go out to lecture? You know while the other one stays here at the farm? That way we won't wear her out and have to draw straws for turns."

"Well there's nothing in the legend that says we can't share her." Andrew ads,

"I don't remember hearing about any rules, you know about what to do if there is only one woman left."

"So, how do we decide what is right?"

The two of them debate back and forth in as serious a manner as they can muster. Both are trying hard to maintain seriousness in their discussion. But their voices are giving them away. They're voices keep cracking as they speak.

"Hey, wait don't I have a vote?" I chime in, and they continue talking, ignoring me completely.

Robert chimes in, "Well it's not like she doesn't enjoy being with either one of us."

"Yea, but I don't like to share her knowingly. It just doesn't feel right, and one of us should marry her before the baby gets here." Andrew Says

"Hey Andrew, you can marry her, that way I'm still free to have fun while I travel around."

I'm starting to get mad now. The joke is over as far as I'm concerned. "First of all, there is no baby on the way.

I took a test and it's negative. Hey, what do you mean! Andrew gets me by default? Is that it then? The both of you can go to hell! I don't need either of you, and you know it! When or if I get pregnant, I have your father to help me to guide the boy when he reaches puberty. And if the boy eats me, it will be entirely your fault."

I get up to leave, feeling that I'm going to cry. Damn female hormones! Where in the hell did I get these things? It's not like me to get mushy feelings.

"I think we are done here, good bye Robert, good bye Andrew." I snap.

I stomp away leaving them sitting there. Andrew shouts out to me, "Kim, wait we're just playing with you. Kim, you know how much I love you. I couldn't live without you in my life every day. See the only problem, is that there's only one of you and we can't be with regular women physically. We could hurt them. Remember the bruises?" I put my head down I know he hurt me just about as much as Robert.

"If you think about it, not all of them were from Robert. Some were from me. We can't be gentle unless we really concentrate. And add in the unnatural desire thing with us and it's even worse." I stop in my tracks, arms folded, and facing away from them.

"Believe me, I know, all control is lost in the desire as it takes us over."

"Kim, that's what we were fighting about, what Robert wants to do. Well, you know what he wants. I don't think that it's fair to you, for us to share you."

I look over my shoulder at him and he turns his head away. I know this conversation is getting to him. I look to Robert to say something, but he keeps his mouth shut and mind letting Andrew continue.

"Kim, Greg was sure that you were the one, and that you could handle the roughness, which comes with making love to someone like us. Truly, we don't want to harm you but, as you know it is unavoidable."

With melancholy in his words Andrew tries to continue explaining. "Kim, when we touched that first night, I knew right then and there. Greg was right about you being the one. I didn't want to rush anything. But I wasn't going to not try to have you for myself. If I had just backed down, none of this mess would have happened and you would be happy with Robert.

You are part Indian and that part of you is what makes you the one chosen. You are the one who must carry on the werewolf blood line. Your blood comes from the ancient medicine women. Their blood lines are the only ones capable of carrying and caring for our offspring."

Andrew comes over to where I am standing. He places his hand over top my sleeve on my arm. Robert continues on, where Andrew stops in a fatherly manner.

"There were times through our history that the men could not stay with the mothers, or were killed. But the mothers being strong and becoming werewolves themselves, they could endure anything that the young child tried. You have been chosen, and there is no going back now, but you must choose which of us you want."

"Do the two of you realize that having to choose between you would be any girl's fantasy? I can choose one of you, but that's no guarantee that the other one won't touch me. Then, I can't help what happens next. Both of you are well aware of this problem. I can't say that I don't love the both of you.

Though I really should, I don't hate you Robert. In your own way you are good. I can't blame you for most of what you have done. The feeling is just…” I close my eyes, this is getting to me. “So intense… even though I now know a lot more about the legend. Still I must follow my heart I’m still just a human woman.

Hey what about other werewolves like Jasmine? Have either of you tried to be with regular women or other Indian women?” They give each other a troubled look before Robert answers me solemnly.

“Well, the lectures that we go on are not only to teach the knowledge of the Indian way of life to the young. We were also looking for, well you, in so many words. The people that we meet while touring know what we are. The young women would willingly go with us in an attempt to try; however it never went very well.

The feeling that we knew should be there, wasn’t. Like Andrew said, we are too rough for normal women. They would leave with bruises and the word spread quickly through our people. So, it didn’t take long for the girls to stay away from us. Other werewolf women like Jasmine can have sex with us. Though, she cannot bear children for us, only you can.”

“Well, I honestly don’t know what to do. The one I don’t choose will have a life of misery. Not just the sex part, but, not having someone for all of the other things that a partner is for.” I say with deep sorrow in my heart.

“I think we should go back to the farm and think about this a little more, and get some clothes on you two, before I do something that would be against my morals.”

I’m thinking so much about the desire and how it affects me. How can it be controlled? And then there’s their bodies just as naked as can be, oh I'm so hungry. I shouldn't have turned around.

Robert clears his throat gaining my attention in the process.

"Andrew, I'll go on ahead of you two. I think you better take care of something before I lose myself control." Robert says looking directly at me as he drops the shirt, the very one that was covering him. Exposing that, I'm not the only one turned on by my thoughts.

"No, that will never happen trust me. Stay out of my mind Robert!" I know I'm blushing. I am trying not to look at either of them. Robert smiles deviously.

"Never say never Kim."

"Never!"

"We'll see you later at Greg's house ok?" Robert nods and takes off running. Shifting as he disappears into the deep woods. That was cool to watch.

Andrew takes my hand in his. The shirt that was covering him falls to the ground. Smiling, he grabs me around my waist holding me tight to his naked body. We enter the tent and wait. We want Robert to be far enough away not to hear us.

Caressing my face with his right hand, he puts his finger to my mouth to hush me. Slowly he slips my t-shirt off over my head, softly he whispers,

"I'm going to try to be as gentle as possible for as long as I can, just be patient with me…"

Through the woods back to Greg's farm, Andrew and I walk silently beside each other. He is covered with my flannel shirt, fashioned like a loin cloth, he resembles Tarzan. Finally, after a very long silence, Andrew is the one that breaks it.

"Kim, you know we still have an issue to resolve. What we are going to do about Robert?"

"Andrew, I can keep my hands to myself unless he touches me…I can't control the rush. You know exactly what I'm saying. You can't control it either when we touch."

I stop walking and fidget with my hands, uncomfortable. I slowly turn toward him. I still have many questions that are unanswered. But I don't think that he is ready for them yet.

"Andrew, really how do you feel about all of this? You haven't said what you think about this truly."

"I never thought that it would come to this but, as long as I don't know, I won't ask."

"What are you saying Andrew?"

He talks very somberly."I'm saying that if you can deal with keeping Robert happy too. I won't judge, I just don't want to see it or know about it, ever. He can hear your every thought. I can't, so I won't know just like before, you should be with him anyway. According to the legend, that is. Greg had no right to push me at you."

"He did this on purpose. How could he know that I would fall for you?"

"He didn't, he was hoping that you would have feelings for me, long before Robert ever had a chance, and that's what happened just like he planned."

"What does he have against Robert that is so great he would interfere like this? It's not his place to interfere. It's not his legacy it's ours."

"Kim, you'll have to ask him yourself, we're almost to the farm. He'll be watching for you. He's been watching the woods every day. He's worried about you."

"He knows that I can take care of myself. Nick was with me the whole time. He even brought me camping stuff. Your father is a good soul."

"Kim, just when did you figure it out?"

"I thought maybe when Robert didn't challenge him in the hall. But I didn't know then that you were a werewolf."

"Lilly also told me that he was your father. She explained that he was staying around to help in the raising of our child. You told me to go to him when I ran from the house remember?"

"No, I didn't tell you that, Robert did."

"Andrew, how did they explain about your mom's death? I don't mean to be morbid but, I was wondering about that."

"No it's ok; she died when I was away, Nick said that she was poisoned. He wouldn't let me open the casket to see her, it was nailed shut. She obviously was not in the coffin. A long time later she came back to us, but I knew she wasn't the same person. I accepted her as what she had become. Robert has never gotten over her being a vampire.

"Sorry to bring it up. I didn't mean to hurt you. Just one more question, what kills a werewolf?"

"Silver and beheading are the only ways to kill us."

"Well that's good to know for the future."

I think about this as we walk on towards the farm. I need to remember this just in case. I guess that's why Greg put his mom's silver set in a locked cabinet. Come to think about it, all the utensils are stainless steel. I guess I never noticed that before.

"Kim, I see the farm through the trees coming into sight. Are you ready to face Greg?"

"More like is he ready to face me. I should kick his ass for this whole mess."

"I think I agree he is in need of an ass kicking, but maybe not right now."

I look at Andrew with a why not look, and he simply shrugs his shoulders. I guess he couldn't come up with a good reason. As we clear the trees, Greg runs up to us, grabs and hugs me. Like a mother would a lost child.

"Greg, can you let go now, I'm fine really."

"I was so very worried about you. You could have called and let me know you were breathing or something."

"I was in the middle of a forest remember, what was I supposed to use smoke signals?"

"No, I guess not, just don't do that again. You had all of us worried sick. You're not a werewolf you know you could have been killed." Greg says with great stress in his voice.

"Greg, I was with Nick their father, I was in the best of care. We met a pack of wolves that stayed with us for a while. I was safer with them, than in my own room here. They protected me, I was fine really."

"Pack of wolves around here, the only wolves in these mountains are" … Greg stops and gives Andrew a worried look.

I catch the look and ask, "Werewolves, right Greg, you knew everything about the legend when you called me here, didn't you?"

"Well what do you mean by everything?" Greg answers bashfully.

"Greg, you set me up for all of this didn't you? You literally fed me to the wolves. You could have warned me or something. Any clue would have been nice of you!" I shout at Greg as he cuts me off.

"I was bound, I couldn't tell their secret, besides we had to be sure you were the one."

"But because you knew the legend. You know that you should have steered me toward Robert, not Andrew like you did. You know that he is the one I was supposed to… I hate to put it this way, but mate with!"

"I can't explain it right now, Robert would know what I did and why. He'll read your thoughts. I prefer that he never knows my reasons." Greg pauses to think.

"He may not scare you but, I'm not messing with his rage." Greg looks down at the ground to hide his embarrassment.

"Greg, your weakness has caused a lot of unnecessary pain for all of us. Didn't you think at all about what you were doing? You're supposed to be my friend."

"Hey, have you seen Robert? He should have been back long before us?" Andrew asks Greg

"No, I haven't seen him. Not since the two you left looking for Kim."

I close my eyes concentrating. "I don't hear him and none of the animals have seen him for days."

"Kim, by the way, you have a long list of messages in the kitchen waiting for you. I think most of the town has called here looking for you. Would you care to explain why?"

"I'll be busy for quite a while thanks to two wolves, who decided to fight in the street, in the middle of town, where everyone could see? Not their brightest idea." I say scowling at Andrew as he smirks.

"I had to break them up in front of a lot of people and Officer Barren. Luckily, he recognized me from your farm. I had helped him with his dog before. Otherwise, I would have had to hall off their bodies because he was going to shoot them both. You know, Greg I think that Andrew can fill you in on the rest. I really need to shower pretty badly." I kiss Andrew and head into the house and up to my room. I find a letter on my bed in Roberts hand writing. My hands tremble as I slowly open it:

Dear Kim,

I'm having a hard time writing this letter but it's for the best. I'm going to stay away from you so that you don't have to make a choice. I know you are in love with Andrew. But, I also know that you love me too. So, for you, I leave. This will be the first unselfish thing that I have ever done. Be happy and I'll keep watch from afar, in case you happen to need me. Or, change your mind. A wolf can dream too.

Please keep this between just us.

My love always,

Robert

With a heavy heart I sit on my bed. I softly sigh "I love you too Robert, be safe." I quickly hide the letter in my nightstand. I am so exhausted that I roll over and fall to sleep. I wake sometime later in the night and drag myself to the bathroom. I start crying softly as I undress for the shower. When I'm almost through with my shower, I hear Robert call to me.

"Can I come in one last time Kim?"

"Yes."

What else could I say to him? He joins me in the shower, looking so very sad. His pain is transparent for the first time since I've known him. He looks almost childlike as he gazes into my eyes. Gently, he runs his fingers over my face and through my hair. He tenderly caresses my body. Neither of us utters a word as he lifts me gently into his arms and carries me to bed. Both of us are dripping wet from the shower. He lays me on the bed slowly, carefully. He whispers with great tension in his voice,

"Kim, I can't control myself any longer."

I simply smile shyly back at him. Afterwards he lies next to me, staying until he thinks that I am asleep. I feel him kiss my forehead as he quietly leaves me.

19

In the morning, I can feel the sunlight on my face but, I refuse to open my eyes. Because, if I do, that would mean Robert is gone. He has left his home and brother because he loves me. Funny, I know that everyone thinks he's some kind of monster. But, I know he has a better side to him. He just refuses to share it with a soul.

How did it come to this? How did I fall in love with both of them? What was I thinking; sharing them would be wrong, right? Maybe I can find some Indian legend where I can have two husbands? No, that would be crazy especially if they were to both touch me at the same time. I might explode at least my heart would, no doubt.

I slowly become aware that someone is knocking at my door. "Kim you awake yet?" Greg yells through the door. I cover up with the sheet, tucking it around me.

"Yes, come in, I'm up."

"Good morning sunshine, you feeling better now that you slept in a real bed?"

"Yea, much better physically, but I still feel bad about Robert."

"Kim, it's for your best interest to be with Andrew, not Robert, he can turn in a minute like a wild animal."

"Really, a wild animal, you couldn't think of anything original?"

"Kim, how he treated you, the bruises he gave you, like the ones on your arms?" he says with suspicion in his voice.

"Kim, where did the bruises on your arms come from?"

I reply calmly as I look over my arms. "I really don't know which one they came from. I guess, they must be from Andrew."

"Wait, he hurts you too?"

"Yea Greg, they both do. But it doesn't hurt when it happens. I don't feel the pain when we are making love. I don't feel the bruises until after."

Greg gives me a look like he wants to slap me. "It's hard to explain but there's nothing like it. The magic, the electricity my heart racing when their skin touches mine. It's just beyond description, the pleasure it brings." I say breathing a little harder as I explain to Greg.

"Ok, Ok Kim, I've got it, you can stop now."

"Greg, I'm sorry I got carried away." I get another visitor as we talk.

"Good morning Andrew," I say feeling my face light up as he enters the room. He walks right over to me and kisses my forehead quickly, causing just a little spark.

"Morning Kim,"

"Andrew we were just talking about you." Greg angrily gets up from the corner of the bed. "Andrew this shit has to stop now," he points to my arms.

"I'll just leave the two of you alone. I don't want to see any new marks on her, understand me!"

Andrew doesn't say a word as Greg slams the door. Quickly, before Andrew has a chance to move, I wrap the sheet around me and jump up from the bed. I hurriedly head for the bathroom. "I'm going to take a shower, then let's get some breakfast, ok?"

"Yea, sure ok," Andrew looks at me suspiciously. But he doesn't ask any questions as he lies down on my bed to wait for me. When I come out of the bathroom, Andrew is sleeping soundly. I lay down next to him for only a moment. The next thing I know its afternoon.

We freshen up then head outside looking for Greg. Walking around the farm, finally we find him in the front barn. He's working hard as always. Right now I think he should be. I'm still pretty mad at him for all he's done.

"Well, I was starting to worry about the two of you." Greg states sarcastically when he sees us.

"Greg, we're going into town for some food. Do you need anything while we're there?"

"No Andrew, but thanks for asking. I'm surprised you two have any energy left or are you refueling for later. Cause, if you are, I'll stay at my girlfriend's house tonight. I really don't need to hear all of that moaning and groaning, let alone the sound of breaking furniture. The breaking of my furniture that is," he says agitated.

"We were sleeping Greg." I snap back at him.

Andrew states, "That won't be necessary Greg, we'll see you later."

Once Greg can't hear us anymore, Andrew says to me. "Let's take the van just in case."

"Andrew what do you mean, in case of what?"

"In case you can't behave yourself little flower."

"Yea, I'm the bad influence." I say teasingly. We both climb in the van and head toward town.

"So where do you want to eat?"

"Let's go to a small restaurant. Some place where they won't recognize me hopefully."

"Well they won't recognize me, but you my little flower, will be known everywhere by now."

"Yea I guess you're right. Still let's try to keep a low profile."

"Speaking of a low profile, have you seen Robert? I haven't since he left us in the woods."

"I think he's gone from Greg's."

"Why do you think he's gone?"

"I just have a feeling he's gone away. I have the animals looking for him. If they see him, they will tell me and there's been no word yet."

"You can what?"

"Oh, I asked the animals to keep an eye out for him as a favor to me."

"They do what you tell them to do?"

"Yup, why not let them help I'm not telling them what to do, they asked if they could be of assistance to me. They know what is bothering me." I say as I gaze out the window. "I'm worried about him he's all alone out there."

"Robert is a big boy Kim, he'll be just fine. I wouldn't worry about him."

"About that, you two heal quickly and you can't die either, right?"

"Well, not exactly like I said before, we can only die from silver in our system and beheading. We can die from old age, but our old age is like 500 years or more.

Robert and I will live longer because, our blood line is pure. However if we were to have children, they would live closer to the 500 year mark. Simply because you bloodline is not pure. "

"Well, if that's true, how many relatives do you have running around in these mountains?"

"To tell you the truth, I have no idea how many are out there."

"Who told you again about us?"

"The wolves in the woods told me some. And Lilly, she told me all about your upbringing. She said that you told her I would come, looking for my answers at the library, where she works."

"Kim, do you mean my Aunt Lilly?"

"Yes."

"If she knows about you, then every werewolf now knows about you. My aunt has a hard time keeping secrets. Our low profile just went out the window, I'm afraid."

"Andrew, we're only eating lunch together, friends do that all the time."

He gives me a sideways grin as we pull into to New Heights. As we walk in we seem to instantly draw a lot of attention. I cover my mouth with my hand and whisper to Andrew.

"Andrew, is my shirt cut too low?"

"No, why"

"Well we just got a lot of strange looks from the natives."

"Kim, just ignore them, they're just jealous because I have the prettiest girl with me."

"I don't really think that's it." I look around at the faces staring at us they aren't looking to friendly to me. We both say hey to Brian behind the bar. We find an open table and sit down to order our lunch. Andrew gets a burger, medium rare. I just order a chef salad.

I try to eat my salad, but I am getting very annoyed at being watched. I even glared back at them. They still keep watching us. I continue to forget, women don't matter as much in their culture.

"Are they friends of yours at the table over there?"

I point towards a booth to Andrew's left, where there are four American Indians eating lunch. They continue staring at us while they talk.

"No, I don't know them all personally. They are werewolves at the table. The old one is an elder his name is Isha, why?"

"I'll be right back Andrew. Don't follow me. I don't want a fight started. I just need some answers."

I get up from my seat and walk right over to their table. I pull up a chair and sit at the end of their table. They all look at me in surprise.

"Hi, my name is Kim but, I think that you already know who I am, don't you?"

I slowly look at each of their faces, to catch their reactions to my boldness.

"So, why am I so interesting to ya'll? Is there some question that I can answer for you that might be burning a hole in your heads?"

I pause for an answer from any of them. They exchange looks back and forth. They all stop on the oldest one of them. He appears to be around fifty years old. He finally, not happily, speaks to me.

"My name is Isha. I would like to know, why you are out with Andrew instead of Robert."

"That's really none of your business, got another question?"

I think I struck a chord with Isha. He looks like he just grew another gray hair. I've pissed off an elder and I'm not even a wolf yet.

"Yes, why are you out in public with minimal protection. There has been a vampire in the area. Your safety is in jeopardy especially after nightfall."

"No, I don't think the vampire is the one I should fear. He has shown me more kindness than any wolf I have met so far."

"But, are you not with child?"

"No, didn't Lilly tell you I wasn't pregnant? Why would that make a difference anyhow?"

"Well, if you were to become pregnant, you would need protection. Come to think of it. We would need it from you as well." He states with a serious tone.

"Wait, I will become dangerous when I'm pregnant? Are you kidding me?"

"Well, not exactly, didn't Robert explain this to you?"

"No, what do I need explained now?" I say disgusted.

"Robert should be with you. He can explain everything to you. Andrew was not told everything. Robert is the oldest son alive. He should be the one you mate with."

"Ok Isha, I am a human being and I don't mate! I really wish that all of you could learn to trust, hiding things from those involved is never a good thing. It only leads to people getting hurt and hurt bad."

I look back to where Andrew is to make sure he is still there. I can tell that he's agitated, but he is letting me handle this, as I asked him to do.

"You need to be with Robert! He is the next one in line. He must continue the blood line. You must have his children not Andrews. Well of course, unless Robert is dead, then that would be ok. You'll know if Andrew starts to hear your thoughts, Robert is dead. That is how you will know if it happens."

Isha spoke with such an unemotional tone that I just stare at him at first. I want to slap the smug look right off of his face. Then as sarcastically as possible I holler at him.

"How cold can you be? I will find Robert when and if I want to. Just how come you know so much when Andrew was kept in the dark?"

"I am one of the elders, which is why." He states with the utmost confidence.

"Like, I didn't know that already!"

I guess I will try to get Robert to return, not that I really want him around. I know he will attack me shortly after besides, I don't know that he will return.

"Is that why they were fighting in the street? You slept with Andrew also?" Isha announces. I couldn't hide myself if I tried. Andrew rushes over to the table where I am still seated and stands behind me with his hand on my shoulder.

"Kim, is everything alright here?"

"No, not really we need to go. Robert has some important questions that apparently we need answered. Isha would you tell us what we still need to know?"

"No, the rightful father he has the answers you need." Isha states bluntly as he stands up. He tells the others at his table that it is time to go. The other men don't even hesitate and follow Isha out of the bar.

"Kim, what is going on, why do we need Robert? I think that you are better with him gone."

"I agree one hundred percent, but we need answers, that apparently only he can answer. I think we already know most of it but, maybe someone else can clarify for us. You know, like your father. I'm getting the idea that honesty is not part of this fairy tale."

"Kim, let's take our food with us. We should get back to the farm and look for Robert. But, can't my dad give you the answers?"

"No I don't think he will. He had a chance when we were wondering in the woods. He didn't say a word. Maybe he is not allowed to tell us?"

We pay the bill and start towards the parking lot to my van. We pass a large crowd of people standing around talking. I notice their eyes and heads are following us. This can't be good.

"Your dad must know where Robert is."

I'm keeping my eye on the crowd it appears to be all Indians. As we near the rear of the van, some of them shout unkind things at us like.

"You've messed with the legend; a true Indian woman would have never slept with both brothers."

"Like, I really had a choice in the matter."

"Shut up, you know nothing about it!" Andrew shouts.

"She's a tramp, you've disgraced us all Andrew."

"None of you know what happened. So shut the hell up!" Andrew shouts. We keep walking fast towards the van.

"Andrew, I don't think they really care that he was forcing me. They think I am his property and his birth right. I am just a vessel for the blood line to continue through, nothing more." They continue shouting things at us, so we walk faster and faster.

"A real Indian woman would have honored our legend and our ancestry…tramp!"

"I wish I could shift and bite them all in the ass right now." Andrew snickers at my remark as we hurriedly walk to the van. However, before we reach the van, I hear many dogs in my head. They are telling me they have the crowd surrounded from the rear. What do I want them to do next? I chuckle when I turn around to see a pack of dogs circling the crowd of men. The tables have turned. They call to me for help from the angry dogs.

"Guys, back down I didn't mean what I thought. Please don't harm them. They don't know any better they are just stupid humans."

As I have a chat with the dogs the crowd is suddenly quiet and very still.

"Thank you all. Come over to me let them leave. Are you all strays?"

The dogs tell me they live on the streets. None of them have a home to speak of. They also tell me they'll do whatever I need them to do.

"Andrew, they heard my thoughts and knew that I was in danger so they came to help me. We'll take them to Greg's with us."

I address our jury, "The dogs won't hurt you if you all stay away from me and Andrew. They are coming with us so don't try anything stupid. I will tell them to attack you, if I have to. Do you understand me?"

The crowd of people just nod or stand as still as statues. Their faces are all angry, but some are covered with real fear. I know they could easily shift and kill the stray dogs, but that would bring a lot of attention to us. With all the noise that would come with a dog fight. I'm getting the idea that werewolves are a closed private type of community.

A line from a movie comes to my mind. 'With great power comes great responsibility.' Knowing that I can control animals with just my thoughts is kind of scary. I never tried to use my gift for protection. I get all of the dogs into the van and Andrew gets in behind the wheel. I look at Andrew's face and see he is as scared as the crowd is, I giggle

"Andrew, are you ok to drive?"

"Kim, when did you find out you could control the dogs like that?"

"Honestly, right now, I didn't ask them to help they just came because I was in danger. They said that the fight was uneven. They wanted to even the odds in my favor. Apparently the local dogs all know about me. Especially, since you were fighting in the street with Robert. They trust me enough to do whatever I ask." I don't remind Andrew about the dogs that protected me from Jonathan. I didn't call them to me either.

We ride the rest of the way in silence. We both have a lot to swallow right now. We arrive back to the farm safely. The dogs easily follow Andrew to the barn, where he feeds them and puts them in a large pen.

I shout for Nick to come as soon as he can, then I sit on the front porch and wait for him. It doesn't take him long to come to me. He comes up to me and licks my face.

"I'm happy to see you too Nick. I can't believe that I need you to explain more to me, preferably with some clothes on." He tilts his head in question.

"Andrew and I went out today. We were almost attacked by an angry crowd. If not for the stray dogs we could have been seriously injured. I need to know what the hell is really going on. No more secrets Nick! Andrew deserves to know what's happening as well. Nothing more should be hidden from him or me."

Nick runs into the house and returns shortly thereafter. He is dressed in someone's jeans. I don't ask whose. He sits down next to me.

"Nick, first, where is Robert?"

"He didn't want you to be able to hear his thoughts."

"I know he loves me too but he shouldn't have forced me to bed. If any of this had been explained to me from the beginning, I might have chosen Robert, who knows?" I pause, "none of this has been easy to accept."

"Kim, what would you have done, if I shifted the first time we met? Then told you that you have to marry one of my sons and make werewolf babies?"

I look at him a laugh, "I honestly don't know what I would have done at that moment." Not happily I ask, "How long will it take to bring him back?"

With hesitation Nick replies, “I have to search for him, he’s hiding in the mountains away from everyone.”

“Great, I would like for all of us to be together, when the rest of this is explained. You, being their father, should have never kept any of this from your sons.”

Nick puts his head down in shame. “I know your right. I need to tell them as soon as they are both together. They probably won’t talk to me afterwards.”

“Nick, you need to be honest with them. You have some time to come to terms with it however, Andrew and I are supposed to start out on a lecture tour this weekend, and we will be gone for at least a month. Will that be enough time to find him?”

“Yes, that should be more than enough.”

“Ok then, we will see you both then.

20

The weekend is here and we are all packed and heading out on the road. There is little to no conversation between Andrew and me, I think he realizes that I have a lot on my mind. I'm not sure what to worry about more, Robert, wolf puppies, Jonathan, or Victor.

As Andrew and I start out on our trip, I stare out the window worrying. What will happen when Robert returns? Will he help me learn everything? They have been keeping so much from me. Will he make me pay even more for choosing Andrew? I know he is suffering.

We make it to Gainesville Florida in good time, since Andrew has a heavy foot. We check in at the motel with time to waste so we rest a bit watching TV, something we never have time to do. Then we freshen up before leaving for the first lecture. We plan to spend a total of three days here.

Since it's so hot here in Florida, I decide on a very flattering black spaghetti strap dress with one inch heels. I know a lot of the audience will be looking at me, if the word about me spread as fast as he said it would, with his aunt Lilly having knowledge of me. Andrew wears his navy blue suit. This way we won't have to come back to the motel to change between engagements. I have a fund raiser after his lecture, where I am a guest speaker. I'm not sure how I got talked into it? It will be my first time on a stage.

Andrew had suggested that I pack dresses and skirts. He said that it would be more appropriate for me to wear dresses then my usual jeans, since I'll be sitting in on his lectures. I think he just wants, it to be easier to undress me at night. We don't have to worry about being caught by anyone.

His first lecture is at three o'clock and the second is at six. Then after that we will go to the benefit for the local animal shelter. The first lecture I sit in on, I learn some things about the American Indians I hadn't known before. I must not have paid that much attention at the last lecture I attended. I look around the hall and notice that there are about fifty people in attendance.

We grab a bite to eat at the cafeteria between the lectures. Some of the younger men join us. They talk with Andrew about a new way of breaking horses. It is the method that I use. I read their body language and gain their trust long before I try to put a lead on them, this way you never need a bit. Andrew keeps trying to direct their questions to me but they don't want my input whatsoever.

Andrew finally tells them that if they have any more questions, that they have to ask me or leave the table. Some look at me then they all get up and leave at once. I glance at Andrew none too happy and he knows it.

"Sorry Kim, they are young and ignorant. They haven't evidently been taught how to respect. The older wolves will be at the next lecture. They will show you respect."

"I sure hope so; I'm not crazy about the way women are treated by the werewolves. I have met many American Indians before you and not one of them was disrespectful to me. Let's get going; the next lecture is on the other side of the campus."

As I look around the room this time, the second lecture is standing room only. I can see that all of the people in the hall are American Indian. I personally don't think that his lecture is all that interesting. Shouldn't they already know this stuff about their heritage? It must be my presence that's filled the hall.

As Andrew lectures, I hear a lot of whispering going on around me. I start to get upset, they are being so rude. I look around and realize that it's me they are talking about, oh great. I get out my makeup mirror and check my hair and makeup. Nothing is wrong there and my dress is fine. Oh crap, they are looking at me because of this damn legend. They are checking out their new chosen one.

I wait until Andrew looks my way. I smile politely at him, get up from my seat and quickly exit the room. I avoid eye contact with everyone. I don't stop walking until I am outside in the courtyard. I find a bench and sit down. I am not a happy person. I am so tired of this shit!

The sun has set while we were inside. I sit there enjoying the cool night air. I see a man with a dog walking in my direction. The man seems to be hesitant in his progress, as they are about to walk in front me. The dog suddenly jumps into my lap. The man tugs on the lead and pulls him off. He babbles as he apologizes profusely.

I pet the dog automatically, not thinking about what I'm doing. The dog grabs my hand to get my attention. The man starts overly apologizing to me, but the dog is telling me to get back inside of the building. They are there as diversions for my kidnapping, that they are a decoy suppose to lead me into a trap.

He tells me that there are vampires hiding down the path. They don't want me to breed. I thank the dog telepathically. I don't give any clues that I know what the man is up to. I make sure to look the man directly in his face, so I will recognize him if I see him again.

"I'm sorry but will you excuse me? I must get back inside." The man shifts his eyes around us nervously. I guess his back up isn't in place yet.

"*Thank you dog. I'll remember your kindness.*"

Quickly, I get up and walk fast back into the building. I stride gracefully back into the lecture hall right back to my seat. I smile nervously when Andrew spots me. His face shows confusion. I smile politely back. I figure sitting in a room full of werewolves. I couldn't be in a safer place.

When Andrew finishes his speech I walk up next to him. I put on my fearless face and stand tall. The people come up to him asking questions and such about his speech. I shake their hands and most of them just say the usual greetings. But a few elders place their hands on my shoulders and eye me up and down. Then they nod an approving nod to Andrew. I know they are not checking me out. It's more like they are checking over a horse for strength and endurance.

The whole thing feels very strange. But what did I really expect them to do, hug me and welcome me to the pack?

The crowd slowly thins out until it is just a few people left. The small group follows us out to the van which I am grateful for. We say our goodbyes and leave the parking lot without incident. Thank God.

We arrive at the benefit and walk in without any trouble. But now that I am aware of possibility of trouble, I have my ears and eyes open wide. We find our table near the stage and take our seats.

We are served our salad and then dinner as the speakers talk. A few speakers talk about an animal they helped. One's that had a bad beginning and how the animal turned around, despite the abuse and neglect it once suffered. Others talk about their organizations and what they hope to accomplish in the future.

When I am introduced I start to get nervous. This is my first public speaking engagement. I walk up to the podium, and by some small miracle, I don't trip. I look over the audience and start to get so nervous that my hands tremble. Andrew makes a loud cough catching my attention. I keep my eyes on him and regain control of my nerves. I paste on a smile, take a deep breath, and begin my speech.

"Good evening, I am Kim McConnor; I am going to try to explain my gift. I am able to communicate with animals. I have been doing this since I was a small child. Some people think I'm nuts but I assure you that I'm not." I pause as they laugh on cue, thankfully.

"I travel all over the country, staying with rescue group members in their homes. I don't make money doing what I do; it's because of my love for the animals that I do it. I can communicate with most animals, except for wolves and alligators. Ironically, the wolf has always been my favorite animal."

By the look on his face, I could have knocked Andrew out with a feather. Now I'm flustered again, shit. I desperately try to stop my legs from shaking. I'm grateful that there is a podium in front of me to hold on to. Otherwise, I might be on the floor.

"Since they say, to see is to believe. The local animal shelter has brought a not so willing volunteer here. They have told me that he is afraid of everything and everyone. He also bites out of fear. This behavior, if it continues, will keep him from finding a forever home.

Now keep in mind, if he shuts me out, I will not be able to help him right now. If that does happen, I will continue my attempts over the next couple of days. If you would like an update, please leave me your email address, and I will email his progress."

I turn myself to face the right side of the stage.

"Ok Izzy, you can bring him out please."

Izzy is a skinny gothic kid complete with multiple piercings. He drags the shepherd mix out to me. I walk to meet them half way and take the leash from Izzy. The dog looks up at who has his leash and relaxes a little. I kneel next to him and in a very soft voice. I explain to the audience that if I translate everything as I speak with him, I might confuse him. To please be patient and I will fill them in, as possible.

I ask the dog if he will speak to me and he asks what he is doing here. I tell him, "You're here because you are scared. I want to help you understand that we mean you no harm. We just want to help you."

He looks at me and the audience, then at Izzy. *"Ok lady, hold me, that kid Izzy scares the hell out of me."*

I grin moving closer to him. I hold him against me putting him in front of me so that the audience can see him clearly. They are in awe.

"Are these nice people lady?"

"Yes, what is your name?"

"Vlad,"

"Vlad, these people and I would like to see you happy and without this muzzle. Can I take it off of you without you biting me?"

"I promise not to bite you, as long as that Izzy kid stays away from me."

"I won't let him near you. Did he do something bad to you?"

"No, it's just that he always dresses in black, like the vampires."

I look seriously in the dogs eyes. Think over his words as I undo the muzzle. Where in the hell would this dog see a vampire?

"What do you mean Vampires? They are folklore not real things."

"Maybe in your world lady, but in mine, they are without a doubt real. In fact, I detect a faint hint of one around you. You must have been near to one earlier tonight. I guess that he didn't bite you though because, your still here."

I give a quick snort at that, and then I look down at him perplexed. Animals don't lie so he must have met his own vampire, and why not, I met my own personal vampire, Victor.

"Lady, you know Victor?"

"Yes Why?"

"Oh nothing, he is one of the good ones I've met."

"Ok Vlad, we'll talk later about the vampires when we are alone."

I massage Vlad's head and ears as I talk to the audience. I explain to the audience, "Not every dog is the same, some take a long time, others just minutes to trust. I believe the reason that my method works so well is that they can clearly read my mind, and my body language always matches my words. They know that I am telling them the absolute truth."

I explain some things to the audience. Vlad starts to wag his tail slightly. He then walks towards the tennis ball. I loosen his leash so he can reach it.

They had put various dog toys on the stage earlier. We play a short game of catch and retrieve, while I tell the audience about William. I also tell Izzy that he can go. I will take Vlad with me tonight. I'll bring him with me in the morning, when I come to the shelter.

It couldn't hurt to have my own little vampire detector with me. I close my stage demonstration with answering some of the audience's questions. Then, I tell them my email address for any remaining questions they may still have.

I tell Vlad that he must sit at my table and be polite until the benefit is over, and then he will go with me back to my motel. He promises me that he will. I show him what chair he is to sit in and he sits there like a person.

I put a plate in front of him with a few meat scraps on it. I hear people near me say how amazed they are now. This dog who was dragged across the stage not thirty minutes ago, is now sitting properly at a table.

There are a few more speakers that follow after me. Finally, the night comes to an end. I find my friend Melanie from the shelter. I tell her that Vlad is afraid of Izzy, not because he has done anything though. He just looks scary, always in black. I also tell her that I will see her in the morning.

We get to the motel exhausted from the long day. I tell Vlad which bed is his, while Andrew and I ready for bed.

"Hey Kim, you guys aren't going to, you know ah... do it?"

"Do what Vlad... oh that, no we are too tired tonight. We won't do it in front of you anyway."

"Oh thank God, I just can't understand why people do it anyway, they do it all wrong."

I stifle a snicker because he was very serious; I shake my head as I climb into bed.

Over the next two days, I spend my time at the shelter, while Andrew lectures at the university. I take Vlad for long walks as he fills me in on the vampires that he knows. It's all the usual stuff, night creatures that drink blood. They burn in the sun, so they sleep during daylight hours.

He tells me that they are only pale when they haven't fed in a long time. If they go for a long time without any blood, they will turn sickly white. They may become visibly dehydrated. I didn't want to know how he knew that part, so I didn't ask. He also said that they aren't cold like people think; their bodies are closer to room temperature.

When I asked him how he knows so much about vampires, he explained that he was raised by them. He said that they use guard dogs to protect them in the day time. The breeds they usually have are Rottweiler and Shepherds like himself.

He put his head down ashamed because he wasn't mean enough for them. They taught him to attack people and kill them, but he couldn't kill. That is how he got to the shelter they dumped him there. I asked him if he could remember where they lived. He said that he couldn't remember. He never saw anything more than a brick wall that surrounded the compound.

After talking with him and listening to all of his stories, I still have a hard time believing. I know that the werewolves told me that Victor is one but, he was so sweet to me. Not at all like the ones Vlad has been telling me about. Then again, last year, I wouldn't have believed that werewolves were real either. It never occurred to me that the vampire books I'd read could be real stories.

I wonder if they are all gorgeous like Victor or, evil and mean, like Jonathan. I also wonder if the sex is as good as they write it is? But, I guess I'll never know since I'm with Andrew now, not that I am complaining. Long term boyfriends don't come along very often for me. I believe Andrew is much more than a boyfriend.

I don't count Robert as cheating, he gave me no choice. I decided that I'm not going to share with Andrew. What I've learn from Vlad about the vampires, I don't think that it would do any good to tell him about it. I know he knows about them already.

When our time is done and I have to leave Vlad at the shelter with Izzy, Izzy promises that he will not wear black every day. I also show Izzy how to use his body language to communicate with the dogs.

The next morning, Andrew and I head out for North Carolina. We are going to a small college this time. We take our time traveling. We are in no rush to get there. We stop at a few road side stands along the way, picking up some produce and honey at one. At this one particular stand, an old Indian is selling handmade jewelry. Andrew buys a wolf necklace made out of wood. He gives it to me and I put it right on.

When we arrive, it is night time already. With my new found enlightenment, the night takes on a whole new meaning. I know that I am being watched not only by werewolves but also by vampires. My life just keeps getting better and better.

21

We decide to go out to a diner instead of having takeout. We find a little family type diner. The place is like one of Jimmy's restaurants in Jersey. Translation, the food and service are great. I enjoy my chicken and Andrew loves his steak.

After we've eaten, I use the rest room, while I am washing my hands, I notice a woman enter. I really don't look at her that well.

"I see that you have chosen the weaker brother." She plainly states. I recognize the voice instantly, as Andrew's mother. I turn to face her.

"Excuse me, Lea?"

"I would have chosen the older one myself. He has zest; the one you chose lacks something, the older one is a better fighter, stronger and wiser."

"I'm sorry, Lea why are you here?"

"Robert will be a better defender. I'm surprised that he let you leave with Andrew. I guess it's good for you though. They don't have to rush now in taking you."

I look her directly in the eye, "You're a vampire aren't you?"

"Yes, am I the first one you have met?" she smiles a bit sideways.

"No," I say calmly, "But may I touch you? You are the first female I have met. I wouldn't have guessed it when we met before."

"Yes"

She extends her arm to me. I touch the back of her hand. Her skin is so smooth and not cold at all, Vlad was right.

"Kim, you must know that I am not the only supernatural one in this room. Any regular human would have run in fear from me by now."

"You know Lea its funny. I have never had to fear anything before. But now that I know you're kind exists. I guess it's time to reassess things. Since you revealed yourself to me you must have a reason?"

She smiles kindly, "I was sent to check on you. They think that I will not protect you from them." I remove my hand from her skin and try to appear relaxed. I'd forgotten I was still touching her.

"Kim, I was in your place over a hundred years ago. Some of them thought that if they killed me, the line would stop. They didn't know that I had already produced my three sons. I had done my part already. The night that they chose to kill me," I see sadness fill her face as she continues.

"One of them took pity on me. He stopped them before they could finish the job. He changed me into a vampire to save me." She looks down at the floor and with sorrow and continues,

"What they got was a very miserable vampire, and now it's your turn, they know that to kill you won't stop it and neither will changing you." She pauses and takes a deep breath. Well, mimics a breath.

"Lea, do you need to breathe?"

"No, it's out of habit mainly, Kim what they plan for you is much worse than my fate."

“Ok Lea, why are you telling me all of this? You are starting to scare me.”

“Kim, when they do try to take you, please believe me, that I’ll do everything in my power to protect you from their evilness. However, I fear I cannot stop them from taking you. I’m sure that I can appoint myself as your keeper when the time comes. You should really go back to Andrew now. I will watch over you as much as I can.”

She hugs me and pushes me out the bathroom door. I stumble right into Andrew. I have no idea what expression is on my face, but Andrew looks alarmed. Even more so when he sees his mother is in the bathroom behind me.

He hurries me out of the restaurant and into the van. He drives us quickly back to the motel. I dash in the room and when he asks what’s wrong. I just scowl at him and grab a beer out of the mini fridge, then collapse into the closest chair.

“Not right now Andrew, I need a few minutes to think.” He sulks over to the TV and flips nervously though the channels until he lands on a ball game. At least he is smart enough not to pry. I ponder all that I know up until now. I think about what Lilly has told me and now Lea. My life is in danger. This is so much more serious than I had thought. Andrew keeps looking over to me with fear in his eyes. He has never seen me angry like this before.

“Kim, are you alright?”

“No, not really, guess what I found out tonight.” I say sarcastically,

“Something that scared you, I guess?”

"Yes, it was something that made me rethink what I know about the world." I say solemnly. Andrew sits down in the chair beside me. He starts to reach for my hand.

"Andrew, don't you dare try to distract me! A vampire, your mother, came to warn me that the vampires plan on taking me away from you. She was not my first vampire either." He just stares at me, speechless. "You knew your mother was protecting me, didn't you?" He simply nods yes.

"Oh, and did I tell you she said that I should be with Robert, because he is stronger than you. I don't really want to fathom the consequence that would bring right now. Did it ever occur to any of you that if they have come after the other women like me, that I should be warned about them, or at least told what I am? A long time ago, before the fight with Robert, before at the moment we met, and you touched my hand, you knew then, and that is when you should have explained it all to me!"

I give him a minute to swallow this before I tell him to sleep on the other bed tonight. I am so pissed right now, that I wish I could hit him without being turned on. My emotions are running so high right now that I need to cry but, this room is so small. I decide to take a shower. Maybe the sound of the water will block out the sound of my tears. Sadly, I'm madder at myself than anyone else. I've trapped myself in a corner with no safe way out. There were big bright neon signs everywhere. I just chose not to pay attention to them, I am such a fool. The only bright side is if I do live long enough, I will have a child and turn into a wolf. That will be so cool.

The rest of our time in North Carolina, neither of us brings up the subject. He does his lectures and I visit the shelters and work with the dogs. We don't do much talking at all about anything.

When nighttime comes, I watch for Lea. Over the next month I see her in the shadows from time to time. I smile at her when I do. Seeing her looking out for me gives me comfort. It's funny, me having a vampire as my guardian angel and a werewolf as a boyfriend.

We are nearing the end of the lecture tour, and I just can't ignore Andrew anymore. It's our last night before we head back to Greg's. So I come out of the bathroom naked. When he looks at me there is no hesitation, he strips faster than I can think.

We have sex in every possible way. I'm surprised that the bed isn't broken in the morning. I have to remember not to make him wait this long again. I try to get up and walk to the bathroom. It hurts like hell. My legs are bowed, but the pleasure last night makes it well worth the pain, well mostly.

I understand why they are so ruff, I could however do without the bruising. The shower helps me feel a little better and the hot water soothes some of the tenderness. I glance at the clock when I come out of the bathroom, its two o'clock in the afternoon. Andrew is not in the room. He must have gone to get some food.

I start to pack up our things a little slower than usual. When Andrew returns, he has food for us both. After, we finish packing up our stuff and load the van. We start for home, it's around four. Going west on route 40 from Hickory North Carolina to Tennessee, back to Greg's.

Once we cross over the Tennessee border, we run into road construction. I start to get warnings from the animals in the woods that we are passing. Something must be wrong up ahead, but what? Because of the road construction we are going very slowly. I get a glimpse of information from the wildlife we pass.

"Andrew, something is wrong. The animals are sending me warnings about something up ahead. They are running from whatever it is. I can't get a clear thought. All the images are cloudy. Andrew, I have no idea what it is."

He starts to look as worried as I feel. The traffic finally begins to clear. Andrew doesn't hesitate pushing the gas pedal to the floor. I turn around after a little time, to see if any cops were behind us. But all I see are two black cars following very closely.

"Andrew, how fast are we going?"

"65, I'm not speeding at all, why?"

"Where did all of the other cars go, from the traffic jam we were just in? They seemed to have just disappeared."

Andrew doesn't get to answer me before we hear some noise at the back doors of the van. I turn to look and see Lea. She is flying in through the rear doors. Andrew can't see who it is and I try to tell him it's Lea, as he keeps screaming at me to tell him what's going on.

"Lea, what's happening out there?" I yell, she just shouts, "Andrew, drive as fast as you can! And keep it on the road. She's still only human."

"Lea, what's going on? The animals are going crazy with fear. Their thoughts are so scattered that I can't make out anything coherent."

I cling onto my seat as Andrew punches the gas pedal. It feels like we are soaring down the road as Lea shouts to us, "The vampires have decided that tonight is the night that they will conduct the kidnapping. They think that it's good timing."

I scream, "Why?"

She shouts back, "They reason you are headed back towards Robert. That only Robert and you can make the legacy continue."

"They don't know that Andrew being the second born, can still produce a full werewolf do they?"

Andrew takes his eyes off of the road just long enough to catch my lack of reaction. "I'm not surprised at all what they think. They must be reading too many books. Shouldn't they know how this all works?"

"No Kim, which is why nothing is revealed until it is necessary. I myself couldn't tell you, as I was supposed to. Being a vampire now I had to stay away from you as long as I could, I didn't want to lead them to you. They put it together between me staying here in Tennessee and then when Victor helped you in the woods. That sealed it. Then they knew you must be the one."

"Lea, was the name of the vampire that saved you Victor?" She just smiles.

"He has a kindness that even I cannot understand."

"Why did your sister in law Lilly tell me that you were dead?"

"To her and the other werewolves I am dead. They don't acknowledge me any longer." She smiles, "Except for my Nicholas and Andrew all others consider me dead. And that is what I am."

"Kim, you ok with this?"

"Well, it's not like I have a choice in the matter, do I Andrew?"

"Well not really, you kind of don't, sorry about that."

Not that any of our conversation is relaxed. We are all in a panic and with the way Andrew is driving. He is swerving the van back and forth, all over the road. I know he is trying to avoid us getting hit. It's getting real scary in here.

Suddenly, we are rammed hard from behind. The van is all over the road as Andrew tries to maintain control. He swerves back and forth, between the trees on either side of the road. He scarcely misses them avoiding a head on crash. I seriously wish that this was a 3D movie instead of real life.

I can't help but scream my head off. "I'm going to die! I'm going to die!"

Desperately, I try to stay in my seat. I'm so frightened at the thought of them killing us all. Lea as calm as can be, touches my shoulder and asks me,

"Kim, do you want me to change you if need be?"

The world stopped moving all at once as I turned to face her. All of my senses returned. I regained control over my emotions and calmly replied to her,

"No Lea, but thanks for the offer."

The van is being rammed hard from the left and then from the right. We are being bombarded from both sides, from the vamps in the two black Lincolns. We can't see inside of the windows of course, they're tinted black. After a few more hard hits to the van, we are slammed one too many times for my old van. It wobbles at first fighting hard to maintain its control over gravity, but it fails with a mighty bang.

The van crashes onto its side and skids down the road. I'm pinned against my door. Sparks trail high behind us. It looks pretty cool. That is, if I weren't in the van making those sparks.

One final blow sends us rolling over and off the road. Over and over we tumble down an embankment. Lea instantly rips my seat belt off of me and heaves me out of my seat. She covers my body with hers on the mattress. Her actions are faster than lightning. Lea is shielding me as we roll down the hill. I know she is trying to keep me alive the best that she can.

The van finally comes to an abrupt stop. The back doors are ripped off of their hinges by two large male vampires. They reach in the van for me, but they can't get their hands on me. Lea has me blocked from their reach. Then two black wolfs attack them from out of nowhere. They drag the protesting vampires away from the van doors.

I look around for Andrew but he's gone. He must have shifted to fight. "Lea," I utter unsteadily,

"Kim, I've got you, and I don't smell any blood on you. Do you hurt anywhere?"

"No not yet."

"They only sent three vampires. They didn't expect me to be here helping you. The wolves in this area must have smelled the vampires. They are very strong and could possibly win the fight."

Lea and I stay in the van. We can clearly hear the sounds of the wolves snarling and snapping their jaws. We also hear some screams and taunts from the vampires.

The fight seems to be all around us outside. Lea keeps me in her grasp. I feel safe with her arms wrapped around me. It's a good thing she has me, I would fall to pieces, my body is quivering so fiercely!

When it goes silent, we both watch the hole where my van doors once were. Lea suddenly holds me tighter. This cannot be a good thing, my vampire is scared. I must be in serious trouble.

"Kim, you're not afraid of heights?"

"No, I don't think so, why?"

"Then turn around to face me and hold on tight. We are going to try to escape."

I turn around and she puts one arm around my waist. Securing me to her she then attempts to fly out of the vans open hole of a doorway. We don't get too far though damn it. Two vampires are holding onto her feet. They yank us back and we hit the ground hard, of course, I am on the bottom.

"Lea, we told you not to interfere with this!"

"But on the other hand, at least you saved us some time having to hunt you down. Jonathan will not be happy with you for your betrayal. He will however be pleased with us for catching you so easily."

"Fuck you, Clint!" she hisses.

"You know how much I would enjoy that sweetheart. Maybe later, I'll give you a tumble, if you behave that is."

The larger vamp snaps at him, "Enough Clint! Both of you get up the hill and in the car now," he says as he shoves us towards the top of the hill. He looks down the road in both directions.

"Before some dim-witted humans come along, they might want to stop and help the naked men lying around."

Once we reach the road way, I look around quickly, searching the bodies on the pavement for Andrew. I spot him lying on the road near the tree line. I struggle to go to him but Clint grabs a hold of my arm.

Without thinking, I bite his arm. What a dumb thing for me to do. He quickly back hands me. It dazes me and instantly hurts like hell. I shake it off then shout since I can't get free from Clint, "Andrew! Andrew!"

"Kim he's just knocked out. They aren't allowed to kill them right now." Lea informs me,

"Lucky for them," Clint grumbles, as he pushes me in the back seat. The other one shoves Lea in the front with him. Clint grabs a hold of my arm, tightly squeezing as he sticks me with a needle. He smiles wickedly and whispers. "Nighty night princess, sleep tight."

22

When I open my eyes again, I'm in a Victorian style bedroom, complete with elaborate wooden trim and antique furnishings. It resembles something from the eighteen hundreds. I can't help but admire it though. It's the most elegant room I have ever been in. This is not at all where I thought I would wake up, that is if I were to wake up at all.

The ceiling appears to be hand painted with cherubs on it. That's a little creepy, naked babies up on the ceiling. The four poster bed is adorned with plush velvet curtains. I wonder just how old this vamp is.

As I get out of the bed I notice, my clothes have been changed. I'm dressed in a chenille night gown. It's very soft and not one of mine. I wonder who changed me. God I hope it wasn't Clint. He was pretty scary last night.

I get inquisitive and check the windows. I find them blocked of course, this must be a vampire's home, and I'm guessing it's daytime. The metal stuff blocking the windows is like the kind you would find on a closed business front.

I figure that if Jonathan took me, I might already be dead. Another vamp must have me. Maybe they took me to Clint's place. Nah, it's too nice in here. I don't take him for an elegant person. More rustic would probably suite him.

I check in the drawers and see they are full of brand name clothing. All of them are my size. This is real disturbing, yet good. I guess that I'll be here for a long while. Well, at least they aren't planning on killing me just yet.

I check the entire room over for possible hidden cameras. I think I've watched way too many horror films. I might as well take a shower and get cleaned up. I use the adjoining bathroom to shower. The warm water feels nice against my skin. The shower has multiple pulsating heads, a luxury I have never enjoyed before.

I dress in a black pair of slacks with a delicate flower print blouse. I couldn't find any jeans. I did find the wardrobe closet full of party dresses and many pairs of shoes. I wonder what they could be for.

Soon after I have dressed, I hear a light knock at the door. Oh shit, time to meet my captors. But isn't it still day time? I sit myself down in a well cushioned chair, beside a cherry table. I try to prepare for who might come through the door. I grasp on to the chair arms tightly.

"Come in please,"

Slowly, the door opens. I breathe a sigh of relief, as a middle aged woman enters. She is dressed in a black and white maids outfit. She's carrying a covered silver tray. She gently places the tray on the table next to me. Shyly she looks at me,

"Your breakfast, madam?"

She is noticeably nervous, I can tell because her hands are a bit shaky. How could I scare a woman that works for a vampire?

"I wasn't sure what you would want to eat, so I made a little of everything. I don't get the chance to cook for humans very often around here."

I slowly lift the cover on the tray, and I see that there is way too much food for me to eat. She made pancakes, eggs, bacon, waffles and grits.

"Is it daytime?"

"Yes"

"Then they are all asleep right now."

"Yes madam, sorry but there is no way out of here for you." She plainly states.

"I kind of figured that, I want to know if you can help me eat all of this food."

"But I'm the maid?"

"And I am the prisoner, Kim, pleased to meet you. Now join me."

She starts to giggle, "Does that mean that I out rank you madam?"

"Yes, I think so, let's eat."

"My name is Rose."

As we eat, Rose informs me that my vampire captor is over a thousand years old, yet she won't tell me his name. She also says that during the ten years she has worked for him, she rarely has seen him. She explains that she works until just about sundown, she always leaves the grounds before the sun sets. I find that hard to believe. But she could be lying to me.

I also find out from her that I am to be locked in my room until further notice. She had been instructed to make sure that I eat well, that while I'm here my comfort is of the utmost importance.

She lets me know that the mansion is guarded by alligators now. But it was guarded by dogs yesterday. She hasn't a clue why she claims, but I know the reason. The dogs would let me escape. Wolves I have figured out why I can't hear their thoughts, but I don't think I want to know about the alligators.

As soon as we finish the meal Rose clears away the tray. She leaves me alone in my chamber. I find a remote for the television and flip through the channels. I land on Buffy reruns. I Might as well bone up on my new captor. If Joss only knew how right he was about vampires, then again, maybe he does know. He tends to stick to the old time myths. Either way, I enjoy watching the episodes over again, I just pray my captor isn't Jonathan.

At four o'clock Rose brings in a tray for me with my dinner on it.

"Kim, I don't think it is wise for me to eat with you for dinner, he will be rising soon. I hope to see you in the morning, good night."

"Yea, me too Rose,"

That wasn't too promising, but there is nothing I can do about my fate at the moment. Night fall is almost here. I will find out who my captor is soon enough. I try to eat my meal, though my stomach is flip flopping. Rose appears to be a great cook. The chicken she prepared melts in my mouth. I'm trying to distract myself from the anxiety that is building inside, but my mind drifts to Lea. I'm worried about her and what she said. The part about the vamps plans for me being much worse than death. My distraction isn't helping my anxiety any.

I hear a small motor behind me and see the windows are now unblocked. I truly jump to my feet out of fear, as soon as I hear a soft knock at the door. My whole body is shaking, I must keep it together. I squeak out a pitiful, "Come in?"

The door slowly opens and Victor enters my room. I swear that the world stopped spinning for a moment. I fight an overwhelming urge to go to him and hug him. I am so relieved that it's not Jonathan. I quickly remind myself he's my captor. At least I have the knowledge that Victor can be kind. His liking me must be why I am still breathing, that alone should ensure I live a while longer.

I sit back down in my chair, and I look at the floor sorting through my emotions. I want him to think that I am calm being here, but my rapidly beating heart is giving me away, I just know it. I do know his kindness and Nick trusts him. He could have been tricking us though, I really don't know if I should trust him or not?

"Kimberly, I hope your accommodations are comfortable, and your meal, is it enjoyable?"

I slowly look up at his handsome face. I just gaze at him perplexed for a long moment. My mind is running through a range of emotions and comments, which wouldn't be wise to share at this moment. So for now I play it safe.

"The room is exquisite as is the food. The clothes however are not quite my taste, but now I understand why they seem familiar to me. They are nicer than I usually wear. Just like the ones you brought to me in the woods."

He smiles politely and nods his head as he takes the chair opposite mine. Someone knocks and enters. The servant has a single red glass on a silver tray. Without looking at either of us, the servant places the glass down in front of Victor, then swiftly, quietly turns and leaves, closing the door behind him. I glance at the glass and see that it is not red but the contents are blood, Yuk. I turn my head away. In a matter of fact style Victor begins.

"The clothes my dear Kimberly are what I think you should be wearing. They are of the finest quality from the finest stores."

"Victor, why am I here?"

"Kimberly, I will ensure that your every need is met while you are here. I had no choice but to bring you here. I must protect you from the vampires that want you dead."

"Jonathan?" Victor frowns in response to my question.

"Victor, how long will that be exactly?"

"I'm afraid that it could be a very long time."

I pick at my plate with my fork. I think this over for a few minutes before I reply. I'm worried about Andrew and Lea. I really want to go home, but I know that it is not going to happen, so I might as well be comfortable while I'm still breathing.

"Well, if it's not too much to ask for, could I have a radio to listen to? A dog if possible, you know, to sleep in here with me. I am not used to sleeping alone." He actually roared into a burst of laugher.

"What's so funny Victor?"

He composes himself quickly. "It would figure that you would sleep better with something furry. I may honor that request at a later time, as for now, I will not. The radio will be in your room by morning."

"Fair enough, at least you will consider it."

He sips on his blood in silence, as I pick at my plate some more. "Kimberly, I believe that you appreciate the craftsmanship of old houses such as this one. Am I correct?"

"Yes, Victor I do love old homes. They have such character to them, not at all like today."

"Would you like a tour of the house?"

"I can leave my cell?" I say sarcastically, he looks offended oops. Watch your mouth girl, you need him.

"I am not a monster, despite what you might think of me. I have shown you my kindness in the past. You should not think that would change while you are here. You just cannot leave my house for your own safety. Please, do not think of my home as your prison."

"Victor, I do know your kindness, I will never forget how you helped me when I needed someone. I am sorry for my tone. However, I also know that you have watched me since I was a teen. All the while knowing what I am to become."

"Kimberly, let me show you my home. I will explain my actions to a point for you."

We go from room to room. I admire each one as they all are Victorian style right down to the wood flooring. He shows me the entire house in a matter of hours. This house, as he calls it, turns out to be a large mansion. He even shows me his bedroom. He must have some trust in me that I don't understand.

The mansion looks like something out of a traditional home magazine. There is even an indoor swimming pool complete with a Jacuzzi. He ends our tour in a cozy room full of books, it must be the library. There is a huge portrait of Victor above the fireplace. Positioned in front of the fireplace are two straight back chairs. Beside each chair is a small table. One of the walls has several paintings covering them, most of which are landscapes. The other three walls are book shelves, which go from floor to ceiling.

"Kimberly, did you enjoy the tour of my home?" He asks as he motions with his hand for me to take a seat. We each sit in the chairs facing each other.

"Yes, very much, your house is breath taking. I have never seen a house so beautifully decorated. I feel as if I have taken a step back in time. Do you share it with anyone else other than the vamp guards?" He laughs at me again; I didn't think my question was funny.

"No, I do not have anyone to share my home with. The last woman that lived here died many years ago. I do not wish to go through the unpleasantness of the human aging process."

"Oh sorry, don't vampires date one another?"

"You know very little about us don't you Kimberly?"

"Well, excuse me, but I recently found out that your kind is real, you do seem much more civilized that I would have imagined."

"I think I will take that as a flattering remark." He places his empty glass down on the table. He then walks to one of the bookcases. The servant replaces his glass with a fresh one. I can see the steam coming up from it. I didn't even know the servant was standing anywhere near. The servant looks to Victor then to me.

"Kimberly, would you like anything to drink?"

"A glass of water would be nice." The servant leaves and quickly returns with a glass of ice water.

I thank him and he is gone. Victor returns to his chair with a few books in his arms, he extends his arm handing me some very old books.

"Here Kimberly, read these manuscripts, they will enlighten you about my kind. But some caution, not every vamp, as you refer to us, is civilized. Still you will learn some things. Mostly about me, I feel I owe you this much, since I know all about you. It seems only fair that you know about me."

I open the cover of the first book he hands to me. I don't think this is how kidnappings usually go. I see that the book is hand written, and look up to him, a bit bewildered.

"Yes, they are my personal journals. Every detail of my life after being turned is within the pages. If you feel that you can learn more after reading these volumes, please feel free to help yourself to the rest on the shelves."

"Victor, why would you share such personal things with me?"

"Kimberly, you will be here a very long time I believe. If you are already pregnant with a pup you will be here even longer." I guess he means forever.

"I cannot allow you to have a child and carry on the blood line of the werewolves. By removing you, the next generation will hopefully never be." He pauses and turns his back to me facing the fire place.

"I could never bring myself to harm you, I was awe struck the first time I saw you. I had come to find out if you were the one, the one I was supposed to destroy, like I have done so many times before to those who have come before you."

Well, he isn't sugar coating this at all it seems, but I already knew he had killed the rest.

"We didn't know that killing one of the chosen would not stop the blood line from continuing on. We did however assist the white men in killing as many Indians as possible, but that was a long time ago, during the 17th-century. We had no idea that even mixed blood could still create werewolf heirs. We only discovered that information in the last century"

He pauses for a few moments returning to his chair facing me. "I came across you that night. I do have to admit, I was… I have enjoyed watching you grow into a beautiful woman." He gazes at me approvingly. Ok he must like what he sees. The rumors must be true about him loving me.

"If we find that you are with child, I promise not to harm the child. But I say this only because the child would be yours; I fear the pain that it could cause you. Well to take your child from you would be unthinkable."

I sit here trying to digest what he is saying to me. He must truly love me. Not many men would raise another man's child, especially a child that would come from his enemy.

"Victor, you are willing to raise a child of mine that is not yours?"

"Yes, Kimberly." He hesitates a moment, "I believe that you should return to your room now. Its eleven o'clock and I have a few things to tend to. I will escort you to your room, now."

He extends a hand to me. I hesitantly place my hand in his. He then places his other hand over mine. Holding it there briefly as I stand, just long enough for me to notice the difference in our temperatures. He isn't as cold as I thought he would be. Thinking back to when I was in the woods, our hands touched, but that was a very cold night.

He leads me slowly to my room up the stairs. Once we are at the top of the stairs he takes my hand in his again. He holds on to it until we are at my door.

Reluctantly, he releases my hand so that he can unlock my door. He again takes my hand, looking directly into my eyes. Quite seductively he whispers, as he lifts my hand to his lips, "I very much enjoyed our evening together." Tenderly he places a kiss on it. What a gentleman.

"Victor, I believe that I also enjoyed myself." I think to myself. You do get more flies with sugar.

"Kimberly, my house now feels like a home with you in it."

By the way Victor is acting I think he really must be in love with me. Then again, he has had centuries to master his performance. Still I blush as I entered my room. I lay the books down that he had carried up for me on my bedside table. I'll read them in the morning.

I dress for bed in sleep pants and a tank top. I climb into bed and turn on the TV. On the news I see my van overturned on a back road. The reporter states that there are signs of a struggle, but, they haven't found any bodies. The policemen states that they have DNA samples. And they hope to have the results by Monday, that's only a few days away.

"Oh shit, my DNA is all over the van and so is Andrew's. Maybe his will test as canine, but mine won't."

I start to bang on my door calling Victor." When he finally opens my door he is curt.

"What is it Kimberly?"

"Victor, did you see the news?"

"No why?"

"The police have found my van and now they have my DNA, I'll be a missing person."

“And that is my problem how? I know where you are?” He crosses his arms across his chest. I mimic his actions.

“If the cops start looking for me and post my face on news, the rescue people I’ve helped over the years will get involved. That won’t be good with all of those people and dogs looking for me everywhere. I know they won’t find me here, but I don’t want any of them getting hurt. They don’t know that vampires and werewolves are real. Our world could be exposed. They could get killed poking their noses in to this. That would only do more harm than good for any of us.”

I pause but, he has no reaction to my words. So I continue on,

“Also the werewolves and other vampires will know I’ve been taken, it won’t take them long to figure out that you have me.”

I start pacing back and forth in my room, finally sitting in the chair. I don’t really want to show how concerned I am. I can’t reason with myself. I’m more worried about Victor being exposed than anything else. Why? I must really be a screwed up person thinking the way I do. He seems to be thinking over what I said. Maybe he is worried that I am trying to escape from him.

“Victor, do you have any friends in the crime lab? They can make my DNA disappear.”

“No, I do not.”

“I have an idea that they might buy.”

He hesitantly joins me in my room. He decides on sitting in the chair opposite of mine. He places his hand under his chin,

"Continue Kimberly."

"Ok, this is what I have thought of, you find me wondering down the road a distance from the crash site, then take me to the hospital to be checked out. Or, it could be one of your assistants, whichever you choose. They will stay with me at the hospital, ensuring that I stay put.

I will tell the doctors and police that I can't remember the accident clearly. I only remember waking up on the side of the road. The doctors will probably keep me for twenty four hours just for observation. After which, I can freely leave to come back here. We will tell the cops that you will see to it I get back home to Greg's." He thinks this over with his chin resting on his fingers.

"It needs some ironing out but it could work. You are right; you are very well known, not just by the rescue people. Especially now that Andrew paraded you around like he did. The werewolves will be looking for you as well, that could cause me unnecessary problems. I don't need a war with the werewolves yet. I'm not worried about the police at all, they are just stupid humans."

"I resent that statement Victor."

"Kimberly, you are not stupid my dear." One point scored for Victor.

"Victor, I want to thank you for not allowing the vampires to kill Andrew last night."

"Kimberly, I didn't stage your kidnapping. I took you from your captor." I swallow hard. I don't need to know the details right now. I know Jonathan was the one behind it.

"Ok, if we plan to pull this off, I will need my clothes from last night."

"I will make some calls and have someone bring you your old clothes right away. I don't believe that they have been burned yet."

"Burned?"

Smiling, he turns to leave my room and abruptly stops in the doorway. With his back to me he asks, "Why would you come back to me willingly?"

"If I run, what would be your next move?" He turns his head halfway in my direction.

"Oh that is quite simple. I take Robert and Andrew, and hold them until you come for the one you love."

"I believe you just answered your own question. I also believe that you would not be as kind to them, am I correct?"

"I suppose that you are right in your assumption. I am aware that you must have fallen in love with one of them. And that would most likely be Andrew correct?" I just raise my brows and cross my arms.

"I believe I have my answer Kimberly. That means that I must work harder, then I originally thought, to win your affections."

I am completely surprised by his statement and he sees it on my face. He lets a grin cross his lips.

"Victor, I will not confirm nor deny whom I have feelings for. I may be human, but I am not a naive human."

"Kimberly, you are not really human at all. I guess they did not tell you that?" I stand frozen in disbelief as he closes my door and locks it.

23

Not too long after he leaves my room Rose returns. She has in her arms my old clothes. She's wearing a smile from ear to ear. With humor in her words she asks.

"Kim, I guess that you met Victor? I assume that things went well?"

"Yes Rose, however it was not the first time that I met him, and I thought that you left here before sundown?"

She clearly had no idea that I had met him before last night. Her expression was priceless, a mixture of surprise, confusion and embarrassment all rolled into one. She composes herself quickly. She didn't add a thing to what I said. She just starts to discuss the plan for my hospital trip. She informs me that Victor will have everything worked out soon. And that she will take me to the hospital. He plans to sit with me during the night and Rose will sit with me during the day. Insuring someone is with me, I'll have twenty four hour coverage, not that I couldn't take Rose.

Victor joins us within minutes. He sits in the same chair as before, and goes over the whole plan with us. Rose huffs, knowing that she just told me the whole thing. But I notice she will not interrupt Victor. She quietly sits in the other chair until he is done speaking.

Rose expresses concern, "Kimberly will you have enough bruising on you?"

I show them some on my stomach, ribs and lower back. Then I lift my sleep pants high enough to show them the bruising on my legs. I don't look at either of them as I do this. I know where most of them came from and it was not the accident that caused the bruises. I was glad that Rose didn't ask me where they came from. I guess some are from the thrashing I took when the van was rolling. However Victor knew not all of them were from the crash, the disgust covered his face. I lowered my head from the embarrassment. Victor didn't say a word. I sat still on the edge of the bed, my eyes glued to the floor.

Rose seems satisfied that all is set. So she leaves us to get the car ready. Victor rises slowly from the chair, pauses momentarily when he stands. Then swiftly walks over to me.

He extends a hand to me; I accept it, but I keep my head down avoiding eye contact. I don't want to see the expression on his face. As I stand, he gently embraces me. I inhale deeply and close my eyes. I've thought of being in his arms for so long. Damn it, this is not how this is supposed to go.

I should not enjoy his embrace. Perplexing me completely, I know Victor is aware where my bruises came from, but, I have no idea why he is holding me. I think maybe I better try to speak in defense of my werewolf.

But before I can utter a word, he whispers softly, "I'm so sorry for what they have done to you. Love making should never involve pain."

As he comforts me an eerie feeling creeps up my back, I ignore it.

"Oh, thank you for your concern Victor. However it isn't painful when it happens." I state defensively, "I'm just a little tender afterward." More than a little tender at times. Especially after Robert attacks, but no one needs to know that right now.

He holds me a little tighter to him. "Still, if you ever grant me the chance Kimberly. I will show you that it should be enjoyable for both partners. We are not all monsters."

Quickly he releases me and steps away the instant that Rose's hand touches the door. She enters the room and informs us that she is ready to go, as soon as I change my clothes. Rose gives me a wink and, they both leave so I can get ready.

Rose and I get into her little blue two door car. I figure that Victor is following us. When we get to the crash site I get out. I shiver from the thought of what happened to me last night, how fast my life changed without a single warning.

Then we drive exactly one mile from the where we could tell was the crash site. I get out and find a patch of ground that isn't too wet, and I make sure that dirt is on my hands and my face. I lie down and roll around just in case they check my story out. This way it will appear that I slept here. We have planned to tell them that I walked to this spot, and then passed out from exhaustion. We hope that they believe the injuries were sustained from the crash.

Rose then starts to drive us to the hospital. But before we get too far, her cell rings. She doesn't say a word she just hands it to me. I roll my eyes and smile.

"Hello Victor,"

"Kimberly, I will be watching you."

"I know Victor."

I close the phone and hand it back to Rose. She doesn't look at me when she speaks, she just looks straight ahead.

"Kim, don't you ever tell him that I told you this, but he has been waiting a very long time for you. He has watched you for years. I believe that he… has..."

"Fallen in love with me? Rose, I know he is in love with me, that's why I'm not fighting you for my freedom. I have to admit, that I'm a little curious as to why. I know that he should have killed me years ago."

"He has held off the other vampires. When they found out you were a possibility. Ones like Jonathan, they all wanted you dead. He waited to detain you. He wanted you to have some understanding as to why he would have to take you. He'll tell you eventually, but he is protecting you from vampires not the werewolves. And by the way, he's not the one who took you."

"I sort of figured that there was more to this. I know that Jonathan wants me dead in the worst way, he told me himself." Concern crosses her face then quickly fades.

"You know Rose, Victor gave me his journals to read tonight. I've never been kidnapped before. But I didn't think that is how it was done. You know, tell the prisoner all your inner most secrets." We both giggle.

"No, I don't think most kidnappers do that."

We drive on in silence to the hospital. We both have our own thoughts to entertain us. As we pull up in front of the Hospital, Rose breaks the silence.

"Ok Kim put on your acting face we're here."

Rose does most of the talking. I try to look battered and bruised. It's not really much of a stretch for me.

Rose explains to the front desk nurse that she just found me, that I was walking along the side of the road looking like hell, and thought that she should bring me right in.

They take us back to an examining room to wait. The nurse notifies the police department. They send out two detectives to interview us. The doctor clearly doesn't believe me when I tell him that all of the bruises are from the accident. The doctor explains to me about many services for battered women in the area, that he will give me some pamphlets to read over. He finally lets the subject go when the police enter the room. They split us up to talk Rose and I alone.

We both tell them the exact same story. I also tell them that I can't remember how the accident happened, that I probably swerved to miss an animal. The officer gives me a strange look and asks me, "Ms. McConnor, you starting a new habit of crashing your van?" Perplexed by his question, I shake my head.

"No Officer, what do you mean?"

"Well Ms. McConnor you seem to have done the same thing in Tennessee about a year ago."

"Wow, has it been that long? Yes, but I remember that time. It was a wolf I tried to avoid hitting in a snow storm." Somehow I don't think he really believed my story.

I over hear the doctor tell the detective that my bruising couldn't have all come from the accident, that he wants to take x-rays. He also wants to keep me overnight for observation.

When Rose and I are finally alone in my room, I ask her if she thinks that they bought it. She just shrugs her shoulders. Then she settles into the chair next to the bed. I'm exhausted myself so I lay down to sleep.

Sometime during the night I wake up and Rose is sound asleep. I thought Victor said he would stay with me at night? I sneak her cell phone into the bathroom. I call Greg's house phone, it rings three times before Doris answers.

"Doris it's Kim, I don't have a lot of time to talk so just listen please. First, I am fine and am being well cared for by my captures. Tell the boys not to come looking for me. As long as they stay away they will be safe. I don't want anyone to get hurt because of me. I just couldn't tolerate that, I love them too much. Vampires are not something to piss off." thinking fast…

"And Doris,"

"Yes Kim,"

"Tell them that I will miss them both, as I will you and Greg. Oh and don't call this number, I stole someone's cell phone and have to give it back to them. I love you Doris, take care of them for me please."

"Of course honey, you take care of yourself. The boys know that Jonathan took you. They are out searching now."

"Really they are? But Doris, he doesn't have me. I would already be dead if it was him. He told me himself that he plans to do just that. I believe the one who has taken me, did so for my own well-being." … I become aware that I am not the only one awake in my room, I hear someone open my hospital room door. I know it's not Rose, because I can hear her snoring softly. "Doris I have to go now, love you."

I hang up the phone and slip it back into Roses pocket book. I try to quietly slide back into bed.

"Kimberly," damn he is hiding in the dark room, I thought I felt him near. Why do I sense him?

I speak softly, "Victor, are you upset with me?"

"No Kimberly, I expected as much. Your words were wise to warn them away. I noticed that you told them who didn't have you, but you didn't say who did have you, why?"

"I'm not really sure why I didn't give you up."

"I'm afraid that I can never allow you to see them again."

"I know, but a girl can dream can't she?"

He smiles, "Yes I guess she can, but I will soon replace them in your dreams."

"Victor, if that is the way it is to be then it will be I guess."

He comes to the bed sitting down beside me, taking my hand in his and holds it for a long while. There is so much to learn about this man. I hope he stays honest with me. My eyes are getting heavy again. Despite that, I do enjoy looking at his face. I somehow find kindness in his ice blue eyes.

"Good night Victor, I could use some sleep."

"Yes my dear Kimberly," and he kisses my forehead like you would a child. I fall asleep with him still holding my hand.

In the morning the doctor comes into my room and looks over my chart and x-rays.

"Ms. McConnor, everything checks out fine. You are free to leave now. Do you have a way home? The nurse gave you some pain killers, I wouldn't advise driving at the moment, especially if there is an animal out roaming in the streets."

I know he was making a joke at my expense. I give him a sideways smile. But I am glad that he is concerned enough about my bruises to push getting help.

"Yes Rose, said that she would drive me where I need to go. Thank you doctor for all you've done."

"I do believe that your first stop will be the police station."

The doctor motions to me that someone is outside the doorway. I look out to see who it is. It's one of the detectives from last night. Rose and I exchange a worried look.

"Is my van totaled officer?"

"Actually Ms. McConnor, your van was already towed by a friend of yours. He is waiting at the police station for you."

On the outside, I put on my pleasantly surprised face and excuse myself for the bathroom. Inside, I'm in a panic. Someone I love is going to get hurt. Who would dare expose themselves? What do I do if it's Andrew or Robert? It can't be a vampire its daytime, otherwise Victor would be here to get me. Whoever it is, I pray for their safety. I calm myself down before I leave the bathroom and don't ask who is waiting, because I don't want to know whose death warrant is signed.

Rose and I follow the detectives in her car. "Kim, do you have any idea who it is waiting?"

"No idea Rose, I was hoping that you would know."

As we pull up in front of the police station. I gather all of my strength to walk inside. Rose holds my hand for support.

"Kim, he's not a monster."

"I'm not so sure of that just yet." I take another deep breath and face my soon to be dead friend.

I almost laugh when I see Izzy standing there. He hurriedly walks to me. He whispers as he hugs me,

"Victor set this up, play along."

Continuing to hug me he says noisily "I've missed you Kim when you didn't show up at the shelter we got worried. Then we saw your van on TV, we knew it had to be yours. I came down town and picked it up to get it fixed. It's at my house, I'll drive you there."

I suppress a snicker. "Oh Izzy, you are too kind. That was very nice. I'll have to pay you back as soon as I can. How is Vlad?"

"Oh he's just fine now thanks to you."

"Excuse me for interrupting your little reunion but. Ms. McConnor, where do we contact you? We might have more questions for you."

"Oh I lost my cell phone. I think it was when I crashed. Did you fine one near the crash site?"

"No we didn't log one."

"Rose, can you give them your number until I get a new one?"

"Yes of course, here officer."

The officer has me take a seat at his desk. He has me rehash everything that was already said the night before. When he appears to be satisfied with my answers I ask.

"Can we go now?"

"I have just one more question. Can you explain the animal hairs in your van?"

"Yes, I work with rescue animals. Sometimes I have dogs with me when I travel."

"Ms. McConnor, what about the wolf hairs we found in there?" I can tell he must know something, but just how much he knows I'm not sure. I try to play it cool answering casually.

"On my last trip prior to this one I had a hybrid with me. I am sure some of his hairs are still hanging around. Can I go now?"

"Yes. If we need any more information we will call. Here is my card, call if you can remember anything that's helpful."

"We will officer, thank you. Izzy, we will follow you in Rose's car back to your house, where I can pick up my van ok?"

"That's the plan isn't it?" I shake my head then Rose and I grab an arm each and rush him out of the police station.

"What? What did I say?"

"Nothing Izzy, now you get in your car and keep your mouth shut."

"Rose, we are going back to Victor's right?"

"Yes Kim, unfortunately I will have to lock you in your room until Victor wakes tonight."

"I Figured as much. I won't hold it against you."

"Izzy will be keeping your van for you for now. He can't return it to Greg's. The wolf brothers would torture him until he broke and told them that Victor has you."

"I'm sure you are right, they can be downright mean when they want to."

"You can tell me about that sometime if you need to talk."

"Thanks Rose, I'll keep that in mind."

We follow Izzy to his house and I grab a few of my clothes from the van. I search for my cell phone but to no avail. I find my laptop under the front seat. I can at least keep up with my email. I get a lot of animal inquiries. I can't email the boys, neither of them have computers.

I just stare out the window on the way back to Victors. Rose hopefully thinks that I am daydreaming, but I am putting the street names into my memory. We return back to the mansion. I follow Rose upstairs to my room and wait while she opens my door. I go in freely.

I am shocked as I walk into the room. I find a Chihuahua sitting on my bed with a pink bow around her little neck. I give Rose a puzzled look, she smiles back at me.

"She is a gift from Victor, for returning to him."

"I love her already. Does she have a name?"

"No, she is from Izzy's shelter. You get to pick a name for her. I'll go get our lunch."

While Rose is away I play with my new friend. She tells me that she was born at the shelter. I figure she is about eight weeks old. She is fawn and white with a tiny pink nose.

Rose and I enjoy eating our lunch, grilled cheese and tomato soup. She tells me that she thought that I would give her trouble on the way back here. I assure her that I would have run if it was only my life I was risking. I cannot have any deaths hanging over my head, especially those of people I love. She asks me which one I love the most. I tell her I'm not that stupid.

I name the puppy Bonita. She gnaws on my fingers before she gets worn-out and sleeps. I spend the rest of the day reading Victor's journals. I still can't believe that he gave these to me so easily. Robert and Andrew guard their secrets so much. But Victor just handed me all of his, the good the bad and the very frightening.

24

Later, when the night falls, Victor comes to my room. Bonita and I are playing on the floor when he enters. The first thing I do is run into his arms to thank him for her. I'm actually thrilled to see him, though I shouldn't be and I know it.

"Thank you so very much for her, she's beautiful. By the way, why did you pick a Chihuahua for me?" He wraps his arms around me, smiling. He pulls me close to him, holding me longer than I had planned, so I rest my face on his chest.

"Kimberly, anything larger you could train to attack me, I am well aware of your gifts."

I snicker, "I named her Bonita." I give him a peck on his cheek, and return to her on the floor. Not sure why I did that? I know that I am in love with Andrew, right? But there is something about Victor.

"That is the perfect name for her." I watch him as he gently picks her up placing her into his lap. They sit together in the chair as he pets her tenderly. I notice she is very at ease with him. A servant soon enters with a covered tray for the both of us. Victor's is of course blood. My meal is Chicken parmesan, complete with a baked potato & peas. He seems to have done his research on me. I think it is safe to say all of my meals here will be enjoyable. I don't eat much red meat except for the occasional cheeseburger. I mostly eat chicken or fish.

While we are eating dinner, I decide to ask about when he was changed. I also am studying Victor's every movement. Everything he does is so graceful, maybe there's a better word for it? I myself am a big ball of nerves. My hands keep shaking every time I try to use them. I am trying so hard not to spill anything. I don't want him to think that I am completely undignified.

"Victor, can you tell me what it was like when Jillian changed you? That is if you are comfortable telling me. You didn't write the details of that in your journals."

He gives me a long look. I'm not sure what his thoughts are about me asking, and his face gives me no clue whatsoever.

"Kimberly, it was not a bad thing at all really. Jillian bit me, drained my blood then fed me hers as I fell to sleep. I awoke as a vampire, no burning or nightmares, it actually was very simple. But the hunger that followed was so intense, my thirst was insatiable I drank from anything with blood. I did some awful things during that time." He looks away from me. I can tell he is distraught about reliving what he did. I want to comfort him but, I stay planted in my chair.

"That is until I discovered some helpful techniques to control the hunger. Still it took me a very long time. I had to teach myself moderation. I don't believe that Jillian was taught by her maker. She had little knowledge about being a vampire. After all when she turned me I was a king, I was a nobleman. I had to have control over my actions. My family was very wealthy and well respected. When I changed, Jillian had to remove me from my home land, she had no choice. The whole kingdom searched for me. I know that my family searched for me for many, many years.

My mother and father both passed from old age. I made sure to visit each of them on their death beds. I had to tell then I still loved them. Both my father and mother wept. That was something I hadn't expected from my father, he was such a strong man. I didn't change either of them. I do not wish this existence on anyone"

"Victor you do not look unhappy to me. You have done very well for yourself." I look around at my room with the expensive furnishings and exquisite artwork on the walls.

A servant comes in to remove the dishes. He does his task quickly, and retreats from the room. The room fills with a silence. I look at Victors face. I think I made him nervous or brought up unpleasant memories. I resort to my gift to break the silence that is surrounding us.

"Victor, Bonita likes you; she thinks that you smell very sweet." I say a little too cheerfully.

"She told you this?" He simply replies,

"Yes, she says that you are kind. And that I should trust you."

"Well, I would have to agree with her. I think she is a very nice dog. Kimberly, I may have wealth but the loneliness that comes with being what I am… can be very hard to endure… Do you know how really special you are?"

"Victor, you don't need to sweet talk me. You must know that I enjoy your company, you fascinate me."

He lets out a short laugh, "I am not sweet talking you. I mean what I say. The gift of talking with the animals makes you special. You will also become a werewolf as well, well that is if you ever have a child."

"Victor, I do want a child someday. Not yet and not just because I have to have one. You really will raise a child of mine?"

"I mean what I say. I do not take back my words."

"Then at some point you will have to let me leave here permitting me to do so."

"I am aware of that fact. We will cross that bridge when we get to it. My dear Kimberly, I must attend to my work now. I will see you tomorrow evening for dinner."

He comes to stand in front of me. I stand up not sure why I am doing this. He simply, softly hugs me as he kisses the top of my head, then he leaves me alone in my room.

I know he must work. He is a king after all. I am so restless when he leaves me alone. I begin reading more of his journals. I learn that since he was changed. He has loved only three women in the last one thousand years.

The first one who changed him was staked in the middle ages. He was with her for the longest amount of time. It was about four hundred years they hunted together. That's a long time for any relationship!

Jillian was her name. She convinced Victor that they were the angels of the night. Together they would travel from town to town feeding on the wicked. She would delight in torturing the sinful men and women. She especially enjoyed torturing the harlots. The poor girls would beg her to kill them in the end.

This is what eventually led to her demise. Jillian killed the wrong harlot one night. Her name was Valerie she was a favorite of a very wealthy man of the time. When he found out what had happened, he had Jillian followed to her place of rest. The wealthy man waited until the next evening. He staked her as she was about to rise. Victor thankfully was not with her that night.

Victor came across what was left of Jillian which was nothing but her clothes, jewelry and dust.

He writes later that he regrets the actions he took because of her that night. In his rage he destroyed the man and his entire family. He killed them all one by one as the man watched in horror. Once all were dead, he set fire to the house. He sat himself a short distance from the house, on a hill as he watched it burn throughout the night. He didn’t feed for a week after that night. He was unaware that he could not die from starvation. He was ashamed from his actions, he was filled with remorse.

A nurse later found him, looking as if he was near death. The nurse, Ana, took Victor to her home. She lived close to the hospital where she worked. She knew from the moment she saw him what he was. She brought him blood from the sickest patients, the ones nearest death. She considered it to be a merciful act on her part. She relieved their suffering much faster. Otherwise, they would slowly painfully wither away until death.

With her help Victor slowly regained his strength. She never asked anything of him for what she had done. He later found out that Ana’s mother had been changed by a vampire when she was two years old.

Ana’s mother had somehow found a way to raise her baby girl to an adult. It must have been hard for her not to feed off of her child. The nurse never saw her mother again after she turned sixteen. Ana had showed Victor a picture of her mother hoping that he might have seen her.

Though Victor told her he had not known her, he knew that he was the one responsible. She was one of his victims. Ana’s mother had been a harlot. Luckily for her mother, Victor heard Ana crying from the next room.

He instructed the harlot to care for her baby, because the child is the only reason he spared her life. He gave his blood to her so that she could heal and remain alive. What Victor didn't realize at the time. Was that the woman's master had come in directly after him. He strangled her completing her transformation to vampire.

Victor stayed alone for well over two hundred years. Then he met the second woman he fell in love with. She was a human named Elizabeth. She is the one whom he loved the deepest. He composed poems for her and commissioned portraits of her. Funny, I have not seen one in the mansion. He showed me every room the other night. Maybe he left out one or two rooms.

He wrote in great detail about everything he did with her. The love making was so detailed. I had to stop reading those parts. My curiosity was brewing and that could bring me only trouble. Thank God for cold showers.

They were so very happy together, Elizabeth never cared that he was a vampire. This meant a lot to Victor. They did share each other's blood. However it was mostly done during their love making. I don't understand why she liked the taste of his blood? She was seventy when she passed from heart failure. They both knew her heart was weakening. She begged him not to save her. It didn't take her long to die after she stopped drinking his blood. I guess she knew all along, his blood was keeping her alive.

The next was Maria she was a very young feisty Italian. He met her in nineteen fifty two. She gave him hell the entire time she was alive. Their love life, to put it mildly, was blazing. He wrote that Maria never did anything calmly. He had suspicions of her being part werewolf. He couldn't imagine a human being capable of such aggression.

Back then he still had to go out to hunt for his meals. So he had to leave her when she slept. This continued on for years until one night, he returned home to find her drained. He recognized the scent of the vampire who had killed her. He knew it was a political move from his rival. At the time, Victor was working his way up the vampire ranks to become king.

He was filled with rage like never before, more rage even then when he had found Jillian's remains. He knew that Jillian had killed so many humans just for the pleasure of it. But Marie never harmed another person. Marie didn't deserve to die like she did.

Victor relentlessly hunted down his horrid foe. When Victor finally caught up with him, he tortured him for several nights until boredom took him over. Then without any second thought he beheaded his foe, that's where I fell asleep reading.

25

During the first couple weeks at Victors I decide to be cautious. I don't do anything without weighing the possible consequences of my actions. I choose my words very carefully. I study Victor's ways and scrutinize his words.

One day I did try to use my laptop, but there is no internet anywhere near here that I can tap into. When I am alone in my room I read his journals. It's not like I have much of anything else to do. I watch some daytime TV, something I never had time to do before.

Rose and I talk some when she brings me my meals. She gives nothing away about Victor, his intentions, or plans for me. I have tried to talk with Brad, Victor's body guard, but I don't think he is all into me being here. Brad grunts or nods his head I haven't heard him say a full word yet.

However there is the broken heart, the one I'm nursing caused by my love for Andrew. I wonder if he really is looking for me. I thought he was in love with me. I ache to be in Andrew's arms again. To feel the warmth of his body surround me. The desire rush filling me, igniting me, overwhelming me. On the other hand I do enjoy Victor's company.

As I take yet another cold shower, I can't help but think this isn't hurting as bad as I thought it would be. I had my heart broken once many years ago, a long time before I met Andrew or, even Greg. He, who I won't name, left a giant hole in my heart. I thought that the hole he had left in me would never close. I walked around in a haze for a very long time. It was so bad, that sometimes I didn't even know how I drove home. I was in a really bad place because of him. I even lost a lot of weight from it all. It's really hard to eat when you want to die.

When I finally started to let go of the pain the hole slowly closed. I told myself that no one would ever get inside of my heart again. I guess that Andrew did get pass my wall, but not nearly as deep as I thought he had. It still hurts like a bitch. But, it is not crippling like my first heart break. Maybe I am stronger now, with all that I have learned recently. I have no choice but to be stronger than I've ever been before.

Victor does help the healing process a great deal. I'm sure he knows what he's doing. I may not be as old as he is, however I know he is courting me. He kisses me on my cheek every evening when he greets me. This has become the norm. Then we walk down to the dining room for our dinner. He never pushes me for anything more, only a kiss on my cheek, even when he leaves me each night.

He holds my hand every chance he gets. He always pulls out my chair at the dining room table. He is very "old world" with his manners. I secretly enjoy every bit of his attentions. I've never had a man treat me so kindly. He makes me feel as if, and I know this is going to sound funny, but like a princess.

We usually spend our dinner talking about the news events of the day. He then escorts me to my room, where we talk or watch television. On other nights we go to the library, and we talk or read as we listen to his music. We also play board games. He has started showing me maps of how the world was divided when he was young. I find it interesting, I have always liked history.

I notice that the nights we study the maps, he sits very close to me. The table is rather large but there are only two chairs beneath it. Our arms sometimes touch when we sit this close. He has also begun to remove stray hairs from my face at every chance. I think he is testing the waters.

One evening after I have been with him for about a month, Victor comes to my door. I can tell by his expression, that he is very happy about something. Somehow tonight feels different as we enter the dining room. The servant comes in and lights the fireplace, then he lights the candles on the table. Before leaving the room he turns off the crystal chandelier, which hangs above the long dining table.

I think to myself this is just a little too romantic in here. Victor is pulling out all the stops, that must be why he is happy tonight. He has something up his sleeve. I'm not going to lie to myself, though I miss Andrew a great deal, and I know I will feel guilty. I believe that if Victor feels tonight is the night he wants to make love to me, I won't stop him. But that would not follow with his character. I don't think he will go that far, just yet.

After dinner I lose another game of chess to Victor, although my chess skills are improving a bit. My mind keeps wondering back to what he is up to. So far, he has not done anything out of the usual. I can't help but wonder what it will be like; I know it will happen before he releases me, if he even has plans to release me. I look at the grandfather clock and see the time is almost midnight. He closes the book he is reading placing it on the table beside him. He looks to me and finds I am watching him again, and flashes me a smile.

"Kimberly, why do you watch me?"

"I really can't say, maybe I like your face?" He looks puzzled, "Victor, I want to know what you truly want from me."

"Well that was straight forward. So, I will do the same in turn. Kimberly, I want you to love me as I love you."

"Victor, it would be hard for me to just give my heart away so soon, that may take a very long time."

"I am well aware that may be the case. I have all the time in the world to wait for your love. You on the other hand, do not Kimberly. I would have set you free, if not for what I find in your eyes when you look at me. Also you are safest here in my home."

I didn't know how to answer that. I didn't realize that my budding feelings for him were so transparent. "Victor, you have known me a very long time and I understand you have deep feelings for me. I respect that. I have allowed someone into my heart that my brain told me so strongly not to allow. I am in no hurry to have my heart broken again. You can't blame me for wanting to be cautious, I wish there was an easy way to handle all of this, but, I know nothing in life is easy, especially for supernatural beings."

"Kimberly, I don't want to cause you any stress or discomfort. Do you wish to leave me?"

He caught me completely off guard with his question. I couldn't answer him for a good five minutes. And still it was not really an answer.

"Victor, I really can't answer that, I don't know for sure."

He smiled at me then extended his hand to me as he rose from his chair. I accept his hand. I know it is time for me to be locked in my room. As we walk up to my room, we are both somber.

"Kimberly, if you decide you want to leave, I will make it happen."

At my door he stops to kiss me. I tilt my face for him; he always kisses my cheek before he leaves me in my room. But tonight he cups my face gently in his hands, keeping his eyes locked on mine he leans in slowly and kisses me full on my lips. So gently, so perfectly, that I can feel my insides stir. Mystified, I stand there in his arms not sure how I got there. Did I really just cave that easily? What the hell is wrong with me? I should want to leave.

"Victor, is that what they mean by glamour?" I breathe,

He chuckles, "No my dear we cannot glamour; there is no need. I take it that you enjoyed our kiss?"

"Um, yes very much."

"See, I am getting to you, my Kimberly." I try to think quickly to get away from him before I regret something. My libido sure wants him but my mind is screaming no!!

My voice fails me and I Stutter, "Victor, I think I better ah, get in my room and check on Bonita."

"Kimberly, may I have one more kiss?"

"I shouldn't… really I shouldn't."

I gaze in his eyes. Oh hell! Yes, I do believe that he can glamour me. I don't care what he says. I allow him one more kiss. My libido may be failing me, but my principles are fighting hard to hold their own. The race is however neck and neck at the moment. The longer the kiss the weaker I am. I wrap my arms around him hoping he won't stop.

Victor lifts me in his arms cradling me. Our lips still joined together. I keep my arms around his neck as he carries me into my room. To my dismay he puts me in the chair. I don't really want him to let go of me just yet. I like how this makes me feel.

Bonita barks at him to stay also. But he swiftly walks away from me to the door. Obviously, by his smiling face, he is very pleased with himself. That was so not fair. I know he is trying to win my love, but he plays dirty. As I recover I think should vampires really be able to kiss like that?

I ready for bed and as I start to drift off I begin to worry about Andrew and Robert. What will happen to them when they do come looking for me? If they ever come looking for me. They should know where to start looking by now? Shouldn't they? Will I go with them or stay here? I'm safer here, no one is attacking me. Then again, I'm not having any sex good, bad, or Robert.

I cringe still when I think of how Robert treated me for so long, I can't understand why he was so mean. They could have been honest with me. Victor has been honest as far as I know. I haven't found any holes in what he has told me.

I also worry if Lea is safe somewhere. I pray that Clint didn't hurt her. Or, did Jonathan destroy her for trying to help me? I sure hope not, I like her. Will Victor kill them all or will he spare them if I agree to stay with him? My thoughts seem to keep me very busy most nights and days.

It's now been two months that I have been at Victor's. He has not tried anything since that one night. He only kisses my cheek as he leaves me each night. No more dimmed lights at dinner. I really don't understand what his game is. I don't know what rules he is playing by. Some days, I feel like my head will explode I worry so much. I can't believe they haven't found a way to contact me.

Rose tries her best to keep me company during the days, having her as a distraction helps some. I have earned Victors trust enough that, he gave me the key to my bedroom door. I can now roam freely throughout the mansion. With one stipulation, if I want to leave my room after midnight for any reason, I must be accompanied by Brad. He is Victor's right hand man.

Victor figured there was no need to lock me in my room any longer. The main doors are dead bolted and the grounds are guarded by alligators anyway. Victor knows that I can't talk with gators. So pretty much I can't escape from the mansion if I wanted to, I have to hope for a rescue. I am starting not to want to be rescued though, I rather enjoy living here.

He treats me like a lady, with respect, he has not tried even once to have sex with me, though I know I won't deny him if he should try. Yea, I know I'm his prisoner but, I can't complain about my captor. I do believe that I am falling for him.

I have now finished all of Victor's journals. He has had quite a life. He traveled all over the world after being turned. He has dined with kings and queens from many nations: he is unquestionably of the upper class.

I often wonder why he is attracted to me; I have next to no class. I prefer my jeans and a tank top, to his expensive designer clothes. Though, I find that I do love ballroom dancing. He has started to teach me how to dance correctly, as he puts it. I think because he can get real close to me. Not crossing his invisible line of proper etiquette, though some of the older dances he has shown me have no touching involved.

I do keep in the back of my mind what he truly is. I think of the wars he wrote of in great detail. He wrote of every bloody detail. I could almost smell the blood of his victims as I read the words. He truly was not always kind but as he writes it, only those who angered him did he kill without mercy. He never killed a child or pregnant women in all of his years. He also never drained a person to simply quench his thirst that is after his maker was gone. I get kind of jealous of him. He has lived a full life. I never will witness all that he has, a lot of which I am glad I won't see. But, the history he has witnessed, that is what I wish I could have seen.

26

My nights now revolve solely around Victor's agenda. I find myself longing for the sun to set just to see him. He keeps me entertained by simply talking; no man has ever been able to do that before. He more often than not enjoys talking about the arts. He was friends with some of the great artists. He simply revels in teaching me. It doesn't matter what the subject is. I think he enjoys having a student.

Dancing is something else that Victor has a great knowledge of. I have mastered the waltz, so now he is teaching me every dance he can remember. His kind of dancing is something that is completely new to me. I find that I really love the dances of old. I'm even getting good at them. I don't step on his toes as often as I once did.

Tonight he plans on teaching me the salsa. Most of the other dances I have learned, where there is minimal touching involved. But tonight our bodies will touch. It's going to be hard to resist him. I might be the one to make the first move.

As night approaches, I get myself ready. Excitedly, I put on a deep purple dress with a long twirling skirt. It's easier for me to dance this way. Pants would be to constricting for the movement of the salsa. I put on a low heel and my hair up in a ponytail. I'm pretty sure all of this was in his plans. Why else would he have bought me a closet full of dresses?

I go down stairs to the dining room for my dinner. This is where Victor will join me. As I sit here at the big empty table, I feel a sadness start to overtake me. I've gotten good at hiding my pain but, I still miss Andrew so much. Though I am starting to think he has given up on me. I really thought that he would have come to get me by now. Maybe he found another woman that gives him the adrenaline rush. I really shouldn't think about him so much. Before I know it I'm balling like a baby.

Victor catches me crying at the table. Without a word he easily sweeps me up in his arms. He carries me up the stairs to my room. Tenderly, he places me on the bed and sits down beside me. Almost instinctively, he holds me in his arms. I stay there until I stop crying. He doesn't say a word, just wipes the tears from my eyes.

I pull back from him slightly and look into his face. I can see the sympathy in his eyes. I know he doesn't like to see me in any pain. With hesitation he brushes a stray hair back from my face. Slowly he leans in to gently kiss my cheek. I close my eyes as his lips touch my cheek. He draws back from me I open my eyes with a longing in them, I hope he sees. He hesitates for just a moment or two. Then kisses my lips quickly, pausing again momentarily, looking into my eyes once more. Searching for some clue, as to how I am reacting to his advances. He kisses me like he did that one night, with great passion. My emotions overwhelm me I kiss him with my own hunger.

I melt easily into his embrace. He continues to kiss his way slowly down my neck. The dress is very low and he continues to kiss every inch of my bare skin softly, slowly. My excitement grows within, making my engine purr, she has been idle much too long. I know it's not right, but I can't help myself.

Easily, he slips me out of the dress. I try not to think about what I am doing as being wrong, it feels so right to make love to him. I know he has had over a thousand years to learn how to seduce a woman. He has definitely perfected his technique.

Slowly he parts my legs and eases his naked body between them. I close my eyes overwhelmed by the anticipation. He slowly enters me, as I look up into his eyes. I can see he is studying my face. I smile slightly letting him know I am happy about this. He smiles back at me. His love making is sensual and tender. His pace only quickens when he is about to climax.

We make sweet love throughout the night multiple times. I discover he has many talents. Not once do I feel an ounce of pain caused by him, I allow him to set the pace, easily I follow his lead. His tender and considerate love making is like none other I have ever experienced. I delight in more orgasms, than I thought was possible.

Sometime in the afternoon I wake. Bonita is nosing her dish and barking at me. I start to get up and see that Victor is sleeping next to me. I long to kiss him, but I don't know what to expect. What would happen if I touch a sleeping vampire, during the daytime? Maybe I should ask him first.

I feed my little girl and shower. When I come out of the bathroom there is a food tray on my table. I guess Rose is avoiding our meeting today. I dress and eat then I go in search of Rose. I find her in the study dusting franticly.

"Hello Rose, thank you for the food." She doesn't look at me at all, she just continues dusting. Finally, she breaks her silence, after a long time.

"Kim, I figured that you wouldn't be able to walk this far today. I was just saving you the trip down stairs." She continues to avoid eye contact with me.

"To be honest Kim, I'm not sure how I feel about this."

"To be honest Rose, I'm not sure how I feel about it either."

I sit down in one of the wing back chairs and she takes the other one. We both sit silently for a bit, until I break the heavy silence that fills the room.

"He found me crying in my dinner. He carried me up to my bed … I've been so lonely… I just gave into him and let him have his way. I guess I let my emotional needs override my logical reasoning."

"Kim, he wasn't using his logic last night either. He stayed in your room to sleep. He must trust you very much. You could have staked him and be free right now. So, if you're ever questioned let's keep that between us." I look at her like she is crazy,

"Who would ask me Rose?"

"I don't know. I'm just saying."

"Ok then, if my werewolf ever tries to retrieve me, I don't think it would be a good idea. Him knowing I could have escaped so easily either."

"Kim, which one do you miss the most?"

"Good try Rose I still would like to protect him. He might be looking for me. I hope that I'm not that easy to forget or replace."

"I don't think that you are forgettable. With the way you have effected Victor all of these years."

"I feel guilty and happy all at the same time."

She chuckles, "You should, how did you make it down the stairs? I heard the two of you were at it until dawn."

"Rose! You didn't hear us? I really didn't need to know that we were heard either."

"Well, our master being happy has been a long time coming. No pun intended." I smirk at Rose.

"Did he bite you?" She asks with great interest on her face.

"No, nothing like that, but his fang nipped his lip when we were kissing. A drop or two of blood fell into my mouth before the wound healed. You know Rose, it tasted familiar. It has sweetness to it. Like the blood I tasted when I woke up after crashing my van. The time I was heading to Greg's. When I met Nick for the first time."

"Kim, that night I know Victor was here at home. He didn't know you were headed to Greg's that night. It couldn't have been his blood."

"It must have been Lea."

"It very likely was her."

"I've never made love like that before, we were… so in sync. It was so beautiful, as if we have always known each other's deepest desires."

"Too much information, I didn't need to know. But it could be partly because of the blood Kim. Are you sure that he didn't take any of yours?"

"No, I don't think so. I did check everywhere I could see. I couldn't see my back all that well though."

"Kim, lift up the back of your shirt!" She orders me, I don't hesitate and I do as she asks. She inspects my back I hear her gasp.

"This is not good, not good at all." She turns me around to face her and the look of fear on her face scares me.

"Kim, do you know what this means?"

"No, not really what does it mean?" Now I'm in a panic too.

"Kim, you better sit back down. He bit his lip on purpose. He plans to keep you for himself. He must really be in love with you. He only shared his blood with Elizabeth, no other women was good enough. Kim, he will never let you go now. You belong to him."

"Just because I was weak once Rose?"

"No because he was waiting for you to except his advances. This way when he gave you his blood, he knew you would freely drink it. That makes you his."

I look at her quite puzzled. "Rose, please explain this some more. I don't get it."

"Kim he will now know exactly how you feel at all times. And you too will know his feelings instinctively. I don't know how long the effects will last. A few days at first I think. But if you continue to exchange blood it will become permanent."

"That means even if I get away from him. He will be able to find me?"

"Well he can't track you exactly. However the closer he gets to where you are, the stronger he perceives your emotions. You will sense him nearing you as well."

"Well, isn't that special, my very own personal radar system. So even if my werewolf grows a set of balls. I still will never be free from Victor."

"No, but being tied to Victor isn't all bad. No other vampire can kill you with his blood in your system. They will smell his blood on you. Think of it as vampire repellant. No vamp would dare cross Victor. Maybe he did this just to protect you?"

"I know that he did give Lea his blood. But that was not for love it was to save her."

"It was the kindest thing he could do for her. At the time the other vampires had tortured her so badly. Did you know they filled her blood with silver? She was slowly painfully dying.

Victor has a kindness that I have never seen in the other vampires. Most of them are quite vicious creatures. That is why I lock myself in my bedroom late at night. I keep a stake under my pillow just in case. I take all of these precautions because Victor conducts his vampire business in the mansion between midnight and dawn."

"I read about what he did in his journals. Do you know where Lea is? I've been worried about her?"

"She should be fine now. She was sentenced for 35 days without food, for trying to help you avoid capture. It will take a little while for her to recover. When she does she will come here looking for you."

The grandfather clock chimes five o'clock. I had no idea that it was so late in the afternoon.

"Kim, would you mind taking Victor's dinner up to him? Then I'll be able to finish fixing your dinner. I'll leave it on the kitchen table, before I go to my room for the night."

"I was going to ask to take it up anyway."

"Follow me, I'll heat it up and you can serve him. Oh silly me you already did that last night."

"You're not funny Rose."

"Oh yes I am, I just need to know. Do you plan to service him again tonight?"

"Rose, don't you make me smack you."

"I just want to know how much food I should make you. You're going to need the energy if you plan on…"

"Rose, that's enough. Seriously, how could I deny him? He's very handsome and his body is well… Rose honestly, I haven't been able to not think about him since I first saw him in the woods.

I ran away from Robert and Andrew when I found out what they were. One caught the other trying to…is the blood ready yet?"

Rose looks at me knowing that I had more to say but, luckily she decides not to push. She gives me a judgmental glare. She then hands me the glass with the warmed blood.

"Kim, he should be up in minutes. I'll see you tomorrow."

"Have a good night Rose."

I pick up Bonita and carry the glass of blood up to Victor. I take a deep breath for courage before I open the door. Opening it slowly thinking he is still asleep. I put Bonita down in her dog bed, a gift from Victor for Bonita, the little queen. It's pink and frilly. I walk softly to my bed and whisper his name.

"Victor"

"Yes Kimberly, I am awake. I see that you have brought me my breakfast."

"Yes," I wait as he props up against the pillows. I look away quickly embarrassed. I had forgotten that he would still be naked. He adjusts the sheet quickly to cover himself. He then takes the glass from my hand.

"Victor, you were so kind to me last night but I have a question or two." He smiles smugly. After he has taken a few sips from the glass.

"Yes Kimberly, what would you like me to answer?" There's that smug smile again. "Will you be honest with me?"

"Well, I will not lie to you. However if your questions are ones I do not wish to answer as of yet I may decline."

"Fair enough, why did you give me your blood last night?"

"I wish to protect you in every way I can. By giving you my blood no other vampire will try to harm you."

"It wasn't to keep track of me should I leave here?"

"No, but it will do that as well, come to think of it."

He's not fooling me. I know he thought of that before he fed me his blood. He takes his hand and cups my face. It gives me butterflies. I know it shouldn't but I can't control it. He slowly inches closer to my face, and kisses me lightly on my lips. Damn butterflies.

"Victor, I shouldn't have done what I did last night." I murmur between his kisses. He pulls himself back away from me. But he keeps my face cuddled in his hands.

"I'm sorry Kimberly, it was my fault. I shouldn't have taken advantage of you when your heart was clearly hurting."

He inches himself closer to me and the sheet shifts. He puts his arms around me pulling me to him. I tell myself no, you can't do this… you're in love with another man, a man that loves you … well I think he loves me; he never did say it. Besides, Victor's a vampire I can't have a future with a vampire, he will outlive me by forever. Victor begins to kiss the nape of my neck. This is not helping me at all while my inward struggle is rages on.

"Please," Is all I get out before his lips are covering mine. He covers me with his body. Damn the butterflies, they just changed to birds or bats. Why do I feel this way towards him? Abruptly he stops the seduction, pulling himself back from me. He grabs his robe and ties it shut. I sit here confused. What just happened?

"Victor?"

"Kimberly, I'm sorry, let's go downstairs you should eat something."

"Ok, I am hungry anyway, I guess."

Why did he stop like that? I follow him down the stairs. I replay the last few minutes in my head. He waited all this time to get me in bed and now he is backing off?

In the kitchen I can see that Rose has left a covered plate for me. And a warm mug of blood for Victor. We sit down together and eat. We both seem to be lost in our own thoughts. It has become very quiet; I wonder what he's thinking. Well there is only one way to find out.

"Victor, what is on your mind?"

"I was thinking back to the first time I saw you."

"Victor, you started watching me when I was a teen right?"

"Yes, I spotted you one summer night playing with the wolf dog. Some of those werewolves can't stick to their own kind. There are mixed breeds running all over the place." I find it hard to shake that image from my mind. "So not all wolves are werewolves then? Victor she never shifted. Can any of the mix breeds shift?"

"No, they cannot, that would be an awful abomination. She was a pure wolf from many generations of true wolves. The werewolves can only make wolf pups while in wolf form. However, once a wolf pup is born it can grow up to make more wolves. Throughout time many did this just to be able to have babies of their own. It's sad but it was the only way they could."

He drinks some more blood before he continues. "I watched you and the way the two of you interacted. I knew that there was something more to you. I didn't know that you were a chosen one yet. The werewolf scent came a year later when you turned thirteen. But you somehow intrigued me even then. I never looked twice at a young girl before you.

You know I should have killed you then and there. However on the night I had planned to carry it out, I just couldn't do it. I looked at you sleeping peacefully in your bed. A cat curled up next to you. You looked like an angel. Your father came into the room to check on you, I hid myself in the shadows of the ceiling. I don't kill needlessly, Kimberly, remember that please.

He stooped to kiss your forehead before leaving your room. I let you be that night. Except that I stroked your face, then I flew away. I tried to watch you from a distance at first. But then I had to know you, protect you. What you liked and what you did and didn't care for. What made you happy and what made you sad. I am ashamed, but I even would peek into your room when you slept. Although, when you started dating I was so enraged, I almost took you then. I did stop looking in your window however. I just couldn't witness that; I would have simply killed the poor boys."

I smile nervously. "Victor, I wouldn't have gone willingly. I didn't believe in vampires then."

"I Know I had someone ask you. I put people in place to watch you. I couldn't tolerate seeing you date. Sadly I had to force myself away from you. Those stupid human boys have no idea how to treat women properly."

I coo, "Oh, Victor, I never knew that I had my own personal stalker."

"Kimberly, I didn't stalk you." he states defensively.

"Think about it, what would you call it then?" He pauses and laughs slightly;

"Yes, I guess you are right; it was stalking, but I would never harm you, keep you to myself yes. I'm not above that obviously, but harm you, never!" He leans toward me and kisses my cheek.

"Nonetheless, when you started traveling all over the country, I had a hard time keeping track of you. I cannot travel in the day time, as you know. I kept losing track of you. I became very irritable over time. Lea had figured out that I knew what you were. She also realized that my interest in you was much more than your wolf destiny. She said that I was obsessed with you, maybe she was right. She volunteered to be your guardian. Lea wanted you to be her personal responsibility. Although she knew about you she didn't share it with her boys.

She knew that Robert would never believe her. He stopped talking to her after I changed her.

The werewolves have such strange rules and laws. They can be very confusing at times. Lea couldn't tell Andrew because Robert should be the one with you. I know that you are aware of that. But being who you are as a person, I'm guessing that you picked Andrew." He looks at my face for some sign that he is right.

I smile coyly, "I'm not talking about that right now. I understand perfectly well why you took me. Doris tipped you off that Jonathan had made contact with me, didn't she?"

"Yes, as a matter of fact she did. But I wanted to take you before you became pregnant with a werewolf baby."

"But why didn't you take me, when I was out in the woods?"

"Nick asked me not to. He and I decided that you needed more information about your destiny. Lilly was the obvious one to tell you, being that she is Nick's sister. She was the next best choice with Lea being away at that time. I didn't detect an extra heartbeat, so I knew I had more time to waste. Lea knew that Nick and I were protecting you. She didn't know why you were alone in the woods. She hadn't found out yet that one of her sons was forcing you to... None of them will tell me which one it is. Will you?"

I think about this first but I know that he will kill them both. He'll kill Andrew for loving me and Robert for hurting me. It's probably only a matter of time before he kills them, but, I am not going to hurry things up.

"Well Victor, the one who hurt me, he was beaten by the one whom I favor." Knowing how secretive werewolves are, Victor should not have that information.

"Kimberly that was not the answer I was looking for."

"I know, but I still cannot give them up. Victor, why didn't I feel it? When you bit me last night, aren't your fangs sharp?"

"Yes, very sharp, but I do not wish to inflict any pain on you. I gave you my blood first, so that you would not feel my fangs puncture your skin. Vampire blood acts like a powerful pain killer in humans."

"Oh, how thoughtful of you" I say with a hint of sarcasm. "Victor, when I crashed my van. Was it your blood I tasted in my mouth that night?"

"No, Lea was watching over you that night. I had business to tend to that evening. She gave you hers otherwise you would not be here now. Vampire blood also can heal to some extent. You had a punctured lung. She fixed your broken rib and her blood repaired the tissue of your lungs."

"She stuck her hands inside of my body?"

"Yes, there was no other way to help you at the moment. You slept in your van with Nicholas. For over a day and a half repairing, you were out cold. We feared the worse that you would wake up a Vampire."

I mull this over a few moments. It does explain the loss of time. Also the cut I found on my body without any blood. Oh but how gross, but I'm still here I guess that's a good thing.

"Lea took my clothes and washed out the blood?"

"Yes, she did."

"Ok I think it's time to change the subject. Victor last night was something. However can we practice the salsa tonight? I would love to dance."

"Kimberly, you're sure that you want to be that close to me?" I smile at him slyly.

"Do I have to answer that question?" I struggle inside with what I asked. I know where it will most likely lead.

"No, let's go and change, so that I may teach you the steps to the salsa."

After we change our clothes, we meet in a room that has been mostly cleared. Except for a few remaining chairs that are up against one wall, along with an old fashion record player. There is also a floor to ceiling mirror that covers the opposite wall. We call it the ballroom of course. He tries to show me the basic steps and then we begin to attempt to salsa together.

"I seem to have two left feet tonight. There are a lot of steps to remember."

"No, the dance that I'm teaching you is a difficult one to learn, here let's try it this way."

He positions himself behind me with his hands on my hips.

"I seriously don't think this is going to help me learn the dance."

"Flow with the music Kimberly. Follow my lead."

Easy for you to say I think to myself. He starts to sway his hips keeping my body secure to his. My mind is not on dancing anymore. I close my eyes and just sway with him. Suddenly for some reason, I really don't feel like dancing. I turn around in his arms to face him. I know I shouldn't be feeling what I'm feeling, but I can't help myself. The feelings are real with Victor. Not some kind of magical desire that I can't control. Well at least I believe they are real. I hope he is not tricking me.

I look up into his face. We both stop swaying and I kiss him. He dips me as we continue our kiss. He slowly returns me to an upright position. He kisses down my neck. I'm a goner… no hope in retreating now… and it's entirely my fault, I kissed him first.

"Kimberly, if you are not ready, I will not…" I kiss him again hoping he stops talking.

"Rush you. I know that you are having mixed feelings." I kiss him again a little harder this time.

"Victor, I desire you. It's not because of an enchantment. True, I do still carry a love for another, but he has not come for me. I have been here with you for over two months, in that time you have shown me nothing but compassion and kindness. More that I have ever received before in my life.

You have broadened my knowledge of many things. The most important thing is that you have been honest with me from the first. You haven't hidden anything from me. What you have done has touched my heart." Oh crap, I can't believe that I said all of that out loud.

"I wondered why you have not tried to escape the mansion yet."

I smile, "Well Victor, you do know that I cannot speak with alligators or wolves. Since wolves would assist me in my escape. You guard the mansion with alligators."

He chuckles, "True, but as clever as you are, I thought that you would have found a way out of here by now. I worried about that every night as I fell to sleep, that I would wake, in the evening and you would be gone."

"Victor, you have been nothing but good to me as I've said. A lesser man would have harmed me long ago."

I shudder with my words. I didn't mean to reflect on one of Roberts's attacks, but my mind went right there. Victor holds me tight to him. His mood mimics my own instantly, turning to rage.

"Which one forced you, I will kill him myself."

"No Victor, I'm ok, just a bad memory, it's gone now with your help. I believe that he is paying for what he did. The toughest exteriors have the weakest interiors."

"True my dear, so true. Let's finish this dance; it will help you forget the unhappiness of your past."

"Victor lets go upstairs. That will help me forget the unhappiness much faster, by replacing them with happy memories."

"If that is what you wish?"

"Yes, it is what I wish."

When we are both exhausted. I ask Victor again why we exchanged blood the night before. His answer is slightly different.

"I needed to know that you were making love to me because you wanted me. I do not wish to make you do anything that you don't want to do?"

"Victor, I have read all of your journals. I already know that when you love, you love with your all." He just gazes at me perplexed.

"Victor, I would not have given myself to you otherwise. You know that I have only met two other vampires, excluding the ones who kidnapped me. Prior to a few months ago vampires were a myth to me. You know like werewolves, only in stories. Not real things, just props for horror movies.

I knew Jonathan was a vampire. However I didn't allow myself to believe it really at first. When I met Lea the second time knowing she was a vampire, I was so in shock and awe, she was so not threatening. Aside from you she was the first honest supernatural being that I met. Sadly, even Nick was not honest with me." I think of the first time I met Andrew and we touched. He could have told me right then and there, but he chose to lie to me as well. I feel my anger building. "You know they still haven't told me things. There are still some missing pieces about my part in this whole legend thing. Lilly was in the middle of telling me, when the two of them began fighting in the streets. They should have spilled it all the first time when I met Andrew. Greg knew what he was setting me up for, they all knew!"

Victor pulls me into his arms and holds me against him. He gently strokes my hair down my back, calming me down.

"Kimberly, I didn't know you could get so angry."

"Sorry, I forgot you can feel my emotions now." I turn to him and kiss him lightly. I fall right to sleep in his arms.

27

Over the next couple of weeks it becomes very obvious to the staff. That something had changed between Victor and me. I start to sleep in later in the mornings. Victor still leaves me at midnight to run his business. Yet I'm not confined to my room during these hours. We agree for my safety that if another vampire is in the house, I am not to come down stairs. Should I need anything from the kitchen, Brad will get it for me. He is now stationed outside of my bedroom door. Brad is a bit scary, being that he is so large.

Now that Victor has shared his blood with me, I can feel his emotions and moods as clearly as my own. I figured out fast that if a visitor stresses Victor, I should stay far away from them. I know some of them could smell me in the house. From my bedroom window, I watch everyone that comes and goes. I want to memorize their faces just in case.

Victor started to share with me, what it is that he actually does as the Vampire king? To me, it involves a lot of boring things. There is the politics, like in any empire. There is the one on top, Victor. Then there are his top commanders André and Angus. I don't know all that much about those two. Victor is not volunteering anything about them either. Then there is the regular population, the ones who must obey and do whatever Victor commands.

Victor and I still practice dancing but always before midnight. I also have a lot of books to keep me busy from the library. I have read many books that you will not find in any ordinary library. A lot of them contain the history told by vampire's point of view not humans.

I have become quite comfortable here with Victor. Maybe a little too comfortable, one night, things became a little too scary for me. Brad and I were in the kitchen getting a snack. He got himself a warm glass of blood. He and I always say hello to each other, but not much more than that in the way of personal conversation.

He asked to sit at the kitchen table with me, before he just sits down. I love supernatural's that have manners. I've observed him with Victor. I have noticed that he takes his job seriously. His responsibilities are to protect Victor, period. Me, being an extension of Victor, I am now included in his duties.

We sat there in silence for a minute or two. Then he shyly asked me if I was going to become a vampire someday. I told him I hadn't made up my mind yet. He kind of shrugged his shoulders and sipped on his blood. Then, another vamp came in the room. They all know it is off limits to all visitors. Brad stood up right away and glared at the intruder. It was written all over his face the new vamp was up to no good. The intruder tried to come after me through Brad. What an idiot, Brad floored him instantly, and held him to the floor. With his huge hand planted squarely in the center of his chest.

"You are staying down Paul, or am I ending your life tonight?" There was not a hint of humor in Brad's voice, no misinterpreting there. Brad was ready to kill to protect me. Though it was all over in a few seconds the time seemed to go in slow motion.

The intruder tried to over throw Brad but to no avail. Brad ripped his head right off in front of me. There instantly was dust everywhere. I stared at him with a new found respect and fear. Very monotone he asked me, "Miss Kimberly where is the broom and dust pan?"

"Brad… I'll get it for you."

I help him clean the kitchen including mopping the floor. Rose will have my head if I leave even a speck of dirt on it. We wipe down every exposed surface and free it of the filth. Neither of us utters a single word as we clean the entire kitchen. It took us about twenty minutes to complete our task. I had just put the broom back in the closet. Brad had just reentered through the back door from taking out the trash.

"Brad, Kimberly, What is going on in here?"

Victor was clearly not a happy camper. Instantly I stopped walking. Brad looked towards me with an expression I've never seen on his face. Pure fear,

"Victor," I stated flatly. He turned towards me his look softened a tad. I swallowed hard, "Victor, Brad protected me gallantly. A vampire that I didn't know came into the kitchen while I was getting a snack. Brad was getting a glass of blood." Brad nodded in response to my explanation.

"Anyhow, the vampire tried to attack me, and Brad took care of him quickly. He did give him a chance to walk away, but the vamp was dead set on getting to me. Brad did what he had to do."

Victor looked back and forth between the two of us with questions on his face, he finally stopped on Brad.

"Brad is what Kimberly says correct. Did you not have a choice in killing him?"

I try to protest, "Victor?"

He put his hand up to me. Which of course pissed me off instantly but, I shut my mouth for Brad's sake.

"Master, Miss Kimberly is telling you the truth, Paul was the vampire in question. He strongly believed that all werewolves ought to be dead. The guard at the gate must not have known Paul was not on the approved list. Maybe Paul used a different name to gain access. He took one look at Miss Kimberly and went mad with his hatred."

Victor seemed to mull this over a minute before he spoke again. "Very well Brad you may go. I have no more business to be conducted this evening. Except… replace the gate guard, before you retire to your room."

Brad nods then begins towards the kitchen doorway. Victor placed his hand on Brads shoulder firmly before he could pass by. I drew a deep breath and held it.

"Thank you Brad; you did well tonight." I exhale with relief as Brad leaves the room. I go to Victor right away.

"Honestly, Brad only protected me from Paul."

"Kimberly, Brad has never lied to me. I know you both spoke the truth tonight."

After that night, Brad became my shadow, especially if any other vampire was in the house. So I taught him rummy and he taught me how to play poker. We began to enjoy each other's company. Though he is not a man of many words, it's a good thing I almost always keep the radio on in my room.

About a month later Victor and I are seated at the dining room table when Lea enters. Victor must have known she was coming by the way he is smiling at me. I leap to my feet and run to wrap my arms around her.

She is just as happy to see me. I'm so ecstatic seeing her that I actually squeeze her too hard. We laugh and she walks with me back to the table. Victor rises and gives her a kiss on her cheek and a polite hug. She sits next to me at the table.

"So Kim, I see that Victor has been treating you well. You look healthy, and I like the blouse you are wearing. It's not really your style though is it?"

I look at the blouse I choose to wear today. Smiling back at her, "You're right Lea it is not something I would buy myself. However, Victor likes this type of blouse on me; he says that it complements my shape. But you're right my usual attire is very simple. I find I do like to wear things of quality some days."

Smiling back at me politely, "Kim, I was simply stating that you look very nice. I am happy to finally see you again. I have missed you so."

"Sorry Lea, I meant no disrespect to you either. I have to admit I wasn't sure how you would perceive my ease, living here in Victor's home."

She reaches to place her hand on mine, "Kim, you must do what your heart and mind tells you to do. I am not the person to judge anyone in their love life decisions." She smirks, "I myself am in love with a werewolf, and I am a vampire; we should be sworn enemies." We all let out a slight laugh. Victor rises up from the table placing his napkin on his chair.

"If you ladies will excuse me, I have work that needs my attention. Brad will be right outside of the doorway if you need him. I will let the two of you catch up on things." He kisses the top of my head then leaves us alone.

Lea waits to say anything, until she believes that Victor is far enough away. She still whispers every word as do I.

"Kim, is he treating you right? Does he take blood every time you two make love? Has he threatened you in any way? Has he threatened my boys?"

I grab a hold of her hand. She looks as frightened as a vampire can possibly be. "Lea he has been only kind to me in every way. I am sure he has taken my blood more than I am aware of. As I am sure that you know if I try to leave him before he is ready, that there will be a high price to pay."

I pause a minute thinking of how to phrase my next statement. "Lea, he has mentioned to me, he knows that I want children. He hasn't decided if he will allow it yet. He struggles with that decision almost nightly, he gets a certain look on his face when he thinks about it."

"He is thinking of letting you carry on the werewolf blood line?" Lea's face was unreadable with her question.

"Yes, he is crossed between what is expected of him by his subjects, and what I want. It troubles him greatly. I didn't even bring it up, he just knew. Did you tell him I wanted children?"

She grins at me, "Remember he has been watching you for decades, he knows things about you that even I do not know." Lea drifts into heavy thought. She begins to play with a loose thread in the table cloth.

"Lea, what are you thinking?"

"My boy's safety, they are the only ones who can get you pregnant. What will he do to them once you are with child? Will he raise the child as a friend to vampires? Have you asked him any of these questions?"

"No Lea, I was waiting for him to reach his decision. If his decision isn't the one I want him to reach. I am prepared to do my best to convince him, that I should carry out my responsibilities. My desire someday to become a mother, I don't think he will deny me."

I pause and reflect on the pain that is still in my heart. "Lea, I still ache with a great longing for… I can't say his name within these walls."

"Oh my child," She holds my hand tightly. "Will you ask for his safety afterwards?"

"Yes, but of course, I cannot live with the knowledge that anyone suffers on my behalf. Lea, I think that it all will work out in time."

She smirks, "It will work out in Victor's time not ours."

"You're right all in Victor's time. Hopefully I will still be able to bear children, when and if he reaches a decision."

Lea and I decide to take a walk outside so that she can fill me in on the boy's whereabouts. Not a long walk, we can only go as far as the balcony but, it is a rather large one at that. Brad keeps an eye on us from just within the balcony doors. It took some convincing on my part to make him stay there.

Lea and I sit on a bench at the far end of the balcony, away from Brad. Making sure neither Victor nor Brad can hear us. She promises me that the boys are getting closer to where I am, and that neither of them has given up hope to find me.

I myself am not so sure of all she says when it comes to her children since she is fighting her own inner war. She owes loyalty to Victor, for he allowed her to live. But as a mother she fears for her children. She wants them to find happiness and live a very long life. I sympathize with her torment. I wouldn't want to be in her place, where I am is bad enough.

Lea stays with me for two nights. She fills me in on the few things that were left out before by Lilly. It's not that bad; really, at least I don't think it is. I'll change into a wolf days after I give birth to my first child. I think that part is really cool. She can't remember if it hurt or not, the birth of her sons was so very long ago.

After I shift I will be almost as strong as Andrew and Robert. I won't heal as quickly though when injured. But after I shift the aging process slows to a trickle. I will most likely live around five hundred years. The children will shift for the first time when they hit puberty; that should be fun.

There are three elders that make up the werewolf tribal council. I have met two of them so far. White Feather I met in the woods and Isha in the bar with his buddies. They maintain all of the laws of the werewolves. When and if a rule is broken, or a crime against another werewolf is committed, a tribal council will be called. Judgments are swift and brutal she tells me. Community service never crossed their minds as a punishment, I guess.

She also tells me that when I do become pregnant that my hormones will be off the charts. I should not be too far from the father during my pregnancies. That disturbed me a bit. Lea refused to clarify it for me though. I'm guessing I won't have to talk with Robert about that now. I'm guessing somehow she believes that Victor will allow me to have a baby. I on the other hand am not so sure that he will. That would mean he allows me to sleep with another man. I don't think of Victor as the sharing type, but I also know he is struggling with this possibility.

Her visit is short but informative. She promises me that the boys are looking for me. But that she cannot tell them that I am here. We both know that Victor will most likely kill them if they enter his home. Or they will kill him. I don't want anyone dead. No matter whom, my heart would be shattered.

I have become quite comfortable in Victor's home. I actually worry when my fairy tale world will bust? What troubles me most is which man I will choose. I don't even know my own heart at this point. I still cry at times for Andrew but not as much as I did. I've been here for six months with not one word from Andrew or Robert. I was sure that after Lea's visit that they would show up quickly. I'm beginning to think that I was just a piece of a puzzle they played with, yet really didn't care if I was lost. Maybe I can go and make a baby then return to Victor? I do want at least one child. I always have wanted children. Maybe Andrew will come for me?

28

"Kim, it's almost dusk, I'll get the glass for you."

"Ok Rose, I'll be right there."

I did it again I got lost in my own thoughts and lost track of the time. This wolf puzzle I'm working on will never be finished if I keep daydreaming. When I get up stairs with Victor's drink, he is waiting for me. He has a big white box tied with a big purple ribbon sitting on the bed. I smile broadly at him.

"What is this?"

"Open it Kimberly, it's a surprise." I open the box hastily and inside there is a beautiful black dress. I'm overjoyed.

"Oh Victor it's beautiful, but what is it for?"

"There is more Kimberly look in the bottom corner. You will need something to go with your dress." The jewelry is a silver heart necklace with matching earrings and a bracelet.

"Silver huh, are we going out tonight?" He simply nods. It must be a public place for him to want me to wear silver. The silver proves to others that I have not become a werewolf yet.

"Where are we going?"

"We are going to a special place where we can dance." I throw my arms around his neck and Kiss him.

"Really, we are going out?"

"Yes Kimberly, now shower and get dressed quickly."

I grab everything off of the bed and run to the bathroom hurriedly. When I return he looks me up and down approvingly, then he takes me in his arms.

"My love, you are breathtaking!"

He backs me to the bed, kissing my lips neck and the exposed top of my breasts. The dress pushes them up greatly. I can sense his desire growing, among other things.

"Victor we will never leave if you start this. Victor… Victor…" I breathe. He completely ignores my pleas to stop. He unzips my dress and it falls to the floor. He removes his suit and in one liquid motion we are both naked.

"I'll make this one quick."

He whispers in my ear. He wasn't lying either. I could barely keep up with him. I hardly had time to draw a breath, until he bit into my neck.

"Kimberly, I am sorry. I would never make it through our night out. You just looked so… tasty."

I withhold a laugh, "Well then, I'm glad you got that out of your system."

I shower again, redress and look at myself in the mirror. I smile and turn to Victor.

"I'll wear my hair down then?"

He snickers, "Yes, that would be wise."

As I fix my hair, I think to myself that sex seemed somewhat familiar. My mind flashes Roberts face. I dismiss the image as quickly as it appears. No need for unpleasant memories right now.

Once I am ready we head to the front door. It will be my first time outside the gates, since my trip to the hospital. Victor unlocks the door and then hands me the key. I take it questioning him with my expression.

"This is your key, after tonight you may come and go as you please."

Well hot damn, I didn't see that one coming. I try to contain my excitement the best that I can. Calmly I say, "Are you sure about this Victor?"

"Yes, I trust you. You have been told everything there is about your legacy. Knowing you, you will somehow fulfill it. I only ask that when you do. Please only carry it out in the day time."

I stand there just looking at the key in my hand. I feel my eyes suddenly fill with tears. I am so overwhelmed, by his unselfish actions that I can't stop the tears rolling down my face.

Placing his hands on both of my shoulders, "Kimberly what is wrong? Isn't this what you wanted, your freedom from me?"

I gaze in his eyes lovingly. "Victor, I am very happy here, with you. I can't say that I don't miss my work with the animals." I pause, trying to compose myself, taking in a couple of very deep breaths. "I have learned so much from you. I now have a better understanding of the world around me. Both the one I once lived in as a so called normal person. And the one I now live in knowing what I am to become. No one has ever given me so much and asked for so little."

"Kimberly, your heart is not a little thing. The choice is now yours, after we enjoy tonight. You may leave whenever you want."

He places his hand tenderly on my cheek. He looks directly into my watery eyes. "I love you my dear Kimberly, which is why I'm giving you the freedom of choice. I know you long to be with the animals. And they need your special ability. It will not be easy for me to see you go. However, you must do what you feel is the right thing to do. I will always be here should you choose to return."

With each word he speaks about my leaving him, I can see the pain in his face intensify. I am not in any rush to leave him now, not at all like I was when I first got here. I wrap my arms around him and hold on for dear life.

"Kimberly, I have also placed your cell phone in your purse. Please wait until the morning to check your messages, they are all still there I didn't erase any of them. I didn't read nor listen to them; they are not for my eyes or my ears." I hold onto him with tears refilling my eyes.

"Victor, I don't really know if I want to go back to my life as it was." I pause, searching for the words I need. "You know what? Let's not discuss this matter anymore. Tonight is a night for enjoyment. We will go out and dance the night away. We'll forget all about the troubles of our world for now."

"That is an excellent idea my love."

We leave the mansion to a waiting stretch limo. Brad of course is our driver. He fills out the chauffeur outfit very well. I'm, positive that no one will dare try to get past Brad to Victor or me. He has got to be the largest man I have ever seen. Brad is about seven feet tall and three feet wide, and he is all muscle. I'm glad that I've gotten to know a little bit more about him. I find that he is as gentle as a kitten that is until he has to protect Victor or me. I never ever want to be on his bad side.

Brad opens the door for us then takes his seat behind the wheel. The windows are of course tinted black. No one can see inside. I take in the landscaping as we exit the grounds.

The first time I was out front at nighttime I was in a rush. We were going to cover for the accident. I didn't take the time to look around. The grounds are very well lit. It's almost as bright as the day in the courtyard. The trees that line the drive are illuminated by white rope lights.

As we drive along I somehow talk Victor into listening to my music. I have found only one alternative rock station in North Carolina. I catch him tapping his foot to a couple of the songs. Though he protests, my music is lacking class, I'm gonna make him a rocker yet.

We make a turn up a long drive that leads to a plantation type house. The drive is lined with Cyprus trees. Other than that there is not another tree in sight. The place is in the middle of nowhere. It is surrounded by open farm fields. The wires must be underground because I don't see any poles. It's like going back in time.

When we enter, we are seated immediately. They place us at a tiny table near the oversized fireplace. The interior is very tacky to me. The walls are dark red with black trim. The tables have crimson red table cloths on them and the chairs are all black leather. The lights are also very dim. I hate to think what might be crawling around in the shadows.

Everyone in the place is dressed to the nines. Many of the couples are dressed from different time periods. Some are dressed in colonel wear. Others are dressed like the twenties. They all seem to be pretending to be something they are not. I chuckle to myself.

"What is so amusing Kimberly?"

"The people here appear to be trying to outdo each other."

"Yes, they are entertaining creatures."

"Victor, are they all vampires?"

"No, but they are all supernatural's. You are the only one even close to human in here. Do not trust any of them. They all know who I am, so they may know who you are. Jonathan is not one to keep his mouth shut when he is unhappy, as we both know, since he was unable to keep you as he had planned when he attempted to kidnap you. Kimberly, let's dance once before we order. I want to show you off."

"Victor, is that wise?"

"No one will harm you here. They know my wrath is great. However, they may tell you stories that are not true."

"Good to know."

Victor leads me to the dance floor. We match each other's steps perfectly and glide across the floor effortlessly. I forget all about the world around us. We are both considerably happier when we return to our table, the sorrows stored neatly away, deep down inside.

We order our meal. Victor orders a rare steak and I order a medium well filet mignon.

"Victor, I didn't know you could eat human food."

"Yes, I do enjoy it from time to time. I simply love chocolate also."

"Oh, now I know why you always have chocolates around. I was wondering who was eating most of them." I grin but it fades fast. I stiffen instantly as I see Jonathan walking up behind Victor.

"What is it my dear?"

"Victor, Jonathan's coming." I whisper, Victor and I are well aware that all eyes are now watching us intently.

"Victor, who is this lovely creature accompanying you this evening?"

Victor humors him by saying who I am. Both of us know damn right well, that he is the one who tried to abduct me. I'll play the game as well. If only I could convince my heart to stop racing from fear.

"Pleased, to meet you Jonathan." I feel Victor's dislike of him intensify as we shake hands.

"The pleasure is mine, Miss Kimberly. Would you care to dance? I couldn't help but notice how you glided gracefully across the dance floor."

I'm not playing it that far. "I'm sorry but I will have to decline. I must visit the ladies room. If you gentleman will excuse me?"

"Perhaps when you return?" I smile as I bite my own lip, not too hard though, I don't want the scent of blood in the air.

"I'm afraid that my dance card is full for the evening."

I quickly walk away for the ladies room. I wash my hands, and then check my makeup to kill a few minutes. As I open the door to exit the ladies room, Jonathan grabs my arm, backing me against the wall, pinning me firmly.

I am more than sick of being man handled. I refuse to show him how scared I really am being trapped by him. I glare at him as he brushes my hair back. He stops short when he sees the bite mark from Victor. Yet he still whispers, "Let's have a taste of Victor's little toy."

He puts his lips to my neck and snarls, "you are protected by him. How dare him! Protect the little werewolf maker?"

I clench my teeth full of rage, "Jonathan, let me go right now, don't cause a scene. Victor will destroy you."

"That he will,"

He releases me and walks away as Victor rounds the corner. They brush shoulders hard. Victor lets out a low growl as they pass.

"Kimberly, are you alright?"

"Yes, I'm fine. He wanted a taste until he smelled your blood in mine. Thank you for that Victor."

He scans the area around us before we step out from the hall. He holds me close to him, just in case. As we walk back to the table, both of us maintain a calm attitude. We sit down at our table as if nothing happened.

"Would you like to leave now Kimberly?"

Victor motions for Brad to come to our table, he has been sitting at the bar with the other chauffeurs.

"No, I'm not leaving, this is our night and no one is going to ruin it for us."

"Yes sir, what can I do for you and Miss Kimberly?" I look around to see Jonathan has disappeared. I relax with that thought. I do however recognize that he is far from done with me.

"Brad, I would like for you to join us at our table. Jonathan is here and somehow you have always scared him greatly." Brad smiles not an often thing. He sits opposite of Victor, me between them. With my two protectors no one will even come near the table.

The three of us enjoy our dinner none the less. Victor and I dance after dinner, while Brad watches us the entire time. Then we return to our table for dessert. We order Death by Chocolate. After which we dance just once more, the salsa. Good thing it was our last dance.

We get up from our table and walk toward the entrance, on our way out. Victor receives many head nods. We get into the car and Victor closes the privacy window. He kisses me with a hunger unlike him. Before I know it my dress is on the floor of the car. He sheds his clothes as well. As he nears his climax he bites me hard on the neck. I truly feel his bite for the first time.

As he drinks my blood the sensations mix. I go from delight to becoming frightened. As Victor continues drinking, I grow weaker and weaker from the loss of blood. Finally he realizes my weakness and stops in a panic.

"Kimberly, Kimberly, open your eyes." Victor cries in a panic. I try to but my eye lids are so very heavy. He holds me in his arms watching my face for any expressions. It takes some time but I manage to open my eyes again.

"That was different. Was that all about Jonathan?" I gasp, it's hard to talk.

"My love, I don't think that I've ever experienced jealousy before tonight. I didn't hurt you too much did I?"

"Well, it was the first time that I felt your bite. I believe you also drank more than usual. I'm ok you just will have to help me in the house."

"That is the least I can do for you after my assault. The audacity of Jonathan to even think, that I would not protect you. How dare he even try to challenge my authority?"

"Victor, that was not an attack as far as I'm concerned, trust me. I was very much enjoying your show of jealousy. You are always so gentle with me. I sometimes wonder if you're holding back. Like maybe you are afraid you might damage me."

"Kimberly, I don't ever want to hurt you. Making love should never be like that. I am so ashamed of myself."

"Victor, I am not mad at you just hold me until we get home." I snuggle into his arms until we get home. I can't do much of anything else. I'm surprised that my eyes stay open that long. When Brad opens the door to the limo, he was not happy to see me so weak.

"Master?" I hear the alarm in Brad's voice.

"Brad get the door, I will carry her up."

Victor carries me up to the bedroom and sits me on the bed. I feel very light headed. I can hardly undress myself though I try to. I didn't want him to feel guilty. But of course he realizes what is wrong. He helps me undress. I see the sadness in his eyes.

"Victor, I cannot break your skin bite your lip for me?"

"Kimberly, you should sleep, I've treated you wrongly."

"No, the night is still very young. I don't want to sleep yet."

"You can't want to make love to me after what I have done?"

"No, not right now that is not what I had on my mind. But, I don't want to sleep just yet. Tonight, you put me above a vampire. You showed your subjects that you have chosen a werewolf for your lover. What you did tonight took a lot, I know this. Truly your feelings for me are deep. I believed your words when you said them, but your actions proved them to me."

"I do not play with the matters of the heart. You really are not mad with me for biting you that hard?" He looks so wounded,

"Victor, bite your lip and kiss me."

I fall right to sleep anyway but in his arms. This is the place that I feel so much love.

29

I wake in the morning just before noon. I eat lunch with Rose and tell her most of the evening's events. I leave out the biting and the blood loss part. She completely catches me off guard when she asks.

"When will you be leaving now that you have your own key? You know the alligators are gone as well."

"Yes, I kind of figured they were gone a while ago."

"And yet here you stay, I don't understand why. You spend hours daydreaming about your werewolf. I've seen you lost in thought, I can't count the times, that I have called your name and you didn't answer me."

I smile at her she has no idea what I dream about. "Rose, I really would like to start working with animals again. I do miss that part of my past life. The rest I'm not so sure about. If you must know, I daydream about staying with Victor and having babies." She was honestly caught off guard by my statement. The look of shock that covered her face was priceless.

"Rose, you must already know that he gave me my cell phone."

"Yes."

"I checked my messages and I only had one. It was not from the one… who I thought loved me. Maybe they found another to replace me?"

"Kim, only if you die will another be born Right?"

"Well, there were three brothers born. There are two more possible women out there somewhere around my age. The ones that Victor killed were all much older than me. They were from the last generation of humans. So there must be at least one more if not two out there somewhere, just waiting to be discovered, the poor things. If all of us are dead, then I guess the next two will be born sooner or later, or maybe they are children already."

"Do you really think that they were able to find another one so fast? They searched for you for decades? Wait! Babies you want babies?"

"Yes of course, but it doesn't matter right now anyway."

"Kim, would you be willing to stay a while longer?"

"If Victor will allow me some freedom to work with rescues again."

"I think he will allow that, he loves you a great deal."

"I am well aware of his love. Mine has grown for him as well."

"Well, I hope you stick around a while longer. I sure could use some help around here."

"Rose, you know, all you have to do is ask."

"I know I just like being a smart ass."

"As I'm well aware, and you're very good at it."

We both laugh, then I help Rose with her cleaning around the house. I have already finished every book in the library. I know things now that I will never ever have a use for. Since I can go outside alone now, I take Bonita out back for a walk. It's late in the afternoon. It feels nice to have the sun on my face. I can feel Rose watching me from the kitchen window. I think she is sure that I will leave at the first chance I get. Although I don't know that I really want to leave.

"Rose," I yell for her as I enter the kitchen. "I want to make sure that I am in the bedroom when Victor wakes up tonight."

"That's a good idea he will not be expecting you to still be here. You know that don't you?"

"Yes, I don't want him to panic. So please hurry with his dinner." She gives me a sideways glance. "Please," she grins as she gives me the mug of blood. I hurry up the stairs to wait in the chair. I place it next to the bed and wait.

Victor opens his eyes slowly. I know he didn't expect to see me. His face instantly lights up with the sight of me. He is delighted that I am still here. After dinner we take a long walk in the fall night air. There's a slight chill in the night, so Victor wraps his cloak around me. We hold hands as we walk, he is oh so the romantic.

We talk about music, his and mine. The groups that I name he has never heard of, I'm not surprised at all. I tell him that I will have Rose take me to a store. We'll get a few for him to listen to. I know that he most likely will not care for them, but at least I'll have some of my favorite bands to listen to.

He leaves me at midnight like always to conduct his business. Brad stays with me in my room. He likes to watch the old westerns, the same as I do, so I turn my TV to AMC. He takes a while before he asks me if I am ok after the night before. I reassure him that I am fine and that Victor promises not to ever do what he did last night again.

"Miss Kimberly, I shouldn't say this but if you ever feel your safety is in danger, even from my master, I will protect you regardless."

"Oh Brad, you like me; don't you?" I coo,

"I'm not joking Miss Kimberly, you are very important to me."

"Thank you Brad, we will keep that between us. It is good to know that you care so much for me."

"Well, for a werewolf, you're not half bad."

I smile, "Thanks, let's watch John Wayne win again."

When I get tired, Brad leaves me alone. I know he is outside my door until sunrise every night, especially now that I have my own key and can leave the house. I don't think he will stop me that is, unless he has been told to do so.

The next day Rose and I go into town after breakfast. We have a blast shopping. Victor left out his credit card for me. I don't have any money here. He put a note on it to spend however much I want to.

I keep an eye out just in case anyone recognizes me. We eat lunch at a fancy bistro after we have a few bags between us. I bought a few CD's to listen to and Rose purchased some new shoes. We also stop for ice cream on the way home.

When we return it is almost sun down, so we have to rush and get the blood ready for Victor. I set up the CD player and decide to go easy on him with the first one. We listen to Pink, her softer stuff. At least he is amused by the music. I think she was a little too much for my old vampire to handle. The next one I put on is a newer piano piece, he enjoys this greatly. We go through the rest over the next month. He mostly does not care for my newer music. I keep forgetting how old he is.

I tell Rose over a late lunch one day about Victor's reaction to my music. She laughs at the thought of him listening to alternative rock music in the first place.

Rose and I go out about once a week shopping. She is careful to take me only to high end stores. I doubt that I will run into anyone I know. My friends can't afford to shop in these places. I know she is playing it safe. She never lets me drive or hold the car keys. I have told her many times that I won't run away. I like living at Victor's home. I do believe that I have fallen in love with a vampire. That leaves me with just one question. What in the hell will I do when they come for me?

Victor and I are reading together in the library one night. I have the latest book by my favorite author, Ms. Harris that I downloaded from one of the few websites I can access now. I still cannot get into my email. The company claims that I haven't paid my bill and they refuse to activate it. I know that it is paid electronically from my account. I know it has a pretty penny in it, so they must be lying to me.

I hear Victor chuckle, so he must be enjoying his paper back. He prefers to read murder mysteries. He puts down his book on the table next to him, clears his throat, "Kimberly, have you spoken to Doris as of yet?" I know what he is asking, but I will play along.

"Yes, she said to say hello."

"I hope that she is doing well."

"Yes, she is in good health and she said that she lost ten pounds, with the boys away she isn't cooking so much."

"Did she say where they might be at this time?" And there it is his main question, I knew it was coming. I keep my expression plain, though I want to smile.

"Why yes, they are in Oklahoma looking for me. They received a tip that I was in Owasso. Would you know anything about that?" I look at him skeptically.

"I might have heard something of the like. I think it was from one of my recent visitors" I put my reading tablet down in my lap and glare at him.

"Victor you know damn right well you sent them on a wild goose chase."

He smirks slightly, "I might have had something to do with it. I could lead them right here if that is what you wish."

I frown, "I guess it is time to get this over with, but you must promise not to kill them." He simply rolls his eyes but doesn't answer me. I put my reader on the table and go to kneel in front of him. I take his book from him and place my elbows on his knees. I look intently into his eyes. He cracks a smile.

"Ok Victor, it's time to tell me the truth. Have you been leading them away from me all this time?" He gently strokes my cheek.

"Kimberly, I have never lied to you and I don't plan to start now. I only have misdirected them twice. The other bumbles are all on them." He gives me a slight smile then continues on. "The night that we went out dancing was the first time. They had been getting closer to you than ever before. So I sent out information leading them far away from here. Then, recently I sent word that you were in Oklahoma. I know you will be leaving me soon enough. I just wanted a little more time with you all to myself."

"Victor, I truly never want to leave you, ever. We both know that I have a destiny to fulfill. It is the only way I can have a child of my own, I so want a child." I plead to him as he caresses my hair and I rest my head on his lap.

"This conversation has been coming for a while. Victor, we have both been pretending that everything is right in the world. You said it yourself. I want a child of my own." A long silence passes between us. I don't want to say what I know I must do. Softly, I say it with a heavy heart.

"Victor, when they come for me I will go with them. If I go willingly they won't search the house for you. But just in case we should sleep in your room. The steel door with the key pad lock will keep them out of there for sure. I couldn't bear the thought of losing you forever. The short time that we need be apart will be painful enough."

"For the both of us, it will be most painful Kimberly."

"Master excuse me?" without even looking up Victor replies to Brad.

"What is it Brad?"

"I was wondering sir, do I follow Miss Kimberly when they come for her." Victor and I exchange a look of question.

"Kimberly, what do you think about Brad following after you?"

"Honestly that would be very nice to have Brad there to protect me at night. But I'm afraid that they will stake him the first chance they get. I don't want that to happen. Thank you for asking on my behalf."

Victor snickers, "I would worry more about the brother's safety than I would Brads. Kimberly, you've seen him kill. He is very efficient at that task." I just roll my eyes at the both of them. They both laugh slightly.

"Brad, I will need you here. There will be times I will leave to join Kimberly from time to time. I will need you to take over my business dealings in my absence. You know better than anyone how to run my empire."

The look of surprise on Brad's face showed me that he never expected to hear that. Victor did not see Brad's expression. Brad simply said thank you and left us alone in the room. I know Victor's words meant a lot to him.

That night Victor and I started sleeping in his room. Each morning that I woke I feared they would come that day for me. Victor had leaked information for them to find me. Brad was getting antsy as well. If Victor was busy with any matter Brad was glued to my side. One night Brad confided in me that he didn't want me to leave even for a night. He had become attached to me in a big brother type of way. I had to admit I was happy to have him as a friend too.

Rose and I are cleaning up after our lunch about two weeks after Victor let out the information, on my whereabouts. We suddenly hear a loud pounding at the front door. My heart sinks, my fairytale world is over. She sees my reaction.

"Kim, is it them?"

"Yes, I hear Roberts's thoughts. I'll try to block him from my mind as you answer the door. Victor and I have agreed that I will go with them quietly. Rose please let Victor know that I will return to him as soon as I can." Rose and I hug each other like we will never see each other again.

We start for the front door. I grab her arm to stop her. "Rose, also tell him if my absence causes him too much pain, I will find a way to return."

She hugs me tight again, and then we both move swiftly to the front door. I hide behind the door, out of view. I really don't want to go now that the time is here. As Rose opens the door, I hear Robert's thoughts calling out for me. I block him out, hoping that he doesn't know I'm behind the door. My heart is about to pop out of my chest.

"Let us have her and we won't hurt you or your boss." I touch Rose's hand on the back of the doorknob. For an older woman she sure is ballsy, she stands right up to Robert.

"My master will not be happy with you taking what is his!" Robert pushes Rose to the ground. She grunts as she hits the hard tiled floor.

He proceeds to start up the stairs and I yell, "Stop! Robert, I am right here, let's go, let him sleep."

Robert stops dead on the steps and turns toward me. His face is alive with the delight of seeing me. He runs back to me and gathers me up in his arms and spins me around. Then his body suddenly stiffens when he sniffs me. He wrinkles his nose and drops me to my feet. I blankly stare up at him.

"He has fed on you, the bite mark is fresh." He looks at me with such repulsion. I thought he was going to kill me where I stood, fear runs all though me.

"You have his blood in you! How could you fuck such a hideous thing? He should disgust you. He is a cold dead thing."

My hands firmly on my hips, with all the attitude I can muster. "I didn't fuck him. Victor doesn't fuck! He makes love, unlike werewolves!"

The shock on his face was instant and horrific. Robert shoves me with great force at Andrew. I stumble into his arms.

"Andrew, you can have her. I want nothing to do with her anymore. This was a waste of our time. I told you she would submit to him if we took too long finding her."

No one speaks for moment. Andrew holds onto me for dear life, his face buried in my hair. I would like to enjoy this moment but Robert has another idea. He glares at me, with such hatred, venom filling his words as he shouts at me.

"Kim you disgust me to the core. I should stake him right now. He must have seduced you right? Or, did he put a spell on you? You couldn't have willingly slept with him?"

Robert grabs my arms pulling me from Andrews embrace, and violently shakes me. Andrew starts for the stairs, I shout out hysterically, "No, leave him alone I will go with you willingly and make your babies, just promise not to harm him!"

Rose blocks Andrew with her body, arms stretched out as far as she can reach.

"I am your elder, young one." Andrew backs down the stairs looking defeated. I wonder why he backed down from Rose.

"Who I love is my business. I have been here for a very long time. Not one word, only one message from Robert telling me that he is looking for me. That was months ago. Andrew, you didn't even call to hear my voice."

Andrew slowly reaches for my hand and the adrenaline rush is not there. He looks bewildered to say the least but this happened once before.

"It's the vampire blood in her system Andrew. It will fade and things will return to normal soon enough. Just like it did after we sent her to the hospital. When Lea gave her some of her blood."

I wondered why I healed so quickly. Suddenly I can feel Victor registering my fright. He'll have to feed before he can help me. Besides, it being daytime, he can't really help me right now.

"Andrew, we must leave now!" I plead, "I don't want anyone to be harmed. Please, let's go now!"

I hug Rose goodbye, in a whisper, "I will return soon. Bonita Come!" I pick her up in my arms.

I take one last long look around. With a deepening sadness filling within me, I glance up the stairs. To where I know Victor is sleeping, I mouth… I love you and walk out the door. I can already feel my heart breaking. I can't help but think that I am going from heaven to hell.

Made in the USA
Middletown, DE
25 February 2020

85144046R00203